perfect silence

perfect silence

a novel

JEFF HUTTON

BREAKAWAY BOOKS
HALCOTTSVILLE, NY
2000

ISBN: 1-891369-20-2
Library of Congress Control Number: 00-133192

Published by Breakaway Books
P. O. Box 24
Halcottsville, NY 12438
(800) 548-4348
www.breakawaybooks.com

Distributed to the trade by Consortium

FIRST EDITION

For my wife, Diane,
whose love and encouragement
have made this possible.

For our children,
Kevin and Susan.

And in loving memory of Pam,
my sister,
who has surely touched
the pages of this book.

ACKNOWLEDGMENTS

I will always be humbled by the lyrical histories of Bruce Catton and Shelby Foote and I do not pretend to be a historian. Their work is a part of what kindled in me a love of history, and this book is a modest attempt to write a small story in the enormous shadow of those who have written so eloquently about this period before me.

I have tried to be true and accurate to the time period, and I have blended some some historical figures in with the variety of fictional characters. There have been volumes written on the Battle of the Wilderness. I add little to the historical record. This story reflects only the narrow vision of one young soldier, thrust into battle with no idea of any grand design. This battle itself, it seems to me, exemplifies the fallacy of grand design in any of humanity's wars.

The early years of baseball are being rediscovered. There is new research and exploration being done on the birth and evolution of the national pastime. Games are being played under the restored rules in parks all over, and there seems to be a new appreciation of baseball in its purest form. For my understanding of this period, I am particularly indebted to the work of William J. Ryczek, whose exhaustive study of the post-Civil War boom in the game, *When Johnny Comes Sliding Home,* provides a year-by-year account of the exciting adolescence of the game.

My wish is a simple one: that *Perfect Silence* puts a new slant on these wedded histories, and that placed in this dramatic, historical setting, it is a story that will ring true, and find a small place in the heart of the reader.

I am very grateful to Garth Battista, my editor and publisher, for taking a chance on the obscure voice of an unknown writer; for helping me make this story a better one; and for being through it all—"nothin' but kind."

—J. H.

It's our game, that's the chief fact in connection with it:
America's game; it has the snap, go, fling of the American
atmosphere; it belongs as much to our institutions, fits into
them as significantly as our constitution's laws; is just as
important in the sum total of our historic life.
  —Walt Whitman, 1865

May 2000

A blue Ford sedan moves down Interstate 64 in Virginia. A father, his two sons and their friend are on their way to the Richmond Rivermen game, a Double-A club affiliated with the Atlanta Braves. It is late morning, already warm, and the windows are rolled down so that they are forced to almost yell over the rushing air. The father is telling the boys about the green grass and the blue seats and the digital scoreboard. He warns them against too many hot dogs and cotton candy.

It's not like television, guys. I don't think you can really appreciate the game without the sun on your shoulders. Without the smell of the grass.

The boys aren't listening. They are singing out the open windows.

I've got to pull off for gas and you guys can get a soda or something.

The car pulls off an exit ramp into a rural town. He turns the car into the parking lot and to the gas pumps of an EZ Mart, a cinder-block building painted white and blue. The boys climb over the seat to come out the front door and he gives them a few dollars to get soda and gum while he pumps. Moments later they arrive, sodas in hand, and sit along a cupped aluminum guardrail at the edge of the gravel parking lot. The man emerges and sits beside them. He tells them how much they'll love the game, and his older son spits soda from the end of a plastic straw onto the hot tar. He sighs and wonders if they'll even watch the game with all their silliness, and his eyes wander to the woods behind the small concrete market.

A pile of rounded stones lies along the rear bank in a random pattern. His eyes follow the stones until they become patterned and deliberate and he sees a stone wall running into the sparse woods—leafless stick and vine grow around and behind it but he can see the correctness of it. It is heavy-looking—monumental in its mass—but still made of the moment, stone leaning upon stone. It stretches through the woods and then ends abruptly at a ditch where gravel was removed for the highway—the heavier stones toward the bottom sinking into the earth and the smaller ones choked by vine and grass.

Look at the wall, guys, and they follow the father's eyes to the stones in the woods. His older son asks why anyone would build a wall behind a gas station and his father laughs and tells them the wall was here long before the gas station or the highway. He spends another minute looking down the wall's straight line, placing his hand on his son's shoulder—then the four of them climb back into the car toward Richmond Stadium and the game.

No personal significance or insignificance can spare
one or another of us. The fiery trial through which we pass, will light
us down; in honor or dishonor, to the latest generation.
     —Abraham Lincoln, December 1862

May 7, 1864, Virginia

In the black sky there was nothing familiar. It was a sea becalmed, opaque. If there had been mystery it was gone. If there was glory in some sense of heaven there was no longer. If the human spirit was celebrated in the waltz of stars and the magic of the unknown moon, the celebration was over. The trunks of oak stood sentinel, guarding only darkness. Surely the bounds of the human spirit had been clearly marked. Here on the pasture's wooded border the contest had ended. With the roots of red oak and cedar soaked in the blood of boys, the agony of physical battle had been the final victory of the body over the spirit. The silhouette of thousands of lifeless bodies across the battlefields of this war was the gruesome trophy. The final chapter of human potential had been closed this day—written across the rugged landscape in blindness and in blood.

History would call this "the Wilderness," and so it was. The return from order to chaos. The sacrifice of the spirit where any meaning to human life is bequeathed to the undug grave. A return to bottomless, suffocating barbarity. At this place a body stirred and struggled to breathe the unclean air. The lungs filled. Blood pumped to the human heart and through limbs, and consciousness returned to Joseph Tyler, relentlessly.

Toward the Fire

In the gloom of our ignorance of what shall be,
in the hour when we are deaf to the higher voices,
who does not envy those who have seen safely
to an end their manful endeavor.
　　　　　—Ralph Waldo Emerson, 1844

I.

Dawn feathered across the sky, pouring like ice melting from the eastern horizon. The tall correct trees leaned in and upward toward the enveloping light, casting shadows across the earth. He concentrated on only the sky—its shapeless abundance—until traces of pain crept into his consciousness like water into the clay soil, breaking through finally in waves as blood pulsed against shattered tissue. His hand went quickly to his arm. Looking at his palm he saw no new blood except the black flakes that danced from his hand to the hard ground. The bleeding had stopped and the blood had dried through the night. He still had not tried to move his legs, but he became aware of their weight and their awkward position on the ground.

Joseph hesitated, lifted them, and bent them at the knees while rolling to his side. He was unaware of how long he had been lying like this, most likely assumed dead. He kept his hand on his shoulder, holding the flesh around the wound on his arm. He could see the grass bent where his revolver lay and he reached for it—holstered it without thinking. Thoughts from the night's battle began to creep into his mind and he fought unsuccessfully to clear them and return to sleep among the shattered branches of pine that lay along the ground around him. He looked upward—became conscious of the smell of smoke—and remembered.

Screaming had engulfed the field of battle—not distinguishable language—not orders, nor direction—just the yells of desperate men. There was no organized line. Men were to all sides and around him. A thick acrid smoke lay low across the landscape, almost blinding the troops and making lightless the field of battle, sealing the space around them. Musket balls thumped against tree trunks, against stone, and against flesh. He could see clearly the bayonet, as if it were now flashing wildly at him. He could see Jacob running to the wall, leaping over it and down into a skirmish with three or four Federals and a Confederate corporal. He could feel the jolt of his pistol firing . . . twice . . . three times, could feel the burning of the cutting blade through the flesh of his arm and the field of battle spinning over him and the dark ground up to meet him as he drifted away from consciousness, clutching his arm, his arms clutching the earth as if he were about to spin off it, curling fetal on the ground and drifting into exhausted sleep, unaware of the lifeless bodies around him.

Again he lay without consciousness in the cool shadows of the trees and in the darkness of the shadows—until light again crept in and his hand moved instinctively to his arm. The pain was throbbing now and his teeth gritted tightly and he felt the pain move to his head, behind his eyes, and he squinted them half-closed. With the other hand he pushed himself up from the ground, felt the soreness of bone lying across rock, and rubbed his side with the fingers of his good hand. One button held the uniform jacket closed and it was torn in several places. Joseph pushed his weight down to the soles of his feet, felt the stony ground through cloth boots, and leaned back against the bark of the tree. He was now standing with great effort. An old hemlock held him up, and he felt the texture of the overlapping bark on the skin of his back where his shirt and jacket were torn clear through. Testing his weight, unsteady, shifting foot to foot, he finally trusted his own strength to stand and he stood alone in the gray shadow of the evergreen and focused his eyes on the scene around him.

He saw the body of Jacob first leaning backward against the stone wall, eyes open and arms outstretched as if in receipt, ready for something— perhaps it had already come and he had embraced it full. The blood on Jacob's head was black and caked like cloth around the white eyes, the eyes turned upward, inward. And then yards away another body, face-down, the back of the blue uniform barely showing through ferns. Joseph could see many others and sense the presence of more. Shattered tree limbs covered the ground beneath them and pine needles were piled in awkward drifts as if the wild things of the woodland had emerged and wrestled at this spot and then receded into the thick trees.

Joseph staggered to the body of Jacob and stood before his friend. He put his outstretched arm toward him, rested his hand on the shoulder and then over the lids of the eyes to close them. He let his head sink slowly to Jacob's shoulder and he closed his own eyes in momentary embrace, waited for tears, waited for words. Neither came. He stood straight up and surveyed all the ground around him. The smell was of smoke and the unmistakable stench of death. He walked in the direction of the open field and saw the stone wall continue on into the pasture. He saw two more bodies at the end of struggle. With the thick woods at his back he emerged into the dim sunlight. There were thin clouds but he could feel the warmth of the sun on his face. It felt like it always had and he was sur-prised. Looking up at the clouds he realized that they were mixed with smoke growing blacker, curling up toward the earth's silk ceiling.

He became aware of the pungent smell of fire increasing and the sick-ening smell of burning flesh. Across the brown meadow he could see flames licking the canopy of oak leaf and limb, reaching up to consume the upper branches that reached for the silver sky, pulling the leaves, black and moistureless to the earth.

Joseph began to walk toward the fire as if he were to walk into it, keep walking, and be engulfed by the flame and be finished. He walked to the end of the wall and around it toward the burning woods. It was obvious that there was a raging fire up the hill in the wilderness ahead of him yet he continued to walk toward it. Black smoke filled the horizon and rolled slowly down into the ravine, twirling in a ghostly dance around the tall timber. It seemed to Joseph that even the smoke clung to the ground, unable to escape the deep woods. Many of the areas of the wilderness had been logged out, and the new growth was a tangle of brush and sapling that now snapped and cracked as it was consumed by the flames. In many cases even the stumps of the trees had been ripped from the ground in a primitive search for iron ore, and these tears in the surface of the earth were left to fill with the leaf and debris of the shattered woodland and formed black, swampy pockets across the ground. He walked on the best ground he could see—into the thin smoke holding a torn red bandanna to his mouth and nose. His step quickened and slowed over rock and moss-covered ledge that let streams of sunlight into the woodland between trees and lit the smoke with blue iridescence. He stopped to rest and breathe, leaning against a pine already warm from the fire's heat. He coughed and cleared his throat. He wiped his head above his eyes with the bandanna and ran his long fingers through his hair and away from his face. He was wet with sweat.

Joseph Tyler stood, almost six feet, and looked as he stood part of the tall, thin pine wood—motionless—his shadow lost among the shadows of the trees. Hair the color of copper was matted down and drawn to one side of his head and the threadbare uniform jacket hung from his shoulders like unfitted cloth, ready to be altered. His trousers were short on his legs and his feet were covered hastily with thick cloth that was strapped together with the belts from his knapsack. Across his chin was a thin, spotty beard that he had not had time to clip or shave. Joseph began to walk again with his hand clutching the wounded shoulder, and as he walked he looked as if he would fall at any moment.

The smoke was getting thicker as he penetrated the rugged woods and he turned from it. He could feel the first sense of heat in his wound and it bit deeply into the torn flesh as he set his jaw and leaned his sweating forehead against the tree's smooth trunk. His hands were blackened with sap and felt thick with it. He leaned down to the brook and lay the bandanna out flat on the water's surface and watched as it darkened and soaked. He wiped his hands first and then dipped it again, bringing it up cool and wet to his face. As he held it there he heard a noise—a human voice.

He had been aware of the movement of jackrabbits and pheasants off the hill and away from the fire. He had not focused on the lifeless bodies that appeared in the thicket, blue and gray the same, lying along stones and clutching vines in helpless grasp—but now his eyes moved along the ground. The body of a Confederate soldier lay along the brook's bank, one hand touching the water, palm upward. He watched the motionless body as he knelt at the brook. He heard the voice again and it froze him. It was not close. It was filled with agony, with desperation, and it was the voice of a young man, a boy. He rose up, stood perfectly still, and listened. There was not a sound—crickets, birds—nothing but the crack and roll of fire in the wild brush. There was no other sound.

Just as the absence of reason had drawn him toward the burning woods, the sudden and clear presence of reason stopped him in his tracks. The silence itself stood him still there along the river. Thoughts raced through his mind like the flame through the thicket. How many voices? How many bodies lay clinging to life in the smoldering carpet of brush and vine? How many hands would reach to him and what uniform would they be wearing? And what hand would reach his? And should he himself lie down with them then, a small part of this, and be consumed as well? Or was it just clean breath for which we lived? Clean, smokeless breath.

He began to turn from the water's edge, his feet shuffling on smooth rounded pebbles, moving back down and away from the fire and smoke when he heard the voice again—a low moan, and then almost a shout, a final desperate call, short and definite in its anguish. The war had taught him to ignore the screams, the groans of wounded and dying men, but this time he could not and he turned again in the direction of the fire.

Joseph held the bandanna to his mouth and nose. The hand of his wounded arm fell instinctively to the pistol at his waist. He was surprised it was still there—and felt the cool metal on his hand. He was not conscious of having chosen to move his hand to the gun but was comfortable with it there. He pushed a branch of something—honeysuckle or berries—from his face and moved forward on unsteady legs. The smoke grew thicker as he moved along some kind of path and he began to see clearly the flames. The fire raged in the thick, tangled underbrush—swallowing and cracking the wild barberry and new laurel with furious reclamation. He could hear the snap of moisture being inhaled from limb and bud, could see the thick pine trunks blacken and hear the smaller limbs falling from the upper canopy to the forest floor, snapping other branches as they fell, crashing awkwardly into the engulfing flame. The heat now tore into his wound, biting the newly exposed flesh and then across his face. The bandanna was now dry from the heat. He coughed, slowed to spit, and tried to breathe deeply; but the breath that filled his lungs was poisoned with the smoke of burning wood and he gasped, his face twisted.

A persistent wind had picked up, whipping the flames laterally and sending a stiff shiver through the unburnt foliage as if in warning. The sound of the voice carried now by the unstill air drifted in and then faded away and then drifted back again over the tortured woodland to Joseph's ears. He could not ignore it, could not turn away from the solitary human voice although he was filled himself with terror and unable to bear the gnawing heat, could feel it pressing on his eyes as he raised the bandanna again to shield them. Small explosions occurred: the unspent cartridges of dead soldiers being consumed in the flames, tearing through lifeless flesh and adding fury to the fire. He let one hand drop again to his pistol and pulled it away, feeling the now hot metal of the handle against his palm. The wind that was not yet touched by the fire felt cool at his back and he turned to it and filled his lungs with it and then began to move again.

The fire that he could now see was not endless. It appeared to have boundaries on either side that he was sure were expanding. The fire's voracious front was moving toward him, slowly along the forest floor toward him, and his eyes were now burning and crying as the smoke rolled in advance of yellow flames and engulfed the space of the forest where he stood, where he tried to walk. He turned from it. The pain of his shoulder was unbearable and his feet were hot. He began to move away; he turned and moved and then heard again the voice, this time long and low and not far away. His movement stopped.

Without thought Joseph moved again in the direction of the voice, somehow threading his way through brush and pine, finding narrow avenues that had not been touched by the flames. He was circling now east, he thought, around the fire, toward the place where he again heard the moan—guttural, defeated—and now he thought he could make out a body lying at the base of a shattered oak tree. He moved slowly toward the body, then quickly stopped. The flames were advancing, the heat and the burning in his eyes were again unbearable. No tears formed in his hot, dry eyes. Maybe there would be no more tears. He stared at the motionless soldier before him and then saw his hand rise slowly, heard a low moan, and watched as the hand dropped heavily to the floor of the woodland. The man's chin was down to his chest and his cap pulled low to block out some of the smoke and Joseph could not see his face. He then took notice of the bloody and gaping wound at the thigh, could see the white flesh and whiter bone. He could see the vegetation pressed down where the man had dragged himself trying to escape the flame. Wounded in horrible battle, now set to be consumed in the flames of the battle's aftermath. The horror of the scene and the thoughts of the battle overcame him—or the smoke, the fire, the burning flesh of his shoulder dropped him to his knees. He could go no nearer the flames. The exertion of his walk through meadow and over stone had used up what little energy was left in him. He fell again to his side and clutched his shoulder. He could see from where he lay the body lying against the tree. Joseph prayed silently—perhaps word-lessly—as concentration seeped from him. The body was dead now; the wave of the hand, it seemed, had been the last effort and the soldier would now be consumed in flame, counted missing in battle. Then the fire would roll to Joseph and engulf him and send his unanchored soul up through the cathedral of trees, through the spires of angular pine, along the shaft of sunlight that lit the black smoke, and away from the wooded slope that raged with fire and pain and death. He waited and watched, began to allow his eyes to close, and then saw the hand rise again, then the chin pull up from the chest and the head rock slowly back to lean on the trunk of the tree. And the body coughed and gasped and fell away from the tree to the tortured ground. The Federal shirt could be seen now; an enemy soldier fallen and dying.

Joseph's eyes closed. Deliver us from evil. He could feel the heat closing on him. For Thine is the Kingdom . . . and Thine is . . . his eyes opened. He could see white flames licking at the boy's leather boots . . . The power . . .

He was not conscious of moving, of lifting himself up. He came to no moral conclusion, yet his body was upright and alert and he swiftly moved to the body of the soldier. Coughing, furiously sucking in the sickening air, he lifted, felt himself lifting the body in his arms. His strength doubled from the adrenaline of fear as it moved through his veins and to his heart. The body felt lifeless and heavy like a rotted log soaked from a day's rain. He could not run. He took long strides, stumbled in the thick underbrush, and continued on down the slope and out of the burning woodland. Ahead he could see the light of a meadow and the gradually widening intervals of trees and finally the open pasture and clean, clear air. He walked past bodies at the stone wall and followed the line of the wall across the open field to the edge of the woods on the opposite side. He coughed and breathed deeply the clean air, and his lungs ached from the grip of the black smoke. The body in his arms let out a low wail and a gurgling sound, living sounds. He could see ahead of him through a thin stand of hemlock the sun glistening on what had to be water and he headed to it, moved to it as if the mission were his only purpose on the earth, and finally he saw the trees open to the grassy bank of a still pond.

Joseph lay the body down gently on the grass and walked waist-deep into the water and fell once again to his knees on the soft muck on the pond's edge. He could see small fish, green in the shallow water, swim quickly away. He pulled the water to his face and neck and submerged the bandanna in the cool water then crawled up the bank, slipping, to where the body lay. He washed the face with the cool water and pulled the hat from the matted hair on the head. It was thin and blond and wet from the fire and from the fear. He could see that this was a boy, about his own age. He had a straight-issue blue uniform shirt that now showed little color from the Virginia sun. His trousers, though, were gray, colorless except where thick blood turned them black. Joseph returned to the edge of the pond and scooped mud into his hands and placed it on the wound on the boy's leg.

He placed the bandanna on the boy's forehead and then let his own weight settle to the ground beside the body, and once again exhaustion overcame him and he fell back to sleep, a sleep that brought him closer to some end to this madness. He hoped to dream nothing, to have no thoughts. His arm came to rest on the arm of the enemy soldier and the blood of his body simply pumped relentlessly—and kept him alive.

Then, in sleep, he was on his knees again, only now he had his face pressed to a window, the fire behind him, within a room, and he did not look back at the flames and instead he tried to see through the glass, smeared with soot or with moisture, and he wiped it with his hand and pressed his face closer to the cool glass and he could see his own reflection and the soot was smeared black across it and he felt his hands thick with sap as he wiped furiously at the glass. He could feel himself lifted. The room spun away and the scene through the window surrounded him like liquid.

II.

Through the watery image he could see the pale orange sky then full, the field. The air still held warmth from the spring day, the landscape full and deep with new growth, buds swelled to bursting and the activity of creatures in the pasture and the trees beyond giving voice to the engine of nature. The rocks along river and ravine were washed clean and shone with winter's last moisture and lay like pearls along the sandy banks. The fish were winter-slow but quickening with the silver sunshine washed across the trembling surfaces of a hundred brooks. To the east of the meadow the first dogwood bloomed along the forest edge, glorifying the spring sun and wrapping the still, dark woods with white and then pink translucent blossoms. And Joseph could see it clearly and it was as if he could reach out and hold the blossoms in his hands.

This was the time of day he loved most—before the dark night brought back the stubborn remnants of winter with cool March air. His muscles still ached from a full day's work clearing new stones from the field, helping his father ready the field for plowing.

He could see himself across the curve of the earth, loading the small wooden skid-sled with a variety of sizes—some smooth, some rugged and broken—the surfaces fractured, chewed and buried by glaciers—some appeared to be two stones fused together and he could see himself lifting them, half-expecting them to fall apart and expose some mysterious innards that would make the toil worthwhile—an adventure. On occasion the stones dropped and broke one on the other and revealed the linear file of year upon year and the occasional twist or rupture to ponder. Like the layer upon layer of day and night, season upon season, stone upon stone.

Perhaps fifteen. He could not tell. Probably fifteen—feeling the first pull of manhood, away from this meadow, away from the farm and away from his father. He looked across the field and as far he could see but saw only more hills, forests, farms where men and women labored to eat and feed children so they could grow to labor the same land until the earth itself, exhausted and depleted, forced them to move on.

He was lifting the wooden cart by the handles and jerked its single wheel ahead. He aimed it for the high edge of the ruts made from the day's work. This would be the last of the day and he would leave it in a pile near the wall. He could feel himself lifting the wagon. As if he were there now lifting the wagon. And tomorrow. Tomorrow he would work beside his father, laying stone upon stone, and listen to the few words that his father spoke while he worked—and he would wait for the day he could build the walls himself rather than be the workhorse. He did somehow love the labor of finding the right stone and watching as his father found the place for it and worked it till it lay solid and strong, ready to receive and support the next, as if the space for the stone had always been there waiting.

Suddenly he could hear Terence hollering his name and he turned and saw him walking up the path beneath the dogwoods. He appeared over the curve of the earth and was walking toward Joseph. It was still early enough in spring that the path connecting their families' farms could be walked but soon it would be overgrown with ferns and vines and they would have to go down the bank on the east side of the Salmon River and follow its course until the other's farmhouse appeared. The path through the woods cut the trip in half and was a welcome advantage of the winter weather that beat down even the relentless growth of the Virginia wilderness. He had watched his friend appear through this hole in the woods a hundred times for sure and could feel the relief of human kinship as the last rock rolled from the wooden wagon. The dry wood creaked from the weight and he knew that a new wagon from spring wood would be on his list of chores in the next weeks.

Joseph's heart jumped when he saw that Terence was holding in his hands, the weight of it resting on his shoulder, the smooth cylinder of hickory they had formed together—from a tree that stood tall and straight at the edge of the land they called Fernwood Farm—the land somehow bequeathed to Terence's family from the estate of Thomas Jefferson for services rendered but now undefined. They had sawed it down with the big bow blade, and carved it smooth, and sanded the surface with pumice until the surface was a hard shell and the sound was clear as it hit upon another surface. They tested it first upon their knuckles, knocking, then later against softer wood. They sanded again until they were satisfied with the sound of it, content with its weight as they held it upright, the thinner end gripped comfortably in curled fingers—the cool surface leaning lightly on the palms. The cylinder thickened as the wood grain widened toward the opposite end. A larger protrusion of wood was left uncarved at the handle end so the side of the hand rested on it—so it wouldn't fly out of grip—so you knew where you were in the holding of the thing. This knob they sanded flat with a slightly rounded edge.

Holding the wood aloft—swinging the mass of it in front of you—stretching the muscles in your arms with the weight of the thing—was the most natural feeling for Joseph. When he was first shown the game by Terence's cousin visiting from New York he had laughed at the exercise—called it a waste of time. But as he played that first afternoon in the hot summer sun—as he hit the leather ball and it made a solid thud and he watched it sail over Terence's head—as he watched his friend turn and run after the tiny missile and dive trying to retrieve it—he felt a lightness of spirit he had never before felt. Day after day he had toiled since he put away the games of children, hardening his body against the will of nature and the whimsy of God. Making his plans along the narrow path that he could see before him—leaving little room for fun, for laughter, for physical effort that did not result in some consequence favorable to his sustenance. But this now—this was something. Feeling the weight of the wooden bat in his hand, he could feel the blood pump to his muscled arms and back—and it was not to pull and move another stone. It was not to fight the spring mud with plow and tine—not to rip the saw through logs for winter wood. It was just to swing. It was to meet the ball with wood and body together and to send it away—and for the joy of doing such a thing.

The weight of it lifted him and he had to hold it back, pull it down to his center. Where the weight of stone anchored him and dragged at him, this mass of wood leveled him, like mercury, and he felt himself extended in its grasp. Terence, even, wondered at his friend's grip, at his silence, and at the strength with which he used it. The green ground was slashed by the shadow of the wooden bat and Joseph pressed toward the image.

They call it a bat in New York, Terence had said. And the game is called base, and he said that's what we should call it when we play, but I think we may call it what we like. And they called it base and Joseph could see himself clearly on the field—but the image of his friend turned to silver and, as Joseph pressed closer, to gold and then vanished, liquid, into the collapsing sun and the thick black of sleep.

III.

Hunger woke him this time, hours later, and he opened his eyes with no other thought but that he must eat and soon. He turned to where the boy lay at his side and he could see that the body hadn't moved, wasn't moving at all. Joseph put his ear to the chest and could hear or feel no heart beating. The eyes were closed and the skin was still warm to the touch so that he knew that the boy had not been dead long. The wounded thigh, the fire, the fear: whatever had killed him had allowed him to fall asleep and fall away from his pain, allowed him to fly from the vessel of his life, from this place where bodies were torn apart with steel and lead and great explosions, where boys were left to lie in tangled brush to burn.

In the distance he heard the explosion of artillery and occasional musket fire, but it seemed to be far from here. Without thinking he reached into the vest pocket of the dead Federal soldier and then into a leather pouch that he found slung from the neck and tucked inside the blue jacket. There were folded papers sealed with wax and then the familiar wrapping of hardtack, which he opened quickly and began to devour. He tore it— chewed, swallowed, and tore again into the food. The sun was getting low and the clouds in the west reflected an eerie reddish light across the hills as he sat and ate beside the lifeless body.

He looked up directly at the sun to see light wisps of smoke drifting across the meadow and mixing now with orange clouds, and he thought that this was the same sun that had set over his father's farm. The same last lingering light that had allowed him and Terence to play one more round, one more inning, that when he hit in this light the ball would look like black coal against the pastel clouds, and sometimes when he hit it hard they would not find it until morning—and sometimes not at all.

More shooting in the distance. He finished the small amount of food and stood. He was aware that he had to move from this place. The coolness of the pond, the color of the dusk, the food in his stomach, made his body want to rest, while his mind told him to move, to keep moving. He reached down and put his wrists, fists clenched, under the arms of the lifeless body and dragged it up the rocky bank and sat it up, gently, against the trunk of a towering oak tree. The hat that had fallen from the boy's head was retrieved, and placed properly over the dead boy's hair. Joseph looked again at the pale, blistered skin of the boy's face, noticed the eyelashes had been burned away. The blood of the leg wound was caked, amorphous, and turned shades of brown and black on the colorless trousers.

He thought about burying the body but backed away. There would be months of burying—the landscape would be gouged with a thousand graves in the next weeks—the results of this blind battle in the woods. It was wrong somehow to separate this corpse from the thousands that lay seen and unseen around him. He thought that perhaps they should leave together, having reached their common goal—blue on gray—young upon old—together, lifeless in the burning thicket. Perhaps none would be buried, the fire consuming the whole—perfect union, he thought and turned away—his eyes on the path through the woods that led away.

He hung the empty pouch around the boy's neck. In gold the letters R. M. were embroidered, and Joseph flattened the pouch out on his chest so the letters were clear. He felt the folded paper in his hand and lifted it read. To Sarah Kingsley, it read, From Roger McCleod; Private, 3rd Regiment, New York, and the girl's address was written on the paper. It was folded and sealed with burgundy wax.

Joseph was soaked with sweat and he waved his good hand at the mosquitoes around his head. His strength had been somewhat restored from sleep, and he stood straight and breathed in a good, deep breath of the clear evening air. He took the letter from one hand to the other and stuffed it in the inside pocket of the soldier's blue jacket, decided it was time to leave, and turned toward the woodland and some cover. The smoke of the fires still stained the sky, but the wind pushed it west so Joseph headed north and followed a path near a great exposed rock at the edge of a stand of silver birch. He was not thirty feet down the path when he began to slow and then stopped, leaning on the thick trunk of a tree that bordered the path. To Sarah Kingsley—he could see the words written clear as day in front of him. To Sarah Kingsley. He turned and retraced his steps to the place where the boy lay white against the tree. He reached with his hand under the jacket until he felt the folded paper and brought it out to the fading light. He held it in his hand, closed it in his hand, and slipped it into the thin pocket of his jacket. Then, without thinking, he extended his arm and placed his hand on the shoulder of the dead soldier. He said nothing. The soldier's face was somehow different now—the corners of the mouth turned down—and white. He lifted the letter from his pocket with his free hand—then broke the seal and opened it with both hands. The sound of gunfire was increasing and the night was quick in coming. He could see a long letter written in a handsome hand and he began to read:

Dearest Sarah,

As you can see now by my writing to you I have so far been spared. It is awful hard to understand why sometimes when so many of my friends have fallen and entered God's kingdom long before their time. Perhaps it is meant for me to see you again as I so long to do . . .

He read no more. Joseph closed the letter and looked hard once more at the face of the lifeless soldier and then retraced his steps down the path holding the letter in his hand, past the giant silver boulder and into the woodland, now almost dark. He could hear the popping of guns and realized what they were—the guns of the dead being consumed by the fire, unfired cannon consumed—the armies gone from the woods—the weapons still firing into the emptiness they left behind through the black night and across the burning earth.

The Weight of Stone

Nor the peaceful farmer any peace, ploughing the field or gathering the grain,
So fierce you whirr and pound you drums—so shrill you bugles blow.
—Walt Whitman; 1891

I.

The farm was called Blackstone and it lay like a patchwork blanket over the land between Stone Hill and the Salmon River on Virginia's Piedmont Plateau. Small fields of corn and wheat were carved out of the rocky soil and divided by woodland and ridge. A mix of pine, spruce, and hemlock covered the hills and mixed the colors of the southern sun with their own, turning the landscape to silver and then to blue in the unclear hours of the morning and in the lingering hours before the end of day. A small pond lay still on the westernmost field and mirrored the black birch and pine that clung to its muddy shore. Three cows grazed the land on the far side of the pond, and white chickens pecked at the green ground around a shed leaning far to one side, ready to fall.

His father's father had cleared the two fields and Joseph's father had begun to clear more, pulling the rocks from the soil with pick and shovel, horse and cart, and quite often with the strength of his own hands and back, claiming as his own the exposed soil and moving the stones to piles to be used for walls to frame the field—separating it from the untouched wilderness. From the field where the stone piles lay, the small house was barely visible to Joseph.

Looking back over the rolling pasture he could see only the top half of the shingled roof and a thin braid of smoke that twisted lazily upward and disappeared in the still morning air. A lime-green field of young corn plants lay draped along the black earth between ledge and stone, slowly giving way to a stand of okra. They had left an open space between crops and from where he stood, Joseph could already see the hint of weedgrass emerging and knew that this would be his fight all summer. Pulling at the clenched roots of weeds with a wooden hoe and throwing aside stone after stone.

Beyond the house, over a scar of granite ledge that allowed wild berries and gray birch saplings to burst through its uneven seams, Joseph could see the shed that housed the tools for farming and a small workshop that Caleb used for repairing equipment and occasional woodworking. This only when the work of farm and field was done and his father's hands were free to work with the wood. To shape it with chisel and file, but rarely finish, Joseph thought. Since her death. Nothing finished. The rough-cut shelves that lined the walls of the shed were piled high with scrapers and chisels, iron tools, and parts of plows and harrows long since shattered by the unforgiving ground. Steel hammers and mauls, rakes, shovels—long iron bars used for pulling the stones from the field leaned against the careless walls of the shed, already pulling the wall boards from the frame and allowing cold and damp air to turn the iron brown and the wood to black and green.

Forty feet from the shed a springhouse made of stone and mortar allowed the water of a small stream to pass under it, cooling the milk and cream and affording some protection from the southern sun. The ground around it was always wet, almost swamp, and as Joseph watched he could see the black soil collect the light of the sun and return it in pieces like shattered glass. The coolness of the wet soil on his bare feet. The coolness of it in summer, is what he thought of. The cold as it oozed between his toes.

Barefoot along the shadowless ground of deep summer—even as a small boy Joseph would volunteer to carry the pails and would linger along the black ground while his father waited. He would watch his feet and see the muck as it rose and feel himself sinking in the cool, unsteady ground. He could feel it at his ankles, cool and complete around him. And sometimes he and Terence would wrestle there in the puddles of thick water and end up as black as the earth itself, and even their hair would be black with the color of the saturated ground. And they would run. They would run through the woods to the edge of the river and splash in the clear water until they were clean, until all that was left of the mud were threads of black in the creases of their skin and the laughter that echoed through the trees and along the banks of the river.

But it had been some time since they had done this. Joseph could not remember when they had done this last. It seemed to him that it had been a long time now, though it may have only been a winter away. Or perhaps more than one winter since.

Joseph stood now, one foot on a large stone at the edge of the pile, his left forearm crossing and leaning on his left knee—studying the awkward pile. The textures were varied, hues of blue-green and gray, silver and the deep black from which his grandfather had drawn the name of the land. The blackest of these shone with specks of garnet, and it was as if a night had been captured and encased in a blanket of granite. There were stones with the outer shells shattered, exposing white and pink mineral deposits and empty bubbles of ancient oxygen. Stones that seemed flattened with the weight of the earth itself, while others were rounded and turned by waters long since vanished.

Joseph Tyler's tall frame was singularly erect among the rolling pasture and the timeless, sanded stones. His hands, not yet as thick and strong as his father's, were still powerful, and long fingers added the power of physics to the hardening muscle. His hair was reddish brown, thick and uncombed, hanging straight forward toward his eyes. Anxious to work this morning, he had not stopped at the glass. His copper-colored shirt

was torn at the elbow, and wool trousers that were now too short for him
showed socks over leather boots. He breathed in deeply the cool morning
air, pulled his leg back, and began the day's work.

His father, Caleb, looked up from the field for a moment to see his son
working the stones of the wall, and as he looked he pulled slightly at the
horse's reins and the animal slowed and then stopped.

What's this? Caleb said to no one and gently cracked the leather
against the horse's hindquarters until its steady pace, pulling the plow
through the rocky soil, was realized again and Caleb was aware of the
familiar tension of the muscles of his arms and back as he leaned against
the pull of the wooden plow, resisting its movement forward.

He looked again to where his son was working—careful not to change
the tension of the reins—across the field to the stones that lay in uneven
piles just below the horizon. Beyond the stones, the trees were thick and
green against a low sky that seemed to be leaking clouds the color of the
stone itself. Caleb hurried in his work with the awareness of the coming rain.

Loading the cart, three and four stones at a time, Joseph dragged it
across the field and dropped them onto a pile near where his father had
been working the wall. It divided pasture from the thicket that grew
under the trees and marked the field's edge. This wall was started last year
and would be finished by next spring—and then another one would be
started. It was his father's wish that all the fields and pastures of
Blackstone be framed in these walls—the land clearly marked and the
fields clean of the rocks that broke the tools and choked the roots of corn,
and wheat, and okra. It seemed to Joseph that more stones grew in the
winter and by spring whole new crops of stones emerged from the fields
and the walls grew endless along the woodline. He looked now across the
field in front of him, the deep green trees and the first set of hills—then to
a second rise of hills almost blue in the distance. From here, on the pasture's north side, he could almost see the concave sky wrapping the earth
in its grip, a perfect marriage of color across the land.

As Joseph worked he enjoyed the feel of his muscles as they were tested
and the strength he felt growing within himself. These same stones that he

could not lift last year were lifted and thrown into piles this year. He would keep up with his father this year, would be ahead of his father, and he would have to let him work the wall too.

He worked through the day and as he worked he noticed the increasing clouds until the sun was consumed by the gray sky. He felt the first mist of rain as he loaded the wagon and the wheels of the cart began to slip in the mud and he pulled it harder to the pile and slipped in the wet soil. It rained hard now but he continued to work. The stones made sucking sounds as he pulled them up, their surfaces came away from the clay and left pockets in the earth that quickly filled with water. He worked for an hour—maybe more—and the rain was blinding when he finally quit and he could feel the ache in the muscles of his arms and shoulders as he ran under the porch roof and kicked the mud off his boots in thick clods along the planks and opened the door to the cabin.

He could feel the warmth of the room immediately and walked quickly to the low fire that burned red. Joseph stripped off his shirt and his trousers and his undergarments and laid them on the hearth near the heat and went naked to his room to put on dry clothes and dry his hair and push it away from his eyes.

His father worked at a crude stove with his back to the room and turned only slightly to acknowledge his son's entrance. The stove had been constructed from brick and stone and though it hadn't been finished yet, Caleb had planned to fix an iron door to its front to control the cooking heat. As it was now there was a stone slab that could be adjusted across the opening. He moved from the stove to a thick wooden table and as he did he looked out to see torrential rain across the porch that rattled the windows and caused a loose shingle to clap against the roof's edge. At the wooden table he began to cut with a large knife that he raised to his shoulder and let slap into the thick wood, leaving threadlike slices that filled with juice and blood and the water that ran from the potatoes when he cut them, and the fluid ran to the side of the wood block and to the floor. A cloth hung from the table's edge and Caleb wiped the liquid away with a single swipe and then touched the cloth to his forehead and continued cutting without looking up again.

Joseph reentered the room in night clothes, a dry towel around the back of his neck and across his shoulders. The steam of the kettle rose to the low ceiling and curled lazily around the rough beams, then back down into a cloud that vanished into itself and began again. He could smell the sweet potatoes cooking and feel the hunger growing in him. He picked up a knife and cut the corner off a loaf of cornbread and put it in his mouth. While he was chewing he said, as if to himself, It uses too much of me. It leaves too little.

His father looked up from where he sat on the end of the bench along the wooden table they had made together two winters ago. Rain rattled against the shuttered windows, and the cool dampness permeated everything except the small space directly in front of the fire that burned in the stone fireplace at the room's center. The log that was burning collapsed into the flame and new light flowed from it and mixed with the shadows from the gray windows and washed across the table where they now both sat. Joseph pushed the bench back, rose again, and walked to the pile of split wood. He lifted one he favored, split sharp and straight—exposing small black holes where worms had weaved their way through the old oak, hastening its journey to the hearth and to the fire. Joseph grabbed it with one hand, held it vertically, knocked it clean against the stone floor, and dropped it into the fire, causing a burst of sparks and smoke.

And what is it you would use the rest for then, Joe? Hittin rocks with sticks, playin games?

It aint a stick and if you hit rocks with it it's ruined. And that's not what I mean anyway. I don' know what I mean. I mean this farm caint be the whole of it. There's a war, and that'll change everythin. You just won't see it.

War changes nothin. It destroys everythin. Men'll kill each other for sport—there's your game—and there aint no work gets done. One side kills more and then the thing is done and all that's left is the misery of the thing—and nothin else is changed. Mothers without sons and women left without men and boys who've seen too much to ever be boys again—

there's your change—and that's it. His father knocked his pipe on the edge of the table and the burnt wad of tobacco fell to the floor and he kicked it away with his boot. If this uses you up then sure as hell war'll spit you out, son. You may as well lay out in the field for the hawks and vultures.

He had never seen his father like this. Though Joseph knew that his grandfather had never returned from the War of '12, his father spoke little of it. He had not even seen his father cry at his mother's death. Caleb had sat alone in a straight-back chair by the same fireplace, hands folded in his lap, jaw set firm against the world—eyes dark and set down to the floor. When his nine-year-old son had come to him and laid his hand on the broad, muscled shoulder, the father's left hand lifted and crossed his chest to rest on the small hand of Joseph. The weight of it brought to the surface the pain of the long days—watching his mother die—the coughing— chest heaving and stomach flat and hard with muscles against the exhausting pain. He had dropped his face to his father's hand and let the tears roll across the rough skin of his knuckles and down onto his father's fingers and waited for his father to pull him, waited for the huge arms to lift him up and to enfold him, waited to mix his own with his father's tears—to somehow in the letting go begin the first step together, without her. But his father's eyes remained fixed on the stone floor and the hand gently pulled away and fell to the thigh. The boy's chin then rested on his father's shoulder and he watched his father's hands go to his eyes but he could not see tears. But then his father wiped his hands on his wool trousers—he was sure of it.

The depth of the void could not be understood and could not be breached. Caleb Tyler was left numbed and wasted and dead of heart. He blamed himself, blamed this hard life—and he could not allow his young son into the dark space he now occupied. He was alone and would not have it any different. Joseph could only look in—could not bridge the darkness to his father.

Now, years later in front of the hearth—his father's eyes appeared the same as he fathomed more loss. Though he had little to show for his labor outside food and shelter—and the land—it was all he knew. In the company of the boy he had cleared fields and harvested, butchered and laundered and sewed. They had gathered blankets together in November for winter's harsh nights. They had fallen asleep together under the same blankets—the fire falling into itself and out. They had risen early for chores and breakfasted with bacon and bread. Joseph had read to his father from books he collected in town and from his mother's Bible and the father's expression had softened as he listened to the words and let himself rest in their rhythm.

And what of the work you've started? Who's to finish . . . what about the wall?

The field is cleared, Joseph answered, and I'll work on the wall, maybe finish it myself, and the ground is almost ready for planting but you shouldn't yet. Work the east field and you'll have enough. The yanks'll take the rest anyway. Word is they'll be through here within weeks unless we push em back and that's what I figure I oughta do. Have enough for yerself and then I'll be back and we can work the new field together when the war is won.

He heard his father laugh and watched him turn away. Wars aint won, he said, they're just finished. Little is gained an' a whole lot is lost and you'll not be back, Joseph, but some stranger may return. Find his father alone and crippled with the pain of workin and they'll be nothin left to be said. You'll not be back.

At this his father turned from the fire and walked to the door and outside. The roof extended about five feet over a porch, and the rain poured in clear sheets off the roof and into a trench they had dug so the water would run down and away from the house. Joseph could see through the frosted glass of the window his father's tall figure standing straight and watched him as he stretched his arms out, palms up, and let the rain pour across his callused hands. It was the closest, he thought, his father had ever come to prayer—letting an angry sky and relentless rain wash over him. He knew the war would come to them—to the farm—and he could not stop it. He could not protect his boy any more than he could protect his dear wife, and Caleb Tyler wept as he stood and the tears mixed with rain now on his face so that his son could not tell if they were tears and would never know if he had seen his father weep. His father walked out into the rain and crossed the field to the shed and Joseph turned from the window and laid out along his bed and it wasn't long before he was asleep.

The next morning Joseph rose early, before his father. He mixed some of the coffee with chicory which would give it a bitter taste but would help save the last of the treasured grounds as the federal ships choked the southern harbors. It wouldn't be long until it was all gone and no one knew when it would be available again. He started the fire from warm embers, stirring them into a small flame, and pulled a woolen shawl over his shoulders. He waited until the fire was hot and the smell of the coffee told him it was ready and he poured the dark liquid into a tin cup. He left another cup empty for his father and walked out of the door, onto the porch, cup in hand and sipping the hot, rich liquid between his lips—trying to ignore the slightly bitter taste until his body began to feel warm and his shoulders relaxed.

The rain had stopped some time during the night and puddles lay like glass in the shallow depressions along the front of the farmhouse. The trench was filled with muddy water that trickled its way through the grass, weaving cracks in the saturated earth down the slope, some settling in the soil of the lower pasture, some ending in rivulets and brooks and down the Salmon River and to the Rapidan and the James. He thought of this as the last remnants of the storm dripped from the roof and he wondered at the journey and wondered what it meant that his farmhouse was part of it, that the rain had been a drone surrounding his conversation with his father the night before in front of the fire. What part of this were they? Why did it make any difference except that if his father had not built this house here, the rain would have fallen unobstructed to the fallow earth and the fields would be running with streams and wild berry and the stones would lie uncovered and sink deeper into the swallowing earth. What could be raised up? The stone itself was sinking, the porch falling. He could see his mother's body—the crude box twisting and the ropes pulled tight and then dropped and buried as well. What could be held—raised up and held?

The sun appeared finally, following a deep pink wash and emerging from behind Stone Hill, presenting a portrait of morning as he watched from the porch. Silver light washed across the smooth puddles, and the limbs of the trees lit as from beneath with the droplets of water shining like cut gems on their smallest branches and the swollen buds. The shadow of a hawk fell across the landscape followed by its echoed cry. He watched not the hawk, but its shadow, as it drifted across the field and vanished in the wilderness beyond. He could see insects touching the still surfaces of water, creating gentle wrinkles that pulsed across the natural landscape.

Where he stood on the porch he was covered by the extended roof of pine boards. Rusty nails showed through the bottom, holding cedar shingles black and silver from the southern sun. His father had turned some cedar posts round with varied designs—looking almost like knees and muscled legs as they held the roof upward. The porch had settled on one end, and the wood surface slanted toward the far corner almost imperceptibly. Wooden steps sitting on great stones had stayed straight and were now askew from the porch—separate and correct, but pulling the railing away from itself and exposing the iron nails like teeth.

Joseph took another sip of the coffee and then tilted the cup back high and drained its last gritty liquid and rested the cup on the railing of the porch. He folded the shawl on a bench by the door and sat next to it to put on his boots and lace them. They were cool from the night air but dry from being near the fireplace, and the feeling of them as he stood made him feel somehow strong. They were made of good leather he and his father had tanned and stretched themselves last summer, and he had treated them with oil and dried them carefully and oiled the cracks to keep them soft. He walked off the porch on high ground, above the puddles of water and toward the new field and toward the wall.

The wall to be worked now started on a high knoll where they had cut down the timothy grass with scythes and leveled an area with shovel and rake—and where new grass was already growing around the large foundation stones. It was just over knee height and about as wide, and as Joseph approached it this morning he could look down the top surface the entire length of the wall and it looked as smooth and consistent as a turnpike road—as though a man could walk on it without fearing tripping and without looking down where he stepped. The morning sun sliced the rounded stones and the even spaces between the stones with precise shadow across its face, and it seemed each stone was a different shade of silver and of black and brown. It appeared almost as a jewel necklace across the rolling pasture.

Behind the wall the tall pine and oak stretched to the sun and cast shadows along the length of the stonework, and in the shadows there were snakes that had already found a home between the cool stone and the damp earth and lay silent in the cool morning, and still.

Joseph walked the length of the wall from the high knoll and down the slope across the pasture and toward the woodland, where the wall now ended in a pile of stones about thirty feet short of the field's end. This is where he would work this morning—to finish the full length of the wall for his father—to try to match his father's precision in the choosing and in the breaking and in the setting of the stones. But he knew that he could not work like his father—as if the wall were there to be discovered in the empty air and all that was needed was the filling of it.

The walls frame a man's life, his father had said as they lifted stones together from the raw field in the early winter. They mark us upon the earth as surely as the scent of the wolf. These are our stories, Joseph. Not the words in your books. These walls mark a man's work and measure him.

Joseph began to work at the stone but he could hear clearly his father's words as if they lay across the still morning air along the field.

They're a measure of a man, he had repeated as they worked together and then he had grabbed Joseph's arm with his huge hand and pointed across the fields of Blackstone. Look now—out there—across the field,

Joseph. The rows of wheat, these are our bloodlines brought from the earth ourselves. These walls, these are the boundaries we live our lives within, the claim—the claim of ourselves on the living earth. When you cross the path, Joseph, from the woodland and see the first silver stones that my father laid you know your place is here and your mark will be left on this land as surely as mine.

The large hand dropped from his arm and his father turned back toward the house and to the hills that lay like a swelling tide on the gray horizon.

This war, he muttered, this is not our war. No other man has lifted one stone from this rocky ground, no other man besides my father and my son. No Virginian, no slave, no negro has ever worked this land. Let them fight their damn war. It is this land and our work upon it that I'll defend—our sweat that's altered it. No yankees or any other soldier has any business here, and I swear these stone walls will still be standin when every soldier's buried in the good ground of Virginia or Pennsylvania or Washington. These walls will stand to frame the good work we done here on the land that the good Lord gave us.

Joseph lifted a rounded stone with one flat side and let it sit in the spot where he worked along the ground. It did not quite fit—still rocked when he tried to settle it—and he cast it aside and lifted another stone and this one slid into the space solid and provided a flat surface for the next. One side was rounded and he looked along the pile for a stone that was cupped on one side—that would fit into the rounded face of the last—and found it at the pile's edge beneath some thin ones that he would use later in the small spaces between the larger stones. The stone he had chosen fit perfectly and the wall was extended about eighteen inches at the base and now needed to be built higher.

He worked like this all morning and through the noon hour, his father's words never far from his thoughts. They rang true for his father—Joseph understood this—but he could not accept the words at the level his father did—and he understood this as well. He worked hard at the wall—breaking stones, setting them, and standing back to see the texture of the wall and watch how the light played along its surface. He stood back often to see if the new wall matched the old—but the difference was clear. There was no mistake where his father's work had finished and his had begun— and as careful, and sure as he was with each stone, the difference was clear.

He looked down the field and he could see his father begin working at the rows of wheat and at the earth between the rows. He was sure his father could see him working as well. Joseph stood to stretch the muscles of his back and legs and looked over the close ridge and across the hills to the farthest ridge and to the sky beyond the ridges. At the horizon, a great wash of red crept up the blue sky and stained it in the midday sun. Joseph knew what it was—the dust of a hundred horses along the red clay roads of the valley—of wagons and of men—of cannon dragged on iron-faced wheels of wood against the leather roads. And he knew that his father could see it as well—and that his father knew what it was but would not speak of it.

II.

Later that afternoon it had grown hot and his shirt was soaked with sweat from the day's work and he pulled at the material—pulled it from his wet skin and held his arms out to let what little breeze there was flow under his arms and along his neck. Walter Graham, Gordon Stewart, and his brother Samuel had joined Terence and Joseph after the work hours and supper to play ball, and they were already on the field as Joseph walked down the path to the clearing. They were tossing the leather ball back and forth to each other and when Terence saw Joseph, he caught the ball, turned, and threw it on a line to Joseph, who without thinking raised his hands and felt it slap into his palms. He wheeled around in a full circle and threw it high where Gordon and Sam both ran for it and Sam caught it and cheered himself and then threw it to his brother. Joseph set a stake in the ground, actually an old shovel handle he had cut down and sharp- ened, and paced off forty-five feet where he placed a rock. This would be the place where they would throw it from to the striker. There was a slightly worn place where the pitcher had stood last week to throw and the rock was placed to the side of this worn spot. Joseph signaled Terence to get up to bat and put his hands out to receive the ball from Gordon. Give me a couple warm-ups, he said to Terence, and his friend stood at the staked ground and put his hands up in different positions and Joseph threw the ball and it hit Terence's hands without moving every time.

Terence finally yelled, You're ready. C'mon, lemme hit, and Joseph agreed and settled himself to pitch. Walter, Gordon, and Samuel took to the field ready to catch the ball on one bounce so that the batter would be out. Sam stood almost on the treeline at the meadow's edge and Joseph was already thinking they needed to move to a bigger field soon.

Gordon and Sam had weaved together old leather from haversacks and rawhide from saddles to fashion catching gloves—but the other boys had laughed at them and they put them away and used them only when they played alone at home. The baseball they were using was from New York but had been used a lot and was softening and the leather was worn and the shape varied when you hit it hard and that made it even more difficult to catch. Terence had made some balls but he couldn't quite get the yarn wound tight enough and the balls he made were soft and sort of lumpy, so they tried to use the ball his cousin had sent them, at least until it was all used up, which would probably be very soon.

Joseph felt the raised stitching in his hands and he held the ball firmly but with some space between the leather and his skin. It seemed the stitching actually fell into the texture of his callused skin—rested in the wrinkles of his long fingers as he gripped it and looked in at Terence swinging the bat in front of him and loosening the muscles of his shoulders.

When you're ready, he heard Terence yell, and he shifted his feet and got ready to deliver the ball.

Up to this point the boys who were throwing or pitching were pretty much serving up a perfect pitch for the batter. They threw it until the batter struck it hard and then the fielders would run to catch the driven ball. But Joseph was beginning to feel a new challenge emerging. He could tell from how he threw it that the ball would move in slightly different ways—and that if he pitched it hard enough, nobody could get the bat around fast enough to slug it. He had experimented a little, but for the most part he had put this in the back of his head and practiced a little with the different throws on his own on the back fields of Blackstone. But today he was ready for a new challenge, and Terence was just the one.

You aint hittin me today, he called in to Terence.

Terence looked to him and called back, Whad you say?

Joseph repeated the challenge. You aint hittin today.

Terence laughed and spit and said, You throw whatever kinda throws you want, Joe Tyler, and if I can reach it I'll hit it so far we'll be stitchin new balls by nightfall.

Joseph laughed and Walter called in to him to let him hit it but Joseph concentrated on the feel of the ball in his hand, turned it until the stitching felt just right, pulled the ball down to his thigh and over his head, and let it sail toward the place where Terence stood with the bat and watched as Terence took a huge swing—almost falling down, and then turning to watch the ball roll toward the stand of pine behind him.

Terence looked back to Joseph as he retrieved the ball and shook his head and was laughing as he yelled to him, Even you don't hit it every time, Tyler, and he reset himself next to the stake in the ground and prepared to swing. This time Joseph turned the ball a half-rotation so the stitching crossed the middle of his fingers and he wound up and let the ball fly from his hand, and as he did he turned his hand slightly and could feel the ball spin and watched as Terence focused on it and tensed to swing and then swung the large wooden bat just as the ball changed path in the flight toward him and dropped down to the ground at Terence's feet, and Terence swung at the air and the bat never came near the ball.

What the hell was that? I aint never seen that, Terence was saying and the boys in the field were yelling to Joseph to serve the ball so he could hit it cause standin out here was no fun if he aint gonna hit it, so Joseph sent the next pitch up to Terence in a perfect arc and Terence hit it solid and Walter Graham caught it on one bounce and called one hand down as if

they were in a game, and for the rest of the afternoon Joseph threw the
ball up to the plate and let the hitters hit it hard and let the fielders run
after the ball, but the challenge had been set, and the game had a new
twist in Joseph's mind. Terence looked at him after they were finished
playing and Walter, Gordon, and Sam had left and agreed to meet again
next Saturday and walked off onto the trail through the woods and
Terence asked him what that was all about.

Joseph just smiled and put his hand on Terence's shoulder as they
walked down the hill and along the river carrying the bat and ball. I don'
know. I just think there might be somethin to the throwin—like maybe
hittin aint the whole game.

Hittins what's fun though, Joseph, and he held the bat in front of him
and pretended to swing.

I don't know, said Joseph, I kinda liked throwin it and seein you get all
twisted up tryin to hit it and he laughed as he said it and pulled Terence's
hat down over his eyes and ran along the edge of the river toward home.

They played every week like this, at least once a week, but Terence and
Joseph would practice hitting and throwing even more—sometimes four
nights a week after chores and before the sun went down so low that you
couldn't see the ball, but sometimes they played right through that too until
you had to almost know where the ball was going to catch it because you
couldn't see it in the darkness. On the nights when there was a full moon
they played right through until they were so tired they had to sit and when
they sat, sometimes they lay back together on the grass and watched the
stars and tossed the ball up against the dotted sky and caught it as it came
down to their hands until one of them would miss it and then they'd start
again and keep track of who missed the most and it never seemed to matter
that Joseph always won and that he almost never missed—but he never
pointed that out to Terence and Terence never seemed to shy from the challenge and the best thing was just lying there and looking up at the sky and
feeling the cool grass on your back. Months went by like this and with every
month they came to love the game more and their skills were refined and
the game blossomed in their hands in the cool Virginia nights and the hot

mornings along the fields and in the meadow behind the barn where they practiced their swing and they practiced their throws until Joseph could hit a tin can sitting on a fence post from fifty feet, nine times out of ten, and Terence wasn't far behind. They grew with the game—and the game grew in their hands—and now they always called it base ball and their friends came to call it this as well when they played.

That same summer they sat on a wooden fence that corralled horses behind the barn at Terence's farm. It was evening but the ground still held the day's warmth even as the air began to cool.

They say the yanks play ball in their camps.

Terence said this as he pitched stones across the dirt in front of them and watched their flight across the split-rail fence where the dirt ended and the tall grass bunched up below the lower rails. The sun had turned the split rails the color of old coin and the grass was yellow against it.

They're good, I hear, Joseph said and waved mosquitoes away from his face with his hand. They persisted and he waved behind his head and then jumped from the top rail of the fence to the ground. A single white cloud was being torn in two—drifting apart and evaporating in the deep blue of the evening sky—and although the daylight still held ground, a white moon already sat over the first ridge of mountains. They could see it clear from where they stood.

Terence's father pulled at a horse, dragging something behind it. One of his little sisters appeared at the door of the farmhouse at the edge of the meadow, yelled something, ran across the porch, and disappeared behind the house. She then reappeared at the opposite corner with a boy in chase, naked from the waist down—perhaps five years old, wearing only a gray poncho-like shirt and crying as they ascended the steps of the porch together and disappeared into the open doorway. Seconds later someone closed the door and they could hear it shut. Terence shook his head. He was somehow removed from his own family. His mother had come down with yellow fever after Terence was born and so it looked like he would be their only child. And that's how it had been for nearly nine years. Then his mother got pregnant again, and then every year after that until there were six brothers and sisters in a house that had seemed too small for the three of them. Terence was asked to help with the children and he felt much more like another parent than a brother. Like Joseph's, his time as a child had been short, and this drew them together even more. Joe Tyler was much more of a brother than his own kin. And he believed Joseph felt the same way.

We'll be killin yanks soon enough, Terence said as he followed Joseph down from the fence. He picked up the broken handle of a pitchfork—pretended it was a rifle and aimed it toward a bird that passed overhead—and made a shooting sound and then turned suddenly as if someone was following behind them and shot again. Joseph, laughing, reached to grab the wood from Terence and they fell to the ground wrestling until Terence's grip was lost, overcome by Joseph's strength, and Joseph stood over his friend with the handle pointing down at his chest.

Don't shoot, Terence yelled loud enough to startle a fox at the edge of the meadow, and they watched it dash across the open field and disappear in the woods. Then he said, Go ahead and shoot ya lousy yank.

Again laughing, Joseph responded, Some soldier you'll be, askin the enemy to shoot ya. Might as well tell ole Jeff Davis that he don' have a prayer once you get to soldierin, and he put the handle down to his friend's hands. Terence gripped the handle and Joseph leaned backward and pulled him up with one pull. The sun was now gone behind the hills and clear yellow light was spun along the belly of the torn cloud.

They stood side by side to admire the work of the sun. The barn door shut and they could see Terence's father returning to the house wiping his brow with a blue rag as he walked—kicking at something on the ground—and then walking to the porch and up the steps to the house. The house was darker inside than was the evening sky and its white side-boards seemed to glow and then slowly fade to grays and silver as they watched. Terence reached down and grabbed a smooth stone from the ground, turned and faced Joseph, and, holding the stone in his palm, tossed it up in the air. The wooden handle was resting on Joseph's shoulder but instantly reacted to the stone's flight, intercepted it and sent it hurtling across the dirt path and far into the canopy of trees that framed the open land of the farm. Another stone—then another crack was heard—and another, the swing becoming more fluid, the muscles both relaxed and tense, another crack and the black object disappeared into the fading light.

We'll be killin yanks soon enough, Terence said.

Joseph said, And they'll be killin us, till the thing is over.

He pulled the wood to rest on his shoulder, now letting the last stone fly uninterrupted, and took silent aim at the wilderness around the farm.

It aint gonna be like shootin fox and pheasants, he said as he continued to aim, moving the wooden handle slowly across the horizon—looking for something moving, or something that didn't belong. It aint gonna be like that.

We'll be goin together then, right? Terence asked and put his hands out to receive the pretend rifle from Joseph's hands. Joseph nodded without saying anything as he watched the moon whiten against the deep blue sky and let the weight of his body rest on the rough wood of the fence in a place where the ax had not fallen true and he could feel the rough surface through the folds of his trousers.

Best be goin, he said, and Joseph began to walk and then run toward the path that would lead him home. The white cloud had now drifted in front of the summer moon and the path was unusually dark. The summer's growth was vigorous and choked the path so that only one man at a time could pass through it in many places and even that took both hands pushing vegetation away so that your feet could step solid on the ground. Terence dropped the wooden handle and walked toward his house after the dark figure of his friend disappeared into the thick trees. He took one more look at the cloud, now ghostly gray like smoke in front of the full white moon, and looked to the house. Still no light shone from within and he could hear one of the children crying as he approached. For a moment that was all that he heard—the solitary voice of the crying child across the field and across the night—and he looked quickly toward Joseph who was already gone. Terence Hooker looked across the empty field and listened to the voice for a moment. If not for Joe Tyler, this would be a solitary life, he thought, and hurried up the porch and into the house.

Joseph felt his way down the path and along the river by memory, especially in the thick part of the woods where the trees blocked the light as much as the roof of a cabin. Only along the river, where the water seemed to shine with the moonlight, could he see clearly and then he reentered the darkness to the top of the hill where the woods ended and the earth opened up to a field of wheat. He could see the lighted windows of his father's cabin in the darkness. The yellow light seemed to pulse like blood against the dark night, and he felt uneasy as he opened the door and entered the light of the room. His father sat at the table eating dinner, two candles on the wooden table laying wax along the smooth grain and a single oil lamp glowing on the far wall by the dry sink. The lamp hung crooked along the wall and the light was uneven and strange.

You'll fix your own then, his father said, and nothing else before they both cleaned pans and retired to their beds. Before he left the room, Joseph pinched both candles and there was again complete darkness except for the glowing of the moon from behind the thin sheet of clouds.

Sleepless, he rose from his bed and entered the room. He lit one of the candles and sat quietly so as not to wake his father. The light of the candle flickered in a breeze through the window and the shadows danced along the floor and walls of the cabin and then froze again as if they were painted there. The window rattled in a strengthening wind. Joseph went to the table in the corner where he knew the *Gazette* newspaper was that they had bought last week and unfolded the paper on the table and sat to read in the light of the candle. He was hungry and he unwrapped some salted pork and pulled pieces of it away with his fingers and put them to his mouth.

Joseph turned the pages, licking his fingers, and gripped the thin corners of the paper. He read the black type—about the battles of the war—about the great victories of the Confederate army—he looked at the drawings of soldiers crossing a stone bridge—a cartoon of President

Lincoln with his awkward length exaggerated—his arms and legs stretched so his hands hung down to his feet like an ape. He saw the caption, "Ape Lincoln," and he smiled as he licked his fingers and turned to the next page.

There were death notices, a description of the new capitol building in Richmond, more death notices framed in thick black banners. His eyes were tiring as he scanned over the words and across the pictures until they froze on a picture that hung by itself at the bottom of the right-hand column. He reached for the candle and pulled it closer to the page. It was a drawing of a man, a great drooping mustache hung from the corners of his mouth. The artist had drawn thick eyebrows to match. His shirt and trousers were uniform, with some kind of stitching—some lettered insignia suggested across his chest. On his head was a flat-topped hat, and the bill was darkened with the ink from the artist's pen. The figure's hands were drawn in bold lines that stretched strong around the deep grain of a wooden bat. The figure held the bat over his right shoulder—dark eyes set in focus to the distance— frozen in time by the artist in the position of waiting for a pitched ball, the instant before the swing of the bat. The caption read simply "The Base Ball Player," and nothing else. Joseph searched for more words but there were none. Just the picture. His eyes rested on the lines that formed the figure on the page. He looked at how the artist had carefully drawn the grain of the wooden bat—the shadows of the muscles of the hands wrapped around it. There it was—in front of him. He grabbed a broom from the corner and stood in a stance like the player—set his eyes ahead of him, like the picture—imagined someone drawing him—watching him as he played the game. That's what it was—a game—just a child's game his father had said many times—but here it was in the newspaper for a thousand people to see. So it was not only him. He was not the only one entranced by the game— not the only one who saw that it was more than that. He turned the pages no more—left it open on the table as he pinched the candle again and returned to bed. He left it open for his father to see in the morning and he lay in his bed for hours with the image of the baseball player frozen before him and he could not sleep at all through the night.

III.

The next day he worked harder than ever in the fields, and in the long days after that until the skin of his hands was cracked and coarse and the muscles of his shoulders and arms tightened like the roots of young trees. He waited for his father to say something about the picture in the paper, but nothing was said—nothing changed, and the work went on as usual.

Joseph rose most mornings before his father, and after eating biscuits or cold meat from the previous evening's meal he would walk from the porch to the small barn and, with a long stick, knock the canvas feed bags that served as poor distraction to the field mice and woodchucks. The noise would draw the white chickens from the morning shadows of the barn and Joseph would push them gently away with his boots as he spread the feed along the ground with a tin scoop.

This past year Caleb had traded a large pantry he had made years ago from red oak for a milking cow, and Joseph set out the pans that his father would use for milking and then walked from the barn, leaving the door slightly ajar to let in the air and light of the morning. The chickens pecked at the ground and two of them followed Joseph through the door and into the thin grass where yesterday's feed might still lie undiscovered. He walked, as he almost always did, to where the horse, Samuel, stood grazing in a small pasture. The first wall of tumbled stone framed the high grass and discouraged what little inclination the horse might have had to wander into the wilderness.

It was on these mornings and in these moments that Joseph loved Blackstone the most. With the earth awakening and the breath of the animals thick and close. In the light of the sun not yet risen, the forest yet embraced by night, and only the field and the young corn illuminated like some spectral image of itself. Suspended in the acquaintance of new light and old light as it must have been at some beginning. Stars to sun, sun to stars. And again the morning.

The months passed this way as well, mirroring themselves and changing ever so slowly. He was, for the most part, comfortable with the rolling of time and the way life slid from season to season. In the spring he worked at his father's side, just as his mother had before him, behind the moldboard plow. The plow broke the soil and pulled more stones from the ground and Joseph would drag them on a wooden cart to a pile on the field's edge where they would dry and turn silver in the summer sun and finally find their place along another wall. Then Caleb would hitch the horse to the harrow and Joseph would follow, setting corn seeds in the black furrows, pushing the wet soil over them gingerly with his fist. Planting used most of the daylight hours in the spring and it wasn't until the days lengthened that he had any time for ball. Still, there were those nights even in spring—the day's work done, supper eaten—when he would walk the trail to meet Terence at a clearing by the river, where the day's light lingered longer, and there they would stand and toss a cowhide ball back and forth until the night crawled up through the tall trees and they would return home for sleep and the morning's chores. Caleb was usually down by then, either in his chair by the fireplace or retired to his bed. Joseph would go quietly to his room and lie in the dim light of the moon. These quiet moments were his own. The hours—before sleep—were completely his own.

On this night he lay in his bed with the quilted blanket pulled close to his chin and then pulled to beneath his eyes, covering his cheeks and his mouth, so the warm breath stayed within the blanket. He breathed in— he could remember when he could smell his mother in this blanket after she was gone, and he would sleep with it even in the hot summer, sleep with it twirled around him or with his face buried in it as a pillow. His father would come to take it from him and he would protest and pull it back to himself and his father would walk away and say, You'll be hot then wrapped in that—and Joseph could not see the tears in his father's eyes as he walked away and left him in the room wrapped in the quilt that his mother had made for him. But her scent was long gone—and as hard as he tried he could not see her face.

His eyes were becoming heavy and he let them close. He could hear in the distance the roll of thunder over the hills and through the window. Through his half-open eyes he could see the unmistakable blue light of an approaching storm. Then his eyes were closed when the rain came and the storm whipped around the house and it did not disturb his sleep.

And just as the storms crept down the hills to embrace the valley, so the light would emerge again—the infant sun peeking below the blanket of clouds to lay its new light across the streams and the wood. The days would be filled with the work of the field and the nights roll one to the other like the rows of corn and of wheat and the ancient stone of the walls that lay draped across it.

Autumn came and turned the sky to thick glass, reflecting the rich colors of the earth and spinning them clear until it lay across the valley the color of granite and white water. And the leaves of the trees curled into themselves and then paused before breaking free—to dance down—to join their shadows on the cool grass of the valley and the hills. And the pine set out a fresh blanket of brown needles beneath themselves and in folds across the woodland paths. And one storm led to another and the rain turned to wet snow and sleet—and the winter, thinly concealed in the changing sky, settled into the valley and across the fields of Blackstone.

There were many days when they could work—repairing cart and wagon, continuing to pull the stones from the reluctant ground, dragging manure to a pit along the pasture's edge, where it was left to dry and rot and then be shoveled again and spread for spring fertilizer. And on the days they were forced inside his father would go to the shed to work with wood and clean and repair the tools for the next season, and in the hours that Joseph was not needed he sat by the fire and read whatever he could. He had taken two of the Waverley novels from the book wagon that passed through town in September and then had grabbed a copy of something new called *Great Expectations* and he read this without stopping and then read it again and wrote down these lines and tucked the paper away.

It was one of those March days when the sun shines hot
and the wind blows cold—when it is summer in the light, and

winter in the shade. We had our pea-coats with us, and I took a bag. Of all my worldly possessions I took no more than the few necessaries that filled the bag. Where I might go, what I might do, or when I might return were questions utterly unknown to me; nor did I vex my mind with them. . . . I only wondered for the passing moment, as I stopped at the door and looked back, under what altered circumstances I should next see these rooms, if ever.

He could remember no colder winter and the world around him was frozen for weeks and then months and the woodpiles near the house shrank and they pulled wood from the far piles and dragged it across the frozen pasture. And when the days started to lengthen, he couldn't wait to be out again and watch the shrinking shadows, anxious even to work the fields.

It was a few days before March. Joseph had risen early this morning and had some cornbread and was already out in the field before the sun's full light. He was working the stone wall—trying to discover what his father could feel in the work, practicing the art of laying the stones in place. Maybe he would finish it then—and his father would be proud—and they would have something to talk about in the cold evening. He had been working hard for an hour or so when he heard Terence's voice calling from the woodland path. Joseph, he said, a whole reg'ment's comin—a whole compn'y. Joseph did not know the difference and he doubted Terence did either. He dropped the large stone in his arms and let it fall and settle on the ground. A whole comp'ny along the turnpike road, he repeated. Headed east I think—along the Rapidan.

They looked back across the field to Joseph's house and could see his father emerge from the door and descend the porch steps. He was walking slowly toward them in the field, and they could see his white breath in the clear morning air. They were silent as they watched him.

He walked along the wall to where they stood. I'm goin to town, they heard him say. You know the day's work. I'll be home before sunset and I'll be needin supper.

Walkin? Joseph asked.

His father told him that he was walking and one of the chores this week was to repair the wagon's axle, which was split, and that it was a good morning to walk anyway. He nodded to Terence and turned away.

There's a reg'ment comin, Joseph said.

His father stopped in his path and stood still. Then he turned to the both of them. His eyes met Joseph's, and then turned away to look across the field and back to the cabin. I know, Caleb said. I could see the firelight over the ridge last night—knew it had to be campfires. If you see them you tell em to keep movin. They got no business here. And stay to your work.

He turned and began his walk toward the path that led down to the river and to the road. Joseph watched him as his long legs stepped over rocks—his hands tucked into the pockets of his jacket, a black felt hat covering his head and drooping toward his broad shoulders. He watched him until he was a dark figure between the trunks of pine and bare oak—until he had vanished into the woodland—and when he could no longer see his father Joseph let his weight settle onto the thick rock wall and crossed his arms to warm himself.

Terence sat next to him and stretched his thin legs out in front of them. S'pose it's time, he said to Joseph.

Joseph Tyler looked down the almost flat surface of the wall. There were thin veils of snow across the broad surfaces of the larger capstones but the morning sun was already licking at its edges, turning it to water. Thicker snow clung to leaves and sticks in the cracks between. The surface of the ground was hard but Virginia's frost was not deep and soon the fields would be wet with spring.

He could see the long length of the wall his father had spent years building, and he could see the difference where he had started laying stone—not the same tightness, not the same even, predictable texture—and he wanted to go back, and to pull stones from the wall and start again.

I s'pose it's time, he said to Terence. I s'pose it's comin to us so we don't have to go to it. It don't seem like a thing a man can turn away from.

They sat like that for a while, feeling the cold, hard stone beneath them and watching the morning envelop the field and the white stone turning black. As they sat Joseph tried to regain the image of his mother's face, tried to see her but he could not.

I caint remember my mother's face—what she looked like, he said to Terence.

Terence nodded and put a hand on Joseph's shoulder and they both rose to walk across the field. I don't s'pose you would, he said to Joseph. I don't s'pose we could see the dead once they gone, not that way anyway. But maybe she can see you, and Terence and Joseph both looked upward to the clear sky. Wouldn't that be better? added Terence, if she could see you right now?

Joseph looked across the farm and to the hills beyond and said, I s'pose, and then, Don't s'pose she'd like what she was seein.

And the boys walked together to Joseph's house and then to Terence's to gather their things and they left together. They carried a blanket and a crude mess kit and an extra pair of woolen socks and they left down the trail, still frozen with winter—walking in the direction of the turnpike where the red dust danced like water over the Army of Northern Virginia and they could see it clearly through the soft needles of pine.

THIRD

Breath to Vapor

The mystic chords of memory, stretching from every battlefield,
and every patriot grave, to every living heart and hearthstone,
all over this broad land, will yet swell the chorus of the Union,
when again touched, as surely as they will be, by the better angels
of our nature.
        —Abraham Lincoln, 1861

I.

Virginia that spring had experienced heavy rains and the earth in all the ravines and low ground was saturated. The colloidal soil, fallow and unturned, had presented an uneasy surface for the marching armies. Since March the sun had only shone unobscured for seven or eight days, and the souls of the soldiers weighed down by loneliness and fatigue were further crushed by an oppressive envelope of fog and rain. Still they clattered on, canteen and haversack, rifle and saber—on paths cut through the woods by hunters, on the gravel roads of loggers, and sometimes on the paths they were forced themselves to hack through the thicket and brush—trampled by ten thousand bootsteps and the dragging wheels of cannon and wagon.

The men of the 2d Army Corps walked this way—it could not be called marching—leaning forward, dragging foot ahead of foot, touching the pack of the man in front, stumbling to slow down and leave space. Most men's eyes were downward. The key was to avoid tripping on exposed stones, which would mean falling forward under the weight of haversack and musket into the cool, greasy mud and hours of discomfort and prayer for the warmth of sunlight. Staying upright was the thing. Balancing and stepping and staying upright under the crushing weight of the war.

A boy-soldier carried the Stars and Bars near the front of the line on a thin shaft. It was tattered and not quite red and blue and it snapped occasionally in a breeze but mostly hung down along the pole. The uniforms of the Confederacy, once steel-gray, were now the yellow-gray of the walnut hulls and copperas that were used to dye the thin cloth—leading the yanks to nickname them "butternuts." Joseph had received one of these uniforms and put it on proudly at first but now pulled it to himself at night against the dampness as he cursed the thin thread and the seams pulled away from themselves.

Each man was the harbinger of his own soul, the protector of his particular humanity, so the essence not be lost in this horror. Dreams of farms, of mothers and fathers, of sweethearts; dreams of boyhood games; dreams of stillness and quiet had replaced any dreams of glory or of victory. Abstract notions—bravery, loyalty, slavery—were meaningless, crushed under the weight of war, under the weight of fog and rain, crushed with the reality of torn tissue and exhausted spirit.

This is where ideas die. When the water starts to seep into the seams of boots and human flesh discolors, ideas are dead things—things for other men to consider. Men who sit where fires burn in the hearth and whose feet rest on firm ground. As these boys—dressed as soldiers—moved through the woods, the mosquitoes swirled around their heads and came to rest on the moist skin at the backs of their necks and in the sweat-soaked folds of their uniforms and they tried to wave them away with their hands as they walked. Almost as one, they walked—as a brooding beast, awkwardly quiet—lumbering along a trail too narrow to contain it but providing the only path available. Eyes down. Always down.

Joseph walked all morning this way, concentrating on the movement of his feet along the ground, and as he did he became aware of the woods as he had known them before. By afternoon a weak spring sun created a mosaic of light upon the gravel path as it turned its way through new oak leaves and pine. The dogwoods that were not shattered by shell were still in bloom and the canopy of trees danced with the short frenetic lives of insects. Concentrating on the play of light and the changing ground as he walked, Joseph allowed his mind to wander away from the shuffling feet in front and behind him. He saw the stronger sun wash the pink flowers of a dogwood at the bend ahead—the outstretched branch holding shining pearls in its palm, offered up to the boundless sky—away from the deep woods; and he let his mind relax and his thoughts wander.

To a moment long before his mother's illness—and he could see it clearly. She picked him up from his bed and let him lie laughing on her shoulder—let the blankets fall to the floor. She carried him that way from his room to the great room, as it seemed to him—where the fire was. Along the mantel there were herbs drying, which leaned over the stone and clung to their color and to their fragrance—even as the air inhaled the moisture from them and left them lifeless across the stone. A crude white vase sat at the center of the table, at the center of the room, and was filled with yellow daisies that spilled over the thick top of the clay and dropped petals along the table, where they dried and curled like worms along the wood. He could hear the sounds of the ax against logs, the steel blade slicing through the thick grain of oak as his father split wood, preparing for winter. The sound of each cut ended as suddenly as it began. He could hear it clearly through the thin walls and the rhythm was comfortable and familiar.

She sat him down on the table, his feet dangling down toward the bench. Joseph could smell molasses cooking—saw the plate of peanuts on the table next to him. His mother pulled the heated molasses off the stone and twirled it gently, spinning the thick, golden liquid in the pan and cooling it in the air of the cabin.

Almost, she said. Almost.

There was a larger pan at the table's edge and she picked up the plate of nuts and let them slide into the larger pan. Joseph could see every movement she made and watched her intently. She took the handle of the pot containing the warm molasses, wrapped it in a thin cloth, and lifted it with both hands. She slowly let the thick liquid slide over the peanuts, coating them in a dense glaze that seemed to sparkle magically in the slats of light from the shuttered window. Joseph could almost feel the texture of the nuts in his mouth—taste the sweet glaze as he rocked back and forth on the edge of the wooden table—waiting.

Let it cool now, Joseph heard her say. Let it cool.

She lifted him again to her shoulders and he laughed and flattened the strands of her hair with his hands—covered her eyes and she pretended to walk into objects in the room, into walls, and into the table—and then finally to the door where she stumbled out to the porch.

Caleb Tyler looked up from his work to his young wife and smiled. And what do ya have there?, he asked as he approached them, then turned to drop the ax blade into a stump of wood by the porch.

It seems it's a boy I found—sleepin in the other room.

His father looked sternly at him . . . and Joseph could not help but smile at all he understood. Ah, better it were a hog or a young calf then— we'd get some work outta it—or a meal I'd say. Or at least half a meal, he said as he lifted Joseph up and pressed him up over his head—slowly spinning, Caleb laughing and Joseph in tears of childish laughter.

Better it were a calf then, rather than a boy.

Caleb stop, he heard his mother say through laughter. You'll both be sick-dizzy. Come inside. I've made pindars for you both, though I don' know why. Come in while they're still a bit warm.

Joseph could see the three of them, together on the porch, clearly— then almost as silhouettes as they moved to the door. He concentrated— tried to remember her voice—the sound of his father's laughter—but he could not. He could not remember a time after that when his father laughed. He watched the shadows move into the doorway and saw his mother raise a hand, clutching the white apron to her mouth, and cough—and then the three of them disappeared one after the other, into the open doorway—and he saw clearly the wide-plank door as it shut, leaving the empty porch.

A cool wind blew to the lower part of his back and made his shoulders shudder and then his whole body shook—and he heard the clatter of the canteen in his haversack and then a voice call, Fall out, and the feet of the soldiers in front of him stopped and then left the trail, and Joseph moved with them. He put his thumb under the canvas strap of his rifle and tried to hear the laughter of his father as he left the trail, but all he could hear was the soldiers breaking line and hollering to set camp in the clearing to the north side of the trail.

Since early morning they had marched, mostly through dense woods but occasionally into the fields where the sky opened up to them and they shook the woods from themselves like they would a heavy coat. They had been fired upon once, probably by jayhawks, which was what they called the small patrols of yanks that fought and ran. No one was hit and the enemy had fled and disappeared into the wilderness. Joseph's regiment had an advance guard but it was almost useless with such impossible visibility. Like the Confederate Army, the yankees moved in the shadows of the larger trees and in the thick new growth of saplings—sometimes fifty yards from the enemy—undetected—instructed by officers to keep silent—to muffle the sounds of tin canteens and utensils and cooking pans, so that the soldiers moved through the woodland like silent predators—and unlike any grand army many of the men had imagined.

Not far off, Confederate scouts watched from behind brush and stone, as Union supplies lumbered wagon after wagon from the harbor at City Point, pumping the Federal Army with food and supplies—along the tattered makeshift roads, along old logging trails—as if transfusing the blood of the North into the swelling artery, toward the rebel heart, toward Richmond. Fresh Union conscripts in new uniforms, boy-faced, sleepy-eyed, excited. Determined, but not quite eager—feeding the forces of Meade and of Grant, now gathering at the threshold of Virginia's wilderness, like the first snow of winter. Trampling sage underfoot in new leather boots—bivouacking in the clearings along the James River, along the Rapidan—building pontoon bridges to cross the other great rivers of the south.

General Lee hoped the yankee army would be drawn into the backwoods of Virginia—hoped the whole army could be dragged through the wilderness, and Grant was about to accommodate him—to bring the battle to the rebs wherever they might be. To begin the end of the South by bringing the battle to them.

The southern boys watched from trees and from behind rock ledges and stone walls. Joseph had been on a scouting party last week and had seen for himself the great river of blue that seemed continuous, unending—and horrible. He could see in the endless line of wagons, of infantry, of cannon—the end of the war. He could hear the drums. Hear even a moment of music—the sound of brass instuments carried across the changing breeze. And he understood that the end of this was near. But he knew also that they would not go quietly—the southern boys—and there was much killing to be done and to be seen before the thing was over.

Joseph was right, and in the weeks that followed a new line of wagons would weave its way through the wilderness as the ambulance corps would haul its cargo north, wagon upon wagon—until the roads were empty and silent once more.

Rocker Falls, New York

The room was long and narrow—a hallway perhaps, if it were not for the thin beds that lay side to side along the far wall—the small pillows pressed against the chipped, mortared blocks. If not for the movement of the bodies and the exaggerated shadows that swam across the cold, tile floor from the arching windows and the thick leaded glass that filled the long spaces. Perhaps a grand foyer—if it were not filled with the sounds of men and boys wounded and dying—the red bandages—the yellowed, jaundiced skin—the vacant eyes.

This building had been started in the late fifties and was to be finished in five years to house the new library for the growing township of Rocker Falls, New York, but when the war broke out the last building blocks were left in piles and the mortar left to dry in huge barrels of useless mass— rolled then to the side to block the path of carriages so the ambulance wagons could unload their cargo and the bodies could be carried through the wide doors meant for unloading books and maps and significant papers that were to be stored in great and meticulous order through the stone building. Unfinished shelves were stacked high with bandages and clips and bottles of quinine and medicinal salts, while the first crates of books lay unopened in a dark corner of the room.

This hallway was the dying place. The men were brought here when the doctors and nurses could do no more. With the beautiful arched windows and the inlaid stained-glass serpents and flowers turning the light to jasmine and to crimson and the shadows into living shapes across the bodies of the dying men. The great planes of glass reflected the giant elm trees that had been moved and planted along the windows, and in certain sunlight the shapes and colors of the trees were repeated again and again in the glass as if the architect had wanted to render less clear the boundaries between the real world and the world that might grow within the walls of the grand library.

Sarah Kingsley could feel her young heart beating as if bursting against her chest—the sound of her beating heart shamefully loud among the weakened hearts of these men—these boys. Her neck and collar were wet with perspiration as she mixed a poultice to apply to the gaping wound on the arm that she held in her hands—as if it didn't belong to anyone. The face of the boy whose arm she held turned toward her, eyes opened only slightly. The mouth formed a thin and silent grimace—almost turning to a grin—and then the light of the face faded and left only a crimson shadow across the closed eyes. Another death. She did not cry. She pulled the thin sheet over his young face and stood, carrying the chair, and sat then at the foot of the next bed and watched another sleeping boy and slowly let her own eyes close.

Sarah Kingsley was just seventeen when she had decided to join the U. S. Christian Commission after the outbreak of the war. Returning quickly from a teacher's college for women, she looked for something she could do—some way to help. She had returned in time to bid farewell to Roger McCleod and she had wept when he left and stayed in her room for days until her mother convinced her to come out and help her with the garden, and as they worked together they decided that they both must do something and together they had signed up for the commission.

Sarah cried very little now. She could see in the faces of the boys and hear in their voices that it was not tears they needed. There were folks to weep for each one. They needed tenderness. They needed quiet. They needed kindness and it was these she offered them and these they received from her. There were trained nurses here, but she was not one of them. She fixed and changed their bandages. She held water to their mouths, wiped their lips and their foreheads with cool cloth. She read to them. She wrote letters for those too weak to write. And when they slipped from this life through the clouds of morphine and anguish, she tried to smooth their way—to hold their hand in the crossing over as if she were some sort of ferry guide—as if she knew where it was they were headed.

All the answers that Sarah had confirmed as a child had become questions again, and the questions horrible mysteries, and she thought as she moved through the murky light of the thick windows—from bed to bed—that she had found an existence in some undefined place where life and death were suspended together and the clarity of the real and the mystery of the imagined were somehow wedded in the thick light from these windows and the shadows that seemed to throb across the tile floor.

She sat and closed her eyes as if in prayer—but she was not praying. She sat with her eyes closed and the white scarf wrapped tightly around her hair and tied around her neck and her hands folded—pressing palm to palm so hard that her wrists began to hurt and she was aware of someone calling her. Three beds down—Michael Toth Jr., who had been an artilleryman with the 3d New York, sat up in his bed and called her by name and she stood and moved toward him and then sat on the edge of the thin mattress and put her hands in his. What is it, Michael? she asked.

Can you write for me, to my family?

She pulled paper and a writing quill from her pocket and reached for the ink that sat on a bedside table and she said, Of course I will, Michael, but you'll see them soon enough. We've sent word to them—that you've arrived here.

I'll see them, I know. But not here. Not on this earth.

Oh you're full of talk, she answered, smiling slightly. Now what is it you would like to say to them?

I should like to say this—he coughed and held his hands to his chest, which had been split open by a part of his own cannon.

Dear Mother, Father, and Simon,

Do not weep for me. There is no need to weep. What I have done in this war I have done proudly and I am sure if you had seen me you would have been proud as well. I will not be here to tell you myself—but we held the hill. It was an important position and perhaps saved many lives. The flag still flies there and until my own cannon exploded in my hands, I stood proud and brave for my country.

Your loving son, Michael

He coughed again and let his head rest back on the pillow and Sarah's hand rested on the paper and smeared the new ink slightly. His eyes were closed. He slept there in the light with Sarah Kingsley at the edge of his bed. She stood and laid the letter on the blanket so someone would see it and have it posted. There was a clock on the wall behind her and she could see from the black, ticking hand that her shift was almost over. Her father would be waiting for her in the carriage. She looked down the narrow corridor of beds and listened to the low groans of the men and thought quickly of Roger—of how proud she had felt for him—could see him in his handsome uniform, freshly pressed, as he called on her the evening before he left. She tried to remember the look in his eyes but she could not see him clearly. She could see only a blank white face and hear the voice of Michael Toth Jr. as he bid farewell to his family. It was as if all men's faces were one—all voices the voice of this soldier for whom she had written a final letter.

She was startled by a loud noise, as if a fist had slammed against the window, and she moved toward it and she could see at the base of the wall beneath the window a lifeless clump of feathers. A small bird—perhaps a sparrow—had flown into the reflected image of the leaves along the thick glass and died—at the instant it had prepared for landing, to settle on the lush green leaves of the tree—its world—its life had ended against a wall of glass. A second bird sat on a thin branch that bounced with its weight and appeared to look down at the still, feathered clump and then took off in a flutter of wings toward the open sky and Sarah watched as it shrank and vanished. She pulled a sweater around her shoulders and walked from the room.

The Wilderness, Virginia

Jacob threw his pack and his rifle down next to Joseph's and lay on the ground with it behind his head. Jacob Skinner had joined up the same day as Joseph and Terence and they had shared the tent and meager supplies issued them since that day. They had each been issued a .58-caliber Richmond musket and a revolver stamped with the words, SPILLER AND BURR. Jacob's was a yankee rifle, a breech-loading carbine that had never been fired and for which there appeared to be no proper ammunition.

He was a city boy—from Richmond—and had just turned seventeen. His hair was so blond it was almost white and he had a sad excuse for a beard and mustache that looked good only in certain light. He was short and thick—had been working at the Tredagar Iron Works, and his body was hard and wired with muscle. The boys had hit it off immediately though. Joseph and Terence and a few of the other boys were hitting a ball with a broken mortar ram and Jacob had asked for a turn at hitting because it looked easy and had just about spun himself into the ground trying to hit the ball until Joseph showed him how to hold his hands together and hold his fingers firm but loose. Jacob was finally able to hit it and the ball rolled through a field of fern and into a small brook, coming to rest in a still black pool under a stand of honeysuckle.

The play did not last long and the late afternoon was spent cleaning guns—their own and those of the officers, who left them on a large table for the new recruits to clean. It was the 13th Virginia, under Brigadier General John Pegram, that Joseph and Terence had caught up with through the gravel roads and thin paths that surrounded Blackstone. They had walked almost three days until they saw the dust of the horses just over the nearest ridge and crossed over, waving their hats at the officers on horses as a party of cavalry rode quickly between them and the officers. There weren't many words exchanged—no swearing in—they just became a part of the line of infantry that followed behind and until they camped that afternoon they talked not at all—not even to each other. They just walked along the thin, gravel road—stopping on occasion to pull the wheels of wagons from the wet soil and the pools of mud, and then marching again. Joseph was thankful for his new boots as he walked. He saw no sign of any generals, only the oxen and mules that pulled the wagons, and the smell of the laboring animals was thick on the trail.

That night, after they had cleaned the guns and eaten a small serving of dry corn and beans, they sat—the three of them—in the canvas tent they had buttoned together and listened to the rain hum against the canvas, an oil lamp rocking lazily from the low canopy—burning low and barely lighting the small space. Joseph and Terence lay silently watching a moth dance through the yellow light of the lantern, while Jacob played cards by himself—some form of solitaire. From the opening in the sash of the tent Joseph could see a dozen or so fires still burning and could see the thick smoke in the rain.

Jacob put the cards in a stack in his hands, tucked them under a coat, and lay down on his back like the other boys, a thin oilcloth separating them from the damp ground. Guess we're in it now, Jacob said, as he swept his hand at the moth and crushed it in his palm and shook it to the wet ground. Been waitin to kill me some yanks, but they wouldn't let me—wanted to keep me in the fact'ry makin guns and cannon, but I finally left on my own—or I figured I'd be barrin the door from the yanks anyhow. We caint let em get Richmond—or the thing'll be done and ole Abe hisself'll be walkin the streets o' Dixie.

Joseph never really thought of killing as what he was here for—though he understood it. He admired the blunt, simple honesty of Jacob's words. He was different, but Joseph liked him right away.

My guess, Joseph said, and then hesitated and put the heels of his hands to his eyes. My guess is it's just the thing we ought to be doin. That there aint much point in talkin about it much. The doin of it speaks for itself.

And then Terence added with a voice muffled in the folded jacket he used for a pillow, We come together—me and Joe Tyler. From down the

Salmon River, and we aim to finish things and go back together. Aint that right, Joseph?

That is.

A new moth took up the dance and they all watched now as the shadow crossed the white canvas. They talked off and on through the early hours of the night and between the thunder of the storm, but finally did fall asleep—one at a time—camped together along the road that followed the edge of the Rapidan River. One by one the fires of the camp died in the persistent rain until the entire regiment was cloaked in the darkness of a moonless night and Joseph slept that night and did not dream.

II.

In the morning the hills and valley were draped in a thick silver mist and the Blue Ridge was a ghostly silhouette against the gray sky. Black skeletal pine and ancient hemlock tore a jagged edge across the distant horizon and the rising sun slowly drew back dawn's silver blanket and revealed the deepest greens and the linear strokes of trees—oak and beech, birch and ash. Over a low ridge of hills and halfway up the next, a clearing exposed straight rows of apple trees whose leaves began to pick up the early sun and turn lime-green like the water of a stagnant pond and it spread as if it had been spilled across the canopy of trees. First light drew forth the color of the granite along the slopes of the hills and the silvers and blacks stood in great contrast to the pale greens and the dark greens and the yellows of the sun. Morning fog still settled in the lowest valleys and rolled up the sides of the great hills—but it lifted in the higher elevations and now a barn or half-finished cabin could be seen along the slope of the hill that led to the orchard, its roof sagging—unfinished or destroyed, with the grass of the field growing through the imperfect floorboards and the dens of small animals taking up the space left vacant by whoever had built it.

The white tents and the spires of smoke from dozens of fires, including the one that Joseph, Terence, and Jacob were now trying to stir, stained the sky and mixed with the rising fog and the first traces of carbon pollution from the iron factories in Richmond, churning out the weapons of war.

Round the clock, Jacob had told them, but the ore was gettin scarce and the steel was weaker and they'd soon come to a stop altogether. Too much war, too many damn yanks. Jacob had spit when he said the last words and repeated, Too many. Spillin down like an hourglass, and I think times bout up, fellas, and he spit again and as he did he looked around to see if anyone else had heard him.

The rising sun now revealed the high white clouds draped across the table of green and brown and yellow—as if preparing for some great feast—some symbolic consumption. Tall cedar and juniper leaned out from the slopes—pushed out from winter's weight and pointing across the valley like cannon. The changing color of hemlock, the drifts of white oak and red oak swelled with spring leaf—coming to color in the morning light— another Virginia morning—the western earth rolling toward the sun.

More than the thousand armed men spoiled the tranquil scene. In fact the black smoke of the factories had already spit tar and carbon across the Virginia sky. Centuries of unchecked work in the fields—first of corn, then tobacco—had left much of the soil spent and wasted. Now the rivers and streams of the Rapidan and the Rappahannock were at some points choked with the rotting flesh of horses and boys—the blood and the waste of armies washing their banks. Still they came. South from the Potomac and Washington—west from the Atlantic—ships of wood and of iron, feeding the Federal troops, arming their weapons—cannon and cloth, rolling across the wooden docks and to the piers—toward the south—to Richmond, to Atlanta—and every soldier in gray knew now that there would be no stopping them. And every soldier swore he'd try—and quietly prepared himself to give his last breath for something he did not fully understand.

The embers that Joseph poked with a crooked stick finally turned to flame, but when they put the damp new wood on it the fire died and the smoke filled the air. Terence and Jacob were breaking down the tent and packing the halves of canvas in their knapsacks. The knapsacks had been issued white with the black letters C.S.A. stamped on them, but now they were handed down and wore the colors of the earth that they crossed and the food that they ate. Joseph finally renewed the flame and put in some of the dry sticks from near the tent and the fire increased while the smoke lingered enough to keep the mosquitoes away. All three stood around it and warmed themselves and tried to get as dry as they could. Already horses were being brought up and the pyramids of guns were being broken down and the hollers of officers to break camp were repeated through the valley and the sound of the waking army replaced the silence of the morning.

I have a feelin, gentlemen, that today's the day. It was Terence talking through a mouthful of old biscuit that broke in his teeth as he chewed. Say the whole Union army's tryin to move through the wilderness and Bobbie Lee plans to keep them there.

Well I guess we're just the men to do it, Jacob added as he leaned against the trunk of a cypress and relieved himself away from the campsite and looked out through the thick woods that surrounded them as he did. Gonna be hard to move through this stuff. Aint you country boys ever hear a roads?

Joseph laughed and said, Get yerself buttoned up and lets get packed up to move. I say it's time we get this thing done and there aint no better place than in the woods. Plenty a trees to duck behind and the yanks wont be able to tell us from a hick'ry. Once they get in here—lets see em get out.

The three of them packed their things and made sure the few shells left were ready to load and fell in behind the increasing line of soldiers. The cavalry rode to the back and the officers hollered to the men and to each other until the army began to move—slowly. Red, yellow, and blue flags—the company colors dotted the line but hung lazily in the still morning air. The Confederate Stars and Bars was held high by a young boy on horseback and the horse walked lazily to the side of the marching army and the boy whistled something to himself as he rode. Already the front of the line began to divide as the army entered the thick Virginia wilderness in search of the enemy that most of the men hoped they would not find.

Yessir, today's the day, gentlemen. Jacob stopped whistling himself to say this—then began to whistle again, then was completely quiet as they walked. Joseph tried to concentrate on the morning—on the cool air—and not on the hunger he felt or the fear—but he could not help it. He could hear the yelling in the hospital tents they had passed the day before—the groans and the screams of men, young and old—the woman—a laundress in one of the camps whose hand had been torn from her by shell fire, a bloody bandage wrapping the stump, her eyes staring straight ahead. Her eyes had been vacant, emotionless—not lost in dreams but in the absence of dreams. Joseph could see her eyes as clearly as when he stood before her.

Anything I can do for ya, maam? he had asked. And the gaze of her eyes had shifted to his, and then away again. She sat on the stump of a tree outside the tent. He had set his pack down and pulled the canteen from it and held it out to her. Her face was like a mask—not a face at all—like a white cloth had been pulled across her features and the hair was matted against the cheekbones and she did not look up again.

Sorry, maam, was all he could think to say and he pulled the canteen away and moved on. He saw her eyes now as he marched and in those eyes he could see the war much more clearly—and it was a look he noticed more and more in the eyes of Terence. A few nights ago Joseph had awakened to feel Terence's hand on his shoulder.

Joseph, you 'wake?

He had rolled over to his side—toward Terence's bedroll—and Joseph could see him leaning up on one elbow. Jacob was snoring on the far side of the tent and the three of them were so squeezed in there that you couldn't fit a broomstick between them. Joseph could see Terence was sweating and his breath was quick for the middle of the night. What is it, Ter' . . . get some sleep. Ya know we'll be walkin for a change tomorrow. Joseph spoke, barely awake, in a gravelly voice and cleared his throat by coughing and leaned up himself and looked toward his friend.

I see yer back, Joe, walkin. I see you leavin the woods alone and hard as I look I caint see myself, caint see myself leavin these woods. Every night I dream it and I never see my own back, just yers. And I holler, just like I would, like I was catchin up to ya to play ball. But you don't stop—never turn around—then you keep walkin right out of these woods and I aint with ya.

Joseph could see the fear in his friend's eyes and pulled his weight up to sitting and pulled the bedroll around his shoulders. You said yerself we're in this together, and we'll be headin back down the Salmon River together and we'll get Gordon and the boys and we'll be playin ball again when this is all over. Joseph brushed the top of Terence's head with his hand and said, Yer so damn short no yanks gonna spot you over the stumps anyway. Terence smiled slightly but his eyes remained down and he repeated, I see you walkin alone outta these woods Joseph, can see it clear as day, and he lay down again and crossed his arms behind his head and Joseph supposed he slept even though he himself lay awake the rest of the night. That was the war, the war that his father had tried to tell him about, the war in the eyes of the woman whose hand lay in the thicket somewhere and in the cold sweat of Terence who lay sleepless at night along the cool Virginia ground.

Now they marched again. Joseph and Jacob walked side by side and Terence walked ahead of them with young Jeremy Higgins from Sharpsburgh who loved to talk about fishing along the coast and of the old Cherokee Indian named One Sky who had taught him the old ways to fish and Terence loved to listen. Terence told Jeremy of his visits to New York and the great ships he had seen there and the hundreds of fishermen and the great piles of quaking fish along the wet docks. They told true stories, then they embellished them and then as they walked they outright lied and they both knew it, so it was okay, and Joseph could hear some of it and just laughed as he marched. It took their minds off the hunger—biscuits and hardtack soaked in bacon grease this morning—and there was no talk of another meal today. No one brought it up as they marched.

The ground on the surface of the trail was beginning to dry and the fog was burned away and was giving in to a thick dust that rose up from the moving army.

Joseph wiped his lips with the coarse sleeve of his jacket. Damn dust, he said.

Don't know what's worse, the rain or the dust, Jacob answered.

Rain.

Yeah, damn rain's worse.

Terence slowed and fell out of line and joined them and they walked three abreast along the road, which was little more than a cowpath. Just ahead Higgins was still talking and it didn't seem to matter at all that no one was listening.

Aint much to this but marchin, huh Joe? Terence asked.

Aint much else to it.

They walked together like this for what must have been an hour. At times the path narrowed so they had to move through it slowly, single file, then rejoin as the path widened. In many places the path was choked with the thick roots of trees that lay like giant fingers across it and the men stumbled and tripped and worked hard to stay upright. An officer in gray with yellow sashes rode by on a large brown horse with a long black mane. They looked up as his shadow crossed them.

Great work, men, he said and headed up the line saying great work and saluting and saying other things like this as he rode along the line of men—ducking under the low branches of trees. Some of the men looked up and some of the men saluted. Terence saluted as he rode by. Joseph did not. He looked up briefly—then ahead again, up the long line of faded gray uniforms, and he could see men marching until the line disappeared in the dense trees. Then there was a single shot and the men froze. There seemed to be a moment of utter stillness, until the officer slumped slowly forward with his arms draped around the thick neck of the horse and the horse began to gallop and the officer slid to one side and then his shoulders and his head hit the ground and seemed to bounce up. One foot remained in a stirrup and the officer's body was dragged beside the galloping horse, a hundred feet or so, until finally it fell free to the ground and the horse slowed and pranced and then finally stopped. A few men fell out to give chase to the sniper but most took up the march again with rifles raised. Joseph passed the body of the officer as three men—one a surgeon—investigated the lifeless body. Joseph could see the black hole that had been the right eye of the officer, and the blood that flowed like wine from a pitcher across the face. He was sorry he hadn't saluted.

There were a few more shots off in the woods and then the men who had left the line to give chase returned to formation. Joseph looked quickly at Terence and saw that he was looking back at the body of the officer.

Ta look at him youda thought he'd be tougher to kill.

That was all Terence said—all anyone said. The battle was coming and they could all feel it and in these hours and moments before—the human spirit becomes a solitary thing—because though we may live together, we die alone. The body of the officer was draped across the horse and covered with a black blanket and the horse was led along the line moving forward and deeper into the wilderness.

They marched for hours that morning until the sun was high and rested on their shoulders and the muscles of their legs ached with fatigue—and when finally they thought they could walk no more, the battle came to them and there would be no rest.

The enemy was sensed before they were seen. There was a high bluff, maybe fifty feet up to their right, covered in blackberry. Joseph and his regiment were now walking along an old logging trail at its base—glad to be free of the thicket and on open ground. They were marching quietly, but still the clatter of guns and packs created a now familiar rhythm through the natural landscape. A thrush of blackbirds from a shattered cypress burst upward into the clear air and the men froze as one. And then—it was not that they heard anything but that they heard nothing. Perfect silence. A moment frozen and empty—or a moment so full that it would explode into the next—and in the silence the men stood, raised their weapons, and waited.

The explosion came with the yell of, Forward and to Richmond, and the blue shoulders of the Federal uniforms appeared on the crest of the hill, bayonets raised and reflecting the noon sun, and then a great guttural holler as two, perhaps three regiments of yankees began an ordered run down the slope through the berry bushes toward them. They were firing muskets as they ran—tripping, leaping over those whofell before them— and in seconds, the air was filled with smoke and lead and the Confederate line dissolved into the woods across the trail, leaving lifeless and wounded bodies along the road behind them like fallen timber. The screams of the wounded men mixed with the screams of the attacking soldiers and Joseph thought it was as if the earth was opening up and they all—blue and gray alike—were being poured into hell.

The man directly in front of Joseph fell in a heap at the first fire and Joseph watched as Jacob dove into the brush and rolled and came up firing at the Federal troops. Joseph tripped and stumbled on the men around him and then fell behind a log at the road's edge. He ducked behind it while he checked his cartridge. Enough return fire had been served to slow the Union troops and Joseph could see hundreds of them crouching behind boulders and in the thicket of the blackberry, and more still at the crest of the hill firing down on the rebel troops. The position favored the Federals and every man knew it.

There was an order to return fire, then an order to retreat and regroup and the men half-stood and scampered back into the thick woods and then an order to stand and fight froze them on the woodland edge and they regrouped and ducked behind thin timber and returned a rain of lead in the direction of the enemy. From where he stood Joseph watched helplessly as wounded men crawled away from the exposed front and toward them. The ground erupted around them in small and final explosions of gravel and dust, flesh and bone, and they moved inches at a time toward the poor protection of the woodland. He recognized the body of Jeremy Higgins draped backward over stones, his back broken, his mouth opened wide and black—his stories forever silenced.

Terence was kneeling and firing but he was slow to reload and Joseph was aware of it and kept fire in front of him. A Union sergeant was standing and brandishing a sword and the sword fell and the officer stood and rocked like a felled tree then collapsed onto the ground and Joseph could see the body rolling down the slope until it rested in the bushes. A bullet exploded in the bark of the tree he stood behind and another whistled by his face and he ducked deeper behind the tree and reloaded and searched the horizon for a target. He could see the shoulder and chest of a blue uniform behind an abandoned wagon on the edge of the slope. He could see a map being looked at, or some other papers. He set his eye on the exposed shoulder and waited until the chest drifted carelessly into view and he fired. He watched the space that had been occupied by the shoulder and chest of a man become vacant and he could see the boots under the wheel of the wagon laying still, the toes of the boots pointing outward.

A second charge began and the sea of blue soldiers reappeared from behind the brush and came full force toward them and an officer next to Joseph stood and yelled, Forward, and the men stood and hollered the rebel yell and reappeared from the woods and into the open space of the trail and fell under a rain of musket fire from the hill. Joseph ran forward and he ran into the enemy line and the barrel of a musket went by his ear and missed him and he grabbed it and wrestled the soldier to the ground and then hit him across the face with the butt of the rifle and he could feel the bone crack in the man's cheek and he aimed the rifle ahead of him and shot once at the stomach of the soldier that ran at him, and then he turned to where Terence had been and did not see him. It was impossible now to see clearly as the air was filled with carbon smoke, and he was unable to walk without tripping on the bodies of soldiers. Joseph tried but fell onto his hands and then felt a hand lift him and he saw that it was Jacob, and he could see Terence at his side firing ahead. All around them there was horrific fighting and the men screamed as they killed and screamed as they died. The Union advantage was taking its toll and the bodies began to pile almost in the line they had marched in and the blackberry bushes were crushed with the weight of the Federal soldiers who lay along the slope, but as quickly as the battle had begun it seemed to be receding.

They're pullin back, Terence yelled over the musket fire. They're pullin back . . . and then Joseph saw the dust of the horses above the road and he could feel the thunder of the hooves along the packed earth and he watched the backs of the enemy as they fled up the hill. He raised his rifle and aimed the barrel at the middle of the back of a soldier who ran slowly, perhaps wounded, up the slope. Joseph's finger was on the trigger and he could feel the tension and the pressure of the cool metal on his finger and he could see the double red stripes on the collar of the soldier's jacket and he watched him—all the way, until the soldier disappeared over the crest of the hill and Joseph let his rifle slowly down. There were already men lifting the bodies of the dead and wounded from the road and Joseph joined in. He was struck by the awkwardness—arms twisted, legs bent— one soldier sitting, his legs straight out in front of him and his upper body leaning forward, his arms draped, hands lying lifeless along the ground. There were new orders from down the line that spread from officer to officer and man to man and the regiment was ordered to retreat into the woods until they hit the road called the Orange Plank Road and so they did—leaving the dead and wounded behind, the cavalry giving chase to the Federal stragglers and the hot breath of a hundred horses filled the air until they had to stop and break up to use the narrow trails through the woods and finally the horses resisted—unwilling and unable to move through the thick and tangled brush of the wilderness.

Guess that's one fer us, Terence said breathless as he joined Joseph and they walked side by side and then were joined by Jacob and the entire army vanished again in the trees and the road was quiet and the sun barely shone through the thick canopy of leaves and as quickly as the day had exploded into terror it returned to quiet and blackbirds returned to the thin branches of trees that held the twisted trails in their grip.

One fer us, Joseph repeated and put his hand on the shoulder of Terence as they walked, and as they did they tried not to think of the exhausted muscles of their legs or of the hunger that gnawed at them or the boys who had fallen, and Joseph kept his hand on Terence's shoulder for quite a while as they walked and he could see the beads of sweat on Terence's forehead and a look in his eyes—a look he had seen—of absolute fear.

Behind them they could hear someone saying, Move to the right—off the trail a moment please, and a soldier led the brown horse by them as they gave way and the lifeless body of the officer lay draped across the back of the horse as they slowly made their way down the narrow trail. Looking back, Joseph could see the yellow sash along the trail, trampled and already half-covered with the dust and gravel of the woodland.

III.

They were marching for hours—kicking the tangled brush from their feet. The sun had faded into gathering clouds and the sky and the ground were welded together in a fist of gray. They had walked from within the trees to small clearings, but with little change. It was if a blanket had been pulled over them and the only light was that which lingered from the past, and once that was used up it would be dark.

Joseph marched with Terence and Jacob. Someone was hollering to keep up, to make time—but they were tripping on the unclear path and the movement of the regiment was slow and unsure. Joseph could see only a few men in front and a few behind him and after that it was just the clatter of pack and rifle in the thick gray mist. They marched without talking and kept their eyes ahead and down, their hands in front of them to feel the trees and brush that blocked their path.

He heard a voice from the front of the line yell that there was a clearing and to keep quiet and stay alert and Joseph waited as he walked for the open space to be revealed and to have the saplings and the thicket behind them—at least for moments. He could see, finally, that the men in front of him had stopped and were standing now—not in line, but shoulder to shoulder along the edge of the field—and Joseph pushed his way through and Terence and Jacob followed him and they stood to see the open field. He noticed the quiet—the absence of birds.

The silver mist lay close to the ground revealing only small pools of the open pasture, and as they looked across it they could see the grass pressed flat where the bodies lay like timber along the ground. Each space revealed three or four bodies clothed in the uniforms of both armies and through the mist they could see white faces and black blood across the faces. The bodies were torn and life had escaped from each one of them as if these empty bodies had been prisons.

Move through—watch your step—and listen.

The men began to re-form the line and continue the march across the open field. As they marched, countless bodies emerged from the foreboding shadows and they could see that the pasture lay covered with the lifeless forms of soldiers—gray and blue, they lay alike across the field. Joseph looked as he stepped over the bodies—as they walked around the bodies of the soldiers—for some indication, some sign of who had won this fierce battle, but there was none.

As they reached the pasture's edge Joseph paused to look back across the battlefield and he saw nothing except the rolling fog and it was as if a thin window had opened to reveal this horror and then the blanket pulled over its face. In the years to come he would often wonder if he had dreamed this—or if the field still lay full with the white bones of these men. He would wonder if that pasture had a name and if it would be remembered as a special place and if the names of the men whose bodies lay across it would be remembered in stories and in books, or had the thick mist that covered that morning simply blanketed them that they may lie undisturbed in that embrace, remembered only by those who loved each one and who had been left on this earth to recall their lives.

That night Joseph lay awake under the stars. They had been too exhausted from marching and from the morning's battle to set up the tents, so most of the men slept where they dropped—leaning on packs—rifles beside them—some with blankets, and some without. Joseph lay in the quiet of the night. Earlier they had heard cannon in the distance, but now all seemed quiet and many of the men slept. Jacob slept sitting, leaning against the trunk of a white oak, and Terence lay half-asleep not far from him, curled on his side—folded hands beneath his head—as a child would sleep.

Joseph looked up at the clear sky and the thousand stars that pulsed against the black sky. He could make out the Big Dipper and searched the busy sky for more and for a moment he was brought away from the battle and to a night as a child, a night he had spent sleeping outdoors. He could see himself beneath his parents' window—searching the same sky for the patterns of stars he had been taught. He could see his mother clearly as her head appeared silhouetted in the yellow light of the window. He had begged them to let him sleep out that night and they had finally given in—his mother folding blankets in half for a mattress and pulling the quilt from their own bed to bring out to him. She set a lantern, its flame flickering on the porch rail, and kissed his forehead and ran her hand gently through his hair before she went into the house.

His father had thought the whole idea foolish, but his mother had won him over and he finally acquiesced, sitting in the chair by the fire—his back to the whole idea, as if he thought that if he turned from a thing, it wouldn't be. He hadn't come out to say goodnight. Then later, behind his mother's figure in the window, Joseph could see his father. His hand on her thin shoulder, they stood together. He pretended to sleep—then could see them leave the window together to their bed and the light going dim and then quickly dark, leaving only the moonlight, the sparkling light of a thousand stars, and the deep and endless sky.

He squeezed his eyes half-shut and watched the shining light of stars blur and swim and return fixed jewels set upon the deep black curtain of night. Joseph reached his hands up—squeezing the stars between thumb and forefinger—and then watched the transformation of his breath to vapor, ascending upward, vanishing celestial and boundless in the night sky.

Sometime during the night he had awakened again, the porch lamp long since burnt out and the stars even more clear and bright in the darkness. He rolled to his side, half-conscious, toward the house. The window was still darkened and the house itself a blue-gray shadow against the night. He rubbed his eyes with the heel of his hand and lay still again—staring at his parents' window until he saw a vague blackened figure—sitting perhaps, by the window—too large to be his mother, he understood it to be his father keeping watch through the night.

His breath streaked the air as he lay now in the camp of the army and he could see it vanish away from him, becoming part of the night sky that seemed so unaffected by these things below. He let the mantle of silence envelop him and Joseph lay there, not asleep, but trying to keep the vision of his father in the dark window fresh in his mind. His eyes began to grow heavy and he was less aware of his discomfort—his flesh on the exposed roots of trees and his head lying on an outstretched arm. He pulled the haversack closely to himself, his eyes level with the ground—following the rolling grade beneath the thicket. He felt suddenly sick in his stomach and tried to swallow to avoid heaving. He had not the energy and his stomach was empty.

He became aware not of noise, but of the total absence of sound. The thrush of birds, the coyote's howl, the movement of rabbits to and from their dens beneath the forest floor—all silent. He let his chin lean on the tin buckle of the pack. There was not the crack of gunfire, nor could he hear explosions—could not hear the dull thud of blade on bone. Silent were the wheels of wagons. Silent was the voice of battle. No horses' hooves on the crushed gravel trail—no whips—no neighing. Silent were the screams of the enemy—the shouts of officers. No drums. There were no drums.

The forest was thick with the stillness. The leaves, the thin branches were frozen as if in fear. A mist circled the canopy of trees and settled in their new wood. Joseph tried to think of nothing but the quiet as he let his eyes close to sleep. A red fox watched him from a slit in stone on the hill beyond, and then withdrew to the darkness of a narrow cavern.

At the Base of Stone Hill

Give me the splendid silent sun
With all his beams full dazzling.
    —Walt Whitman

I.

Hollowed out by the heave of glacier and stone—wrought smooth by flood and wind, carrying with it small particles of sand and clay, seed and seedling thrown against the earth and raised up again to settle further down and manifest in thick grass, wildflower and shrub—the pasture. Waves of wind and rain in great sheets had sanded it flat in a quilt of yellows and greens covering the soft belly of the spinning earth.

On the north side great exposed granite formed cliffs with cracked faces and thin caverns. Hairlines of small trees softened the edge and offset a wall of rock stained in red from bleeding iron and glistening with deposits of garnet and mica. Smooth faces of rock shone, glazed with water seeping from the ground above to the unsettled earth below. Occasional fists of clay clinging to itself tumbled down the cliffs away from the grip of hungry roots, adding to the rich, black soil at the cliff's base, where it lay in the shadow of the mountain and brought forth tall transparent flowers and pockets of grass that hid woodcock and quail and cooled the ancient trails of black bear and fox.

A narrow, deeply cut brook was torn into the base of the cliff with great rock tumbled into black mud and the phosphorescent ferns dividing the pasture from the cliffs. The Algonquian had called it Stone Hill and so the settlers of Virginia had come to call it, and Joseph and his friends knew it by this name as well. Along the south border of the dry brook knee-high grass stood grudgingly and swayed in the occasional breeze as far as the eye could see, interrupted only by great boulders of granite that lay like silver spasms along the flattened earth. In the stones' pores grew blue lichen and green moss and from beneath many of the boulders white birch stretched to the sky as if in some eternal quest.

A hundred or so feet from the cliffs and the brook a second great shoulder of granite rose up from the earth—one whole sloping side covered with soft moss then giving way to a grassy field. It spread out three hundred yards straight to another woodland and a path that led to Terence's family farm and then down to the banks of the Salmon River which framed the whole west side of the open meadow. On all other sides the Virginia woodland stood gracing the outer edges of the field with dappled shade and shadow. One side was all green with white pine. The pine woods had been thinned a hundred years ago by the British, who used the tall, straight trunks for the masts of their sailing ships—or thinned by colonial patriots who had taken down the straight pine to keep it from the British navy—let it lie rotting on the ground rather than give it up to the British—and some of the straight trunks still lay half-buried in the ground, framing paths and adding compost to the forest floor. Under the pine was the cushion of brown needles that let a person walk soundless through the woodland and feel the true quiet of the earth. The adjacent edge of the meadow gave way to cedar, cypress, and oak, and its edges were trimmed in a bright necklace of azaleas and wild berries. Another path lay unused, reverting slowly back to woodland as the first year's saplings already pushed their way through the abandoned ground. Joseph could see the great pointed pine stretching toward a cloudless blue sky. He leaned on a tree at the edge of the meadow.

From the second surge of stone the field sloped gently down, drained quickly to the river, and presented a perfect playing field for the game. This is where they worked now to ready the field for the game and Joseph stood watching them. Terence swung a long scythe and the curved blade sliced through the tall grass and Joseph could hear it as it whispered through the air. A yellow hound belonging to one of the boys ran barking through the grass chasing a terrified rabbit, leaving a wake of shivering yellow and a cloud of pollen and insects unsettled from the thick grass. Two wooden bats leaned against a rock near where they worked, casting unnatural linear shadows on its face. The hollow knocking of woodpeckers could be heard from the dark woods, echoing off the stone face and through the meadow.

He walked down and grabbed the end of the hemp line from Terence and the two of them stretched the line to measure the distance for throwing and striking. They had cut the line to exactly forty-five feet so the full length of the line stretched between them would be the right distance.

They all comin? Joseph asked Terence as they hammered stakes into the ground at the ends of the line to mark the striking plate and the pitching area. Terence assured him that they would all be there, even Billy Spence from Culpeper and Alex Phillips from Spotsylvania. The game had been arranged over the past weeks by note and courier—enthusiastic messages about a ball game on the 12th of June, in the open field at the base of Stone Hill. Bring balls and bats, the note had said, and some food for nourishment, as we might play "till we drop or all the balls have been hit out of the valley," and it was signed Terence Hooker and Joseph Tyler.

They had heard about Billy Spence from friends who had seen him play and had told them of his knowledge of the game. Like Terence he had spent some time in New York and watched the clubs play the game there and brought the new rules back home. Spence was known for his hitting as well as his bravado.

The rules were still not too clear and seemed to change from game to game. A lot of the boys grew up on town ball or had seen some cricket, but Joseph and Terence and most of these boys knew the difference and could tell the future from the past. Some of them just showed up to play whatever was being played, and the guys who knew the game would show it to those who didn't.

Terence had seen a ball club called the Knickerbockers play in New York. They had uniforms and a field all lined out with white lines and a man who would sit and watch the others play and tell the players what the rules were. They would have games of nine against nine and people would come to watch them play and then after the games there would be tables set out with food and drink and the clubs would eat and joke and wrestle and make a big party of the thing. Terence had gone to a few matches and then bought a ball called a base ball and brought it back to Virginia with him and he and Joseph had learned the game together. Terence's cousin sent him a rulebook called *Beadle's Dime Base Ball Player* that set out the right distances and some newspaper articles written by a New York writer named Henry Chadwick and they learned the game together and made up some of their own rules as they went along.

These rules were always changing. Some boys threw the ball directly at the runner between the bases and if he was hit he would be down. This would be called a "hand down." Joseph and Terence preferred the new rule where the ball had to beat the runner to the base and if it did that runner would be down. Three hands down and the next club got a chance to hit. They played both ways and sometimes other ways but they preferred their own and Terence would write to his cousin to find out new rules and some news about the game. Everybody seemed to call it base ball now and so that's what it was and what they were about to play here in the shadow of Stone Hill.

Joseph and Terence, Gordon and Will Fellows and some of the other local boys who had ridden their horses from the neighboring farms were already throwing the balls around the field. They had two balls this day and were hoping some of the other boys would bring theirs. There were some breads and dried apples and somebody brought a rhubarb pie and Joseph went down and filled up a big bucket of water from under the falls and they set it out on the sideline and yelled at Gordon for already eating before they had played a single minute of real ball. They were yelling to each other, throwing the ball up high and trying to catch it before it bounced along the field, and they were exaggerating stories and laughing and the yellow hound was chasing the ball when they missed it and they were trying desperately to keep the dog from getting the new ball in his mouth until they finally decided they had to tie him up with the measuring rope. That dog had never been tied up before and he let out enough yelps and howls to be heard in the next county until he finally quieted down and slept in the shade of pines along the edge of the field.

The others began to show up quickly. From different farms—all from Piedmont County. Jason and William came to complete their team—then Will Calloway and his boys to make up the nucleus of the other team including Joshua the colored boy and another younger negro who was dressed in only shorts—no shirt or shoes, a rope belt wrapped loosely around his waist. Joshua was a huge young man, black and chiseled as coal—head shaved clean—great white eyes shining from a round face, jaw set firm. Joseph had known few black men. They had never owned slaves and had seen them only occasionally walking behind wagons in town. He had once attended an auction in Ciderville with his father and watched the boys and young girls standing on wooden platforms being pinched and prodded and shown like cattle in the summer heat. He had turned away feeling not disgust—he knew nothing different—but solitary and empty. He walked to the back of the crowd hollering numbers, the women laughing—and escaped to the open space and the steps of a brick building where he sat. Eventually the crowd broke up and his father came to him and grabbed his hand and said something like there's no work worth doing that you can't do yourself and they had left on the wagon saying nothing to each other on the hour-long journey home. Along the way they passed large farms—plantations—white fences and gardens—fields of tobacco spotted with the dark figures of men and women and children— great baskets filled with the crop—white men upon horses, the sun washing across the field and framing them as statues—still and dead—while the leaves of tobacco shuffled with a breeze and the colored workers moved in a great unified rhythm across the field.

We're playin with neegras? Gordon had asked.

That's all we could get, someone answered. And they can play the game as well.

We'll see about that, someone else, said and they went about checking the distances and walking the field and comparing bats and newly made balls. There was then much discussion of the rules—will the pitchers throw underhand or overhand—and there was much disagreement and many stories of feats encompassing all the variations of the game. Two boys brought makeshift gloves but it was agreed that no gloves would be worn by either team. Each batter would be allowed three misses, or strikes, and five balls, at which time the batter—the striker—could advance one base. They decided that they would play this day with the rule that you did not have to throw the ball at the runner but rather throw it to your own teammate and try to beat the runner to the next base. Some were unhappy, but all finally agreed to a set of rules. They flipped a coin and Joseph's team walked to their positions on the field while the other boys took to waving their bats over their heads and howling and saying things like the valley wasn't big enough and at two o'clock in the afternoon—in the field along the base of Stone Hill on the eastern side of the Salmon River—the game began.

First up was Will Calloway. It was decided that Terence would start pitching the ball for the batters and Joseph took a place right behind the second base, which was a cloth sack filled with sand. He put his hands on his knees and tilted his cap back slightly on his head so as he could enjoy everything—so he could see the sky and the green field in the same view with his friend Terence right in the middle of it all, practicing his underhand throws to Gordon, who caught most of the balls and threw them back to Terence. Finally Calloway, the first striker, walked up to home plate as Billy Spence had called it, waved a long wooden bat in front of him and called out, Lets play boys, and so they did.

Calloway watched the first throw roll at his feet and past him back to Gordon, who was catching about twenty feet behind the batter. Terence apologized and sent the next toss right in front of Will Calloway who struck it hard and sent it bouncing toward Luke Peters at the third base. Luke bobbled it in his hands and then tossed it back to Terence as Calloway stood at the first base smiling. The next striker hit the ball on a soft line toward Joseph who moved a few feet to his left and caught the ball on one bounce, or bound as it was called, and there was one hand down and a runner on first. Calloway was clapping as the next batter was Billy Spence.

Spence was dressed in loose flannel trousers and a shirt that was cut off at the sleeves. White suspenders crossed his broad chest and a blue cap that looked like a soldier's cap was pulled low toward his eyes.

The baseball clubs wear caps like this, he had said, and they kidded him that he looked like a damn yankee in that cap until they could see he was angry and they stopped mostly because he was bigger and stronger than most of the other boys. Joseph watched him as he walked to the plate. Instead of talking or joking as most of the other boys did, Spence was looking out at the field, at each one of the fielders, and at the broad space of green between them. His eyes were slightly closed as he squinted from the sun and he held the bat on his shoulder with both hands. As he stepped to the plate the other boys were yelling to him and joking about how serious he looked, but Billy Spence didn't change his expression one bit as he knocked the thick end of the bat on the ground once and then stood straight up with the bat in front of him and said, Serve it up.

Terence took an exaggerated loop with his arm and sent the ball sailing on a nice arc toward Spence. Joseph, watching, could see it every second and he did not take his eyes off the ball in its path from Terence's hand to the bat. As Billy Spence swung, the ball exploded in flight on a straight line in the space between Joseph and the other fielders and bounded across the grass toward the edge of the field. The fielder closest to it ran after it as Calloway rounded third and scored and Spence slid into third base as the ball sailed back into the field of play.

Spence stood up and knocked the dirt and grass from his trousers by slapping his legs with his hands. I love this game, he laughed.

Joseph walked toward him from the field. You looked like you aimed that ball, Joseph said, like you knew just where it was goin.

Course I did, the boy answered and went on to say that it didn't make much sense hittin the ball where the fielders were as long as they were keepin score.

Joseph shook his head and said, We'll see next time.

The black man, Joshua, stood and walked toward the plate with a bat over his shoulder.

The neegra's up, someone yelled. Show em, Hooker.

Terence looked toward the man and then at Joseph. Joseph shrugged and stood watching Terence.

It's my arm, Joe. It's been botherin me.

I'll pitch, Joseph answered, and trotted in toward Terence.

Not sure what to do, Joe. These boys don' want him hittin.

Dont worry bout it.

Joseph looked at Joshua. His arms were thick and the bat looked small in his hands. Taut muscle gripped his arm and shoulders—bulged through his black flesh.

Gowna let the neegra hit?, somebody from the outfield was yelling in. Joseph waved to the black man to finish his walk to the plate. Joshua's expression didn't change as he stepped up and raised the bat. Joseph looked at his eyes and he felt a slight shiver slide across his back. He knew this man could hit this ball—and could hit it hard.

Let the damn nigra try to hit Joe Tyler, someone else yelled.

Joseph gripped the ball in his hand and it felt suddenly heavy. He stepped with his left foot, wound up, and threw a pitch that rose up from his waist and crossed the plate uninterrupted as Joshua took a vicious swing and watched the ball settle in the grass behind him.

Weren't close, Joshua, Gordon called out. Not even close.

Joseph was thrown the ball and gripped it again. He could feel the sweat on his palm and he wiped it on his trousers. He could feel all the

eyes watching him—could feel and see Joshua's eyes on him. He wound
up slowly and threw again and the bat in Joshua's hands barely touched
the ball and sent it rolling behind the plate.

That's enough, Will Calloway called out. Sit em down.

Give em one more pitch and that's it, Joseph heard.

One more's all he gits, Calloway added, and Joseph turned to Joshua
who already had the bat held in striking position over his broad shoulders.

Joseph got his feet balanced, shifted slightly backward, rocked, and
swung his arm full circle toward the plate. He could see Joshua's eyes
widen, the wrists cock, and the bat start its violent journey to the ball. The
wood and the ball would meet and Joseph braced himself to catch the ball
as it flew back to the field. At the last second Joseph saw the bat quiver
and drop and its path missed the ball just slightly and the ball sailed into
the grass of the pasture and the black man finished his furious swing and
let the bat drop from his hands to the ground in front of him.

The boys were laughing. Joseph watched the man walk to the side of the
field and sit on the cool grass. Joshua looked directly at him and his expression never changed. The other black boy came and sat next to him nervously.

He missed on purpose, Joseph yelled. He could've sent that ball into
the damn river but he missed on purpose.

What? What the hell are you sayin, Tyler? Calloway was walking
toward him.

Joseph looked at Joshua and he watched him close his eyes and lie back
on the grass. He was motionless as he lay looking up at the sky and sure
not to glance back at the playing field. Nothin, Joseph said. Terence—
here—you pitch. My arm's sore too, and disgusted he dropped the ball to
the field.

Terence picked it up. Wasn't sure what to do, Joe.

I know. Joseph looked over to where the black man sat and he could see
the younger boy staring across the field at him. Guess none of us is. Lets play
ball.

Joshua and his friend took their places in the field, but they were
skipped when it was their turn to hit. They didn't protest.

Nines—that's what they called them in New York, Billy Spence had told them, so that's what the opposing sides would be called. Nines. By the time Joseph's team had a turn at bat the other nine had scored seven aces and Joseph thought that was a good score. Sometimes they played until the first one had twenty-one, but this afternoon they would play until they were tired of it and Joseph knew that would be a long time from now and a lot more aces for both nines.

His first time with the bat Joseph sent a high fly ball off the top of his bat and it was caught in the air before bounding, but the team scored six runs the next chance and by the end of the third inning the score was 18–16 in favor of Joseph's team. Joseph had doubled past third base and scored an ace on a single up the middle by Terence.

It was very hot and the boys took a break and had some water and cornbread and then continued. Joseph could see from where the sun was and the length of the shadow along the edge of the field that it was getting to be late afternoon. A couple of the boys started saying they wanted to start riding so they could make it home before dark and one boy was ready to leave because the ball he had brought with him was torn and shaped like a pear from being hit hard so they all agreed that this would be the final inning. They had only played a few innings but with all the hitting and chasing balls the game had already gone on a couple of hours. One more inning, they agreed.

The other nine scored three aces and had a man on second base with one hand down when Billy Spence came up again. He had hit each time up and the balls traveled in straight lines through the infield. One was struck right at Joseph and he was able to catch it and he could still feel the sting of the leather against his palms. As Spence stepped up to the plate Terence turned to Joseph and said, You pitch again, Joe.

Terence tossed the ball to Joseph, who caught it and walked to the pitching area.

What's this? Billy Spence asked, and Terence said his shoulder was tired again from making the big circle throws and that Joe Tyler would take over if that was alright.

Joseph had been experimenting with different throws, but most of them were overhand. He could throw farther and harder overhand and he could control the movement of the ball a little with the movement of his wrist. Underhand was still the rule, however, so he had practiced the underhand throws with a flick of the wrist right before the ball was released, and he could tell the ball moved differently. Terence could tell as well.

Billy Spence took some wicked swings at the air and said something like it's the end of the day so we don't need to worry about the ball and his clubmates whistled and Joseph laughed and tossed the ball up lightly in the palm of his right hand as he waited for Billy Spence to signal that he was ready. Billy held up his hand as he kicked his toes into the worn grass and dirt and then waved that he was ready and peered at Joseph and the ball in front of him.

Joseph gripped the ball across the seams, leaned back just slightly, raised his arm to his waist, and circled it downward toward the plate. Right before he let it go his wrist snapped and the ball flew toward Billy and past him before he had even moved the bat from his shoulder. From the boys sitting on the grass behind the plate there was a great uproar about unfair tossing and yells about cheatin and Billy Spence raised his hand to the boys behind him and yelled to Joseph, You heard of Jim Creighton?

Nope, answered Joseph, I sure haven't.

Greatest pitcher there is, Spence answered. I seen him throw like that up in New York one time. Made all the strikers look like fools. I never seen it around here though.

I never seen any striker aimin the ball neither, Joseph answered. Least anybody hittin it where they aim anyway.

Well lets do it then, Tyler. Lets you and I show these boys something new.

Joseph laughed and Spence dug himself in on the patch of bare dirt worn into the pasture. Joseph gripped the ball again, slightly different, and wound up and released the ball real low so his knuckles scraped against the tall grass and he could see the ball rise upward in its flight, past the hurtling timber in Billy Spence's hand and roll to a stop in the grass far behind them. The yellow dog began to bark and pull at the rope as the ball rolled just a few feet out of his reach. They laughed and kidded each other and Joseph repeated the same throw and Billy was able to just glance the ball with the bat as it flew past him and there were two strikes on him. The sun was getting lower over the ridge of mountains and all the boys were getting anxious to get going.

One more, Tyler, then we'll see, Spence called out to him.

Joseph felt the tan leather ball in his hand—felt the stitching on the flesh of his fingers—listened to the barking and then the howling of the awakened dog and felt like he could do this—play ball—forever. He raised the ball until it was even with his belt, almost like a pistol in a holster. The rule was you could not bring the ball over your waist and Joseph had practiced so that he was close, but the ball never did come up any higher than his waist. He leaned back again. His eyes and Billy's eyes were locked. This time Joseph lifted his left foot in the air slightly as he rocked back, twirled his arm, and brought it right to the belt—fully extended—and then whipped his hand with a loose wrist and the ball flew past Spence in the second before he was able to swing and rolled into the mouth of the waiting dog and caused quite a commotion as the other boys chased the dog down, pulling the rope in, and finally retrieved the ball. Billy Spence immediately threw the bat down in disgust and walked away kicking the dirt.

Joseph walked to him and put a hand on his shoulder. Sorry. Din mean to show you up.

That's okay. Billy was wiping his face with a dry cloth. That's somethin, how you throw that. I've seen Creighton do it. He's the best they say. I seen him throw in New York. He calls em "slows."

Never heard of him, like I told you.

I can see, Joe Tyler, you and me, this game's different for us. These other boys don't see it the same as we do.

Terence Hooker sees it same as me.

Well, seein and playins two different things, Tyler, and you play a different game than Hooker, though I can tell he loves it too.

The boys gathered around and sat on the grass and talked about the game and the news about war with the North, but mostly this afternoon they talked about the game as they sat on the grass and shared the food and the cool water. There was something unreal about the playing—with the trouble with the North getting closer to these boys—there was something about the playing of this game that suspended things for a while. Joseph watched as the two colored boys walked off into the woodland without a word to anyone. Billy Spence told them what he had seen up north and Terence told them what he knew about it—about the clubs playing the game in New York and New Jersey—and after an hour or so they started to drift away, on horse or on foot, through the pasture and onto the paths through the woodland.

Before he left, Billy came up to Joseph and shook his hand saying, We'll do this again Joe Tyler, you can bet on it, and he turned and walked into the woods.

Joseph watched him until he was gone and then called for Terence to start their walk home. Blackbirds settled on the fresh cut grass that had served as their outfield and pecked their thin beaks at the insects disturbed by the activity. An activity that had ended as abruptly as it had begun and left no trace but the cut and flattened grass that lay like thick, knitted seams across the pasture.

Joseph walked with Terence down the thin path toward the river. They used the bat to hit the branches that overhung the path and when they got to where the path split and they could see the river, they saw the two colored boys sitting at its edge with makeshift pine fishing poles and string that lay flat across the water before it disappeared.

I've gotta get home, Joseph. Don' have time to stop.

Terence ran down the path that led up the slope and Joseph walked down to where the boys sat fishing. The younger one looked up at Joseph as he approached and Joseph could see him nudge Joshua with an elbow and both of the boys stood and faced him as he walked toward them.

Why didn' you hit?

Yessuh?

When I threw that last pitch. I could see you watch it every second—could see your eyes still on it as it hit the grass—why the hell didn' you smash it?

No suh. I couldn' be hittin it suh. Yours was good pitchin and this po man had no chance agin you suh.

That's not true and we both know that.

No suh. I know no such thing suh.

The younger boy had been silent until this moment and he just about jumped up as he spoke. He coulda knocked dat dey pitch over Stone Hill I guiss missuh Joe Tyler. I knows he coulda done 'at.

Shush boy, Joshua, said and put a hand on the boy's shoulder.

Joseph smiled and leaned on the bat that he held in his hand. Catchin anything?

No suh.

Joshua looked at Joseph and put his hands out and Joseph handed the wooden bat to him.

Dis hea's a fine bat Joe Tylah.

Why didn' you hit?

Don' think dem boys wanna see no negro boy hit dat base ball suh. Sho don'.

But I saw it in your eyes—my pitch didn' fool you at all.

Well I guiss if you saw it and know'd I could hit it that be enough for Joshua suh. Sometime it what you know's mo impotant than what you do. What you know is fo'eva. What we do on this earth don' seem to count for much.

You coulda showed those boys. You coulda showed me.

Well I guiss I did' Joe Tylah—o' you wunna be stannin heah talkin at me now would yah?

Joseph shook his head and laughed quietly. Looks like you're better at ball than you are at fishin.

There was a slight smile across Joshua's face and Joseph could see his white teeth and a brightness to the eyes that he had not seen before. He handed the bat back to Joseph and nodded and turned back toward the

river. Guiss that's right Joe Tylah. Guiss I should be usin dat dey bat fo
fishin aint that right Jitter, he said.

The other boy laughed. Dat's sho, Joshua, and he cast a line out onto
the surface of the river and watched it sink.

I'll see you boys, Joseph said as he turned and followed the river, heading back to Blackstone. He never saw them again but he always knew that
Joshua had won the contest that day on the field, and that it was even
more real than if the ball had been smashed past him and rolled to the
outfield grass. It was more real because the two of them knew it and what
we know seems to last longer than what we do, and Joseph thought hard
on those words many times and could always see the eyes of Joshua clearly,
watching the ball as it approached and letting the bat drop at the last second. He would never forget Joshua's eyes. The brightness of them.

II.

Rocker Falls, New York

They were in the garden beyond the patio, behind the brick house thick
with ivy and geraniums and the cool scent of moss and turned soil. Sarah
was pulling thin weeds from around the base of the peonies and singing a
song about a tailor who had made a suit of clothes that had no sleeves—or
something to that effect—a song she had learned at school. Her mother
was standing at the garden's edge pulling a steel rake through the fine soil
and leaving small, smooth rocks in a straight line at her feet. Her mother
was wearing a straw hat with the dry leaves of hibiscus tucked in a white
band around it and white gloves that were stained with perspiration and
soil.

If you would work more and sing less we would be finished by now, her
mother said as she gently kicked wet soil from the teeth of the rake.

Mother—as if you'll ever be finished with your gardens, Sarah laughed.
And what would you do then, if our work was finished?

Perhaps I would sing. And her mother pretended to sing in a weak falsetto voice until laughter overcame them both and they had to stand away from their work to settle themselves. It was Sarah's birthday. The family would gather tonight in the kitchen and on the patio where candles in color-tinted globes would be lighted and songs would be sung and her two-year-old cousin, Sophia, would be running down the grassy paths between the peonies and the unflowered rosebushes and Sarah would chase her and catch her and roll on the cool grass with her while the women talked and her father and her uncles would gather in white wicker chairs on the side lawn smoking cigars and talking about the trouble with the South and the upcoming election. Sarah would long to be away from all the talk and the smoke and when the sun went down she would sneak away to the rear of the yard and lie out on the grass near the blueberries where she could still hear the melody of voices but not get lost in the words. She would watch the white stars until she imagined she could see them swim against the black sky. Sarah wondered what the sky would be like—how bright the starlight would be without all the lantern light from a hundred houses and a hundred shops and office buildings. How black the sky—how white the stars? She wondered at what the quiet would be like—in the country—in the new land out west and the open stretches of land down south. How frightening, how exhilarating it would be to be alone under the ceiling of stars, away from the protection of her parents— the familiar gardens and paths—the comfortable, familiar smell of her father's cigars. Fourteen years old and she had never been anywhere. To the city—she loved the city—but she longed to see so much more—to see the stars shining unabated and listen to the quiet of the night—uncon- nected. Perhaps even to see the image of God in the galaxy of stars—to understand better the message that seemed to be written there.

She stayed like this—lying on the grass—until she was called for cake and in the connection revisited, the sky became ordinary again as the noise from the patio drew her back—enveloped her—and she settled comfort- ably within laughter and the voices and the singing. She stood and pulled her hair back from her face and smiled as they sang to her and her mother carried a large cake and placed it on the table and it shone with the light of tiny candles that flickered with the night breeze that passed in a whistle over the grass and the gardens.

Later that evening Sarah stood in front of the mirrored glass and studied her image in the imperfect reflection. She was thin—shapeless, she thought as she put her hands flat on the mild curves of her hips and turned slightly. The wick of the lamp was old and the light was low and image of her face was muted with shadow and yellow light. She held her chin up and admired her own long neck. With her hands, she again pulled her hair from her face and held it there for a moment, pushing it up—over and behind her head—holding it there for a moment and glancing to the side as she did and then, disgusted with her own vanity, jumped onto her bed like the child she still was and lay there with her arms crossed behind her pillow.

She watched the shadows and the light across the white plaster ceiling and thought once more of the whirling tempest of stars in the night sky and how dim was the light of the gas lamp that cast these pale shadows across the room and she pictured her own face—lighted from a bright moon, her hair blown back with a warm wind and a boundless earth before her. With this image still in front of her eyes, she could see then armies of men—in silly uniforms of blue and red and gold—marching across the green pastures just as she had seen them marching through the village green. What would war be like? How would her own life fit into this new scheme? How would the swimming stars respond to the tiny soldiers she could see spreading across the empty fields and the empty pastures that she could see clearly now in the dim play of light and shadows that lay like blankets across her room as she settled into them to sleep? Later her mother would come silently into the room and watch for a moment as she slept and then pull a wool comforter over her to block the cool breeze from an open window.

III.

Virginia

On the next Sunday after the game Joseph and Terence walked the path through the wild azaleas down to a place where the water lay calm and still, just after tumbling over a mass of shattered rock that lay from side to side across the water. A split trunk of scrub pine hung low across the embankment, its roots weakened by the movement of the water through the soil and across the ground, and Joseph thought that the next time they came down this way that tree would be lying like a bridge across the water and might be fine for diving. The river here was lined with hackberry and Joseph could see the small fruit already forming along the new branches. Dry goose dung lay along the flat stone and he kicked it to the side with his foot and took a seat at the base of an oak facing the pool. Terence leaned on the tree and was touching the water with a long stick and creating circles of current that shivered along the surface of the water. They both took their boots and stockings off and as Terence did this he sat next to Joseph and let his bare feet touch the water.

How long you got? Terence asked him and Joseph told him he had chores in the late afternoon but he had some time this morning. Then without another word Terence stood at the edge of the rock where the water dropped off deep and jumped in the air, twirling halfway so he landed in the water on his back while at the same time letting out a holler that cleaned the trees of birds and wildlife. Joseph laughed and took off his shirt and followed him into the water. It was cold and they kept moving to stay warm. They spent a good part of the morning in the river—skipping stones, wrestling, and splashing—and then they climbed back onto the rock and lay straight out on the cool surface and let the southern sun dry their skin and trousers. They lay quiet for a while listening to the shiver of the leaves as a breeze washed over them and to the sound of the falling water downriver. As they lay there Joseph could feel Terence nudging his arm and he opened his eyes and looked to where Terence was pointing to see five wild turkeys walking their jerky, determined walk through the brush by the river's edge.

Guess I wish I had my rifle, or something like that, Terence said.

Joseph said, Guess so, and they were quiet again as the turkeys seemed to be absorbed by the woodland and disappeared as they watched.

Where's the river end up? Terence asked as he lay there next to Joseph.

Joseph could have fallen asleep with the warm sun on him and he opened his eyes and held his hand over them lazily. Lantic I guess, he answered. Don' all the water end up in the 'lantic eventually?

Guess that's right, Terence responded. You never been, have ya?

No. Never have been as far as the ocean. Been to town. Been to Richmond twice. Been mostly around here, just like you.

Terence had been to New York and he began to tell Joseph the same stories of all the dry goods and the shops bursting full of things and Joseph never really tired of hearing about it so he just lay there and listened to the same stories. When Terence was just about finished with the last one, Joseph chimed in and finished it for him and they both laughed and splashed each other with their feet.

Joseph told Terence that he had to be getting home and they both stood to put their shirts and shoes back on. As Terence buttoned his shirt with the two buttons that were left on it he asked Joseph if he planned on seeing things—seeing the world?

Don't guess so, Joseph responded. No, I guess I don't need to see the whole world.

I will, Terence responded. When I'm a grown man I'll be gone from Virginia and I'll be travelin all over the world doin business and such.

Joseph smiled. I guess it's not what you see or how much you see as much as how you see it, Joseph said as he tied the laces of his boots.

Terence groaned and said he was always saying these things that don't make much sense and asked just what he was supposed to mean by that.

I want to see things for myself. I want to see things clear.

Maybe you ought to wear spectacles then, Joe Tyler.

Terence jumped off the rock onto the dirt path and they started walk-

ing up the slope and away from the river. Joseph came up behind him as
they passed through a huge stand of mountain laurel and jumped over the
half-rotted trunk of an old oak. Terence hesitated and knelt down at the
rotted log. He picked up a stick and carved the thick speckled moss from a
large crevice in the wood. The log was soft and wet and the moss and the
rotted wood peeled off like the skin of a peach.

Joseph stood and watched him with his arms folded across his chest. I
want to see things with nobody tellin me what they are. I want to see
them clear and understand them that way.

What kinda things you talkin about? How else could you see things
cept for yourself?

I guess I don' know much what I'm talkin about. Guess I'm just talkin.
He was almost out of breath from climbing the rocky ledge up from the
river and he stopped at the top and looked back. Terence stopped a few
feet in front of him.

This river, Joseph said, looking down at the place where the water tumbled white over the smooth, black rocks.

When I'm here with you, or my father, he hesitated and walked back to
edge of the ridge—I see this river one way.

Terence walked up beside him and they both stood at the slope's edge
with their shadows reaching down the embankment toward the water.

But when I'm here by myself, alone, I see things different. He leaned
down and picked up a small round stone and tossed it toward the river. It
landed in a thin splash and the water settled flat again, mirroring the trees
along its unfinished edge.

The sound is different, and the smell of it, I can smell this river when
I'm alone. It's a whole different river and it's as if it exists only for me
sometimes. And that's how I want to see some things. I want to see them
for myself, without anyone else deciding what they are or what they mean.
Like base ball. When I hit a ball things are real clear and I know I hit it
myself in the way I wanted to. When I throw it with a little twist to it it's
a Joe Tyler throw and it's something that's my own—and the decidin of
how it was thrown was mine.

They started walking again down the path and away from the river.

Just want to see things clear is all.

Terence only laughed and encouraged the idea of the eyeglasses and gave a wave behind him as the path split and they each headed home. Then from the path toward Terence's farm, he hollered, One thing's for sure Tyler, you sure can throw that base ball. Then he added, That much is clear.

Joseph smiled and laughed as he continued down the path. That does sure seem clear, he thought. It sure does. He picked up a long stick and snapped it through the overhanging branches as he ran the rest of the way home.

That afternoon he was in the barn with his father and there was a light rain that fell from the clouds that had crawled along the hills and settled in the valley. Caleb had traded for a sheepskin and they were in the process of tanning it along with the skin from the buck he had shot last week with his Kentucky rifle. It was late afternoon and the barn was poorly lit. The skins were stretched out on a crude wooden table where they covered their surface with salt and would leave them there in layers of skin and salt for several days. Then the salt would be washed off and his father would brush on a limestone solution that would help remove the excess hair before it was brushed down. They would treat it with a liquid made from boiling the wood and bark of hemlock. The tanned leather would be cut with shears, then stitched into coats for winter or boots, and the sheep hide would be used for gloves.

Out of this leather Joseph would make new boots for himself, with his father's help. They worked together silently in the barn until all the salt was spread evenly over all the surfaces of the skins and the animal hides lay in a thick layer across the table as if the table itself were held in some morbid embrace. His father wiped his hands with a gray cloth and tossed it to Joseph across the barn and told him to feed the horse before he came back into the house for supper.

When he entered the house his father was removing a large slab of pork from the salt brine for supper and Joseph could see the water boiling for

field peas and the steam rising over the cooking stove. It was a hot afternoon and beads of sweat were across his father's face and his shirt was
black with it. Joseph left the door open slightly but then closed it, as the
flies and gnats were terrible this time of year. He walked over to stand by
his father, to help him with the preparation of the meal, but his father said
nothing—didn't even acknowledge he was standing there—and Joseph
finally walked away and went in to sit on his bed before dinner.

Sometime later, maybe an hour, he could tell from the smell that the
pork was ready and he walked back into the room. The table was set for
both of them and the roasted slab of pork was on a dish and there were
green peas on each plate and a slice of cornmeal bread. Joseph went to the
dry sink and dipped into the bucket next to it for two cups of water and
set them on the table next to each plate. They sat and ate silently, dipping
the bread into the pork grease and scooping up peas with wooden spoons.

I'll be needin those boots before winter, Joseph said, and Caleb
answered without looking up that he better make them before winter
then, and as he spoke they both heard horses approaching and looked out
the small window at the same time.

Three riders approached on what appeared to be workhorses—with
thick legs and slumping backs. Two of the men were dressed in faded
flannel and cotton shirts like Joseph and Caleb, but one had on some kind
of uniform. His trousers were deep blue and his shirt was burgundy red
with double buttons up and down the front. He wore a tall cap that did-
n't fit him and when he saw him Joseph could not help but smile and
choke back a laugh. Caleb and Joseph rose at the same time and walked
out on the porch. By now the afternoon sun had reemerged from the thin
clouds and sat on the far ridge and spilled a stain of pink along the horizon. They could see clear sky where the sun was even as a light rain still
fell on the porch. The sun set early behind the hills but the daylight lingered long on these summer afternoons and would later turn the puddles
the colors of the late sun and the painted sky.

Two of the riders dismounted and walked to Joseph and Caleb on the
porch.

Evenin, one said, and they both took their caps off politely. Wonderin if we could get some water for ourselves and the horses, and some directions. We was on the Orange Turnpike but we seemed to have been, we seem to be lost.

That there is Stone Hill that you can see in the first ridge and you're close to the Salmon River, Joseph replied.

Thank you.

Caleb said nothing and pointed to the well near the barn where the men could get some water. Help yourself and move on.

Where you headed? Joseph asked as he wiped grease from his hands with a cloth and then dabbed it to his mouth.

Richmond. The army.

What army?

Aint you heard about Sumter? The rebel flag flies over her now since the yankees went runnin in April. The man talking hesitated to spit tobacco juice on the ground. And this here man is the son of a hero of the War of '12 and we're going to sign up for the Army of Virginia and serve under him and kill us some yanks.

The man in the uniform looked away. Joseph could see the material of the red jacket almost bursting through the buttons at his stomach and he didn't guess this man had ever seen a battle or an army or ever fought anything but the tits of a dairy cow and sure didn't look like he would be leading any kind of army.

We're fifty miles from Richmond. You got to find the Rapidan River and there's good roads along it, Joseph said.

Caleb spoke up. Get your water and ride on. We're in the middle of supper. He turned and walked back through the open door and Joseph followed him and they both sat back down at the table and finished their meal. Before they rose from the chairs they could hear the fading sounds of the horses and from the window Joseph could see the riders disappear into the edge of the woodland.

His father picked up the dishes and Joseph picked up the cups and they started out cleaning at the dry sink when Caleb suddenly stopped and leaned on the wood along the edge of the sink.

How old are you this year, Joseph?

I'll be fifteen . . . February.

Fifteen. I was workin Blackstone myself at fifteen.

I can do more work, if that's what you mean.

Caleb didn't answer and continued cleaning the plates and the large pot that had held the peas. He spilled the yellowed pea water onto the stone floor. The water was still warm and a mist rose up from the floor and vanished quickly.

Stay close to home now. There's no need to be wanderin off to the river or off to play any ball. They's plenty of work to do here. We don't have half the wood for winter and you need those boots and you'll have to make them yourself this year.

Joseph listened as he wiped the plates dry and twisted the cloth around the inside of the cups until they shone clean and dry. What's gonna happen? Is it gonna be a war?

It aint our war, Joseph, and it aint your business. Finish up and we'll split some wood I cut in the north field before it's dark.

Caleb threw his cleaning cloth down across the edge of the sink, sunk his hands in his waist pockets, and walked out of the open door. Joseph finished and followed him and they walked across the north field to a pile of oak logs that had been cut into short lengths with the bow saw. Caleb took the splitting wedge from a wooden box by the pile and set a log upright. He raised the big hammer he had made from iron and oak and let the weight of it fly to the wedge and the oak log burst open into perfect halves. Joseph picked up one of the halves and set it upright again and watched his father raise and split it down into burning size. Rabbits scampered from the pile as Joseph threw the new logs onto the stack and he watched them vanish in the high grass at the edge of the field. He and Caleb split and stacked for hours without talking. Joseph copied his father's concentration and when it was his turn to split, the logs fell open in perfect seams. They took turns splitting and stacking the wood along the edge of the field until it was almost dark. When they were finished

Joseph leaned the hammer against the neat stack of split wood and looked back to where the sun had set in the west. He wondered if those men would even find Richmond, let alone any army. He looked across the dark field and to the silhouette of Stone Hill that sat like a black face on the horizon and then back to the house where he could see the dark figure of his father already on the porch and then disappearing through the open door of the farmhouse and then he heard the door shut and nothing else.

The rain had stopped but a splash of light across the sky, pale pink— the color of a child's flesh—was the only remnant of the day and Joseph watched as that evaporated, leaving only a dark and starless night. Caleb watched Joseph from the window and turned away. He poured fresh oil into a lamp and pulled the wick up slightly. With a cloth he wiped black soot off the glass and then set the lamp on the table in the center of the room. Caleb held flame to the wick until the oil-soaked cloth took the fire and glowed yellow and white—and the flame of the lamp appeared to be the only light in the valley, as if Blackstone Farm was all there was.

Lighted from Somewhere Unseen

Skyward in air a sudden muffled sound, the dalliance of the eagles,
The rushing amorous contact high in space together.
　　—Walt Whitman

I.

Caleb Tyler was a tall man—legs slightly long for his upper torso and his arms long as well, as if the wrong parts had been applied in some haste to make a man. Despite this he was considered handsome, with great broad shoulders, a strong angular face, and deeply set hazel eyes. His fingers were long and thin and the strength of their grip and the power of his arms had won him many wood-splitting contests in town. But this was when he was young, and he was no longer young. Gray hair persistently mixed in the strands of brown. Where he had been able to work the fields for days without rest, work the walls with relentless passion—he now could feel the ache of yesterday's work in his back, and the ache stayed with him even after sleep.

This morning his fingers were curled to his palm in a fist and tucked deep within the side pockets of a wool jacket as he walked along the turnpike road. The night had brought frozen rain that clung in crystals to the empty branches of oak that reached to touch over the road and formed a great shining glass tunnel in the wilderness. Caleb did not see this—not in this way. He pulled one hand from a pocket and turned the collar of his jacket up around his neck. Should've worn a scarf, he thought.

The road was rutted and had the look of old leather—dry and cracked —an occasional sliver of ice giving way to small stone and then to mud along its sides.

The road had been well traveled and was hard-packed from the wooden wheels of wagons and the constant pounding of horses' hooves. The water drained to trenches on both sides along the woodline and these formed partially frozen lines that glistened like the metal blades that had cut away the wood. By late morning the water in the trenches would thaw with the warm Virginia sun and form narrow arteries running slowly with leaf and branch, coming to stop at dams of debris and slowing the water to pools of cracked and shining mud.

It was twelve miles to town. He made the trip once every two weeks to load his wagon with supplies, trade what he could, and talk as little as possible to the folks in town. Last week along the same road the wheel of the wagon had gone heavy into a rut and the shaft of the axle splintered and broke at the hub and he was not quite finished repairing it. He would need Joseph's help. This day he preferred to walk. There was much on his mind, and he was not completely unaware of the magic of the sun on the frozen trees and the stillness of the morning.

He turned, following the lazy bend of the road, and passed the familiar cypress tree whose low branches would catch the top of his wagon when he came by if he did not steer the horse all the way to the left. As he thought of this, his movement froze. On the road in front of him a young deer was pawing at the frozen turf, uncovering the rich growth just below the new ice. Their eyes met and stayed fixed for a moment—maybe only seconds—and the deer turned and trotted in the opposite direction, its thin legs graceful over the frozen and rugged ground. Caleb stood still, listening to the cracking sound of the deer's hooves on the cold ground as it grew quieter until the sound disappeared. He could see the deer for a while in the leafless forest—but then it vanished in the tangled thicket and brier and the world froze in silence again as he began to walk—listening to his own steps now on the frozen ground and the quiet weeping of the thawing ice.

He could remember his childhood, but not well. He remembered hunting with his uncle and fishing with nets along the river. He remembered the happiness he felt at times, when he was with his uncle. He could not remember his father, who had left for the war in '12 and never returned. Caleb was born just months before he left and was told as he grew up that his father had died in the fires when the British burned Washington. Caleb thought of him not at all except in the work he did on the fields of Blackstone. His father had started the stone fences that lined the fields and he had continued the work, quite often at his mother's side, extending the walls along the fields. He started working the farm at an early age and had known little but work as a child. He could remember his mother reading to him in the dim light of candles as he struggled to stay awake and listen to the words, but the fatigue of his labor—even then—the weight of plow, ax, and shovel, the weight of the bales—had left him little of himself to listen. His strength and his spirit were spent and he used the sounds of the words to rest upon and vanish in deep sleep until he woke before dawn to return to chores.

He remembered one morning in very early spring. He could see the trace of snow on the ground, perhaps a day just like this one. He woke to the sound of his mother crying in her bed and he went to her.

He asked her what it was and she had said nothing, but as he left her she held his hands and said, Things will be better for you, Caleb. This work we do will reward you with a better life.

But this is a fine life, he remembered saying, and she held him in the new light of morning. He could not remember how old he was at the time. He could not separate the years or the winters from the springs. His mother performed every deed, every chore, beside him and as he watched her beauty fade beneath the mask of labor and the shortness of the winter days that finally took her from him, he grew more silent and withdrawn.

He had watched the doctors draw blood and he waited for her to sit up and reach for him but she lay there, moving less each day, until the last breath left her without her having spoken a word to him.

His uncle and his aunt had taken him in as he was only nine years old, but he was solitary and sullen and he missed the home of his mother so at twelve he left and returned to Blackstone. He scraped sustenance from the land. The neighboring farmers helped him and were generous in their barter with Caleb and the land prospered at his hand. He began to clear new fields, felling trees and building stone walls to draw boundaries to his world. This was all there was of him—this piece of earth—this house built by an unknown father. This land that his mother had died working—and lay under now even in death.

He learned carpentry and began to mend and then improve the structure. He built a barn from the cedar he thinned from the woodland and then a shed for storage and woodworking. In the winter months with little fieldwork to do he sat by the fire planing and carving from wood. He carved a chair and a case for his rifles. He began tooling bed posts and carved porch posts from white oak and in the spring he replaced the old posts of his father with the carved ones. His long fingers held the chisels firm and he loved the resistance of the wood as grain was pulled from grain and the smooth, hard surface was revealed. He worked hour upon hour, candles burning out, wax lying along the table, another candle lit, another log carefully placed on the fire. The wood became like silk in his hard hands and shone from the reflected firelight and seemed perfect to his touch. He worked entire winters on these projects and finally was able to sell pieces and was asked to make pieces for neighbors, but mostly he worked the wood for himself and made the things he needed at Blackstone—simple riggings for the horse and plow, skid-sleds for the stones and handles for the axes and the hammers that he used to break the stones and cut wood for winter. By early spring the fields called him back to his work and the unfinished projects lay in the corner and some were forgotten and left incomplete. The bedposts were still there—where she had seen them that first night.

It was on this very road on a hot summer afternoon that he had met her. He was taking a routine ride to town, this time on a horse with no wagon, to trade for grain and paraffin. The treeline was flushed with summer growth and the woodland was swollen with life along the dirt road. The road was newer then—the stumps of trees still green along the sides and bayberry growing in patches along the path. As he walked he was planning the afternoon—perhaps of the stew for supper or which pile of wood he would work at in the last hours of daylight. Alone on the trail he was always quite content and relaxed. In the evening, he thought, when the sun was down behind the hills but the blue-gray light still allowed enough sight to see the stone in the open field, he would work a wall. He would work with the sweat dried and cool on his skin and then would return to the house and lay upon his bed for sleep—his body exhausted and his mind free of thought except for the dancing shadows along the wall—until the last candle was pinched and darkness filled the room where he slept.

As he rode that day his mind had been on the evening's order and he did not even see the crippled wagon until he was almost upon it and it startled him and his hand reached across his chest to the rifle that hung loosely over his shoulder. He let his hand rest on it. He could see the wagon wheel cracked almost clear through, and the wagon itself lay tilted like the stone cart he used to clear the fields. The wagon was empty and two horses whinnied and shuffled hooves in the dry gravel as he approached on his own horse. He pulled at the reins and the horse circled around the right side of the wagon and it was then that he saw the barrel of a rifle aimed square at his chest and he froze and the horse could feel his body tense and his heels dig into the leather stirrups.

There was a massive boulder bursting from the edge of the woods, trees somehow growing from its base and moss covering the smooth face of it like cloth. On top of the stone sat the girl with the rifle pointed at him, and next to her lay an older man—perhaps her father—holding his leg and in obvious pain.

Don't move, he could hear her saying like it was yesterday.

He answered that he had no intention of moving but he could not say the same thing about his horse and so she directed him to dismount slowly from the horse, which he did, kicking his leg up and over and hopping to the ground on both feet and holding the reins in his left hand.

There are thieves, she said, on this road and I suppose you might be one of them.

I suppose I might, but in fact I aint and I don't look kindly on gettin stuck up with rifles.

How do I know? she asked and he explained who he was and where he lived and enough about the countryside and the farm that she could tell he was settled here and not a wandering thief and the father rested his palm on the rifle and the weight of his hand pressed the barrel down to her lap.

Looks like you folks have some trouble, Caleb said. He looked directly at her and she at him. He could see her eyes were reddened from crying. Her skin was slightly pink from the sun, but her blouse lay low on one shoulder and he could see the thin bones and white skin of her neck. Her skin was glistening with sweat from having carried her father into the shade. They had been sitting for hours, she explained. They were almost out of water.

I caint move him myself, she said, and lay her hand on her father's leg.

Caleb could see that the wheel needed major repair. He inspected it carefully and ran his hand across the shattered wood.

Clamp might do.

You got a clamp?

No.

He walked down to the river and refilled their canteens. Caleb Tyler, he said.

Margaret Fisher, Mr. Tyler. And this is my father, Mr. Andrew Fisher. We are on our way to Arlington to visit relatives. Thank you. I've been afraid to leave him, she said as Caleb handed her the canteens of water.

Well you won't be gettin to Arlington on that wheel, maam. My farm's not far up the road. I'll fix the wheel there and then you can be on your way. I have some pork and some bread to share but not much else.

That will be fine, Mr. Tyler, she said, and she smiled and let her head rest on the shoulder of her father. You're very kind.

Don't see much choice, Caleb responded, but then for some reason as soon as he said it he was sorry.

But he knew there was no choice. He would have to go to town tomorrow and it was strange but it didn't seem a great burden that his plans for the evening were changed and his day was to be used up on these strangers.

I'll have to come back with a wagon for you, he said to her father. The lady should come with me to get out of this heat, and I'll be back for you in less than an hour. Margaret protested, he remembered, but the two men convinced her to leave with Caleb and he helped her mount his horse and led it down the trail holding the reins in his hand as he walked beside them. As he walked he remembered feeling light—as if his steps went easily over the rough road—and he could not remember what it was he had needed in town. He walked toward the side of the road to keep her in the shade of the tall oaks and he was silent as he listened to her tell her story and he repeated her name to himself, Margaret, and he could not think of what on earth he was doing before the moment he had come across this girl and her father along the road. He could see only her chestnut hair and the wet shine of her upper lip as she spoke and he listened as if she were the source of all truth—of all language.

My father has not been well, she said, and we're going to live with his brother in Arlington, to see if that would work out. He was a teacher but he has been too sick to work for this past year.

I've tried but I just can't keep up the house and look after him properly, so when we were invited we said we'd come as he's been now worried about my health. I was in school—wanted to be a teacher like my father—but now there's no time and I'm thinkin it's not the right thing. Mama died a few years back and I'm refigurin what it is I'm going to do. I'll be twenty-five next year so I'm no child anymore. She went on like this in a quiet voice and Caleb listened and did not speak except to nod his head or to agree, and they walked like this until they rounded the ridge and could see the farm and the house in front of them, the barn not quite finished, the shed half-framed. He stopped the horse at the turn and let her—let himself take the view in full.

This is it, Caleb said and then was silent.

She said nothing, just smiled slightly. Then she said, Blackstone. That's what you call it?

Yes maam. My father named it.

Your family?

No family, maam. Just me and this land. Most times it seems 'nough. I guess sometimes not.

She laughed. It's beautiful, Mr Tyler, quite beautiful.

She looked at him. He was older, she could tell, but quite handsome. And honest. And she thought she had never seen such a look of pride on any man as he showed her his home.

Caleb, he said. Thank you, but it's just a farm. Small piece of Virginia. But I guess I'm glad to have it.

He led the horse down to the house and tied him off on the porch rail and set her up on a wooden chair with a pitcher of water while he left to get her father. He took a wheel off his wagon to use on the broken one and strapped it to the saddle and let it hang along the side of the horse. He returned down the road to her father and lifted him carefully onto the wagon and led the horses and the lopsided wagon down the path to Blackstone. When he returned she was asleep in the chair and he let her sleep there while he set the old man up on the bed and raised the leg up with a pillow. The ankle was badly swollen and the man groaned from the pain of the rough ride, but he was soon asleep himself on Caleb's bed and Caleb went out to begin work on the wheel.

He remembered he woke them both for dinner. He remembered that night like it was yesterday. Her father had been quite uncomfortable so Caleb gave him some rum in a tin cup and he slept well. The wagon was almost finished but it was too dark to leave, so they sat, he and Margaret in front of a small fire and amid the candles that burnt around the room, and he remembered thinking how small and ugly was the room, and how pitiful he must look, and tried to remember the last time he had even combed his hair. He had shaven that morning with a straight razor, thank God, he thought. How I must look to her.

That night they talked all night it seemed, and they laughed, and he remembered showing her some carving—the bedposts that still lay unfinished—and he watched as she ran her thin fingers over the wood he had carved, and he knew that everything was changed that night. Finally she covered her mouth as she yawned and he apologized and put fresh blankets on the other bed and said he was sorry again, for the simplicity of his home and how he did not know all the right things to do, and he remembered her saying, You're doing fine Caleb Tyler. And then, Goodnight.

He lay awake the rest of the night and in the morning rose early to finish the work on the wheel. By the time he returned she had a pot of coffee on the stove and some biscuits uncovered on the table.

I hope you don't mind, she said, and he just smiled and continued to the other room to wash up. He came out wiping his hands on a cloth and told them the wagon was fixed and they could go anytime they were ready. After breakfast they both thanked him. Caleb gave the father a crutch he had made and they hobbled together to the wagon and shook hands.

Thank you, Caleb Tyler, she said. Caleb said nothing. He waved casually and returned to the porch and through the door. When inside he sat on the chair without moving. He could not return to his work. He could not go on about his day as if nothing had happened. He couldn't remember if it was moments—or an hour. He remembered watching the dust of the wagon settle as it rounded the turn of the road. He sprang up from the chair, raced out through the door and onto his horse. He remembered the horse in full gallop and smacking the horse's side with his cap to get him to go faster. They were gone—a different road—maybe the east fork over the river—across the shallow part where it straightened out after the slow bend—maybe turned around and headed back—and then finally as he made a turn and ducked under some hanging branches of an old sycamore tree he saw the wagon. It was moving slowly on the road in front of him, and he slowed the horse suddenly to a trot and in doing so made the horse groan with frustration and they were heard as they pulled up on the gravel road.

All he could think of was the sound of her laugh—could see the chestnut hair lying on her shoulders—he could see the light as it washed across her fingers—her white teeth as she laughed at his choice of phrase—and the kindness—the kindness in her eyes. He could see her fingers on the wood he had carved.

He saw her turn to him now, and then to her father at her side, and the wagon slowed and then stopped. She came off the seat and walked back on the road to Caleb as he approached on the horse. She was wearing loose pants that were tied at the ankles and the material seemed to pulsate in the morning air as she walked toward him. He could see she was smiling and he was relieved.

Somehow I knew we would see you again, Mr. Tyler.

He asked her if that were a good thing.

She answered that it was indeed a good thing. You're a bold man, she said.

No maam. But I would like to ride with you, maam, for a while if I could.

Margaret, please call me Margaret, and ride with us then Caleb Tyler and tell me more about your farm and about the walls you build from stone—and more about yourself. I can't do all the talkin. It's already hot out here again and we've a long ride still.

And so Caleb rode with them and stayed two nights in Arlington with Margaret's uncle and his family. They were married that fall in a small chapel there with only her family in attendance. She returned with him to Blackstone before winter and he seemed now to remember every moment of that first winter and struggled hard to remember all the moments of those years together as he listened to the rhythm of his feet on the ground.

He walked along the frozen road until he came to huge rock covered with the thick roots of trees and tangled brush. It was here that he had first seen her. This was the boulder, although now covered in wild growth and almost unrecognizable. This is where she had sat on that day with her father and he could almost see her now. He imagined her on the rock, the rifle pointed and lowered, but then the image slid into a silver, and he could

see her in the muted light—moving as if floating on the air—spinning —
arms spread . . .

II.

Why do you dance?

She had been humming and that had turned to words—a song about a
journey and a girl's dreams—and Margaret had begun to rock back and
forth as she sang softly and then quite suddenly she twirled, holding her
arms outstretched to her sides, and spun slowly around the room as she
sang. She bent her legs ever so slightly as she turned. Her arms seemed
suspended—to rest on a pillow of light that surrounded her.

It was twilight and the light inside and out was equal. It was that sliver
of time between day and night when everything is close and important.
The ancients would worship at this hour when the real world seemed blanketed in the mystery of the enfolding night. The Algonquian still living in
the mountains and in great tracts of land along the Virginia shore would
sing plaintively and beat on the skins of animals stretched to drums and
worship that part of themselves that was the earth and that part of themselves that belonged to the sky and that came together in the twilight.
The negroes in the cabins along the dirt paths and in the low fields along
the plantations would sing to worship the coming of the night that would
give them some rest from the cruel, relentless day. Here at Blackstone it
seemed to linger, as if it were grasped in hands and spilled slowly to the
earth around the farmhouse where Caleb sat and Margaret danced—
spilled like silent sand along the ground.

Caleb Tyler, she responded, you've never danced?

No.

Never?

Never. But that's not what I mean.

You mean why do I bother dancing—like an old sow?

No, not at all, Margaret . . . it's good. It gives me pleasure to watch you. I mean something different. I don't mean, I mean I don't mean to ask why you dance person'ly.

She laughed and resumed the gentle sway of her dance, trying not to let the song leave her head. What then? she asked.

Nothin.

She stopped and came to rest on his lap and wrapped her arms, moist with perspiration, around his neck. He breathed her in and was full of the scent of her. Her youthfulness seemed to flow into him.

Caleb Tyler, what are you gettin at? she asked as she ran her fingers through his hair.

I mean, he said softly, staring at the light that seeped through the window, why do people dance?

She was about to laugh but she could see in his dark eyes how serious the question was and she knew him well enough. The part of him that could ask such a question was a part of him she cherished, though she didn't always understand.

Why do people dance? Caleb, you are a different sort aren't you? My father could see that clear enough.

Guess he could that. I don't see—why people dance.

She pulled her arms from his shoulders and held his coarse hand in hers. Darkness began to swell within the room but they did not light candles and the shadows of the hills and of the trees consumed the space where the dim light lingered and melted until it was almost black.

It's something people feel, she said.

I don't feel it.

You don't know, Caleb, perhaps, when you're feelin it.

I never felt like swayin in the wind, like a scarecrow. That'd be a sight, wouldn't it? Never will—and the last time I twirled I was starin at the bottom of a glass a whiskey. Never did dance, not even after drink.

It's like . . . I don't know.

She looked down at his hands stacked together like old books with covers cracked and dry. She searched for words for something that should need no words.

It's like . . . when the two come together, maybe . . . the body and the soul.

Caleb was silent as she spoke and he watched her mouth move and listened.

And the soul takes over for a moment. Like the soul is always dancin but these bodies of ours just keep em grounded like anchors and every once in a while the soul wins out and the body's caught up in it. And when that happens, Caleb, when that happens, it's a pleasure to live, to be alive.

The sky was pitch now and there was no moon. Neither of them moved to light candle or lamp but rather settled into the darkness. They could hear the sounds of insects and the other sounds of the forest and field as they sat together in the single chair. She let her head rest on his broad shoulder.

I caint dance. His words sat there in the stillness like paperbark floating on still water.

Don't see it, he said.

She let out a sigh and she pulled his hands to her belly and pulled the thin cloth of her dress up so his hands could rest on the warm, swollen skin and so he could feel the movement of the baby—the life within her stirring, and they sat for over an hour in the darkness until they imagined they could hear the baby's beating heart in the quiet.

Our child will dance, Caleb Tyler. We shall teach him. We shall teach him together.

He remembered lying with her at night—his body hard against her as he let his hand skate across the skin, barely touching, and wondered at the softness of it, smoother than the carved wood, and he lay weightless with her in the darkened room and clung to the waking moments so he could watch her sleep and wondered at how she had effortlessly transformed his tired life.

On many nights she read to him from the Bible as his chin dropped to his chest in the firelight, and then he would catch himself and wake to watch her fingers turn the yellow pages of the book, its binding cracked and dry on her crossed legs, and he would watch and listen until he slept and she took his hands and led him to bed.

They worked side by side in everything and he watched the soft skin of her palms turn hard and callused much like his own. He could not see the skin of her face and shoulders tighten, could not see her eyes becoming less clear, but he noticed she read less and fell asleep at his side some nights in the chair. The long days, the longer winters leaned on her and pushed at her.

When Joseph was delivered to them they had both rejoiced and he could see the new youth in her face and a smile he had not seen for months. She protected Joseph as an infant and as a young boy from the harder edges of their life and held them both, Caleb and young Joseph, in her arms late at night and hummed songs to them as they slept. And when the boy fell asleep in the wood and rope bed that Caleb had made for him, they would lie close together and explore each other in the night and he would hold her tight to him and fall asleep with the smell of her hair in his nostrils. And when she began to cough—when she began to cough he would hold her and bring her warm tea and would rub his palm at the base of her back.

He could not remember when it started. They thought little of it at first, thought it would pass with the warmth of summer and the dry air of fall, but as winter came again it persisted and seemed to worsen slowly. He could remember the first time he saw blood on the cloth she held to her mouth as she coughed and watched her mouth twist with the pain of gasping for air in her lungs in the early-morning hours.

Doctors came then from Alexandria, Fredericksburg, but nothing changed and he had little to pay for a trip to the hospital in Richmond. The doctors at first said it would pass and then said very little at all and he remembered realizing that her time was short and seeing that she knew it as well. In fact she knew it before Caleb knew it, but she let him believe in their future together because he seemed to believe in so little else. He saved through trading, enough to take her to Richmond, but by now the months had turned to years and she was too sick, too weak to travel.

He could see her eyes wet with tears when she thought he was not looking—shining like diamonds in the corners of her eyes in the quiet times between coughing. He could see her shining eyes as she held Joseph and read to him quietly, could see the silver tears roll down her cheek as if she was before him right now. In those days he would reach and touch her face and mix her tears with his own as he wiped his own eyes.

As he stood here today even now, he could see the light bouncing off the silver tears and reached his hand out to steady himself, feeling only the cold bark of a tree and shivering. He looked up at the ice-laden branches with the light bouncing and settling to the bare ground of the turnpike road. It was here he had first seen her, and he choked back tears even now as he continued down the road toward town.

He thought of Joseph and he could see in Joseph's face the beautiful eyes of Margaret, as he had first seen them that day along the road. The eyes before they were clouded with illness and exhaustion. He could see her in the brown strands of hair that were mixed in his. He could see his young wife in the boy's smile on those days when they could laugh together as they worked and in the evenings after work. He tried to rejoice in the boy but it was just too painful, and he withdrew again into his work, and how had Joseph put it? It used him up. He had little to give to his son except the life he had received—that was all there was to it. There were days when he wanted to reach for Joseph, bring him to him and hold him in his arms. The night of her death he needed to pull his son to him but he could not. He tried but he could not touch his son with his heart—could not break the barrier that protected him from further pain. And as the months and years went by he could no longer see her face, could not imagine her expression, could see only her tears and her struggle for air and when he looked at his son it came to the surface—just under his skin—and it froze him there and he moved away from it and to his work. His work was his life, as it had been before her, and it was all he had to give to his son.

He found peace in the walls—in the stone—his son pushing the cart full to where he worked and letting the stones tumble solid to the place where the wall would be. And even hearing the solid thunder of their fall as they settled into the grass of the field was the sound of life to him and all there was of it. And now, he thought, as he walked—now the thunder of cannon would be heard and he knew there was no stopping it and he knew that Joseph would be lost to him as well. His father, his mother, his young wife, and now his son and all that would remain was the land and the stone walls that his father had begun. The war would destroy, that was for sure, because that's what wars will do. Wars destroy those things they touch and those who dare to touch them. He had prayed silently at night that Joseph would ignore the approaching war—that he would work the farm and help him protect Blackstone from the world around it. And this game—he could not understand this game that his son seemed to love. He could see no point in it—it did not bring forth food from the earth, it did not provide warmth in the winter night, it did not lay claim to field or meadow—it was a game. He could see no room in a man's life for games. He could not remember a game he had played. He could not remember the looseness of limb and muscle that would allow him to do anything but labor to live upon the earth and bring forth from it what he could, and to claim for him and his son that which would be their own. But even now as he thought on this he could hear her voice, gentle in the early night.

We shall teach him to dance.

And he could see them moving—dancing awkwardly, Joseph's small feet upon hers. He could see it clearly as he walked this day and he held the image of the small boy for moments as he walked. But even as Caleb saw it this day, Joseph had always seen it differently.

Joseph had grown quickly with the work of the farm and the love of his mother and father. He had attended school off and on, but always his mother read to him and taught him to write and he practiced his lessons as Caleb slept near the fire and his mother watched and listened to him reading. But then when Margaret had fallen ill, as they struggled together with her illness and then as they had watched her die—the pain had drawn them apart rather than together. They rarely spoke of her once she was gone. As if speaking of her would prolong some pain.

And there were no lessons.

I've done well, Caleb would say to his son, without no regular schoolin. And it seemed to Joseph that he had—that his father had done well. And as Joseph grew he respected the clarity of his father's opinions and his unmistakable wisdom. His vision, or the assurance that came with a lack of vision. His woodwork, the walls: these were all great accomplishments to Joseph and his father had his undying respect. But what did he feel—or did he feel anything?

He did not see his father as someone awake in the night dreaming of some other life—dreaming of his young wife, of a life that had been denied him—but he saw him in deep sleep resting his body for the morning's tasks, the preparation for planting, the uncertainty of harvest, the readying for winter and the compact days full of staying warm and nourished—the days that ended in the walls of darkness that surrounded candlelight. The quiet that his father wore like a blanket around him.

But there were those days—of bright moonlight and an earth blanketed with white. Joseph would walk with his father from the house and down to the east pasture, a dome of stars and a pure white moon as if pinned on the black sky and turning blue the rocks and the meadows of their farm. They spoke little on these walks and Joseph could remember that when he was very young he would look back at the yellow light of the farmhouse to suppress his fear of wandering too far into this night world, the tall cedars casting ghostly shadows and the blue spruce at the crest of the hill—its branches weeping downward, vertical, covered with white— reaching down to the earth even as it grew up toward the sky—as he was reaching for his father, and was drawn back down to the working soil— the trunk their common center, the roots their eternal connection.

One night when they walked, stomachs full from supper, through a cold night like this—he watched as his father walked ahead and away from him, and he waited and let his father walk on without him. Joseph stopped and leaned against the cold, rugged trunk of a sycamore tree towering sixty or seventy feet straight up. He was leaning on it and then realizing how wide it was and he tried to reach his arms around it and he could not. He looked to see that his father was not watching him.

His father walked toward the stone wall he had built the years before and sat on a large stone at the wall's end. He seemed suddenly unaware of his son's presence, or of his absence. He was lost in the reflection of the sky's light on the snow. Joseph watched him—longing to know his thoughts—what was in his heart.

He wandered down the slope to what he and Terence had named Skull Pond because of the rounded formation of stone that seemed to emerge from the shallow water—two gouged eyes at the surface that in the morning, when the sun hit it from the east side, were deep and dark and seemed to them to stare out across the pond and directly at them.

Now the pond was smooth with ice that slit the eyes in half and the moon cast a short dark shadow on the frozen surface. Joseph stood there on the frozen grass that rose up through a silk-thin snow. Looking back he could not see his father but knew he would still be sitting silently under the winter sky. Joseph picked up a handful of small pebbles and, reaching back, threw them across the pond's surface, watching them skip along and settle on the opposite side. He wondered what creatures the sudden pebbles had disturbed and if the mild intrusion had caused the total evacuation of the pond's edge. He picked up a larger stone—the size of a ball—and threw it to the pond's middle—waiting for the plunk of broken ice as it sank into the water. He was surprised as it landed solid and skipped along and then, sliding, settled into one of the eyes of the rock skull.

He looked back but could not see anything beyond the slope and he felt alone. He walked up to the top and he could see his father had lit tobacco and could see the thin drift of smoke in the clear night as he sat on the stone wall. Joseph climbed down the slope again, slipping once on the slick ground, catching himself with a hand behind him and then standing upright at the pond's edge.

The first step was cautious and he hesitated between steps—pushing his weight down and then the second foot—and he stood stiff and upright on the ice. He shuffled a few more feet and stood again, the flat ice illuminated blue by the full moon. He had never stood here before. The pond seldom froze and he loved the unfamiliar feel of the surface beneath him. He walked carefully toward the middle—across the black shadows of the tree and toward the rock. He imagined the water beneath him, lapping at the underside of the ice, fish slowly circling in the milky water. He imagined the murky bottom, protected by this ceiling of ice—shielded from the winter air—the dark eyes of Skull Rock brightening as he came nearer to them—the surface of the hollowed granite smooth with ice—the shore behind him, though close, already dark in the shadows of the leafless trees.

The ice on the south side of the pond was thin and still wet. The surface somewhere between solid and liquid—water frozen to solid in the shallow areas but only a mask of ice in others. As he walked he stopped and listened to the quiet of the night—and then to another sound. It was a groaning, unmistakably ice pulling from ice somewhere ahead of him and then perhaps behind him. He thought to turn back quickly to the shore from which he had come, thought maybe the rock was closer, and he shifted his feet and he could feel the movement of the ice below him, could feel the sway of the surface on which he stood, and he dropped to his belly—lay forward as the black water rose up and engulfed him. He sucked in breath quickly, deeply, instinctually and felt his knees touching something and sink into the pond's muddy bottom—felt the icy water around his shoulders and his head weighing down on him and for a moment the black silence devoured him. His young heart pumped furiously and his lungs, longing for air, forced him upward. He was unaware of breaking the water's surface except for the rush of air that filled his lungs, but his feet could not find anything firm to stand on and they slipped and he plunged again into the black water. His hands grabbed for the ice he could see in front of him, but it gave way, it had no strength. It was broken and breaking more from his attempts to escape it and his thrashing left no solid ice around him. He gasped once more at the air but felt a mix of air and water enter him—felt his thrashing legs begin to slow and could feel even the beating of his heart slow. He felt the darkness enclose him and pull him downward—his knees sinking—mud to his thighs—his arms wrapped to himself and he curled his body forward—folded instinctually into itself—his face toward the muddy bottom.

And then he was aware of sound—from above and then all around him and he could feel the water move around him, but he could not focus—could not understand what it was. He could feel himself drifting into the black eyes of the stone skull—away from the noise and the light—perfectly still—and then he could feel himself being lifted. Hands were under his arms, arms around his back—under his knees—and he felt himself surging upward and breaking the seam of water and air and pulling it into his lungs. He became aware again of the painful cold, and he coughed and spit and then lost awareness, except that he could feel himself flying—suspended above the earth's surface and looking up into stars—skipping along the earth, barely touching the ground like the pebbles across the ice. He looked up again to the stars and saw instead the face of his father—red and frightened—wet with water and with tears and written across with anguish and with fear and that which Joseph could not see in this state between life and death, but it was unmistakable and it was love. As surely as the moon shone down on the blue pond and the shattered ice, it was love that was written across Caleb Tyler's face if only Joseph could see it in the night.

Caleb had been sitting quietly under the canopy of stars and the winter moon. Sitting upon the stone wall that stretched maybe seventy five feet downpasture, every stone placed by his hands, he sat on a large one that he could remember pulling from the ground and hauling on the cart to this place. He could remember lifting it into position in this place and setting it hard on the ground and building along its surface with smaller stones.

The stone was cold now against his trousers and he pulled a coat up around his shoulders and watched his breath drift into the space between himself, sitting on the wall that he had made, and the stars. His left hand reached for and felt for the tobacco he knew to be there and with his right he drew the pipe from his chest pocket. He stuffed the bowl of the pipe with the leafy wad, struck a sulfur match against the surface of the stone and sucked the hot smoke between his teeth and lips. It was a comfortable warm sensation and, breathing out, a cylinder of gray smoke mixed with his breath and mingled with the air and vanished into the night sky. He breathed in again and clamped the pipe in his teeth and felt the bowl warm in the palm of his hand.

He was aware that Joseph was no longer near him and looked across the path they had walked to see him throwing rocks down into the pond below. He wanted or thought to call out to him—to bring his son to his side under this winter sky, but he did not. Rather, he sat smoking and measuring the texture of the stone wall as it drank the light of the moon and cast consistent shadows along its surface. The regular pattern of the light was the true test of the texture of the wall and he could see it as if it were the embroidered pattern of a quilt draped along the field. Here was where he felt himself centered—his work to his back and the deep, uninhibited sky above him. He could see the black silhouette of trees beyond the field—the trees that framed the site where she lay, the grave barely visible from the working fields beyond the wild blueberries and the red osier dogwood. He looked up as he sat and smoked and watched the drifts of smoke and tried to see her face, or the face of God in the night sky as she had often seen—but he saw only the clear white of a thousand individual stars scattered across the ceiling of night. He looked down again. This field was his measure, this stone that he sat upon the vessel that he would ride through this life. He had heard the words of people, the words in books of people flying through their life, enabled to look down or around and judge the merit of their life, as if somehow removed from it—to see themselves as part of some larger thing—larger than the feel of the cool grass at his feet, the feel of the river's water through his fingers and across his lips, the feel of cold stone against his skin—larger than this.

He thought that perhaps he had felt this once, with her against him on a cold December morning when the fire from the night before had burned itself out and the wood lay cold on the stone. He had awakened before her as he so often did and he lay his head on her shoulder, watching her sleep. His own breath he could see in the air, but hers—she hardly breathed at all and only the slow, gentle heave of her chest showed her as living, as part of this world with him.

There was only the faintest light of dawn reaching over the eastern ridge of mountains and it shone from the window white across her face—strands of hair across her cheek that he pushed away with callused fingers felt weightless and he touched her quietly so as not to wake her. She had begun her coughing that month. It was before he was overly concerned, but he pulled the thick blanket higher to her chin and draped his arm around her waist and pulled her gently toward him.

She did not wake—but stirred slightly—and he remembered a thin smile, her lips colorless in the cold morning air. And he remembered that at that moment he felt as if he could see himself with her, lying together there—he could see as if from above with the cloak of darkness all around them and only the two of them—lighted from somewhere unseen—covered in the calico blanket and holding each other—somehow ascending and looking down on himself as he lay near her. He tried at that moment but could not think of a reason he should raise himself up from this bed and could not think of what work was to be done, could not separate himself from her and that this—this was an end in itself—a journey in itself—that they should be together on the earth under a cold winter sky—draped in a blanket together.

He watched a single star shoot across the black sky away from a thousand stars, and he tried once again to see the exact lines of her face—the slant of shadow across her features—but he could not, and he knew that she was gone to him. He wanted yell out to her at this moment, to fly up to her, to be with her again like that morning—but he could not. He was anchored here by the stone itself.

He tried to hear her voice again—to remember the sound of words as they came from her—but he could hear only something new in the night, another voice, and he tried to focus on it, gritting the pipe in his teeth and closing his eyes. The sound was clearer and he suddenly felt an empty space within himself as if he would collapse into the space—the sounds of splashing, of ice breaking, of Joseph's voice across the cold air, mixed with the sound of his own heart beating and the pipe dropped from his teeth into the thin snow as he leapt over the wall, ran down along its length and down the slope to the pond that sat at the edge of the pasture.

He could see the ice broken and the black water moving, lapping the frozen, shattered edges—and he ran directly into the water. The weight of his boots cracked through the thin ice and sank in the mud below. He saw suddenly in the moonlight Joseph's face and arms appear over the black water and disappear again. Caleb could not swim but he pushed his way through the ice and water, the weight of the mud pulling his boots and his legs down, pulling him down so he had to bend his knees and drag his legs through the water. His legs were anchors as heavy as the largest stone—keeping him from his son—just as this earth stood between him and his wife.

He plunged headfirst into the black water and could see nothing. He pulled up grass from the pond's bottom, and black mud that clung to his fingers. He dove again into the darkness and reached out—felt nothing but kept moving and reaching until he felt the weightless body—the body of his son as it floated into his arms. Caleb found something solid and pushed against the ground until they broke the water's surface and gulped in the frigid air. He moved his legs and tried to walk on the mud. One boot was gone and Joseph now spit and coughed and gasped for air. But the body of his son was so light. So light compared to the stones he lifted, and suddenly Caleb felt himself almost weightless as he moved through the water to the shore. He could feel his feet on the gravel—on the snow along the edge of the pond—and he ran, slipping as he went, across the frozen grass toward the house. The fire was still burning and he lay Joseph on a blanket in front of the fire, banged the palm of his thick hand on Joseph's back, and Joseph spit out more water and gasped and coughed and finally breathed deeply and was shivering violently. Caleb wrapped the blanket around him tightly and pulled him to his chest and wrapped his arms around Joseph as he shivered until Joseph stopped shivering and fell asleep there.

Caleb got more blankets and covered him and boiled water for tea in case he awakened and cradled his son. He threw split logs and then unsplit logs on the fire until the room was hot from the burning wood and the flames licked the blackened stone of the fireplace and the warmth finally found its way through the skin and bone, to Joseph and to himself—and they slept together in front of the fire this night. Caleb lay next to Joseph and let the warmth of his own body transfer to his son's.

For five nights and days Caleb sat next to Joseph as he lay on blankets in front of the fire. Caleb kept the fire going through every hour and sat in a thin nightshirt next to him. He kept stew ready and tea and there were moments when he thought Joseph was waking, but the fever raged and he could not leave him to get help and Joseph lay sweating, covered in thick blankets by the fire. Caleb took cloth and soaked it in the snow and placed it gently on his son's forehead and watched as Joseph fell back to sleep. Caleb cursed and pulled the blanket up across Joseph's chin and sat in the hours of the day until the noon sun turned to blue dusk and to the sixth night, the fire lighting the room with yellow and amber, Caleb sweating from the heat—sleeping moments and then awakening to feel his son's slow pulse through his wrist. And then finally he prayed—as Margaret would have—for her son.

Dear God this boy has brought no harm to no one and has not had a fair chance at life and his mother does not need to see him just yet—but he could not and did not finish the prayer.

In the early hours of the following evening Joseph finally opened his eyes long enough to focus and could see the yellow light of the fire along the walls and reaching up toward the ceiling. He could see the blackened glass of the lamp and knew that it had been burning long. He could then see his father's back at the stove and then he could hear his father say that they had missed many days and that the ground was soft enough to clear the lower field before it snowed again. Through the window Joseph could see only black—and the reflected light from the room. He could see his father's reflection in the crude glass and he saw his father take the back of his hand to his eyes while he continued cutting the fat from a slaughtered hog. He could hear the knife land hard in the wood as it slit though the fat and meat of the hog. A log settled into the fire and sent sparks upward into the lightless chimney. He rested one more day, maybe two, and in the morning of the next day they began to clear the lower field, working until dark and speaking only of the weight of the stones and the thickness of the soil still held in winter's grip.

III.

Caleb could see now the ice melting on the branches that hung over the road and watched them and listened to them drip and turn black against the sky. As he made the next turn he could see the smoke from the tavern ahead and knew that he was reaching town. He didn't stop. He passed the gray clapboard house that William Hanson had built, passed the sheds that stored tobacco, the church. He walked with his hands in his pockets and stayed away from the few other people he saw on the road. He walked toward the far edge of town to the stone building that sat on the edge of the river and housed Samuelson's Sawmill. The road in front of the mill had given way to yellow grass and two young children ran across it chasing each other. There were stones set in the ground that led to the front door, and the door was held open by a large square piece of timber. Caleb walked into the mill and it took a moment for his eyes to adjust to the dim light. He looked up into the vaulted space and could begin to make out the great linear stacks of lumber. Broad planks, finished and unfinished stacked across each other. Some of the piles were twenty feet high and the air was full with the dust of the wood. Caleb walked through the alleys between the mountains of lumber. He had never been inside. He had cut all his own wood and saw no need for milling like this, but he could not take his eyes off the stacks of lumber and he loved the smell of the wood in the cold room.

This time he would find the wood ready to work. He needed it dried and straight and he did not have time for drying. He needed a hardwood—maybe ash—and he did not have time to cut it. He needed a block of wood with perfect grain, maybe four feet long—ready to plane and sand, because he knew he had little time.

Samuelson entered from behind an interior door. He had a cup of something in his hand and he was drinking from it as he entered.

Yessir, he said, and continued toward Caleb. Tyler, I thought you had no need for millin. Never thought you'd be lookin here for lumber.

Aint got no need except for a particular piece.

He didn't care for Samuelson and he realized he didn't even know his first name even though he'd lived here for as long as Caleb could remember.

What is it you need?, he asked Caleb and Caleb said he needed a hardwood, maybe ash, and he needed it ready to tool and that he didn't have time to cut his own or he certainly would have. Samuelson raised his hand and waved Caleb down the aisle and across the next until they were standing in front of a large stack of rough-cut posts. They had been roughly planed but not finished.

This is all the ash I got. What size you need?

Maybe four feet long.

Samuelson pulled one out of the stack that measured at least six feet and let it drop on the dirt floor in front of them.

That's all I got. You may need four feet, Tyler, but you'll be payin for six feet.

That's fine, Caleb answered as he looked at the wood and studied the grain and could see that it would carve up nice. He paid the man one dollar Confederate and hoisted the rough beam onto his shoulder. Samuelson was following him out the door inquiring as to what he might be making when they both stopped where they stood and listened. They could hear the sound of horses' hooves along the road, a lot of them. Wagons—they could tell the sound of the wheels—and then suddenly the men appeared from around the bend in the road about a hundred yards north of the mill. It was army—cavalry, with the colors flying and Confederate flag sitting on top of a long staff and held upright by a horseman. They kept coming and they stopped in front of the mill and Caleb could see that the whole army hadn't even rounded the bend of the road.

An officer greeted them and asked, Which one's Samuelson? And Samuelson responded that it was him and spilled the liquid from the cup that he still held onto the ground.

We'll be needin lumber' Mr. Samuelson, and as he said it two empty wagons pulled up around the bend and came to a halt in front of the mill.

How much lumber will you be needin?

As much as fills up these here wagons. It's a valuable service you provide for the Confederate States—for the cause—better than servin in the army I guess.

Guess that means you won't be payin?

Guess that's what it means.

The wagons were loaded and the lumber tied and the wheels of the wagons turned on the icy road and the soldiers trotted by, maybe a hundred horses and then infantry. The line that passed before them had still not ended when an officer, accompanied by a couple of other soldiers, rode back to the two men standing at the doorway of the mill. The horse that the officer rode trotted up directly in front of them and blocked their view of the army as it passed.

We need you to keep your mill workin. That's fine—but what about you?

Caleb could see that he was talking to him and he stepped from the shadows and stood in front of the officer. He was holding the thick wood in both of his hands. What about me?, Caleb responded.

They lifted their voices over the sound of the falls that drove the great cutting wheels behind the mill. When the cold breeze changed they could hardly hear each other as they spoke.

Why aint you fightin? You're a little old but why aint you fightin for
Virginia?

Caleb stepped toward the young officer just as Samuelson stepped
between them and put his hand on Caleb's shoulder. You think one man
can run a mill? There's work for ten men here but there's but two of us left
and the damn army's gonna need more than two wagons a lumber.

After the fightin's over we got to rebuild what the yanks burn down.

The officer looked at Caleb and then at the beam of ashwood that
leaned next to him now. Caleb had put it down and taken another step
toward the officer.

Now that's a piece a lumber. What's that meant for?

A farm tool.

That's about six feet long. What kind a farm tool you makin outta
that?

A six-foot farm tool, Caleb answered.

The officer stood straight up in his saddle and put a hand on the
revolver at his waist, but the other men with him laughed and he relaxed
and smiled himself and his hand rested back on the leather saddle.

Well, I guess that's as good a answer as any, he said, and held his hand
to the brim of his hat and Caleb and Samuelson watched as they rode
away. Caleb put the lumber back on his shoulder and nodded thanks to
Samuelson and started back down the road. He wondered where the army
was headed and how many days' ride they'd stay from Blackstone—and if
Joseph would have supper ready for him when he got there. He wondered
all of these things as he walked along the road, now slick with mud from
the melting ice and the weight of horses and wagons and from the weight
of a thousand boys dressed and armed as soldiers.

SIXTH

The Black Horse

The regiment melted away like snow.
Men disappeared as if the earth had swallowed them.
—A New Yorker, 5th Army Corps

I.

Weeks into the war Joseph could recognize the difference. The veterans told him it was rifle fire. The usual thunder of artillery was replaced by the wicked scream of a thousand muskets—the woods too thick for cannon, the views obscured—the armies afraid to fire on their own troops. Cannon lay useless in the thicket along roads that ended abruptly in groves of black birch and blueberry. Along the ground shattered branches of trees, some as thick as eight inches around—torn to the ground from the rain of rifle balls—leaving jagged stumps, knee height, shoulder height—stumps to hide momentarily behind, to reload cartridges behind.

The enemy emerged and vanished, rising like ghosts from the tangle of brush and vine—showering rifle shot—yelling forward and retreat—the lines obscured, the usual organized front of a Federal advance turned to a torrent of advance and withdraw and blind firing.

Great lines had been drawn on incorrect yellow maps by generals unsure and wavering—seeking separate goals—Lee, Grant, George

Meade—questioning, doubting themselves, doubting each other—planning flanking maneuvers that became onslaughts and forward thrusts that became the tortured battle of man on man. Feet slipping in swamp and tangled to their knees in thicket, the soldiers of the two armies wrestled for the wilderness ground. Men who fell to the ground next to dead comrades used the lifeless bodies to protect themselves, fired at the spaces between thick, choking vegetation—fired blindly at shadows that moved and changed before them. Thousands of soldiers from both armies filled the woodland. It was as if a nest of hornets had been disturbed and had, in some terrible frenzy, turned on themselves, disoriented, vengeful.

There was fighting every day now and rest only for the hours in between battles, and even then there was preparation for the next fight. The battles had become even more fierce—less organized in the thick underbrush of the woodland. They had fought again today in the early-morning hours and lost twelve men and three wounded and now they were camped in the late afternoon in a clearing near a brook that tumbled over smooth rocks in a series of small waterfalls and many of the men bathed briefly and then cleaned guns and readied for the relentless fight.

Joseph was chopping and splitting logs and Jacob dragged them to a clearing where a dozen or so men were stacking the logs into a breastwork of some kind. Over the low noise of the encampment he could hear officers yelling for volunteers for a scouting mission, and then with few volunteers he could hear the orders barked and a promise of extra rations and then finally just orders and several men were lined up and their weapons checked for the mission.

Joseph was shirtless and the insects swirled and nipped at the skin of his shoulders and back as he lifted the ax high over his head and then let it bury itself along the lines of grain and watched the wood fall away from itself against the steel blade. When the ax was buried into the wood this time he let it rest, and he stood and stretched the muscles of his shoulders. Down by the brook he could see Terence rinsing his shirt and wringing it out in his hands as two officers approached him, and Joseph watched as they spoke and Terence put on his jacket without a shirt—left the shirt hanging from the branch of an evergreen that hung lazily toward the water. Terence was grabbing his rifle and Joseph walked toward him and toward the officers. He could see that Terence had no boots on his feet.

Need a volunteer? Joseph asked as he put his own shirt on and buttoned it awkwardly with his thick fingers. One of the officers looked up at him and smiled and said, Got another one, Sergeant.

Joseph went to pick up his rifle from a stack by a tree and walked to join his friend on the mission but the second officer raised his hand and held it open and flat. Sorry Private Tyler. We've seen you use that ax and you're more useful here than you'll be sneakin around the woods lookin for yanks.

I'll finish when we git back, Joseph offered, and pulled the strap of his haversack over his shoulder.

That's an order, Private. General Pegram wants a breastwork built here and I'm gonna see that it gets made and you're the one to get it done. You'll be the cutter and as long as you keep cuttin you'll keep eatin and the Confederate States'll be indebted to you.

He laughed and turned to Terence and said, Lets get a move on men. We're huntin bluebacks.

Terence stood and turned to Joseph and looked long at him without speaking words until he finally said, Its okay, Joe. We'll be back by dusk and we'll do some hittin . . . after this ole breastwork's built. And he fell in with several other men and one of the officers and they walked toward the narrow trail that led deeper still into the wilderness.

Joseph called to Terence, Hooker—where's your boots?

Terence answered that they were gone—walked right through and he left them by the river in pieces.

Joseph knelt and removed the boots that he had made and ran to Terence with them. Take these. I don't need em splittin wood, but you sure do. The trail's covered in brier.

Thank you Joe Tyler. I'll be bringin em back to you shortly. The boys shook hands until Terence was called to fall in and he ran to catch up to the patrol. Joseph stood and watched Terence and the other men until they disappeared between the thin trees and the tangle of thicket and he did not turn his back to them until they were long gone.

Jacob came to stand at Joseph's side. Where they goin? Jacob asked as he put his hand on Joseph' shoulder.

Huntin yanks I guess.

They'll find us. Don't know why we need to be huntin em. We're bound to trip over each other in these woods.

They're huntin em anyway.

He'll be fine, Jacob Skinner said. S'probly safer than us waitin here anyhow.

Joseph turned to the flat space where he had been working and picked up the ax. With his foot he rolled a long log into the space so that it lay before him. He raised the ax as high as he could and then let it fly downward toward the wood, and as it hurtled downward his wrists moved slightly and the blade barely skimmed the slick surface of the bark and skipped off and the steel blade seemed to lunge at Joseph's foot and just missed his toes and buried itself deep in the soft ground beneath him. Jacob moved quickly to his side. You okay there?

Joseph dropped the ax and turned toward the trail and yelled after his friend, Terence, he yelled through cupped hands, Terence, we'll be hittin hard tonight. After dark—full moon—we'll be able to see fine. I'll pitch easy.

No answer came from the woodland and a sudden shift of wind turned the leaves of the trees and sent a shiver through the forest that went right through Joseph. Right through him.

He finished with the wood and walked through the encampment. Most of the men were cooking or already sleeping in tents and on the ground with their bedrolls laid out near a tree or in a bed of pine needles, bellies half-full of tanglefoot whiskey and little else. Some were sitting reading old letters from home or having their friends help them make out the words they could barely read. Joseph himself had been asked to read many of the letters of the men around him; even Jacob, who was from the city, could barely make out written words. It had been many weeks since the last mail and most of the men read the same letters over and over, trying desperately to recall a different reality.

There was a short line at the commissary wagon. The wagon carried so little that it was hardly worth dragging with them but still the men waited—for hardtack and flint, linen for bandages, paper and writing tools—and they shared what little came from the wagon with their tentmates if they had lived through the day's battle.

Rifles were stacked neatly between the groups of men and stones rolled into circles on the ground, smoked with cooking fires. Some of the men gambled with worthless coins—as if the blind hope inherent in gambling somehow ensured their tomorrows. They played checkers and poker, and they didn't talk much as they played.

Over the quiet sounds of the camp Joseph could hear a shrill voice that echoed along the river's edge and pierced the quiet encampment like the sound of artillery. He walked in the direction of the sound and as he crossed under a canopy of pine he could see a large group of soldiers, perhaps twenty-five or thirty, standing at the river's edge. Knee-deep in the current of the river was a man, dressed in what appeared to be a long coat that disappeared into the current of the river. Joseph could see in one hand a book and as he walked closer he guessed it was a Bible. Joseph stopped and watched from where he stood as one and then another of the men walked into the river toward the preacher. The preacher put a hand on the shoulders of the men, and the men fell onto their knees in the rushing water and were completely submerged and then emerged again. The preacher spoke more words and the soldiers, their uniforms drenched, walked back to the shore to stand in the group. Joseph quietly walked closer so that he could hear.

And you, my children of God, baptized this day shall go forth and sing praises to the Lord God and call his angels down upon you.

Joseph watched as the preacher swirled in the water and seemed to be reaching as if those angels were in his own grasp and he heard him say, Now pray with me, sons of Virginia, as I read to you from the word of

God, as it is written in the 29th Psalm.

> The voice of the Lord is over the waters . . . the God of glory thunders,
> The Lord over the mighty waters; the voice of the Lord is powerful . . .
> The voice of the Lord is full of majesty.
> The voice of the Lord breaks the cedars, the Lord breaks the cedars of
>   Lebanon
> And makes Lebanon skip like a calf,
> And Sirion like a young wild ox.

Kneel down before these words my friends, the preacher called out to the men who were gathered at the shore. The men knelt down, and without thinking so did Joseph.

> The voice of the Lord flashes forth flames of fire,
> The voice of the Lord shakes the wilderness;
> The Lord shakes the wilderness of Kadesh.

The preacher held the Bible over his head and finished the words from memory: The voice of the Lord causes the oaks to whirl, and strips the forest bare, and in his temple all say, Glory . . . and he raised his hands higher and repeated, Glory . . . and he yelled out to the men to join him and they called out as one, Glory . . . and Joseph could hear, before even the sound of the word had settled from the air, the screech of cannonballs mixing with the voices and as he watched, the water of the river rose up and there was the thunder of explosions all around the men as they ran for their weapons and Joseph started to turn and then saw the preacher standing alone in the river and yelling over the explosions as the battle returned to them.

The Lord sits enthroned over the flood; the Lord sits enthroned as king forever. May the Lord give strength to his people. . . .

Another explosion of mud and water; he was shouting and Joseph started to approach the river to go to him to bring him away from the clearing and to some protection.

May the Lord bless his people with peace . . . the preacher called out as the river rose up around him and a great explosion of a number of cannonballs that landed in the water engulfed him and sent Joseph backward with the force. He held his arm over his face and he could not see in the smoke any sign of the preacher and he could hear the whip of bullets through the trees around him and so he ran. He ran for his gun, through the camp, where the men were now alive with the anticipation of battle— and some lay dead, with its realization.

Rocker Falls, New York

Sarah Kingsley sat on a wooden pew in a small church. She sat between her mother and her father. Some of the congregation was standing as they sang—not a hymn but a new song. It was a victory song. The words called for new volunteers to the swelling army of the Union and the thin Pastor Howell—hunched over from a shrinking spine—had passed out white paper with the words carefully printed on it and most of the people sang and some stood as they did. A thin rain rolled quietly across the long windows, smearing the glass, and the spring air was cool and damp within the small chapel. Some of them sang loudly, and some not at all . . .

> If you look across the hilltops that meet the northern sky,
> Long, moving lines of rising dust your vision may descry;
> And now the wind, an instant, tears the cloudy veil aside,
> And floats aloft our spangled flag in glory and in pride;
> And bayonets in the sunlight gleam, and bands brave music pour—
> We are coming Father Abra'm—three hundred thousand more.

Alexander Kingsley grabbed his daughter's hand and stood as the chorus was repeated. They had sat, as they always did, in the last pew so they could leave if the sermon became long-winded as it so often did. Sarah's mother stood and followed them as they opened the white door and quietly left the room. Athough there was still a light rain where they stood under a narrow overhang on the church's front, they could see a splash of sunshine along the ground not far off and the faint trace of a rainbow in the unsettled air between.

You would think we were at a rally. Sarah's father pulled a thin coat over his shoulders and rubbed both sleeves flat with the palms of his hand as he spoke. His hair was turning silver and hung slightly beyond his collar. Songs to Father Abraham, now. I think we are losing the concept of separation—church and state—the founding fathers made it clear. Father Abraham—rubbish.

Sarah's mother let out a quick laugh. Alexander, this war. This war has broken all boundaries. You've said it many times in your own newspaper. The slave issue makes this a holy war, didn't you say that yourself?

Sarah folded her arms and shivered from the chill morning air. She waited for her father's response.

You're right. That cause is just. But remember: there are slaves in New York, in Rocker Falls even. They just aren't called slaves. Servants, hand-maidens—slaves nonetheless. Such hypocrisy. It sickens me.

He paused and looked out across the cobblestone road.

These battles become more terrible every day. You should see the news we get from the south—we can't print the half of it. All these boys killing and being killed. It's come to something more terrible than any of us imagined. And now to send more, three hundred thousand more they're singing. Three hundred thousand more obituaries filling the pages I'll guess. Name after name across the page. It has to stop. Does anyone know these names?

He put his hands in his pockets and Sarah put both of her hands on his arm. Lets go before the rain starts again.

They ran through a persistent light rain to the carriage. It was covered with a black canvas roof pulled tight over wooden poles, and the leather seats were cool but dry. Her parents sat in the front seat and Sarah sat alone in the back and pulled a shawl, woven with a pattern of roses, across her shoulders. The carriage jolted to a start and rolled down the narrow street and away from the white church and away, in fact, from the rain, which slowly gave way to a weak sun.

Do you think it will be over soon, Father? she asked leaning forward so he could hear her over the clatter of the horse and carriage along the road.

I'm afraid not, Sarah. I'm afraid men are much better at starting wars than they are at ending them.

They rode past the post office and past the unfinished library that served as the hospital where Sarah and her mother volunteered, and down the narrow road lined in tall elms and sugar maples and past the mottled skin of sycamores. As the carriage moved past the trees they looked in the spaces between toward the broad field of the park, and there they could see children playing in the wet grass. She would teach children some day—so she watched them as they played and wondered when that could ever be. The children were throwing a ball and then they could see a boy shouting toward the others and holding a wooden club in his hands.

Watch them, her father said, and they turned in their seats to watch as the ball was tossed toward the boy with the wooden cylinder and then it was struck hard and the ball was sent high and they watched as the others gave chase and slipped in the wet grass as the ball rolled across the field.

Look at that, Alexander Kingsley said as if to himself. It's called base ball, he said to Sarah and to his wife. He shook his head and smiled as he struck the horse gently with the reins and they clattered on more quickly. Sarah turned and watched the boys playing in the park until she couldn't see them anymore through the thickening trees. She could still hear their laughter though—even as they passed back into a light rain that hummed against the tight canvas roof. There had been so little laughter lately and she listened to it as long as she could as they moved along the road. Sarah looked above them—for the rainbow—but she saw only an uneven pattern of clouds and patches of blue, as if holes had been ripped in a fabric sky and the light that burst through was selective and deliberate.

The Wilderness; Virginia

The enemy was upon them again and the battle was as fierce as he had seen. As Joseph ran through the camp and to his rifle he could see there was some fighting in the thick woods to his right. The air was filled with gunshot and the thick stench of carbon smoke floated through the woodland and gathered in the hollows and along the streams. The smell alone gagged Joseph, as he grabbed his rifle and tried to find position in the battle—tried to define the fronts and find the enemy. He fell behind an outcropping of stone and ripped open a cartridge with his teeth. He poured the powder down the thin barrel, his hands shaking as he hurried, and with same motion withdrew the ramrod from beneath it. He drove the bullet and powder together and in seconds he was looking back at the field. All the men had grabbed their rifles and run into the woodland at the edge of the camp and fired again at an enemy they could barely see. A soldier lay half-naked along the first waterfall where he had been killed as he bathed. He still held his uniform shirt in clenched hands and the water of the stream ran over his shoulder as he lay there and down his arm and then returned to the stream as if he had become part of the natural spectacle. Above him Joseph could see Terence's shirt still hanging from a branch and it bounced slightly as lead bullets crashed through the trees and through all the branches. Below the tree lay the leather of Terence's boots, discarded as if it were skin shed by an animal.

Officers gathered quickly behind him amid the firing. Enemy soldiers emerged and vanished in the light and shadow of the surrounding woodland. Joseph had already fired a dozen times now, knowing some of his fire had found targets as he watched soldiers fall to their knees and then facedown to the forest floor. He watched as one bullet from his rifle hit the left side of a man's face, the force turning the body—reeling and twisting to the ground. He watched the surprised face of another as the bullet crashed through the flesh and bone of his chest. The soldier turned away from the battle—walked a few steps, and collapsed to the ground—a vacant vessel crumpling to the field like stone.

The battle didn't so much come to them as it grew around them, as if from beneath them. As if this battle had waited on them to be. Bullets flew all around them, in all directions. Bodies fell and left empty space between soldiers. Breath that had filled the air and had sucked desperately at it fell still as the lungs of boys emptied onto the cool ground—mouths opened to the dirt floor or closed in painful grimace. Joseph could hear the whine of bullets, could hear them skip off stone and whistle and tear through the thicket. The Federal soldiers were screaming as they fired, stealing the usual rebel yell.

Joseph could not tell who was retreating or who was advancing, could not see any separation, any defined front, any advantage. He saw yanks kneeling and firing from under a low canopy of pine branches and aimed and fired his own rifle again in that direction and every shot was recorded in the slamming resistance of the gun against his shoulder. He saw so much movement in the brush. Figures appeared, then shadows, then explosions and blue smoke. He looked—through the confusion—for the face of Terence Hooker and he could not see it. He listened for his voice to emerge over the chaos, to embrace him with its familiarity—but he could not hear it. The cries and groans of the wounded were fused in a chorus of agony. Grown men were weeping—calling out for water, for help. Any man who moved to help fell to the storm of lead that whipped through the branches and filled the breathless air and added his own voice to the terrible choir. The wounded who were able hugged the ground and crawled behind rock and into ravine, covering themselves with black mud and dry brush—closing their eyes as if in some nightmare from which they might still awaken. The landscape was reduced to a thin plane, like the surface of the sea enveloped in fog. Narrow corridors of terror emerged and vanished in sulfur and smoke and the men were pressed to the earth. And then suddenly there was a pause. It seemed to Joseph the deep breath of an angry God. The battle paused.

They retreated from the clearing of the encampment after the first round of fire, leaving provisions neatly stacked amid the bodies of the dead and the wounded. As the air slowly cleared some of the wounded were dragged from the open space, but others were left in the heat of battle, left where they had fallen. Joseph could see a pyramid of rifles surrounded by a ring of lifeless bodies—soldiers who were shot as they rushed for their weapons and lay now as in some ceremonial wreath around the guns—as if they had been laid out like that—forming a circle—a human offering.

He sank behind a fallen tree—one he had not yet cut for the breastwork—and hugged the ground and the tree and shrank low as the grapeshot skipped off the trees again and sent bark flying. And then he heard an order to return fire and he raised his rifle and shot in the direction of the enemy and was joined by a hundred rifles.

The return fire momentarily quieted the enemy. Joseph wondered if they were flanking them and he glanced behind him.

He could see officers crouched behind a large boulder talking, glancing ahead. Joseph checked his cartridge box. Bullets again flew around him and he lay low and listened to them whine over his head, heard them land solidly in bark and in flesh, could hear them skip off stones and whistle through the thicket. He heard yelling. The Federal soldiers were yelling as they fired and advanced. The rebels yelled as they retreated. He looked up quickly, spotted a union soldier firing from behind a thin pine, and raised up again and shot him and watched him fall as he reloaded.

Someone behind him joined the volley. Something to his left—he turned in time to see a union soldier rushing at him with bayonet raised and Joseph shot again and the boy soldier fell screaming to the ground clutching his knee. The yank raised his rifle to Joseph as Joseph hurried to reload but he knew in these seconds there was not enough time to load and fire again at the fallen yank and he watched the barrel rise to him and could see the smile on the boy's face as he prepared to pull the trigger, then watched the smile explode into anguish as a bullet entered his skull and he went limp in the firing position, his rifle still aimed at Joseph's chest.

Lets go, Tyler, he heard Jacob holler and grab the shoulder of his uniform. Caint you hear retreat? Stay down. Caint you hear, Joe Tyler? Retreat they said, retreat.

Joseph followed Jacob, half-walking, almost crawling deeper into the woods, and then they slid into a ravine and Joseph could see something crawl or slither out as their bodies filled the hole and crushed the fern and azalea that filled it. There was quiet again for seconds, then a new wave of blue coated soldiers emerged from the treeline and a small group of Confederates tried to repel them from the left flank but were mowed down in a tremendous volley of fire from somewhere behind and they fell as they fired on top of the soldier in front of them and one even remained standing with his rifle stuck in the ground and his body wedged upright like an unfinished statue.

Joseph could hardly focus, but he heard the call for retreat renewed and he and Jacob rose firing, backing into the woods—slowly at first so as not to trip—then running.

Lets go Joe, Jacob repeated, and he and Joseph were in full run between the trees and the brush with gray-uniformed soldiers all around them and the enemy fire exploding on the moving and the unmoving things in the woods. They found a path that made their running easier and then ran across a stream ankle-deep in cold water. He heard the water splash around him but he could not feel it. He could see the company colors heading toward a clearing in the woods and he followed, with Jacob right behind.

Keep goin Tyler. We'll find a place to fight from, and they ran with Joseph slowing slightly so Jacob could keep up, until they were in the clearing and the rebel army emerged from the shadows of the trees into the clearing and across it to a shattered stone wall on its far side and they leapt over the wall and hugged the ground behind it. The standard on which flew the colors was rammed into the crevice between two large stones and the carrier fell to temporary safety behind the stone wall.

Miraculously, the yanks had not seized the opportunity but rather withdrew to the opposite edge of the field. There they gathered their wounded and began to assemble and organize. Joseph sat exhausted on the grass behind the wall, his rifle across his lap, and then lay straight down on his back looking up at the clear morning sky. He could see birds—geese, pat-terned against the blue, fleeing the carnage below. He needed moments but had only seconds to gather himself.

You all right?, he asked Jacob.

Jacob nodded without raising his head or eyes. We need to re-form, rest and re-form. We can lick them damn yankees if we're ready for them. Not one can shoot worth a damn.

Jacob was talking as if to himself, his chin buried in the open collar of his uniform jacket—his body clinging to the stone. Joseph could see his shirt drenched with sweat, his eyes closed tightly.

Ordered to hold, he heard someone call out. Hold this position.

Joseph had lost interest in who was ordering or calling out, but he under-stood that holding this position would be very difficult and that the battle would be renewed in moments. He closed his eyes for a moment, then raised himself to his knees to look out across the pasture and around him and as he did he picked briers from his trousers and dried brown pieces of leaves from his hair. He had lost his cap running, looked around but could not see it.

He thought there were a hundred of them behind the wall, but as he looked now he saw that they were lucky if there were fifty. Across the field he could see bodies lying in the open grass and then in the woods beyond he saw shadows and reflections of the enemy army gathering itself for battle—could hear the clatter of ramrod through the thin leaves. Behind him now he could see a group of rebs standing in the protection of the trees and talking. He recognized Captain George Cole, son of a wealthy plantation farmer. He was brandishing a sword and a pistol—one in each hand. He was speaking —saying something about yankees—almost screaming. He had no hat and long blond hair that fell to his shoulders. He had on one of the newer uni-form jackets with blue and red along the buttons and collar and gold epaulets at the shoulders. His shirt was still deep gray, unfaded. A silver chain hung around his neck, supporting some kind of medallion. There were patches on his vest pocket that Joseph could not recognize but assumed to be some kind of awards—for gallantry—or for wealth. It really no longer mattered. He could see, even from where he sat, the officer's eyes, and the unfocused stare of cold fear and rage. That combination would kill George Cole today. Joseph was sure of that. Nothing killed like fear—except rage.

Officers gathered again behind them in the trees, about fifteen feet from the stone wall. One was pointing across the field to a high ridge that rose up, the other gesturing along the length of the stone wall, but the discussion was abbreviated with a tremendous volley of fire from across the pasture and everyone ducked and clung to the ground. They could see nothing to fire back at, but some fired nonetheless—wasting precious cartridges. Then just as quickly as it started it silenced again. There was other firing in the distance, and Joseph could make out voices—screaming voices—in the distance but not the words, which were muffled through a thousand trees. A half-mile away—maybe less, no telling who it was.

Joseph and Jacob stood kneeling, their rifles breaching the flat surface of the stone wall, watching the woodland across the field. The leaves of the trees around them seemed to shiver into silence. Then he could see movement, a rustling of the waxy leaves of laurel on the edge near the enemy line and then through the bent and broken branches walked a black horse.

The horse staggered into the daylight, nostrils flaring as if in fury—the sun reflecting off a polished leather saddle, an undrawn sword. The animal walked uneasily, as if moving across ice, staggered and then righted himself. He walked into the tall grass toward the rebel troops. Joseph watched as the bony legs began to collapse, watched the horse raise his head upward even as the huge body folded into itself—hurtling forward. A great cloud of dust rose over it as it hit the dry ground. Soldiers on both sides of the field watched and listened to the moans and primitive grunts of the black horse. They watched its chest rise and settle, rise and settle, its feet kick helplessly at the air and at the ground. And then a single shot was heard from the woodland and the beast's anguished wheezing and kicking stopped. Silence gathered again and froze the pasture in the moment—the black horse in the green field. The last breath of the horse was unheard but seen—its great broad chest emptying to the cool air and its bone and flesh settling into the uneven texture of the pasture as if it were a part of it. As if it had been there always.

II.

Blackstone Farm

It had been same year—the year he had fallen through the ice of Skull Pond—he remembered his father had gone for his weekly trip to town and left Joseph to groom the workhorse. Samuel was the horse's name, but his father just called it horse. He remembered entering the small barn and could hear the snorting and shuffling of the animal as he entered. He rubbed the back of Samuel's neck, feeling the coarse hair of the mane and the smooth black skin. There was only gray light in the barn as the weak sun crept through the spaces between the rough-cut, shrinking cedar boards. One window was still boarded up tight from the winter and Joseph took a steel bar and pried the boards off and let them fall to the floor. The sun and cool air washed through the barn and the horse raised his nose to it. Joseph continued to rub him with the palm of his hand and spoke to him quietly as he did. The horse shook his great head toward the space of the window, lifted toward the light.

Joseph went to the door of the barn and pulled it open. It was loosely hinged and seem to groan as it opened wide. Joseph dragged a bushel of feed to the door to keep it from closing, and now the barn was lit brightly with the cool spring sun. All the snow was gone but the ground was still slick with frost and the leafless trees filled the landscape with the depth of detail in the spaces between the tall pine and hemlock. Joseph reached to the barn floor, picking up the brown brush, and pulled it across the horse's mane, downward, and then pulled the stiff bristles of the brush across the skin of Samuel's back and then across the great chest. The horse barely moved as he was brushed, blinked his black eyes and lowered them. Joseph could see the breath of the horse in the cool air and the mottled sky move past the open window.

A breeze rattled the door against its hinges and slapped the boards against the bushel and the horse whinnied at the sound. There was little work in winter, but the horse's muscles retained the strength of the exhausting summer of work. It would be very soon that the animal would be tied to the plow and pulling at the soft earth of spring. Joseph took a thick rope from a hook on the wall, draped it over the neck of the horse and holding it in one hand, guided the animal through the open door and out of the barn. Samuel seemed to hesitate at first—to resist—then followed the gentle tug of the rope to the outside.

They walked across the field to the ridge that led gradually down to the river. Joseph walked without thinking through the clearing, through the frozen brush, to the edge of the murky ponds formed from the melting snow and the loose soil. Joseph watched the fading sun and the shadows of the low clouds wash over the dark skin of the horse—watched the black nostrils swell to the clean, cold air—watched the breeze unsettle the mane and the lip raise and snort. They walked together, and Joseph could hear the sound of the river grow louder as they neared it—swelled with winter snow and rain and running fierce over stone and fallen trees. They crossed silently under a stand of pine and when they were through it, Joseph could see the Salmon River below where the water fell over rocks and then slowed in a deep black pool. On the far side there was little division between water and land; the river swelled into roots and grass, turning the ground black with mud. This forest was filled with these shallow swamps, yellow fleshy grass crowding the edges and giving way slowly to solid ground, covered with spores of ferns that would manifest by summer into a blanket of quivering fronds and turn the light of the southern sun into a carpet of yellow green across the forest floor. But now it was black and wet and Joseph could feel a light rain, just beginning, at his neck. He pulled a flannel jacket closer around him and pulled a single wooden button through a hole to keep it from falling open. White clouds vanished and gave way to gray shapeless drifts in the darker sky.

The horse walked up to the edge of the pool. The surface of the water trembled gently with the increasing rain. Joseph pulled the rope toward

him and in one movement was on Samuel's broad back. A single tug of
the rope and the horse began walking along the river's edge. Joseph could
see the great muscles and skin of the horse shining with the rain as he
brought the animal into a trot along the path that followed the river.
Joseph wasn't thinking. He allowed himself simply to listen to the river, to
the beat of the horse's hooves along the trail—felt the rain rolling from his
cap and cascade down his face—felt it down the back of his neck. Thunder
swelled up and rolled as if over the hills ahead and the silver light deepened
the color of green and the leaves of the pine and cedar seemed to swell with
the wet air and the light of the sun, twisted in the storm, seemed liquid and
blanketed the woodland and the river in a thick iridescence.

The horse's step quickened at the sound of the thunder and the pressure
of Joseph's boots at his sides, and horse and rider leaned forward into steady
and then full gallop. The land spilled into the river again and white water
rushed over rocks and raced with Joseph and the horse deeper into the
Virginia wilderness. Suddenly the sky was white with lightning and the
lower branches of pine flashed like fleshless skeletons against the white sky
and the rain fell in sheets now against Joseph's face and across the black
body of the horse. The horse pulled at the slick ground in front of them, the
thin bones of his powerful legs working furiously—the back legs pushing at
the earth and into the saturated air. Joseph clung now to the mane, his body
pressed against the powerful body of the horse. White light exploded again
across the sky and then the deep rolling thunder as they continued to gallop
along the river's edge. Follow it to the sea, Joseph thought. Follow it to the
sea. To where it spilled out into the great sea—crashed at the sides of
ships—washed onto the shores of other countries—wherever it led he would
ride, and continue riding. There was a tremendous explosion of thunder and
horse and rider were both startled, Joseph almost breathless, and then a sudden calm as the rain eased slightly and the horse slowed to a trot.

They slowed, almost stopped, in the moment of calm—but it lasted only
a moment. The rains began to increase swiftly until it was blinding. The sky
was steel-gray and almost lightless. The sound of the rushing river was deaf-
ening, seeming to swell up to the pouring rain, and Joseph finally looked for

familiar markings along the river's edge. He and Terence had come this far last summer. He could see familiar granite cliffs across the river and the thin trees that grew from the cracks in stone—and the caves. He remembered the caves that spread like yawning mouths across the face of the cliffs.

The sweat of the horse was now mixed with the sweeping rain. The river crashing over stone, the rain pelting the skin and clothes of Joseph and the horse, thunder, now distant then close, rolling over the hills. Joseph tugged the horse's rein and drew him through the thick brush toward the caves and was relieved when he saw the broad chasm of the largest one in front of him. He walked toward it—but Samuel stopped and pulled against him. Joseph tried to pull the horse, which he knew could fit through the mouth of the cave and be sheltered—but the horse would not enter the dark opening in the rock face and Joseph was forced to abandon him as he ran for shelter in the great outcroppings of heaved stone. He could feel the cold air against his wet skin as soon as he entered and could see only darkness like the black of unburnt coal. He turned to look away from the storm and into the dark cave to help his eyes adjust so that he could see—and he began to be able to make out shadowed forms that were familiar to him from past visits to this place and the work of his heart began to slow in his chest. He took great deep breaths to calm himself—and then let his weight down to sitting along the near wall not far from the entrance, wrapping his arms around his folded legs to find some warmth in his own body—clenching himself in the darkness.

He could not see the horse, or at least he could not tell if it was the horse in the dark shadows. The rain fell almost horizontally in a powerful wind and he could no longer make out the voice of the river in the howl of the wind and the whipping of the rain against the stone face of the mountain. The earth beneath him seemed to move—to be collecting itself and rolling toward a tumultuous crest—and from the earth it seemed came a great crash of thunder that rolled over the cave as if in a wave, a cracking sound—the splitting of the wood of trees and then a pure white light lit the woods like midday, washed light into the cave, sustained long enough so that Joseph could make out lines of drawings along the cave walls and then faded to black quickly. And then a receding roll of thunder and another explosion of light. The dark walls tunneled his sight to the woodland. The trees were tall silhouettes leaning toward him and in a clearing not far away he saw the horse rear onto his hind legs—the strength of the plow, the power of his life of work challenging the angry sky—the horse dropped and rose again kicking his forelegs upward. Joseph watched him, black against the dark woods lit with white lightning, and then another crash of thunder as if overhead, and he could see but could not hear the horse cry out at the strange sky with a fierceness he could not recognize—and he watched as the black horse raged against the storm and the whipping rain until the lightning finally subsided and the thunder sounded only faraway echoes in canyons unseen and Joseph fell asleep in the uneasy mix of darkness and light.

He remembered waking to the sound of an owl—the last embrace of night giving way to traces of daylight. The woods in front of the cave were lit as if from within with the early-morning light—the sun unseen. He stood and walked out of the mouth of the cave and looked for Samuel. Light streamed into the forest as if on the path left by the torrents of rain the evening before and it illuminated the earth in that way peculiar to the aftermath of a storm. But where was the horse? He was gone. Joseph could see the forest floor torn apart from the great weight of the horse's hooves and could see prints leading down toward the river. He followed the depressions in the mud through a clearing and down to the edge of the river which ran with a new ferocity. There were no more prints—or they had been washed away with the night's rain. The evidence of the horse's presence vanished along the river's edge and the sound of the river's rushing water consumed Joseph's thoughts. He kneeled down at the edge and brought the cold water to his face and through his hair. His trousers and shirt were still soaked from the night. He could see the jagged edges of a spruce that had been torn apart by the storm, the white and imperfect flesh of the tree lying open to the air like the teeth of an animal, the great trunk and outstretched branches leaning to the earth—suspended with the strength of itself—not yet ready to settle to the earth and give in to weightless decay. Joseph began to walk back upriver toward home. He looked constantly in the clearings and in the dense woods for the horse—calling him by name—whistling—and he prayed that the horse had survived the storm.

It was late morning when he walked over the stone bridge and up the last grassy slope to the top where he could see Blackstone Farm. As he ascended the slope he imagined his father's anger at his adventure and at losing the horse. He tried to tell the story in his head—that it had been a simple exercise walk, that the horse became excited, that they had run along the river losing consciousness of time, that the storm came suddenly and the horse would not enter the cave and had become strange in the storm—but he knew his father would not understand—would be angry and would hold the anger within himself and would not speak to Joseph for many days—maybe weeks. He could see the top of the slope and the sun fighting its way through the torn rag of clouds that remained, and as he reached the top he could see the east field and the background of pine and oak and the swelling brush beneath it. There along the field's edge was his father. A gray wooden cart, a sled with no wheels sat angular on the ground with large stones upon its surface, pushing the cart into the earth. The cart slanted up along long wooden poles and the ends of the poles were tied to the horse with thick rope. His father held a thin stick and tapped along the horse's hindquarters urging him onward. The snap of the stick echoed in the quiet morning of the field. The gaze of the horse's eyes was downward at the winter ground in front of him as he lifted one foot at a time in front of the other and then again as the load shook and moved along the wet soil. Joseph could see the breath of the horse and of his father in the damp morning air. He stood on the crest of the hill and watched. He felt cold at the base of his back that rose upward to make him shiver and draw his arms around himself and he was aware of himself shaking and then became aware that he was ready to cry. He stood in the high grass looking down at the field and the farm.

He stood perhaps a few minutes. The tortured sky was close around him. As he stood the strength of his legs gave out as the tears rose to his eyes and he fell to his knees on the wet grass, and he shivered—his whole body shaking—but he did not cry. He wiped the tears in his eyes dry before they rolled to his cheeks. He held himself, his long arms wrapped around himself, kneeling on the cold ground. But he would not cry. He looked across the field and to the hills. Nothing was left of the storm but the opalescent clouds and the shadows of clouds repeated on themselves and pronounced again across the field. And puddles of dark water that lay like steel across the uneven earth.

III.

The Wilderness

On the battlefield the horse's death had caused a bizarre pause in the action and Joseph was awakened again to the present when a bullet skipped off the stone, just missing his right ear. Jacob swore and ducked lower behind the wall and soon there was a resumption of firing from the yankee line and bullets filled the air above them almost like mosquitoes, spinning and skipping and ending in dreadful thuds around them.

Then, again, it was reduced and then stopped. Singular shots rang out and then they ceased as well. He could hear orders being called out across the field. Then there was quiet. Joseph peered carefully over the stone. The Union regiment was forming in a line at the edge of the pasture. He could see the U. S. flag flapping in a sudden breeze and then relaxing again on its staff. Beside the flag bearer stood a young boy with a drum, a wide white strap across his chest and a blue forage cap pulled low over his eyes and cocked slightly to one side. Another order from across the field and the drummer began to pound the surface of the drum. The army began to move. The blue soldiers emerged from behind trees and the dense brush until they were thick across the field, shoulder to shoulder—hundreds, perhaps a thousand of them, Joseph thought—moving in unison toward them. He was waiting for orders to retreat—the position was impossible—but he

heard orders to fire and then a scream or a yell to attack. Attack the yanks
across the field. Joseph watched as Jacob rose up and crossed the wall and
staggered to the grass and the men that were left rose up yelling and
Joseph was drawn up with them, without thought, firing and advancing
with impossible steps across the uneven ground. The regiment spread out
in a slow and awkward run toward the sea of blue uniforms. Joseph saw
the colors dropped, retrieved—raised up—and the line increased in speed
and he could not feel himself running but rather was lifted, buoyant,
toward the oncoming enemy.

Drop and fire, he heard, and the rebels dropped into the grass of the
field and fired low and watched as yanks dropped as they walked and others walked over them in long, exaggerated strides.

Advance, he heard, and he rose up, Jacob a few feet from him, and fired
ahead. His rifle was jolted from his hand as it was hit by grapeshot and he
reached for his pistol and cocked and fired and watched a soldier fall.

Drop and fire, he heard again and they dropped into the grass and held
their ground behind a small outcrop of ledge. Then the drummer changed
his beat and the union army began to run and there was a low roar of
human voices as they trampled across the field toward them. It was an
unnatural sound. It was not the sound of human beings but rather the
sound of an army. It was something different they heard. Something that
those who lived would recall to their children and their children's children
and would hear repeated themselves across a thousand starless nights in
lives far removed from this poor field.

Hold your position, Joseph heard, and then, retreat. Retreat . . .
regroup . . . someone yelled.

And the rebel soldiers, now not more than fifty men, stood and ran for
better cover, firing behind them as they ran.

Joseph fired his pistol once more and turned to run. The field behind
him appeared immense and the trees that framed it small. It was actually
about 150 yards until protection. More yanks had flanked them and were
assembling and firing from the stone wall. Before the woodland began
again there were no trees except one, and no other protection in the open

field. A single white oak emerged from a grassy depression in the pasture and stood alone in the field. After the oak it was another thirty yards to the woodland and the protection of the dense growth of the wilderness. Joseph, along with Jacob and the others, aimed for the tree and ran full speed across the yellow grass—he watched it fly under him—fixed his sight on the tree and watched it grow in front of him. He could see the trunk was split into two thick trunks and the branches flushed with new growth. He began to make out the color of the bark and could feel himself longing to embrace it—to have the huge trunk of the tree between himself and his enemy. Suddenly aware of being alone in his run, he glanced quickly to both sides of him and saw nothing. He pulled his pistol so both hands held it and slowed slightly as he turned to look back across the pasture. His men were a good thirty or forty feet behind him—he had simply outrun them all. He slowed instinctively and they began to catch up but as a few of them reached the safety of the tree Joseph knelt and turned toward the enemy. He watched the runners fall. He could see the enemy walking now—firing in unison at the trapped rebels. He watched a young boy from his company run right into the ground after being shot in the back, the dust flying upward as the body slid to a stop in the grass. He couldn't see Jacob. Next to him, a soldier's cap flew from his head and tumbled to the ground with a fresh hole in it. Joseph looked to see the soldier standing, somehow unaffected. Others arrived at the tree and clung to it and to each other in its protection. They huddled there in the shadow of the oak.

We need to slow them, someone hollered, and they all knelt and fired in unison. He could see the man standing next to him, leaning on the bark of the tree as if trying to enter it somehow—the hair that framed his ears flecked with white—and he could see the man was crying. They fired in unison and at least three blue-coated soldiers dropped from the line to the pasture's uneven surface. Joseph watched as one fell to his knees and his body stayed in that position. But the spaces left by the fallen soldiers were quickly taken by others and Joseph knew that it was only moments before they would be overwhelmed. He stopped firing and sat against the tree with his back to it. He looked into the woodland. It was dense and offered plenty of protection, but it could not be reached. He sat and waited—waited to die—deciding whether to die here behind the single white oak or along the pasture as he ran. He thought briefly of Terence. Was he safe? Alive? And then he was aware of new firing from the west side of the pasture. He looked to it and saw clearly the Confederate flag and gray-clad soldiers firing from the woodline. Standing and kneeling and firing. Then he heard calling from behind. Joseph, someone was yelling, and he stood and yelled, Lets go!

It was Jacob's voice and he stood with a group of soldiers behind a stand of black birch and they fired at the yankee army as Joseph and five or six survivors ran from the sanctuary of the single tree toward the woodland. Joseph ran behind the firing soldiers and then came up to stand next to Jacob. How the hell d'you get here, and where'd they come from?

It's all split up in the woods. Small parties everywhere fightin what they caint see. I could sure see that tree wasn't big enough for all of us. Damn, Jacob yelled, as he fired his rifle at the shadows cast by the enemy soldiers and the shadows of the Confederate soldiers trying to lose themselves, trying to be absorbed by the thick and tangled woods. But there were more blue soldiers. There seemed, at least to Jacob and to Joseph, to be many more who wore the blue.

I saw artillery up on the next ridge . . . and our flag. Looks like six cannon, maybe more. We can make it there. Follow me, Joe Tyler.

Joseph turned to move and tripped over a body on the ground. He could see from the blond hair that it was George Cole. His face leaned against the bark of the tree and the back of his head was missing and the purple tissue of his brain hung through white bone and the blond hair was soaked red. He pulled the face from the tree and rolled the body gently to the ground. He looked down at the lifeless face a moment. Joseph pulled the medallion that was twisted around the man's neck and he flattened it on his chest—took a second to read the inscription, the words SIC SEMPER TYRANNIS were etched on the hammered silver—then Joseph ran into the woods, following Jacob and maybe a dozen other soldiers. No more rage, he thought as he ran. No more fear.

They ran full speed in between the saplings, knee-deep in brier and brush. They ran along a brook and crossed to the other side, where their steps were softened by a thick carpet of moss.

Up here, Jacob yelled, and the men followed. No one was firing now. It was a chase. The yankee army was in the woods and moving in small groups behind them in pursuit. And then as Joseph passed a stand of trees that had been mauled with bullets he saw the flag. The Stars and Bars had never looked better, and just as Jacob had promised there was a stockade of felled trees with the protruding cannon along its length. The rebels yelled as they approached and Joseph could even hear some of them laughing. Jacob was yelling at them to turn and fire when they reached the cannon—was yelling at the men behind the stockade to fire at the pursuing yanks—was yelling as he leapt over the stockade, Yahoo. Fire, damnit! Fire! Give em some Dixie thunder.

But as Joseph approached the stockade and saw the cannon, his heart sank and his feet gave out and he tripped and fell to the ground in front of the great stacked logs. He couldn't hear anything in those seconds—just lay there. Jacob was no longer yelling and he looked up to watch the rebel soldiers climb the breastwork and jump behind it for protection and he could hear them swear and scream as they saw what Joseph had seen. The cannon—protruding from the wall of wood—were not cannon at all. They were logs—mere lumber. Tree trunks—pointed outward to fool the enemy. There were no cannon. The bodies of two soldiers lay behind the stockade, one still holding a sword—the other draped over the fake cannon. This was what we've come to, Joseph thought. He saw Jacob sitting against the logs and went to sit beside him.

This is it, Joseph said. This is the fight, this is the place.

What kinda place is this? Jacob responded. I spent five years makin cannon and now I got logs to shoot. What the hell is this? What the hell. Goddamn.

This is where we fight, I guess.

You fight, Jacob answered. I'm done. There aint no sense anymore. No sense to it.

Sense is livin. Sense is gettin outta this war alive. Folks are waitin in Richmond for you.

Jacob looked to Joseph's eyes and said, I'm finished. I'm done.

At that they became aware of the closeness of the enemy and the five or six soldiers behind the stockade rose to fight. Joseph stood above Jacob. He grabbed the rifle of the dead soldier that lay across the fake cannon and climbed the stockade. There were only a few—maybe twenty yanks approaching the stockade and they climbed the wooded slope slowly. They were so far fooled by the black trunks that protruded from the wall. The soldier next to Joseph said, What do we do?

Joseph said, We fight.

We fight, the man said. And then the few of them left yelled, We fight. . . . Bring it to them. Bring it to the cowards, and they ascended the walls and jumped down onto the ground firing and running full speed into the yankee line. Stunned momentarily and perhaps waiting for the cannon to fire, the enemy did not fire back. Then as if awakened from sleep the blue army rose from the brush and from behind trees and rocks and now surrounded Joseph and the last of the regiment. Some fired, some rushed with bayonets. All of them screamed as they fought. Joseph grabbed the rifle from one who lunged at him and plunged the bayonet into the side of the man until he could feel the blade hit bone and then pushed him away to release the bloodied steel. Someone grabbed him from behind and Joseph could see a knife blade flashing toward his neck and then watched as the man collapsed to the ground. Out of the corner of his eye he saw Jacob standing on top of the stockade with a pistol in one hand and a rifle in the other—firing both of them and screaming, This here's Confederate cannon. He leapt off the wall. This here's Richmond thunder.

His forward motion carried him down into a ravine, and two yankee soldiers followed him. Joseph raced toward them and shot one in the back with a jolt of his rifle and could see the other as he fired at Jacob and he could see Jacob crumple to his knees and fire again into the air—still yelling something as he fell—but Joseph could not get to him. He could hear Jacob's voice as he fired blindly, falling to his side, but he could not get to him. He could not understand what he was saying. The battle separated them. And all he could do was watch as his friend fell back and vanished in the low ground.

A volley knocked the rifle from Joseph's grip and he reached again for the pistol and then, as if rising from the ground itself, a yankee private lunged at him with a bayonet and he could feel the sudden burning in his shoulder and he reached for it even while firing once more and he could feel the earth rise up to him and the trees tumble around him and the air turn thick as he tried to breathe it in and then he could feel the black night engulf him—like the icy water of the pond, the sound muting, receding—drifting away. And then nothing.

Through the rest of the day and through the night that followed, Joseph lay among the thousands. They lay contorted and awkward along the paths and along the streams and woodland—no different. Some blue-clad, some in gray, some in the clothes they left home with—extra clothes their wives and mothers had run after them with. Dressed in jackets and red shirts—in uniforms of past wars and uniforms of foreign wars. They lay facedown in the crushed grass of the pastures, or flat on their backs—eyes to heaven, crumpled where they fell. Bodies leaning on trees and bodies leaning on other bodies. Officers, farmers, teachers, millworkers, blacksmiths, gentlemen—all lay now in the still Virginia night—and the body of Joseph Tyler was indistinguishable among them, one of the many thousands who would die in this Wilderness Campaign. Except for his heart. It would not stop. It was relentless in its beating even as he lay bleeding on the forest floor. Except for the heart that pumped even now—and would slowly return consciousness to the exhausted body—the voided spirit. And Joseph Tyler would rise from this spot and would hear the dying screams of Roger McCleod. He would walk into the fire toward him and raise him up from the flames. And Joseph would walk from the burning landscape—clinging to a letter—and to a life.

I Would Fly from This Place

A Union soldier named George Putman recalled playing between the lines in Texas when, "suddenly there came a scattering fire of which three outfielders caught the brunt; the center fielder was hit and captured, the left and right field managed to get back to our lines. The attack was repelled without serious difficulty, but we had lost not only our center field, but . . . the only baseball in Alexandria, Texas.
—from *Baseball*, by Ken Burns

But if a man would be alone, let him look at the stars. The rays that come from those heavenly worlds, will separate between him and what he touches. One might think the atmosphere was made transparent with this design, to give man, in the heavenly bodies, the perpetual presence of the sublime.
—Ralph Waldo Emerson

I.

They sat together in a line along a wooden bench fashioned from a log split down its full length. The bark hadn't been removed from the round side and the flat surface carried every cut of the saw. They were in what may have been a large barn or warehouse before the war. Joseph's wound had started to bleed again and someone had wrapped a colorless cloth tightly around it. He looked down the line of prisoners but saw no one he recognized from his own regiment. Exhaustion and hunger weighed him down—pressed him into the hard bench and against the plank wall.

One guard stood, musket in hand, at the latched door. He looked uncomfortable and nervous. He was an older soldier, with a long gray beard stained in tobacco, yellow teeth, a fat waist and a red sash that seemed to hold it in place. His blue uniform stretched to capacity, he stood in stark contrast to the starving soldiers of the Confederacy who lined the bench in the long shadows of the barn.

Joseph moved his hands only to find they were bound at the wrist and he was tied to the man who leaned against him and so on down the line. The pain now in his wrists brought to him a new awareness, and he began to recall in fragments—as if his mind would not allow him to see anything whole, or understand anything but the moment—and he let his head rest back onto the cool wall.

He tried to remember his capture. He was walking, he recalled, from the place where he had left the dead Union soldier. Walking without thinking on a narrow path along the brook that may have been a weak branch of the Rapidan. He thought of the larger river—if he could get to it and follow it away from the choking woods, away from this place, following along the cool water. He walked past the dead bodies of soldiers, avoiding their lifeless stares, and he did not slow as he passed them. Small fires burned everywhere and the flames licked lazily at the spoiled air and the smoke drifted in pillows at his knees like milk spilled in water. He should find his regiment, he remembered thinking, whatever was left of it.

And then he remembered hearing them first and then turning quickly to see them as they stood on the bluff, rifles raised and pointed at him. There were six or seven of them and as his hand went to his pistol he heard one of them say, Just as soon kill ya reb. Less trouble for us all.

And Joseph remembered thinking that he might be right and he considered drawing his pistol, but he raised his hands. A young yank soldier ran toward him then and pushed the butt of his rifle into Joseph's stomach and it buckled him over and he fell to the ground. Then there was a blow to the side of his head—and nothing.

Now he could feel a draft—a thin stream of cool air through the cracks between the broad shrinking planks of wood that formed the barn wall. Joseph twisted himself into a position that allowed the cool air to flow to his neck and down the back of his shirt. Across the dark space before them another shaft of light cut through the emptiness and splashed along the dirt floor. A soldier at the end of the bench slumped forward onto the floor pulling everyone toward him—swearing—and pulling his arms in both directions. The men tried to pull him upright with the rope but his body twisted to the ground. The fat guard rushed to him, lifted him up to the wooden bench, and then pushed him up against the plank wall with the sole of his mud-caked boot.

Sit up, damn secesh, or something like that Joseph could hear him say, and then he went down the line and pushed each prisoner back to the wall with the flat butt of his musket and Joseph looked away as the guard pressed with the gun against his shoulder and held it for a moment— could feel the tears of pain growing in the corner of his eyes—but he said nothing and the guard moved on down the line, taking similar time with each prisoner. There was very little noise.

The wounded were too exhausted from the march here—the starving too near death to care in which form it came. Joseph focused his eyes forward, gritting his teeth against the new pain. He focused now on the single source of light. He closed his eyes and let his head rest again on the wall and felt the cool air at his neck and shoulders—and followed the black tunnel that led him again to the only escape—led him to deep, exhausted sleep.

He could see now—a single shaft of light streaming through the half-open door of a hayloft. They were in Terence's barn. Particles of sawdust danced lazily through the light like water. The structure of the barn was of rough-hewn cedar planks and oak beams that stretched from side to side. Great vertical boards were tied with iron nails to an unsettled framework and absorbed the colors of the earth—gray-brown, green with moss, sagging but sitting strong on a stone foundation.

Where the wood met the stone there were spaces where field mice scurried and gathered and slept, and the muted light seeped between the walls and the foundation and washed the floor in shadows. The timbers were wall to wall, thirty feet across, and unplaned bark still clung to the corners and the edges and the black iron nails could be seen in the corners and at the junction of the planks and the beams. Two small stables were occupied by black horses that spit and whinnied and shuffled on the dirt floor—and the smell of dung and rotting grass, not completely unpleasant, hung heavy in the cold air.

They knelt there together, dripping hot wax from a burning candle onto a wad of dampened hay. Joseph squeezed the hot mass in both hands and held it firm, feeling the wax cool as it seeped into the straw. When it was firm, he pushed it into an old stocking that Terence had brought with him to the barn, and they tied the end with two knots. A rope was then tied to the knotted end of the stocking and Joseph took it and swung it around and let the stocking fly upward toward the dark barn loft. It flew in an arc over a beam and returned to them swinging and bouncing. Terence grabbed it, lowered it to his waist, and held it still. Joseph took the other end of it and tied it to a short piece of broken ax handle and threw it over the beam again so it was tethered and would not slip, then tied the end of the rope on a stable door. The filled stocking now swung lazily, slicing the shaft of light like a saber as it slowed and finally stopped. Joseph watched it and then pulled on the rope firmly to check its strength. A breath of wet snow could be heard on the barn roof, and the air inside was thick and still. The horse closest to them made a guttural sound and turned away.

Terence turned and walked to the end of the barn, behind a wooden toolbox with brass hinges on it, and pulled a bat from the darkness. It was unfinished—chiseled with little skill, tooled with a rasp and scraper, but not yet oiled. There were lumps of wood bulging like blisters on the otherwise smooth areas and places where the rasp or pumice had not yet touched, but the handle was smooth and Terence held the fat end as he handed it to Joseph. Joseph put his hands, one on top of the other, along the bat handle and felt its weight and swung the bat from side to side casually. Lets give it a try, he said.

Terence backed away a few steps. Joseph carefully placed the fat end of the bat along, almost touching, the dangling object. As he did he took careful measure of the distance—and the feel of the bat against the thing it would strike. He concentrated on the dark, gently swaying object, imagined its flight, drew the wood back behind and above his shoulders, and brought it around in a swift, explosive motion until the thick carved wood struck it and sent it hurtling upward—adrift in a cloud of straw dust—toward the barn loft. It reached its peak, stretching the rope to its full length—then swung down, bouncing back to the place from which it started.

Awright—my turn, Terence yelled, laughing, and Joseph handed the bat to him and Terence repeated the exercise in the dimly lit barn, the horses snorting at the unfamiliar activity as it was repeated time after time. They took turns striking it and watched the flight of the ball as it reached for the loft and returned each time. Joseph measured each chance, the motion of his arms—the movement of his wrists—discovered the feeling of it as it rushed from light to dark and back. He found he could swing quicker with his legs bent and the weight of his body shifted slightly forward—watching the swaying object, his eyes fixed ahead. Not exploding—no, that would shift the balance—starting the movement suddenly, as if waking with no other purpose—back and shoulder muscles extended—legs pulling against gravity, fingers held firm and feeling the cold wood against his skin. Following the movement of the bat once started, pulling him along with it—watching the black object fly upward while the weight of the wood remained in his hands and came to rest at his back and then returned to the front, held strong at his waist, then resting on the ground—balanced—collected.

They each took thirty, maybe forty swings, commenting on each other's form—laughing as they missed completely and talking about the work still needed to complete the bat. Snow fell silently now outside and floated, whirling through the small open door of the hayloft on a cold whisper of air. Their breath mixed silver in the dampness and then collected and vanished in the air above the rough-hewn beams—each breath a quick cloud of silver, and then gone.

Finally it was getting late and there were still chores to be done. Terence handed the bat to Joseph for one last swing. He gripped the bat firmly—but not too tight, he thought. He measured his step and his weight and focused on the crude ill-shaped ball dangling at the end of the rope, and at that moment nothing else mattered. The moment was filled with the task. He became aware of the blood pumping to his muscles and his hands tensed. There were seconds of quiet, eternal seconds, then the wooden bat whipped through the air and shattered the stillness. The stretched thread of the old stocking had pulled away from itself with the force of the blow—the dry broken straw clinging to wax exploded and flew apart, hurtling toward the beams and the dark space of the loft and filling the air with a thousand bits of gold grass flying upward and then down again—across their shoulders and in their hair—through the silver slices of light and mixing with the clouds of breath and the snow that crept quietly through the hayloft door and settled on the floor of the barn.

Joseph could sense the light as it streamed through the door and feel the strength of his legs and his arms and he was aware of a burning in his shoulder and his hand went to it and he felt a hard object and then pain and his eyes opened to the fat guard who stood over him and who had poked his wounded shoulder again with the silver butt of his rifle. He was aware only that they were now moving. They remained tied together and were being led to the open doors of the barn. Joseph could remember seeing a long train of boxcars and the steam of the locomotive, and little else but the tortured movement of his feet along the ground.

He remembered nothing of the train trip until he opened his eyes to another flood of light and heard the grinding sound of the opening doors. As he adjusted to the bright light the pain of his shoulder and then his legs returned. He was sitting on the boxcar floor; when he tried to move his legs he realized that there was something pressing against them and he could not shift them. He looked up and could see faces—dozens of faces and the upright bodies of men standing. He must have fallen, slid to the floor beneath them, but he had no memory of this. They were crammed together in the small space and he was suddenly sick with the overwhelming smell, even as the air rushed in through the open doors.

He realized it was a man's body lying over his legs and that was why they ached, and he pushed at the man and rolled him slightly to his side and off his legs. A man standing nearby swore and kicked at the motionless body and pushed it with his boot back onto Joseph's legs. Off me, dammit. Leave it be.

Joseph was so crammed in the space that he was unable to resist. He reached to put his fingers on the man's pulse and before he even felt for the pumping blood of the veins he could tell from the cold skin that the man was dead, and had been for some time. He tried again but he could not move the body from his legs. There was no room.

Joseph was aware that he was in the boxcar of a train and he could see now the rifles with bayonets fixed and pointed silhouetted against the lit door. Then he heard voices. Union guards were yelling at the prisoners crammed in the car to stay put and not to move, just to get some air and stay put. They poked their bayonets into the empty air in front of the prisoners and the men crowded back into each other. A boy, slightly younger than Joseph, ran up to the open door and threw cool water into the sweltering space and the men yelled and swore and took the moisture from their arms and hands and put it to their mouths. He saw a body being dragged and handed from prisoner to prisoner toward the open door.

Can we remove the dead?

Stay put, and the bayonets were raised higher and closer and the body was laid at their feet.

These men need water for drinkin, he heard someone call out. It was an officer from the 5th Alabama. Joseph could still see the brass numbers along the tattered color. The man's hair was plastered to his head with sweat and he had a long beard that hung to his chest. He was not old, Joseph thought, but his face was drawn and his eyes reflected the defeated spirit. Joseph could see a gold scarf around his neck and tried to picture him on a grand horse leading men to battle but all he could see were the tired eyes and the lips cracked and dry with thirst.

Who's speaking?

I am, sir. The Confederate officer managed to lift his arm in salute, elbowing the men who stood next to him as he did. Colonel John J. Harwick of the 5th Alabama. General Cullen Battle's Brigade, sir.

The officer put his hand back to his side as the men who could watched him.

These men need to drink, sir. There is barely room even to kneel or sit. The man wiped his lips with the back of the hand he had just saluted with. We are dyin, sir. We are dyin as we stand. Don' see how we deserve that, sir.

Two hours, reb, and you'll have water. You'll be at your new home by then.

Some of these men won't live two hours.

Joseph looked at the faces of the men standing around him—lying on the floor around him underfoot. They were staring at their captors, barely enough strength to protest. Their faces were expressionless, ashen, their eyes only half-open to the new light. The air within the car could hardly be breathed. Joseph had no idea how long he had been here—hours, days, he had no idea—but he could feel the burning thirst now in his throat.

Get another bucket of water, Private.

The boy ran with the empty bucket and brought it back with water spilling over the rim onto the ground. Joseph watched it as it hit the sandy soil and vanished.

Let me have it, Private, the Union colonel said and he took the bucket in both hands and it clattered against his sword. He held it for a moment in front of the Confederate officer and the prisoner took a step forward and the eyes of the all the men opened and they seemed to swell forward. The bayonets rose up before them. Joseph tried but still could not move at all and he felt the muscles of his neck were stiff and painful.

Hold on.

The yankee officer sank a tin cup in the water and let it fill and then brought it full, to his lips. He smiled as the water drained to his mouth and ran down his chin.

Just what I thought. The officer hesitated and then said, Sweet water, yankee water, and he tilted the bucket slightly forward, just enough to let the water drain in a thin sheet to the ground. A Confederate soldier lunged forward toward the spilling water and a single rifle shot dropped him and he crumpled slightly and then remained upright between the other prisoners. There was no room for him to fall. The Confederate officer swore loudly and Joseph could hear screams from the back and then, Close the doors. Keep the train movin—these rebs are used to the damn heat.

The bright light slid back to darkness and the men groaned and swore and Joseph lay there with his eyes wide open and one hand on his wounded shoulder and the lifeless body of the man draped across his legs. He tried to move his legs but he found that he couldn't. They no longer ached, though. He realized as the train jerked forward that he couldn't feel them at all.

II.

Elmira, New York, 1864

The prison had risen up from the sloping hills of rural New York and it sat like an awkward mistake along the graceful landscape. Wooden stockade fences and towers and skinny ramps built hastily cast crooked shadows across the field. The site was poorly chosen, as it lay below the level of the Chemung River and the stagnant water and severe weather caused thousands of deaths before the fighting finally stopped in the south. The southern soldiers were brought here to face northern winters barefoot and dressed in thin cloth. The barracks were not yet finished and the canvas tents provided poor shelter. These were the survivors. Though many of them would come to regret this, even doubt it. And the journeys of many more would end here against the cold ground of New York.

Joseph had survived. He remembered very little of the journey and had no sense of the time. When he had arrived at Elmira he didn't even know what month it was and it took him a while to think of the year. He recalled only the bodies being unloaded and the prodding of the bayonet at him and waking and pulling away from the blade.

We got a live one here, he remembered someone saying. They were ordering him to stand—shouting at him—but as they lifted him they watched his legs collapse beneath him as he fell to the floor and to his hands. Someone prodded at his legs with the blade of a bayonet but Joseph felt only a dull sensation and didn't respond to the pain.

Got a cripple, he heard them say, and they lifted him and handed him out of the car and into the cool air and he sucked the air into his lungs and squinted his eyes to the sun.

He was thrown on a wide, flat board and carried to the hospital tent but they were turned away because his shoulder wound had seemed finally to heal itself and the surgeons could see no visible or treatable damage to his legs. He was put in the quarters with the other invalids, amputees and men paralyzed and dying slowly, and he slept those first nights among the crying and the screaming of the mortally wounded and diseased.

On the third day he awoke to feel a sharp tingling in his legs and then a great growing pain in his thighs and calves, and his hands went quickly to them and he gripped the muscles of his legs. He felt the sensation and strength flowing back to his muscles and to the nerves of his legs and he felt them move as he willed them to move. He could almost feel the muscles relax and the strength return to them and he realized they had been severely cramped by the immobility on the train and the weight of the body and within a couple of hours he felt complete strength in both legs and he stretched them full as he lay under a wool blanket on the ground and at the same time he realized something else. The strength of his legs was now his secret, and as they called him cripple they also thought of him as helpless and unthreatening, and so without thinking it all out he decided to keep the strength of his legs to himself. It was something of his own.

That afternoon as hunger gnawed at him and no food was brought he could see men lining up for food at a barracks across the grass field and he realized if he could not walk he would not eat. He looked around quickly, and then raised himself up. When he was upright he walked toward the line of men with a severe and awkward limp. He made sure to be as slow as possible, shuffling one foot and dragging the next. The guards watched him and he heard one of them say, Looks like we got a walkin cripple reb.

Joseph didn't look up as he shuffled to the food line. As he did, he thought more clearly about his legs and he realized he now had not only a secret but a weapon that he could use when the time was right. For now he would walk as if severely wounded and exaggerate his slowness and his shuffle and in this way he was absorbed into the life of the prison. At night, though, under the blankets or in the cover of darkness, he exercised his legs until the muscles of his thighs were stronger than ever. He would have to find a way to survive until the time was right.

The days in the camp seemed endless. Ragged white tents divided the slanted sun and cast black shadows on the ground. Line after line of canvas tents crossed the field, enclosed by wooden stockade and towers—hastily constructed from the timber of the surrounding woods—and the yankee guards walked along elevated walkways from which they could see the whole camp. The squares of black that framed each tent provided the only shade for the prisoners and on hot days they lay on their bedrolls on the bare dirt between the tents to stay cool.

When it was warm, black water ran like a skinless snake between the blankets and the bare earth. It ran along the ground, sliding under the thin cloth that separated the prisoners from the ground. Melting snow and rain had filled the brooks and the nearby river and the water swelled and lifted black waste from around the kitchen tents and the latrine trenches and then receded, leaving the drinking water and the water used for cleaning mixed with the fouled water, turning all the water gray.

Despite boiling, the water from the kitchens remained spoiled, and most of the prisoners had some degree of scurvy or a similar disease that Joseph had not been aware of before the war. The prisoners who survived illness and near-starvation were digging larger and larger communal graves and there was a little more space within the walls of the camp and shorter lines. Joseph himself spit blood from swollen gums—even as he helped to dig the graves—and as he tried to rub his lips with the water, he tried to feel the water on his tongue—but he did not swallow. As he left a meal he had to ask himself, did he swallow at all?—or should he have swallowed to stop the pain of thirst? And the dreams of the dark night became images of clean water and he tried to see it running over the smooth rocks of the Salmon River but as the nights went on he could no longer see the clean water and he saw only the black water of Elmira as he poured it from his cup to the ground. Between the water and the stench—the disease, the loneliness, the unspoken fear—Elmira Prison Camp may as well have been hell, for Joseph could imagine no worse. Perhaps even battle, clear at least in its own immediacy, was better than this timeless despair. Despair that seemed written even across the faces of the guards who watched them file in and clenched their rifles, expressionless.

You're lucky to be here, a prisoner had told Joseph in his first days here. We're stacking bodies along the tracks like logs. Burying em in big holes all together. You wait. You'll be diggin them yerself, he had said.

Why are we here? Why'd they bring us north?

No room down there. Prisons along the Potomac are fulla rebs. Don' know what to do with us, I figure. They'll never figure what to do with us.

Here, day folded into day. Many men slept as much as they could—many as much as eighteen hours at a time finding sleep their only relief. They let their physical selves waste away in the receding tide of their spirit. So much had been seen. So much had been witnessed on the battlefields of this war that for many, no human connection was dared. Joseph managed to exist in the narrow and numbing corridor of time between food and sleep. He volunteered for whatever work he could accomplish—to stay strong, to achieve some focus in the ill-defined days—and despite his awkward, exaggerated limp, he worked. And sometimes this allowed him sleep.

But on many nights he would lie there and think of a way to die—so that he would not have to face another morning in the camp. And it was on one of these nights that he found the very thing that saved him. It was cool and the wind whistled through the thin canvas of his tent. He pulled his thin jacket around him. The seams were pulled apart completely in many places but it was all that he had to keep him from the cold. As he lay this night he became aware of something uncomfortable between himself and the blanket and he moved but still sensed it. He rolled over onto his back and put his hand to his jacket and he could feel that something was between the cloth and the lining. Something had slipped in between and he had not noticed it until now. He found a torn seam and pushed his fingers in until he felt paper and he pulled it out and held it in front of him. The tent was dark so he leaned toward the opening and held the paper to the light of the moon. There was writing on it and he strained in the dim light to read it—and then he saw the familiar words—*To Sarah Kingsley, From Roger McCleod*. It was the letter—from the soldier he had pulled from the fire. Was that weeks ago?—months?—he couldn't even tell, couldn't remember how much time—but the letter, the familiar writing on the paper, brought him suddenly away from this place and he saw himself standing. He could see himself carrying the body and feel the heat of the flames and then the sun as it lay across the clearing of the pond.

Joseph rolled onto his back and pulled the bedroll around him once again. He held the letter in front of his eyes and waited for his eyes to adjust to the dim light. He quietly unfolded the paper and, lying on the cold ground that night, thinking that death might be a desirable escape, he read the letter.

Virginia, 1864
Dearest Sarah,

As you can see now by my writing to you I have so far been spared. It is awful hard to understand why sometimes when, so many of my friends have fallen and entered God's kingdom long before their time. Perhaps it is meant for me to see you again as I so long to do. If ever I do get out of these woods and away from this war—I will surely fly to you and I trust you will still have me.

I sleep very little as the battle has its own sounds in the night. Sounds that I believe no man should have to hear. When I do sleep my dear Sarah, I dream of you and I can see you sitting in the garden our last day together. I still do not know what you meant when you said you would not be enough for me and I have to protest and ask you not to speak those words again for surely you are more than a man should ever have to himself and I shall make sure you understand that every moment of our lives if we get to spend them together, for surely Sarah the beauty that is so plainly seen when a man looks quickly upon you is only surpassed by that beauty of the spirit that a man sees when he is fortunate enough to engage in conversation with you, both casual or otherwise as I have been so lucky myself to do these past years.

I can sometimes see us together in my dreams. Sometimes I can still sense the breath off your lips that last night we kissed and I can see the silver pools of your eyes as you wept in my arms. If I had it all to do over again I am not sure I would have left you although I know this war has its reasons and it is not right for a man to look the other way when trouble comes down the path.

I will return Sarah, I promise you that. There are no johnny rebs who could keep me from you and I think since I survived today's battle, no other could be more horrible, then it must be that I am meant to be with you in this life and I shall count the moments until that is the thing that happens. This life brings me many terrible things Sarah, but I know this will all be worth it when I am at your side once more and I can see you smiling kindly at me as I remember you have done before.

I have had no letters from you or your family, or my own since March when we were in Washington. We were camped on the Potomac there in full view of the new capitol and it surely was a beautiful sight to see for our nation but it paled in comparison to receiving your letter of March 5. I hope your mother is recovering from her illness and I hope your hours in the hospital with the wounded soldiers are not too long or painful. Oh to be there sick in bed with you to care for me . . . I would endure much for

that chance—if I could fly from this place, this moment, and come to rest
in your arms, I would never stir again, Sarah. Surely I would not.

I can hear cannon and the sentrys are active. I will write again
tomorrow evening. This battle can not rage with this ferocity much
longer and my time as a soldier will be up. Lee's ranks are thinning and
it can not be long, but the rebs do fight fiercely so it may be a while before
they see the thing is done. Everything. . . . I must go.

> *Much love, Roger*

When he finished reading the letter he folded it carefully and slid it back into the space between the lining and the thin cloth of his coat, then pulled the coat around him as he turned over on his side to sleep. He was not conscious of the welling up of tears in his eyes. As he lay there the words of the letter haunted him, and he tried to imagine the feelings that inspired the words and he tried to imagine the woman who would read this letter had this boy survived that battle and walked away from the war. And on that night, he knew he would survive the prison. He would survive no matter what. He would fly from this place. Joseph put his hand on his chest where the letter lay concealed and fell slowly into deep sleep, and had no dreams of black water. And when he woke the next morning he felt a new strength, which he concealed and kept close to himself as if clenched in a fist. His spirit, crippled by war and crushed by captivity, began to grow in strength. And as he exercised his legs under the cloak of night—he did so with his spirit and his will, upon the words of the fallen soldier and the thoughts of a woman he had never seen. It was not the woman that kept him living. Nor was it the thought of a woman he did not know. It was the words of the letter. It was the soldier's words that seemed to soar over the plane of human struggle—and lift Joseph with them. And so, it was the fallen soldier—Roger McCleod—that this time, carried him. And it was as if he could see the burning woods diminish and then go cold and still. And silent.

Outwardly nothing changed. The days and the nights remained seamless and Joseph lost track of their count. The nights were often cold, despite the season, and hunger kept him sleepless and he prayed the clear morning would mean good rations. Potatoes. Beans. Vinegar.

He spoke very little to anyone. He watched some of the men as they played checkers on boards they fashioned themselves. One of the boys from Georgia had taken to carving things from animal bones with a small penknife that he kept concealed. To the guards Joseph draped a shield around his spirit and to the fellow prisoners he only let out what was necessary to survive. He was given the duties of digging the graves, trenches for the swollen water—of trying to clean latrines, of splitting and stacking wood. Prisoners were still flowing in from the trains and he could see in their faces the utter defeat and fear. Many were still dying of the wounds and the diseases of the war and Joseph tried hard to be careful how and what he ate. He collected rainwater and stayed away from the blue beef that buckled the men in two. He ate bread when it was given, and corn and potatoes. He maintained his crippled shuffle even as he worked, and at night he pushed the muscles of his legs hard and thus kept warm as he restored his strength. He had not looked at himself, but he could tell from his wrists and arms that he was growing very thin.

On the nights when there was no screaming or fights, and the camp slept, Joseph would keep his eyes open to look into the depths of the sky and watch the stars pulse with their singular light. This was the same sky. The sky across which he and Terence had tried to count the stars one night as they lay tossing a base ball back and forth—where they had seen the light shoot across a hundred times as they lay with their backs against the ground. And now again. Joseph could see the beauty of the sky, rediscovered. And on this night it carried him away from the prison, and to another place and time.

He must have been very young. He had awakened under a sky just like this one and he could not remember where he was. He rubbed his eyes and recognized the space and knew he must be sleeping in the back of the wagon. As he sat up, the blanket rolled from him and he could feel the cool breeze of a summer night wash across his arms. He was alone and he could remember being scared with the million stars above him and the large trees around the wagon that seemed so large and so close and whose shadows lay across the wagon and the ground.

He sat higher and looked toward the voices he heard and he could see lanterns burning in a circle and a grand tent and he remembered that they had been at a picnic that day and all the children were now sleeping. The grown-ups were talking and laughing loudly and he saw his mother standing with a group of women at the edge of the tent. He saw drifting smoke and followed it with his eyes to where the men sat talking and playing cards and then he watched as another group of men walked with banjos and a Jew's harp toward the center of the burning torches and he listened as they started to play music. The melody was slow and melancholy and Joseph could remember feeling a chill and pulling the blanket around his shoulders. He let his chin rest on the side of the wagon, yawned, and listened to the sweet music of the banjo and the twang of the harp.

His mother walked to where his father sat and put both hands on his shoulders. His father turned slowly, with the wooden pipe gripped in his teeth. Joseph could not tell if they spoke, but he watched as his father stood and turned to his mother. She took his hands in hers and stood facing him and in the light of the stars he could see his father's face clearly and there was a look upon it that he had never seen. He could not see the face of his mother. As the music washed over the last hours of the picnic, Joseph watched his mother begin to move her feet and her hands lifted his father's hands. At first his father's feet did not move. Then slowly, as if shuffling through spring mud, they moved. His eyes were on hers and Joseph thought his father's hands looked light even as his feet moved heavy on the ground. Joseph could see—the clear, starlit face of his father as he looked at the eyes of his mother. They moved like this for only moments before his father turned away and sat again along the table with the men. Joseph lay down along the wagon's wood and fell asleep again and didn't wake up until he could feel the bounce of the road beneath him and see the stars above as they moved across him, and he looked up to the seat of the wagon and could see his mother and his father sitting on the seat. His mother's head rested on his father's shoulder as they rode and Joseph watched them sit like that until the rhythm of the road put him back to sleep.

The prison nights offered the unfettered sky and the dance of stars not unlike that night and he used the stars to carry him from the walls of the prison. Often on these nights he would unfold the letter and read the words and recognize their spirit as he saw the expression on his father's face at the picnic that night and he thought that if he lived through this, he should like to feel this way and understand better the night sky, because it must be more than stars and moon and drifts of clouds. More than flame and vapor. He had seen it that night, written across the eyes of his father.

The days continued relentlessly, and Joseph learned to function quietly and to keep to himself. Until one morning. He was splitting wood near the tall fence. There was an opening in the fence through which supply wagons passed when they came and it was left open and through the opening he could see several guards. They were without guns and they were shouting and laughing. An armed sentry stood next to Joseph as he worked but was watching the activity himself. Then as Joseph looked between swings of the ax he saw a base ball roll by in the grass, and a guard give chase to it. Joseph stopped swinging the ax and watched and the guard paid no attention to him. There was more hollering and then the sound of a bat hitting a ball and running and Joseph heard, Get to work, and he returned to his splitting.

The next day the same thing happened and the same guard stood with him and the guard finally asked him, Pretty interested in the game, hey Reb? Ever seen it?

Joseph let the ax rest across his shoulder and answered, Yessir.

Didn't think rebs played ball. It's called base ball.

I play it.

I'll be damned.

The guard called out to one of the men outside the stockade fence, Got a reb here says he's a ball player. A guard on the overhead walk turned and walked to them and looked down. The yankee players stopped and walked in the direction of the woodpile.

Where ya from, reb?

Virginia.

What kinda ball you play in Virginia, reb?

Same I s'pose.

Before Joseph spoke another word he saw out of the corner of his eye the ball flying full speed toward his face and in a single motion, he dropped the ax and caught the ball in one hand without moving.

Nice catch.

Good throw.

What else can you do?

Not much. I'm crippled. Caint run. Caint hardly walk.

Well come on out here and lets see a reb hit. You can stand and swing, can't you?

I guess I can, Joseph answered, and the guard led him out of the opening to the fields that surrounded the prison camp. In all these weeks, turned now to months, he had dreamed of this. And now here he was. It was a broad open field and he could see clearly to the wooded hills. He was handed a bat and told to stand and then one guard threw the ball to another guard and the yankee wound up and flicked the ball at Joseph and he could feel the bat take off on its own and he swung and hit the ball and watched as it cleared the stockade fence and bounded into the camp, and as he watched it he remembered to fall to the ground and pretend to struggle to return to his feet.

Aint much good if you can't run, but Lordy you can sure hit, one of the guards offered. Now get back to damn work, reb, and the guard led him back to the woodpile and he split wood for the rest of the day. But the image of the field and the hills stayed clear in his mind the rest of the day as well, and through the night and through the next.

It must have been two or three days later when the same guard found him and held out his hand to Joseph, and Joseph took it and shook it.

Private Zachary Plummer, the yankee guard said.

Private Joseph Tyler.

Where you say you played ball?

Just in Virginia. In the fields along the river there we played some.

I played in Philadelphia before the war. We was a club and we played other clubs in other towns. We was called the Athletics. I never seen no one hit any better than you, though. Could tell by your swing you could hit just about anythin.

Thanks. Joseph folded his arms, waiting for what the man had to say.

How would you like to play some? Other rebs with you—against us yanks.

Joseph had no interest in playing ball with these men, but he could see what it might mean and he didn't hesitate to answer. Just tell me where and when and I'll git nine men ready.

You got some time. Here's a ball and a bat. The yankee soldier pulled a wooden bat and a ball from a canvas bag and set them on the ground in front of Joseph's tent.

We'll be watchin you close so don' think about usin the bat for anything.

We'll be hittin ball with this bat and nothin more.

The guard left and Joseph could see that the other guards were watching him and he picked up the ball and hollered down the line of tents, Who plays ball here?

There was no answer.

What prisoners play ball?

There was still no answer, but a few men emerged from the tents. An older man, dark and unshaven, walked toward Joseph and stood in front of him. We're starvin and were sick—how can we play ball?

We'll surely die if we just lie here. You know they want us to just lay here and die I guess, Joseph said. Besides, we know damn well if they put down those guns we could whip em.

Guess that's right. You show me what to do and I'll challenge yanks to anything. I'd be a rich man if they played poker with us, that's for damn sure.

A couple of other men laughed and said count me in and altogether there were eleven men besides Joseph who began to practice base ball inside the walls of Elmira Prison under the watchful eyes of the yankee sentries. Three of them knew the rules and had played and another one had watched the yanks play enough to understand the basics of the game. The others were strong and clumsy but anxious to have a shot at the yanks so they listened to Joseph as he showed them how to grip the bat and how to throw the ball and how to let your hands give a little when you were catching a thrown ball. He showed them how to kneel down on one knee to stop the bounding balls and explained the bases and how to score aces and they practiced some in daylight hours and then thought about the game in the night hours. Other prisoners watched with increasing curiosity.

A week, maybe two went by when the same private came by and said there would be a game tomorrow and the team should report to tent number twenty-five at the dinner hour. When they got there, there was a table set and some bread and a pot of gruel that didn't look spoiled and clear water.

We figured you better eat some before the game. We don't want no damn excuses, rebs.

And so the twelve men ate extra rations and Joseph and many of the other men saved some and brought it back to some of the other prisoners who shared their tents. Cap Porter, from Louisiana, had been bunking with Joseph but Joseph had made a point not to get to know him personally. Without Terence, without Jacob—it was time to be alone. Cap was playing, though, and he caught on quickly and Joseph could tell he was a player.

We caint win when we play them. They won't let us play if we win.

Cap looked at him. What are you, crazy, Joe Tyler? We're playin to whip yanks.

We will—but we caint at first. Joseph explained how they needed to gain the trust of the guards and then they would take advantage when the time came. This is what they did.

They played for several weeks, three and four times a week, and the yanks scored twenty-one aces every time and called the game and sent the rebs back to their chores, congratulated themselves, and then called them out for another game. Joseph was sure to limp and stagger through the games and try to act as more of a coach than a player and they went weeks losing every game. They played within the prison walls and there was little room and

Joseph could see the fields outside the walls and he finally suggested they set up a game on a real field where they could hit the ball full measure and not worry about it bounding off fences and ladders and buildings.

A few days passed when two of the guards came to Joseph's tent. We're gonna play outside the fences—see what you rebs really got. Wait till you see how far the ball goes, reb, when it aint got a fence to stop it. The two guards laughed and patted each other's backs and one pointed his rifle at Joseph. Pick your nine. We're playin tomorrow.

Joseph met with his players that night and told them they were going outside the walls to play a real game. They were to meet at the gate at noon. Joseph picked eight of the younger boys and then told them to gather around his tent.

Once you're outside, you're on your own, he said.

What's that mean?

Once we're outside these walls, I aint comin back in.

They'll shoot ya, Joe. Damn, you can hit a baseball but you caint hardly walk.

You let me worry about myself, but I'm sure I'd rather be shot than to walk back through that gate once I'm out. This here's my last night.

Damn war's almost over, Joe, Cap Porter said. We'll be gettin outta here peaceful.

You're on your own—that's all I'm sayin, Joseph concluded as he turned to the tent. I need to get some sleep and I suggest you all do the same.

Cap Porter came in and lay on the ground next to Joseph. I seen you movin your legs at night, Joe Tyler, and spect those legs work jus fine don't they.

I'm a cripple, Cap, and that's all you need to know.

We aint goin, Joe. It's almost over. Guard showed me a newspaper today that said Sherman's near Atlanta, said we'd all be goin home soon. I talked to the boys. I don' think nobody's runnin. Just give the bluebellies an excuse to shoot us anyhow.

That's fine, Joseph said. You're right. I know it's almost over.

You aint no cripple.

Joseph didn't answer but just lay on the thin blanket on the cold ground and thought that, one way or another, this would be his last night here and he slept well with those thoughts on his mind.

At noon, the next day, the boys met at the gate and the guards marched them through. A playing field had been marked out with sacks of sand as the bases and wooden stakes marking the pitching box. The prisoners were ordered to take their positions in the field. The yankee nine were singing something and two guards fired rifles in the air and the game began. Sentries stood with repeating rifles along both base paths. The Confederate soldiers played nervously, but as the game proceeded the contest and the energy required to play the game took over. The rebs were retired easily and Joseph had gone down with a half-swing that bounded the ball back to the pitcher as he hobbled to first.

Guess I was wrong, Joe Tyler, Zachary Plummer yelled in. Joseph just shook his head and limped back to the tall grass and waited. The yanks scored three aces in the next half-inning and then the rebs scored one on a long drive by Kip Williams from South Carolina that got lost in the grass for a few moments. The game went on sort of uneventfully like this and by the bottom of the fourth it was a tied score.

Joseph pitched the next inning. For moments while he played he almost forgot where he was—who he was. It was a clear day and the river reflected the light down the first-base line and the sun was high so there was no shadow from the tall stockade. Holding the ball in his hands before he served it up felt like he was reaching back and getting hold of his past. Things he hadn't thought of for a long time.

But the game itself meant nothing to him. He simply measured the moments as they passed. Checked distances. Stumbled as he walked. Watched the wooded ridge as it was soaked by the sun and the varied light and shadow between the birch that crowded its edge. And as the game went on the score remained close. The yanks were much better at catching the bounding balls, but a few of the rebs could hit and they played with a contained fury that quivered just below the surface of the game.

Finally Joseph let a pitch go and collapsed to the ground. Can't pitch anymore, he said. Can't do it on these damn legs. He kneeled, holding his legs.

A couple of the yank players talked and then signaled for Williams to come in from center field. Joseph was almost breathless as he waited for the nod. Take his place, Tyler, he heard. Play deep center and we'll try to hit em to you, they laughed.

And Joseph limped across the field slowly and took a position with the playing field in front of him and the birches at his back.

Joseph looked quickly over his left shoulder. He pretended to flex the muscles of his legs and looked again. The guards were talking with each other and laughing and paying attention to the man with the bat. Private Zachary Plummer from Philadelphia was walking toward the home plate, holding the bat over his right shoulder. Robert T. Jameson, a private from Louisiana, was standing in the pitching box ready to deliver up the pitch and a single guard stood just beyond the first base, the strap of his rifle hanging over his shoulder and the gun across his back. Joseph looked closely and could tell it was Sanborn, one of the older guards. He looked quickly behind him again across the grass to the woods.

Joseph looked to the playing field. The prisoners were considered too weak or sick to be much threat and there were plenty of guards watching them, so things were fairly relaxed. And so they played on. It was as if the game had taken a moment for itself. Stolen back from the war some of what had been taken from these boys.

As he looked now, Joseph could see the thin strand of brush and then what appeared to be towering silver birch. The growth of the birch was dense and he noticed that a man could barely fit his shoulders between them and then after about forty feet of birch there was a clear field of high grass and an upward slope.

He glanced again, pretending to exercise his shoulders by twisting, and saw what he hoped would be the top of the ridge and a display of broken rock and ledge that could afford a man some protection. There was little light in the woods that high, so he knew the growth would be dense—good cover. He looked back to the playing field and put his hands on his knees.

The game was about an hour old. There had been little hard hitting up to this point—except the one the yanks had lost in the grass. The shallow fielders—the infielders as the yanks called them—had caught most of the balls. The yanks had taken extra chances at hitting, changing the rules as they played. Now Zachary Plummer approached the plate and Joseph was beginning to fear that he might not have a chance—that the yanks would change their minds and call the game. He cupped his hands to his mouth, Move in, fielders, he yelled. This kid's a rabbit killer.

This was a derogatory way of saying the batter couldn't strike the ball off the ground—that he hit nothing but grounders—and Joseph knew that this would be just the kid to be bothered by the call. Zachary Plummer tensed up and looked at Joseph Tyler in center field. The guards were loose and laughing and saying something about southern rabbits being too slow to get out of the way. Joseph was about thirty-five or forty feet from the woodland's edge. While Plummer looked at him, he limped in a few more feet and yelled again, Reach me soldier, I caint be runnin in too far. Can barely walk, but I'll catch it if you reach me.

As the pitch was delivered he took a few more steps in so that Zachary Plummer saw him, but at the instant before the swing Joseph turned and began to walk quickly backward. He knew everyone would be watching the hitter. He could see Plummer's eyes open wide as the ball approached and he had seen him hit enough to know that this one would be struck and driven high and far and Joseph began to jog backward as everyone's eyes were on the driven ball. They were all watching, the prisoners, the guards—all attention was on the ball as it sailed across the clear sky. Joseph could tell it was high over his head and far beyond where he was now trotting and he exaggerated the limp one more time and then broke into a dead run. As he did this the stunned guards watched the crippled prisoner cross the field. He was running full speed.

Joseph had not intended to catch the ball. The plan was to let it fly into the woodland and run as fast as he could after it and past it and not look back. As he ran, however, he could see the ball sail in the air and he found himself running toward it, his hands wide open and his arms outstretched, and he couldn't help it. At the second of decision—to let it drop and roll and to keep on running—he had no choice but to leap for the ball and he felt it land solid in his hands as he rolled into the brush of the woodland. The runner, having tagged up, was rounding third, his hat rolling along the ground behind him, and Joseph stood, set his feet, and threw the ball on a line toward Cap Porter, who was standing at the home plate waving his arms and yelling. Porter didn't even have to move; the ball hit him in the hands and he reached down and put a solid tag on the sliding runner who was called out by one of the other guards.

The other fielders jumped and yahooed and turned to congratulate Joe Tyler but as they stood and looked toward center field they could see the pasture was empty and the stunned guards were kneeling to fire into the woodland.

Joseph was already squeezing between the birches when he heard the runner called out and he was now in full run in the high grass and up the slope of the hill. The months of faking the limp and strengthening his legs had all paid off, as the guards were too stunned to chase him—waiting for him to trip and fall. They couldn't understand what was happening and by the time they did Joseph was jumping over the rock and ledge at the crest of the hill and running full speed into the woodland. Some of the guards gave chase, squeezing their way through the birch trees and ascending the grassy slope. But by the time they reached the crest the only sign of Joseph was the stirring of animals and birds he had disturbed.

In the days and weeks to follow, the prisoners and the guards would talk about it—about how the leaves shivered with the speed of the runner and how Joseph Tyler had vanished in thin air, and eventually even the guards had to smile at the thought of the crippled man flying through the woodland as if on wings. And the prisoners would remind anyone who listened, And the damn runner was out at the plate. Throwed out dead by Joe Tyler before he vanished, they would say.

In the year that Elmira served as a prison, only seventeen men escaped. Joseph Tyler was one of them.

III.

Joseph heard the shots but never slowed, and the best he could figure he must have run five or six miles before he stopped at all. His legs ached as he ran but he had been exercising them every night in anticipation of this day so his muscles weren't all tight from his hobbling around the camp all those months. He stayed in the protection of the trees for the most part, but crossed a few gravel roads and a small stone building of some sort with its roof caved in—maybe an old roadhouse for the wagons that passed this way. After a couple of hours he slowed down to a hurried walk and then when he couldn't see any sign of being followed, he crawled under a big stand of laurel and lay there to rest. His heart was still racing and he was afraid they would be coming after him so he lay there quietly, listening to the sounds of the woodland and the beating of his own heart. As he lay there he smiled, thinking of what had happened. You caught the damn ball, you fool, he thought, and he laughed as he lay there under the laurel, and then you threw it in, and for the first time—maybe since the war had come to him— he laughed out loud and rolled onto his back laughing.

When the sun was down low and the ground was covered in long shadows he figured it was safe to come out and he got up and shook the leaves and twigs from his clothes and hair. He looked down at his bare feet and could see that they were scratched and bleeding, but they didn't seem to hurt at all. He glanced at his torn clothes—the worn jacket and the tattered trousers—and he knew if he was seen he'd be shot on sight, because whoever he was, any citizen would know that he didn't belong walking these roads. The darkness was closing in quickly and it was a good time to move undetected along the edge of the woods. He found a wider road and followed it, staying behind the trees at its edge. Not knowing exactly where he was, he faced the setting sun and decided he might as well head south, and since this road appeared to be heading south he followed its path. He had run due west, he figured, and now with the sun setting over his right shoulder he was headed due south and that fact put a little bounce in his step as he walked. He was a free man heading south, he thought, and that aint bad. He stayed in the shadows and walked until the shadows grew long and he couldn't see at all in the moonless night.

He awoke the next morning curled up in a mossy crevice between some stone and the twisted roots of an old spruce whose branches hung down like arms over him. It took him a moment to remember where he was and when he did he looked quickly around in all directions. He saw that the forest was still and the sun had not been up long and the light of morning was rising up in a mist from the forest floor. A gray squirrel sat on a rotted log, gnawing at some small thing that it held to its mouth, and Joseph picked up a small stick and tossed it in the direction of the squirrel and watched it scurry away and up the silver bark of a maple tree. Joseph listened again, and then rested there in the quiet of the morning.

As he rested he remembered a morning just like this. He lay on the ground staring into the still woods. His father lay next to him and they both had rifles resting across their arms. They had set up there well before dawn—the branches and leaves of the trees black shapes against the night as thin clouds slipped between the moon and the dark woodland. Joseph could hardly see the ground where he walked as he hurried to follow his father. When they came to a place where they had seen the bark of the small trees and bushes rubbed off, they knew they were at the spot. They knew the buck deer would return.

His father told him to lie down and be quiet. Be ready and listen. Don't miss a thing, he had said, and so Joseph lay there quietly with his finger resting on the trigger of the rifle.

But there were no deer—or at least none came their way—and they just lay there, without talking, as the morning rose up around them. Joseph watched the light of the sun slide across the milky leaves of laurel and azalea. It was autumn, he remembered, and the leaves of the oak had turned red and the silver maple and the birch shone with the yellow and the orange light of the morning sun. As the light slid through the canopy of leaves they seemed to shiver, and the forest seemed to rise up to meet it in a silver mist and the light and the mist did a dance together before their eyes and they could see small animals crawl out of the darkness—rabbits upright, necks stretched, sniffing, sensing their presence and dashing away into the low brush of the woodland.

They lay there for hours, Joseph and his father, watching the morning unfold around them until the sun was high and its light streamed through the ceiling of leaves and the mist seemed to be inhaled by the swelling light and the morning sat upon the forest, clear and quiet.

His father rose first, he remembered, and Joseph followed him again as they found the trail they had followed to this spot and walked without speaking, through the woodland to the clear field and toward the house. When they reached the field Joseph had looked up at his father and said, Bad luck, huh? No deer in sight.

His father looked down at him and without slowing his walk said, Wasn't spectin any. They're in the south woods along the river now. Everythins still green and flushed down there.

So what were we doin?

But his father never answered him and just kept walking back to the house, and when they got back to the house they ate quickly and got to chores and never talked again about the morning. Joseph always wondered if his father had taken him there just to watch the morning unfold and listen to the silence of the forest. And if he did, he knew there was a lot that he did not understand, about the morning—and about his father.

He thought of this even now, as the forest awakened and he rose to walk the path silently. He saw the gravel road and tried not to think of his hunger as he walked quickly behind the trunks of trees and the evergreen bushes that licked the edge of the gravel path. It was beautiful country, framed in hills and pine—not unlike home, he thought, and he wondered just how far he was from Blackstone, from the fields, from the rivers, from the stone walls. He thought a moment of Terence but then forced the thought from his mind and kept walking along the edge of the road. He was heading south, he was sure, but he knew nothing of where he was or where the road would take him. He walked all day, seeing nothing, and spent the night in an abandoned shack along the road, but he found nothing to eat and the night was very cold and as he pulled the thin jacket around him he wondered for the first time since he had run from the prison if he could live. He had to eat. He had to find something. He couldn't just walk.

The next morning he walked the road again and could see it twist its path in front of him and he noticed it was slightly improved and wider. As he turned the bend he slid quickly behind the wide trunk of an oak and watched a carriage and two horses approach. A man and a woman were sitting on the seat of the carriage and there were two luggage bags in the back. They were engaged in conversation as they rode and they didn't look at all in Joseph's direction. From the look of the fresh horses, Joseph could tell that they hadn't been riding long. He looked down the road and then ran through the thin brush to the next bend. He could see a large red house with a great porch around two sides of it and another horse tied to a stone that rose up from the ground. He circled back into the woods and when he was at the edge of the clearing that opened up to the house he lay down and watched. A man was standing in the window and looking out. He was drinking something from a cup and then he seemed to be talking and Joseph saw him put the cup down. Moments later he emerged from the front door and walked out onto the porch. He was well dressed, in a suit and a derby. He had tall boots that wrapped around the calves of his legs. He stretched out his arms and then walked down to the horse. The horse was led to water at a long wooden trough and then brought back to the porch and tied.

The man entered the house and disappeared and Joseph could not see him. He saw a woman, an older woman, near the window and then gone as well. The man appeared again with some leather saddle bags, threw them over the horse along with a leather saddle, mounted the horse, and rode down the gravel road and out of sight. The woman appeared for a moment at the window and then vanished.

Joseph lay there watching. He could see a small barn that extended from the back of the house and then a smaller structure that he thought might be a smokehouse. He stood and followed the line of trees that bordered the clearing and then ran to the back of the silver barn. He noticed it had been built well, but was sagging and in disrepair. Whoever had built it so carefully hadn't kept up with it and the winters had weighed heavily on it. He stood against the wall and turned the corner and then could see the narrow door. He ran quickly to the door, opened it, and entered through the small opening. As soon as he was in he knew he'd been right. He could see the fire pit and even in the darkness he could see meat hanging from a hook and smell the smoke and grease. He could tell that it was already smoked and he walked to it and pulled at it with his fingers and ate the meat from his fingers until he could feel his stomach was full. Nothing had ever tasted like this meat. Nothing in his memory had tasted this good. Nothing.

He opened the door a crack, and he rested there with the door opened. He didn't move at all and he could see there was no activity in the house. He knew they would be coming out eventually so he figured he better find somewhere else to spend the night. Joseph waited and then as the sun began to slip behind the tall pines, he ran from the shed into the shadows at the side of the house. He stood near the window but he could not look in. He crept under it, staying close to the house, and then around the corner. He could see there was space under the porch. There appeared to be some material in a roll and he could see a space where the wooden lattice did not meet the stone foundation and he slipped in the space, pulled the burlap around him, and lay still and quiet. He could hear muted sounds from within the house but no voices. He wondered if the woman was alone. He lay there watching the squares of light darken as the day ended and the night rose up and he fell asleep there under the porch with his stomach as full as it had been in many months, maybe years. He couldn't recall this feeling of being full.

When he woke it was not to the quiet morning, but to the rattle of a rifle through the wooden lattice.

Gettup.

He rolled over with his hands on the breast of his jacket and found himself staring down the barrel of a rifle, and then to an old woman who peered in through the lattice.

Knew it wasn't a fox took the meat—now git out from under there where I can see you.

Yes maam—I don't mean no harm.

Stealin food's harm.

Yes maam but I was starved.

And what are you doin under my porch?

Sleepin.

Well git out.

Joseph crawled through the opening and stood as the woman backed up. As she saw his clothes she raised the rifle to his chest. She was not quite as old as he had thought but he could tell that she took little care of how she looked.

Who are you?

Joe Tyler, maam.

You're a reb.

No more.

The war aint over.

Is for me.

Why shouldn't I kill you.

I guess there's no reason maam.

Looks like you'll be dead in a day or two anyway. Where you from?

Virginia.

And how'd you get to New York from Virginia, Joe Tyler?

Prison, maam. They brought us up by train.

You escaped from the prison? How'd you do that?

Well, I kinda just ran. We were playin ball and I ran and I just kept on runnin.

And Joseph told the woman the story and as he told her of his months in the prison and the ball game that set him free, the rifle lowered and the woman took to laughing out loud and said that was the best story she had heard in many months and even if it weren't all true it was too damn crazy to be all made up and she told him to go into the barn and she'd bring him some clothes so he wouldn't get killed before he had time to tell that story to some more folks, because the damn war was just about over and they'd all need some stories like that one to get through the days that would follow. And so Joseph went to the barn and was dressed and the woman brought him some bread and then as he was thanking her and about to leave she asked him where he was goin.

South I guess.

She laughed. You goin to walk back to Virginia, son?

Don' know—just figured I'd keep walkin.

The only place your gettin is Pennsylvania. Don't suppose you have a map?

No maam.

Paper says the war's bout done. Virginia's bout done, son. I say if you walk this road long enough you'll get yourself killed or back in prison, and then nobody'll get to hear that great story you have to tell. She folded her arms in front of her and looked at Joseph's face. I need some help here. My man's gone, since '63. Signed up to be a cook in the army and I aint heard from him since. He sure could cook. This here is an inn and folk come to stay here a night or two and they're on their way. We'll fix you up in the barn and you can help me—least till the war's over, which I expect won't be more than a month or so, or till the winter's over—'chever comes first. Or you can walk to Virginia. Your choice. Suit yerself.

Joseph looked at the woman and at the house and at the road that ran past it.

I don't guess I'll make Virginia walkin, he answered. So I'd be obliged to stay maam. And Joseph was set up in the barn and she told him to burn his clothes to get rid of any lice and he did that, but before he did he reached in the lining of his jacket and pulled out the letter and he read it many nights as he slept in the barn of Mrs. Constance T. Albright and helped her with chores around the Pine Tree Inn that sat along the gravel road heading through the hills of New York.

Joseph spent the fall and winter with Mrs. Albright. He butchered and helped her cook and clean the linens. He did some hunting and trading for small game in town and he smoked the meat and made bacon and helped serve the guests who wandered by and spent a night or two. Joseph would brush the horses and bring the men brandy and cigars as they sat on the porch and they decided that it was best if he didn't talk because of his accent so Mrs. Albright pretended that he was a nephew who was deaf and dumb and a little slow, and Joseph took to limping again like he had in prison and people stopped asking about him and the folks in town got used to him riding the carriage with Mrs. Albright. He would wave and they would wave back. He figured he'd spend the winter and then find a way to start back south in the spring. Word from the war wasn't good, except for the fact that it would soon be over. Around Christmas Joseph sent a short note off to his father. The mail wasn't moving well down south, so he wasn't sure if it would get through. But in February he received this message from Blackstone.

> *The war has been through here. But here I am. I was pleased to hear you are alive. There's work to be done.*
> *Caleb Tyler, Your Father*

Joseph was relieved. He tucked the note away. The assurance that there was work was somehow pleasant. The assurance that everything hadn't ended. That despite the changes, some things would remain the same.

When there were no guests, Mrs. Albright would often ask Joseph if he would like to sit for supper with her in the house. The rooms were large but rather sparse and simple. Some of the furniture was painted and some was not and seemed to be thrown together. There was a nice lamp with a white tasseled shade that sat on the table in the room's center and Joseph enjoyed the way the light was cast down and through the white fabric. Thick shades were drawn down at night to keep the warmth. There was an iron stove in the middle of the parlor that kept the first floor warm and another in the kitchen, and fireplaces in all the guest rooms. Most of the time they would sit out on the porch after supper, when the weather allowed, and talk and he would tell her about Virginia and his father's stone walls and how he had lost Terence, and that he hoped his friend was safe somewhere as he had just vanished that day and hadn't been heard from since. He told her about the game—about base ball—and he tried to make her understand how he felt when he played it and she laughed as she told her of the games in the fields of Virginia and in the end she would always ask him to tell her again how it was he escaped from Elmira Prison and she would laugh every time he told it and she would say, You must be lyin Joe Tyler, about the part when you catch the ball . . .

And he would answer, No maam, I had no intention of catchin it but it sure seemed like the right thing to do at the moment, and she couldn't wait for the war to end so she tell that story herself to the folks who passed by.

In the evenings he retired to the barn. He had fashioned a fireplace of sorts from stones and an old stovepipe and Mrs. Albright had moved a cot and blankets from the house. He hung a lamp from the rafters and used a stool as a table. They spent the winter like this. Joseph did some repairs to the barn and split wood for the Franklin stove and helped her carve a new sign for the inn out of white oak. She had some chisels and scrapers in the barn and he gouged out the flakes of wood and carved the pine tree she had drawn on the wood and when it was finished he hung it from a post just off the road so that it was clearly seen by folks passing by. He was quite proud of it. It reminded him of his father.

Winter was ending and the days began to lengthen and Joseph began to think about leaving. Mrs. Albright had grown quite accustomed to having him around, so his leaving wasn't discussed much, but it was understood that when the snow had stopped for good, he would be on his way. It was already April but the snow was still on the ground in Elmira and he was waiting. This night he sat in the barn on a milking stool reading the paper from a couple of weeks past when he could hear the door slam at the house and he stood and ran to the barn door. Before he reached it Mrs. Albright pushed it open and the cold air filled the space of the barn.

It's over, Joe Tyler. Word is Lee surrendered to U. S. Grant in Virginia. The war's over.

Joseph didn't know what to say. He tried to picture the proud general giving up—handing over his sword—but he couldn't. But the war's over he thought. It's over.

It's over Joe Tyler. You can go home if you want to. The president says everyone should go home. All you boys should go home.

She said this as she stood in the doorway of the barn. For the first time he saw tears in the eyes of Mrs. Constance Albright. He walked across the barn and put his arms around her. I guess you saved my life, maam.

She looked at Joseph's face and could see his youth through the mask of suffering he had seen these last years. Even wars can't kill kindness, Joe Tyler. You remember that.

He stood with his hands on both of her shoulders and said quietly to her, That I will, maam. I surely will.

Joseph stayed for a while longer as the news trickled in about the collapse of the Confederacy: rumors that Jeff Davis had been caught fleeing south with gold, and then all the troops finally laying down their arms and heading home, some of them walking, some on horses or in the empty military wagons—heading home to whatever might be left. Joseph had always known it would end this way and he felt mostly relief at the news. He spent the week doing final chores for Mrs. Albright and it was understood that he would leave on Sunday. It would be the middle of April and surely the worst of winter would be behind him. He would walk into Pennsylvania and then try to catch a train from there and keep going south until he was back on Virginia soil. He woke that morning early and packed a small bag she had given him and put it on his shoulder and walked to the porch. He knocked lightly and opened the door and he saw there was a man standing at the table and Mrs. Albright was sitting at the table with her hands covering her face. He could tell she was weeping and he went to her and put a hand on her shoulder.

You gonna be all right Constance, the man said in a solemn voice. I need to be movin on to spread the word. She answered yes and he nodded to Joseph and left through the porch door.

What is it?

They killed the president.

What president got killed?

Abe Lincoln. They killed my president, Joseph.

Who killed him? How?

Don't know, but you can't be leavin now. They'll be lookin for an excuse to kill a reb. You better stay a while longer. Joseph sat at the table with her and watched the morning sunlight fill the room, stripping it of its vivid colors and replacing it with an uncomfortable clarity. Color becoming uneven layers of paint hastily applied. The long shadows of things shrinking to chipped and dusty surfaces. He put his hand on hers as she sobbed and he felt some of the sadness pass to him. When would it end?, he thought. What purpose was there in this? He remembered the exaggerated figure in the cartoon and he remembered laughing and he felt suddenly ashamed. He was not sure of what. Perhaps of his small part in all this.

That day passed and the days following and it was already June when Mrs. Albright called him again to the kitchen.

I have someone you might like to meet, she said as he entered the room. This here is Alexander Cooper. Mr. Cooper, this is my friend Joe Tyler.

Pleased to meet you, both men said and smiled and shook hands and then stepped back from each other.

Mr. Cooper is resting here tonight on his way to Terryville. That's right outside New York City, isn't it, Mr. Cooper?

Yes maam, it is. Terryville and Rocker Falls sit side by side along the river just northwest of the big city. Sometimes at night you can see the lights from all the buildings and such and there must be a hundred boats along the river.

Sounds fine, Joseph said.

Tell him what you do there, Mr. Cooper. Tell Joe Tyler what you do.

Well, I play base ball, on a club. I play for the Terryville Niners base ball club and we're always lookin for players. Mrs. Albright says that you have some base ball experience. Is that the truth? Joseph didn't know what to say but managed to answer him.

Yes, I can play the game some.

Tell him your stories, Joe Tyler, while I get some supper. You two men sit and tell each other base ball stories. You tell him your story Joe Tyler, she said as she walked away laughing.

They sat and Cooper told him about the new clubs that were sprouting up everywhere and the fields that were being carved out of empty pastures and the people who were coming out to see the game. He told Joseph about the Atlantics and the Excelsiors and the other big city teams and how they were looking for players and Joseph listened and shared stories with the other man until late that night and then when both men had tired and were ready to put in for the night, Joseph asked him, What was the name of the town—not Terryville, but the one you said was next to it on the river?

That'd be Rocker Falls—you been there? You know it.

No sir. Goodnight.

Joseph walked from the house to the barn and dug the letter out of the pack and looked at the words. Rocker Falls, New York, it said. In the morning he was packed and in the kitchen early. He hugged Mrs. Constance Albright one more time and promised her he would see her again though they both knew that this was probably not true.

I will remember, he said to her.

That's enough, then, Joe Tyler. I'll tell your story, I will, she said with a smile.

Joseph boarded the wagon alongside Alexander Cooper and the two of them left down the road. He waved at Mrs. Albright as she stood on the porch and she nodded back. Joseph glanced one last time at the carved sign that rattled on the pole in a light breeze—at the carved pine tree—and then turned and looked straight ahead. The road narrowed after a mile or so and when other carriages passed Cooper steered to one side and a couple of times they almost got caught in the soft soil at the woodland edge but the horses pulled and the wagon rolled without stopping and eventually the road widened again. The wagon passed clusters of houses, an occasional store, and miles of untouched woodland. Most people greeted them with a wave as they passed and stood to watch the wagon roll by. Children chased them and hollered after them. Dogs barked at the rolling wheels as they passed small farms and villages. They headed east toward Terryville, toward New York City. Sitting together on the wooden seat of the wagon as it bounced down the gravel road and in and out of the ruts from other wagons, they headed toward the game. Toward base ball.

EIGHTH

More Than a Game

In the procession of the soul from within outward,
it enlarges its circles ever, like the pebble thrown
into a pond.
　　　　—Ralph Waldo Emerson

I.

On the day the carriage carrying Alexander Cooper and Joseph Tyler rolled up to the King's Tavern Inn in the village of Terryville, New York, in the summer of 1865 several members of the Niners base ball club were there having a breakfast meeting. As Joseph walked in behind Cooper he saw plates stacked high with ham and plates of eggs being passed around and dished out to the men, who sat around a table. In the table's center was a thick slab of white butter that had already begun to melt and pool up on a green plate and a broad knife that lay on the wood, thick with butter. The ceiling was quite low, indicating the building was probably already a century old and, with a low fire burning in a stone hearth large enough for a man to stand in, the room appeared very comforting after a long journey. The table sat in a corner of the room and the only light was from two narrow windows that it seemed to Joseph had been recently added. The room itself was wide and square, with tables of different sizes. On the far wall hung a blue banner made of shiny fabric and across it the words THE TERRYVILLE NINERS BASE BALL CLUB were sewn in gold. With all its bravado it could have been a regimental flag that hung over the table.

Most of them got up from where they sat and came to the door to greet Alexander Cooper as he returned from his trip, but a few of them remained seated and ate as if they hadn't eaten in weeks and might not again for some time. Some of the men embraced Cooper, while others shook his hand and slapped his back.

Like you fellas to meet Joseph Tyler, he said.

Joseph shook their hands and nodded a silent greeting to each one.

He has some stories to tell you boys when the time's right, but he also plays base ball and I believe he plays it well.

Where you from? the boy who had been introduced to Joseph with the odd name Rooster Nash asked him.

Long way from here, I guess.

Guess we could tell that, the boy answered and looked at the other men and laughed and then looked straight at Joseph. One of Bobby Lee's boys I guess, he said, and Joseph straightened and met the look from Nash's eyes with his own. Cooper stood a few feet behind him and quickly tensed.

Fought fer Virginia—where I'm from. That's right.

This here's a good man, Alex Cooper offered as he stepped to Joseph's side and rested his hand on Joseph's shoulder. And a good base ball man, and if he can play half as good as I think he can, the Niners will be needin his service this season I reckon. Damn war's over boys. Did we lose Calvin?

Went to the Mutuals. They're splittin the gate over there and word has it players are makin as much as five dollars a game. Pass that ham, would ya? A thin boy whom Joseph had heard Cooper refer to as Ned Conway reached across the table to get the platter piled high with meat, and slices of ham slid from the side and slapped onto the wooden table. The slices were picked up with fingers and run through the yellow eggs and eaten.

If Joe Tyler can play we'll need him then. He throws too, aint that right, Joe?

Yessir. I throw some.

We'll see tomorrow, reb, someone else added. Sit down, Coop, and have some breakfast. Look like you boys been ridin a good while.

From Elmira, Cooper answered. Three days. We'll eat, that's for sure, and then get some rest. Is Beezer around?

Just walked to the telegraph office . . . be right back, and the men ate a hearty breakfast together on a long table that sat by a window of the inn. Joseph was hungry and he ate and didn't talk to anyone at all. He hadn't seen this much food set out in a long time. When he was finished he wiped his hands and face with a damp rag and asked Cooper to show him to his room.

The room's provided by the club, Cooper explained and he continued, We'll stay a few days until we get settled. The club spends what little money we get in this tavern and Old Man Beezer's a big ball fan. Comes to most of the matches. He used to play rounders, I guess, but he loves the new game.

The room was small with a wide-plank floor fastened with square nails that appeared randomly across the surface. Increasing gaps between the boards collected sand and dust from the shoes of every guest. There was a narrow window that seemed to sag to the left, leaving a narrow space between the sill and the wallboard. Through the window Joseph could see a small store that sold sundries, with two horses tied up in front of it. A small table and a cot made of what appeared to be wooden poles and canvas sat in the corner. It seemed comfortable enough—and there was a thick blanket. Joseph slept well that first night.

The next morning he was awakened by a knock on the door and someone calling his name. When he answered he was surprised to see Alexander Cooper in baggy white trousers pulled up tight at the calf and a flat-topped white cap with a bill like a soldier's forage cap. He was also wearing some kind of special shoes, Joseph noticed, but he didn't say anything as he greeted Cooper.

Breakfast in fifteen minutes, and then you'll be showin these boys what you can do on a base ball field, Joe. Cooper clapped his hands together and walked away down the hall.

There were eggs again and more ham and loaves of bread that were swollen gold, but this morning they ate quickly and within an hour they had arrived at the field and Joseph held a wooden base ball bat in his hands for the first time since Elmira Prison. As he was handed the bat he looked around him at the field and the split-rail fence that bordered it. Across the outfield there were shops and what appeared to be an office of some kind and in the background he could see the top of a huge building that must be the mill; Cooper had told him about it. The bat was perfectly smooth and had a sanded grip and knob, much more balanced than the ones he'd been used to. But it felt too heavy for him. He looked through a large wooden keg that held a dozen or so bats until he found one he thought might be right. It was smooth and long, thin-handled so he could feel the weight in his fingers. And it already had a few nicks and depressions along the fat part that showed it had been used with some success. That it was good for hitting.

Been a long time, he said to no one as he walked to the plate. He saw the boy called Rooster in the pitching box and heard someone else yell, Show us what you got, reb.

It was still morning, and the sun sat just over the shops and shone across the grass and toward the home plate—right at the striker. Joseph supposed that's why they let him hit first and he smiled just slightly as he swung the bat in front of him and looked at the long shadows of the morning and set his feet firmly in the sandy gravel at the plate. He looked out at the pitcher and then looked away as his eyes hit the bright sun directly. The latest rules moved the pitcher back to almost sixty feet away. Joseph was used to forty five feet, but with this sun that wasn't going to help. He could see the silhouette of the pitcher winding up and then the ball sailed toward him, but at the last minute he lost it and he turned his eyes away from the sun and into the long shadows behind the plate where the ball rolled to a stop in the grass. Rooster Nash and a couple of the other boys were laughing as the catcher threw the ball back to him.

Hold up, hold the ball. It was Cooper, running in from center field, and as he approached the plate he took off his hat and held it out to Joseph. Don't need this out there this morning, Joe. Sun's at my back. Put it on and tuck it over your eyes. It'll help keep some of the sun out anyway—long enough for you to get a bead on Rooster's pitch, I bet.

Joseph took the hat and settled it on his hair with one hand and straightened out again to face the pitcher. Nash was already set and he wound up and Joseph could see the ball but then had to turn his eyes away slightly once again and the bat barely hit it and sent it high in the air behind them.

That all you got, Reb?

Guess not, Joseph answered as he watched the ball being tossed back to the pitcher. He held the bat in front of him, the weight suspended from his hands. He pulled it up slowly and set it just above his right shoulder. His fingers were loose, yet strong around the thin barrel of the bat. His legs were strong and balanced and he squatted slightly and could feel the muscles of his legs strong from lifting stone in the field—strong from the nights of exercise in prison, under the cover of darkness and the thin wool blanket. He hadn't handled a bat properly in years. In the prison games he had to fake his limp and stand unsteadily at the plate and swing with only his arms. Now he could swing full. Now he could stand and swing full. That was simple enough. Clear enough. He wasn't trying to mimic the work of his father on the walls. He wasn't firing blindly into the smoking thicket, following orders that were screamed from behind or below. And the feelings of loneliness, even rage, seemed to vanish here as he stood on this field. He was returned to moments of his youth. Collected. Whatever had brought him here to this spot, to this moment—seemed unavoidable, as if it had been written for him and waiting only for fulfillment.

Nash wound his arm way over his head and kicked a leg up and Joseph could see the ball flying through the light of the sun toward him—could see the parallel shadow on the grass and could feel the bat moving without his conscious effort and without clear thought. The wood flew through the morning air to the ball and did not slow in its journey through the ball and the contact of the two was recorded only on the quick vibration against Joseph's fingers and a thick sound like a horse's whip and the men who stood on the field, as well as Joseph, watched the ball fly on a straight line toward the outfield—not high—but as if it were shot from a cannon and the arc did not change before it slammed against the top of the fence and dislodged the rail. The rail fell out of the post on one side and lay on end in the grass and the ball finally settled on the edge of the street in front of the small shops. Someone looked out the window of one of them and Joseph could see her come to a door and stand out on the porch and look across the field at him.

The swing sealed his fate. He was a Terryville Niner, and all the boys congratulated him and that night they partied with chowder and beer and Joseph was accepted as a member of the club. They kidded him about his accent and a few of his country habits—but it was a new time. Hatred was something that most men shed like a new coat that did not fit. They shed it quickly when they could and threw it to the side. Most men did not even keep what was left of their military uniforms. They had new uniforms. The colors of the game. Off the field Joseph was their equal and he was treated thus. On the field he was considerably more. That was something he had always known. That night when he had returned to his room he sat on the edge of his bed with a writing tablet and quill. His thoughts spun with all that had happened, and so quickly. He smiled and thought of the games at Stone Hill. He thought of Joshua, who was probably better than them all. Finally, with the last light of his first day as a ball player, he wrote this letter.

> *Dear Father,*
>
> *I trust you are well. I was thankful to hear that you are okay and still on Blackstone. We survived, you and I. We survived. I am in a place called Terryville in the state of New York. I have found something here. Base ball. Don't know how long I will stay but right now it seems what is right.*
>
> *Don't expect you'll understand. I will see you again. I am good at this game Father, and it's what I do.*
>
> *Plant enough for yourself. When I return we'll work together. That's a promise.*
>
> *Your son, Joseph*

The game filled him. The club was his family. Hitting the ball, pitching—this was who he was and all he wanted. Joseph settled in as the leading hitter and in no time took over the primary pitching duties from Rooster Nash, who didn't seem to mind at all. He started out slow but by the end of the '65 season and in the '66 season, and then in the seasons after that, he came to dominate the game. He went on to hit over .350 and was the most talked about pitcher in the game except for a sixteen-year-old boy named Al Spalding from Illinois. Joseph had seen Spalding pitch in a match in Brooklyn for the Forest City Club and he recognized his natural ability right off. He had a different way of pitching—holding the ball poised with both hands in front of his eyes, hesitating, and then starting his motion. In later years he would see pictures of Spalding in the newspapers, his striking looks and drooping mustache reminding Joseph of that first drawing he had seen in the *Gazette*. Albert Spalding would go on to win over two hundred games and become an ambassador of the new game of ball all over the world, but Joseph would always see him as a boy —with the ball held in his hands and his eyes riveted to the striker on a hot summer day in Brooklyn. Joseph had just had to smile as he watched him move in the pitching box. He could see himself—and all the others who loved the game. He could see himself in this young boy.

In these seasons everything was easy for Joseph—natural. He could hit line shots to any field or when he wanted send the ball over the outfielder's heads. When he was pitching it seemed the ball went just where he wanted. He could keep the strikers off balance—make them hit it into the dirt or up in the air for a lazy fly. For those months, those seasons, it was effortless. He wished they could play every day and on the rain days he worked on his swing or a new way to release the ball. More and more fans were coming out.

The Niners weren't considered one of the big clubs in the area. Most of the boys held jobs at the mill or in the shops. The Mutuals and the Gothams in New York were more powerful clubs and were supported by the rich folks in the city, and the Brooklyn Atlantics seemed to be the most popular— drawing consistent crowds of over two thousand. The Niners, though, had an excellent reputation. They played the game fairly and were known for their after-game hospitality when they hosted. And they were known for the second baseman Alexander Cooper and their star pitcher, Rebel Joe Tyler.

Joseph was friendly with Cooper but remained quiet and aloof for the most part. The war had taught him not to allow himself to feel too much and he preferred to be alone most of the time. He took a job working nights for a grocer in Terryville who was a member of the club but was considered a "muffin" and never got to play with the first nine. Joseph had never heard the term but that's what they called the less skilled players and when a fielder missed a ball he was supposed to handle he was said to have 'muffed' it. He didn't mind the work—opening crates of vegetables and fruits and stocking the shelves with dry goods. He would ride out to the dairy a couple of times a week and bring in milk and eggs. He swept the floors and got the store ready for morning and this was fine with Joseph because he still had trouble sleeping—waking with visions of the war—of Terence disappearing into the trees—and he preferred to stay busy. He spent many hours reading. He read anything he could get his hands on. John Beezer had taken a liking to him and let him stay on at the King's Inn for a dollar a month, and Joseph was quite comfortable there. He was allowed to take a portion of food from the grocery and on occasion the Niners had special games against some of the big clubs and earned a share of the gate themselves, so Joseph had enough to take care of himself.

The 1867 season was his best as a player. He seemed to be able to concentrate as if nothing else existed. The rules were being revised every year now at conventions that took place most winters. Most of the rules had been set out in *Beadle's Dime Base Ball Player* in 1860, but as the game grew some changes were needed. The first official stolen base had occurred in the sixties simply because there was no rule against it. It seemed some new twist came up regularly. The National Association of Base Ball Players was formed and met regularly to shape the evolving game. Joseph paid little attention to these things. He concentrated only on the game and on the skills required to play it well. The intensity of his devotion to the game became legend in the area and the joke was that he slept with his base ball uniform on. It wasn't far from the truth. The game galvanized him like nothing else. He knew now that in battle, there could be no winners. Life itself had no particular rules—no certain measure—no clear boundaries. But the game—the game was precise, the boundaries marked, the challenge clear—and within this Joseph Tyler existed. He was a base ball player.

The others on the club—even Rooster Nash—had become like brothers to him and although he remained separate and did not socialize too much with the boys, they had become a surrogate family to him. They were trusted and on the field of the game they were bonded—strong only in their union with each other, their exclusive, particular existence on the field—from the beginning of a game until its end. But a true and deep affection developed off the field as well.

They had played in front of ten thousand spectators who paid fifty cents to watch at the new Capitoline Grounds in Brooklyn. The owners of the fields were building grandstands for the ladies and high fences so the people had no choice but to pay if they wanted to see the game. Quite often the Niners ferried across the Hudson River to play at the already legendary Elysian Fields where the New York Knickerbockers had played the first organized base ball game in '46. It was a broad open meadow with drifts of grass and brush surrounding the field, and the spectators would lay blankets around the diamond and help find the struck balls in the tall grass. Sometimes you could smell the sea as a thin wind swept across the field and made it extra hard to judge fly balls. It was Joseph's favorite place to play. It was the fields and pastures of Virginia and it was the game he had played there with no fences, and as he played he could almost hear the barking hound tied up at the pasture's edge.

It was a game he was pitching at Elysian Fields when he first felt the twinge of pain in his shoulder, and he was unable to finish pitching that game. Rooster Nash was the change pitcher and came in and finished up the last innings. The wound had healed, but the constant throwing had aggravated the torn muscles and tendons and from that day on, when he pitched, the night was spent in pain. On one night he sat alone in his room with a warm towel on his shoulder. He reached for a book from the shelf and out of it fell a folded paper. Holding the towel on his shoulder with his left hand, he reached down and picked it up and in the light of the lamp he could see that it was the letter. He held it in his hands. The ache in his shoulder—the letter—reminded him of the past that he had tried to force from his mind and heart as he played the game. The letter brought it back—he did not even read it that night. He decided then to deliver it. He had put it off for months and now years. It was as if the possibility—no, the idea of Sarah Kingsley—of human love rising above this war, was too important to him to risk. He seemed to have so few of these possibilities left. So few ideas that had not been tarnished or shattered. But he knew that he had to deliver the letter. He had often looked across the crowd at the games, across the colored hats and parasols, and wondered if she were among them. He had found out that her father was a newspaperman. Perhaps she had heard his name. Seen him play the game.

It didn't matter. It was time and he knew it. It was part of the reason he had come here in the first place. He would find the courage to meet Sarah Kingsley. She was only a girl. He would put the letter in her hands. It was only words, after all.

II.

Rocker Falls, New York, 1868

It was early spring, just weeks into the new base ball season. Joseph pulled the carriage to a stop at the sight of the number twenty-eight on the brick pillar that cornered a white picket fence. Green grass formed perfect squares framing a cobblestone walk. The walk led to three stone steps, cut from larger stones, that ended at a slate porch partially covered by an extended roof. The house was built of brick, muted orange courses with slight aberrations—the mason's carelessness or purposeful imperfection. Lines of graying mortar—some green with moss and more dry and crumbling at the exposed surface—ran corner to corner; lines of brick ran to the windows where slanted courses bulged from the otherwise flat surface, forcing the dripping rain from the roof away from the window's base.

White window frames divided the bull-nosed glass into small sections—nine on nine—and green shutters thick with paint framed each window. The shutters were all open, some hanging slightly askew, disconnected—and one was shut carelessly to the morning sun.

He tied the ropes of the horse and carriage to an upright stone hitch with a rusty ring and as he approached the steps he could see a statue of a child, arms outstretched, holding a basket of pale yellow narcissus. It stood on the corner of the porch. Joseph was startled by the lazy gate as it closed to a crude clasp behind him, sounding strangely like the clash of a ramrod in the barrel of a gun. As he stood on the porch he was suddenly unable to knock the brass knocker or pull the ringing chord that hung in his reach. He was unsure of what had drawn him unavoidably here, unsure of why he had gone to such trouble inquiring about her. But even as he had found her he hesitated again. As the season ended and the winter came, the decision made—he could not bring himself to risk this sacred illusion to another reality. Until now.

Joseph breathed deeply and straightened himself out. He felt a soreness in his left leg from sliding into the third base in yesterday's game and reached down with his hand to rub it. Probably a deep bruise, nothing serious. He had hardly felt it at the time—aware only that the winning run had scored in front of him, that he had been able to hit the ball solidly again and achieve his purpose on the playing field. His teammates had greeted him as he stood and dusted off his baggy trousers with the palms of his hands and the hundred or so fans that had been watching from the grassy slope had cheered him and he heard them chant Rebel Joe, Rebel Joe and he had once again drunk in the laughter and the sweat and the fullness of an organized base ball game.

He found the courage and lifted the knocker and let it fall twice and it made a sound not unlike that of a steel chisel upon the face of stone. He could see the shadow of someone pass in the hallway behind the door through the glass lights that framed the oak door. The doorknob turned and the door swung open, inward. A man stood, well dressed in black trousers and black vest. A gold chain hung from the vest and disappeared again behind the garment. The man was quite short compared to Joseph, and slightly bald with a perfectly trimmed white beard and mustache—like General Lee, Joseph imagined, although he had never set eyes on the general. He had seen his grainy likeness in the newspapers, though, and he looked very much like this man who stood before him.

Yessir, what can I do for you? The man spoke with a light, friendly voice.

Joseph answered, Tyler sir, Joseph Tyler, and he extended his hand and removed a felt cap from his head.

Nice to meet you, Joseph Tyler, the man answered, extending his own hand in a friendly shake, but to what do I owe the pleasure of your acquaintance, son?

Joseph was relieved at the kindness in the man's voice and breathed more easily as he spoke. It's your daughter sir. Is your daughter Sarah Kingsley?

The man answered affirmatively. Are you an acquaintance of my daughter?

Joseph looked at him a moment and then answered quietly, No sir. I've not met her. I have something for her, Joseph answered. A letter, sir. I have carried it through the war and these months—these years since—and I feel I have to deliver it, sir.

The old man's eyes squinted at the boy's face and he could see no trace of insincerity in Joseph's eyes or expression. Come in then, said Alexander Kingsley. The flies have been nasty and my wife becomes very uncomfortable when they're in the house. And I'm afraid when my wife's uncomfortable, we're all uncomfortable, Mr. Tyler. They don't bother her in the garden but they just won't do in the house.

Joseph entered into the narrow foyer. An adjacent room was full with dark wooden furniture with brushed maroon cushions and carved chair backs and he could see the back of a small couch that faced a large fireplace. Dark mahogany had been carved into cherubs or angels all along the sides of the fire pit, all reaching toward the mantel and the deeply carved rays of a bursting sun that licked the light and shadows and cast them down again toward the wooden floor. Joseph had seen things like this—in the parlors of the hotels in Manhattan—but never in a home and he was losing confidence quickly. But the man's voice calmed him again. You've come a long way then, son, from the South I would presume.

Yessir, Virginia. But I've been in New York for these years, since '65.

And what does a Virginia boy do in New York?

Joseph hesitated, and then not without some pride answered, Base ball. I play base ball with the Terryville Niners. He was relieved to see the look of recognition come across the face of the man.

Kingsley's hand reached to his shoulder. Tyler, you say. Joseph Tyler—of course. You're Rebel Joe. You hit over .350 last season and struck out twenty-two in one game. With his right hand he grabbed Joseph's and shook it. I was there when you hit the sign over Broad Street to win a game in the ninth. Good work son, very good. I didn't recognize you out of uniform, I'm afraid.

He stood back as if looking him over and then said, Of course. Joe Tyler. It's the only part of my own paper I can stand to read anymore, the base ball. The people seem to love it. Enough war stories, impeachment, politics—the readers want to see the base ball scores. Rebel Joe . . . so what letter is it, then? From whom?

It's from a Union soldier sir, from the war. Roger McCleod, sir, and it's written to your daughter.

The man's face darkened and his hands withdrew from Joseph's. He turned half away and rested a hand on the black desk that stood along the wall of the hallway. He spoke quietly. We know that Roger is dead, Mr. Tyler. There were letters from the War Department. We know that he died in battle in Virginia—and I wonder how you came to have a letter by his hand.

Joseph could sense the depth of feeling that Alexander Kingsley had for the young soldier—that this family had mourned greatly the news of his death. Not only the daughter, but the family had lost someone they cared greatly for—like so many families whose sons and fathers and friends had not come home from the war.

Son, tell me this. Did you have a hand in his death?

No, answered Joseph. But I could not save him. The battle was horrible for both sides . . . We were in a place called the Wilderness. I woke—I had been wounded with a bayonet and was unconscious and I woke and the armies had withdrawn. There were fires burning . . . it was all scrub oak and pine . . . the brush had caught fire from the battle and there was smoke and fire . . . and I heard a voice crying for help and I went toward it. I wasn't sure what I was doing but I went toward the voice, and I found Roger McCleod. He was mortally wounded and the fire was at his feet so I carried him to a clearing . . . to a pond . . . and we both lay there and he died while we slept.

Joseph hesitated and took a deep breath. Kingsley was watching him, leaning on the desk and watching and listening to the words that he spoke.

When I woke again, he was dead. I could see that he was dead right off. I went through his pack cause we were all starvin—the Confederates I mean—and the Federals always had food. So I went through his pack and ate what he had and I came across the letter and somethin made me take it. I tucked it in my jacket and forgot about it till one night when I was lyin in prison camp in Elmira. I found it in the lining of my jacket . . . and I read it. And I read it many times after that—and I'm sure it helped keep me alive. These words that Roger had written to your daughter . . . I meant to deliver it, sir, and now I have come to . . . to give it to her.

The father was silent. His hands were tucked awkwardly in the pockets of his vest. He spoke again, quietly. Why didn't you post it?

I meant to, sir, but I couldn't. I needed to hand-deliver it, sir, to make sure.

I am not at all sure it's a good idea. Some memories are better left obscure. It took a long time for her, for all of us to get over the news. He was a fine young man—a friend of the family for years—and they were to marry after the war. I just don't see the point in bringing it up again.

Joseph stood straight and without hesitation said, Here's the point as I see it, sir. It's a soldier's last words, sir. This battle—it was like nothin you can imagine, like nothin human bein's ever seen or will ever see agin.

He paused and closed his eyes for a moment and then continued. Everything was burnin and then these words . . . come from that. These words that Roger put down for Sarah Kingsley to read is what I came from the battle with. It's a human voice that shoulda been heard over all the stink of battle—words I couldn' write . . . not sure I could even feel. Words that she should hear, should read herself cause he died not long after he wrote them. And I feel compelled to deliver . . . and to meet Sarah.

These last words slipped from him and he could see Kingsley's eyebrows rise again.

There was something about Joseph—he could not turn the boy away and he finally waved him into the parlor and asked him to sit on the couch near a large mirror that made the room look much larger than it actually was. I will get Sarah for you. Wait here please. I see there's no stopping you at any rate.

Alexander Kingsley left the room and left Joseph sitting quietly. Joseph pulled the letter from his vest pocket and held it in both hands in his lap. It felt so good to sit on these soft cushions. He needed rest before tomorrow's game and he still had to stock shelves at the grocery tonight.

Joseph turned the letter over in his hands. It was worn—familiar to his touch. He tried to picture Sarah. Would she very tall? Short? Would she hate him—of course she would hate him as the enemy. Would she welcome the letter? Would she thank him, or send him from the house? He thought of this in silence as he sat.

He noticed a large piano, dark wood and ivory keys yellowed from the touch of human hands. He had seen pictures of pianos—but this was the first he had seen, and it seemed much more grand. Its wide surface was washed in sunlight from the window and a likeness—a photograph of a gentleman dressed in a suit and tie, and a derby hat like Joseph had seen around town—but he couldn't make out the man's face in the grainy picture. Was this Roger McCleod? Joseph tried to compare his memory of the lifeless body with this picture—but he could not. He could see the lifeless body, almost shapeless, gathered at the base of the tree like something discarded. He remembered the singed eyes and that was all. The picture stood crooked in a gilded frame and beside it there was a vase of red tulips and a pile of music books.

Along the surface of the wood the sunshine brought out the lines of dusting and polishing, as well as the lines of black grain. He looked at the reflected light and thought of his father's unfinished bedstand that proba- bly still lay in the corner of the farmhouse at Blackstone—most likely never to be finished—not a product of a man's work, but the work itself, left for a world to see—the effort, the labor, the beginning of something to be done but never truly completed. The scent of the wolf. Joseph smiled and thought for a second of his father. The scent of the wolf.

He lay his open hand, his palm, on the cool polished wood. His left hand dropped to the keyboard and he let his finger drop to the tarnished white and listened to the hollow ping of the hammer bouncing off the taut chord and the sound of it stood him upright and he turned halfway, looked over his left shoulder and he could see her. Her image was reflected in the mir- ror. She was standing in the doorway, her hands held together in front of her. He turned full around to face her, knocking the piano stool with his long legs—held it still in his firm grip and stood straight up facing her.

For these months, these years, he had thought of her often—rereading the letter, trying to imagine what she might be like, reading it out loud as if she could hear it—as if she stood before him. And here she was—standing before him, and he could not remember why he had come. He could only rest the gaze of his eyes on the woman before him in the doorway. The hall- way behind her was dark and the sun washed across the front of her. The heat of the sun seemed to press on his back through the great front window. The bent rays of the sun lay across his back. He could see his own awkward shadow spill across the wide planked floor toward her—and he thought, how tall, how awkward he must appear to her. What kind of clothes was he wearing? He wasn't aware—how awkward.

The tulips cast a delicate shadow across the thin cloth of her dress but otherwise she stood clear in the light—clear for him to look upon. He could see her pale blue eyes shaded by a faint trace of dark eyelashes. Her skin was just slightly darkened from the summer sun and the light shone across the fine silk hair of her arms where they emerged from a loose sleeve. She wore a patterned blouse that was tucked in behind a sash at the waist and hung loosely at her neck. He could see a line where the white skin remained untouched by the sun and thin bone began to form her chest. He tried—but could not look away. Unthinking, he reached into his vest pocket for the folded letter. It wasn't there. He looked quickly behind him and saw it on the floor where it had dropped from his hands. Reaching down, he felt the worn shapelessness of it and felt foolish—for having read it—afraid again that she would hate him for it. He held it in his hand for a moment, and then held it out to her—took a few steps toward her—placed it in her open palm, and stepped back again.

There was a moment of silence, and then he said. This . . . is from Roger McCleod, maam . . . addressed to you . . . Sarah Kingsley. And then he realized how stupid he must sound. He could see her eyes shine with tears as she looked down at the folded paper and then back at him, without speaking. He could feel a cutting pain above his heart—wished he had never come here—wished she would strike him, throw him out of the parlor, out of the house—but she said nothing. She moved toward the couch and let her weight settle into the cushions where he had been sitting moments before. She was crying quietly, and she pulled a white handkerchief from the pocket of her dress and brought it with both hands to her eyes.

And how did you come to have a letter from Mr. McCleod? she asked, her voice thin and wavering.

I was with him . . . when he died, answered Joseph. Was he sure she knew he was dead? Yes, her father had said. What a fool he was standing here.

And you're a reb. Did you kill him? . . . and then come to me with this?

No maam. I did not kill Roger McCleod . . . but I did . . . I had a hand in killing many others.

She stood again—leaned against the white wooden molding around the door. She sighed and wiped a strand of hair from her face. There was nothing but sincerity written across the boy's face and she could see this clearly.

Well, it was war—and I suppose killing is what war is for . . . whatever the other reasons they say . . . it comes to killing. He was in Virginia we heard, and he died at a place called Spotsylvania.

Yes maam, but not Spotsylvania, before that, at the Wilderness. A few days I guess before the battle at Spotsylvania. It was a terrible fight. There

were no winners . . . and the brush caught fire and burned for days after-
ward . . . and the trees even caught fire and I found Roger McCleod after I
was wounded. I heard him callin. He was the enemy but I could not let
him burn . . . so I carried him away, and he died lyin next to me. He died
while I slept. I gave him a proper burial, Miss Kingsley, Joseph lied, and I
found this letter in his belongings and I have had it with me ever since.

From what? she cried out.

Yes maam? he answered.

What killed him?

He explained that he appeared to have been shot in the thigh and that it
was bleeding real bad and that it was just too much blood lost. Joseph continued, There were no winners . . . just death is all . . . and sufferin all
around. And Roger McCleod had just been caught up in this and carried
away in it. We were all carried away in it. Just some of us lived and some
surely did not.

She breathed deeply again and let out an anguished, throaty sigh and
crossed the short distance back to the couch and sat on its edge. She
looked childlike on the couch and he lowered his head and spoke softly. I
am sorry Miss Kingsley. He spoke clearly. I should not have come. Some
things are best left alone.

She looked up at his strong and honest face and listened to the drawn-
out syllables of his words. She could see the pain drawn across his face—
the scars of war as surely as the cut of sword or gun. She had seen it on the
faces of many of the young boys who had returned. None of them truly
young anymore. She had seen it in the eyes of the boys at the hospital,
even those well enough to walk away.

It's just that . . . I read the letter and I . . . I thought you should read it,
to see for sure how Roger McCleod felt bout you. That he thought of you
the night before he died . . . and I'm sure that morning as well. I could
never write those words . . . or even think these things . . . so I thought it
was important. And I couldn't seem to help myself anyway . . . like God
hisself had delivered this letter to me, for me to bring to you. And so here I
am. It is hard to find God on a battlefield, maam . . . and it's sure not to

be ignored when there appears to be a glimpse of him.

It's okay, Mr. Tyler. I will be glad to read it. And I shall be thankful to have it.

She began to sob and held her hands to her face and her shoulders shook and her small frame seemed to fold into itself and sink into the soft cushions. He watched, helplessly, as her shoulders shook and she seemed to cave inward. She seemed so very small.

Joseph said something like, Yes maam, and left quickly into the foyer, grasping for the doorknob, pulling the door to him, letting the sun and light wash over him and breathing in the fresh air. He stood a moment on the slate porch and felt the same relief he had felt when he had escaped the heat of the fire—and lay the body of Roger McCleod next to him and slept near the cool water. He could see the white, blistered face—the open life-less eyes—and he felt suddenly hatred—or envy—that this girl loved him so and wept for him so—and that he had been able to say these things to her in a letter. He stepped out and off the porch and felt tears burning at his eyes. He walked down the walk and through the gate and pulled the rope from the stone and pulled himself up on the seat of the carriage. The horse started and then they rolled away from the white fence and the gate.

So it's done, then. He said this out loud.

A black carriage led by two white horses clattered by and the driver tipped his hat and Joseph ignored the greeting and rode on. Far off a train or a factory whistle could be heard, and the barking of one and then several dogs split the rhythm of the evening like rifle fire.

It was early afternoon, not long after Joseph's visit. Sarah and her parents had just returned home from church. The women were setting the small table in the kitchen, as they preferred this in the spring to the formal dining room. The room was drenched in the sweet scent of viburnum, lifted on a breeze through the loose screens of the open windows. Her father was using a long knife to carve a ham that folded into thin slices on a cutting board made of planed oak. Mrs. Kingsley was putting a loaf of uncut bread in a woven basket.

On the way home from church they had stopped at the bakery in town and purchased two loaves of bread and a small pastry for the evening. The heat had still been rising from the crust of the bread as it was wrapped in brown paper and Sarah had enjoyed the aroma all the way home in the carriage. She could still smell the bread as she placed a blue porcelain bowl on the table filled with sliced potatoes and cream with pieces of shallot from last year's garden chopped and mixed into it.

They ate together at the small table in the kitchen, discussing the morning's sermon and the recent death of one of the deacons, Charles Carrington, who had never quite recovered from losing two sons at Gettysburg. They talked about the upcoming election that looked to be assured to go to General Grant. Alexander's newspaper had endorsed the general, but not without some misgivings.

I'm afraid his willingness to kill is what has propelled him to this, he said to his wife and daughter. And I fear this might be his only qualification for the job.

And then just as quickly, as if not willing to ruin the morning with this talk, the conversation changed. Her father was touching a cloth to his mouth and the ends of his mustache when he said, I saw one of the games last week. Your friend Tyler had quite a day for himself.

He's hardly my friend, Father, she said, and felt her cheeks warm slightly.

Perhaps not. But I believe it was a noble thing he did. On the field of battle, and bringing you the letter. And further, I believe that if you were looking for a friend you might have found one.

Alexander, please, her mother said smiling.

I've not been looking, Sarah answered and folded her own napkin on the table in front of her. The shadow of a bird that had fluttered to the window, touched the screen, danced quickly across the surface of the table, and vanished. Sarah continued. I know nothing about him. Perhaps it was he who killed Roger after all.

No. We know that's not true. We can read that in a man's eyes, her father answered. There is something about the boy. Watching him perform on the base ball field, there's a certain grace I haven't seen.

Alexander Kingsley stood and helped his wife and daughter clear the table. Sarah was stacking the dishes gently on her arm when her father continued. Why don't you come to a game with me next week? he asked her. These crowds are getting bigger. It's really quite exciting. I think you'd enjoy it.

She was wiping the last remnant of cream from the bowl and placing the dishes on a wooden rack to be washed later. She thought of the boy standing awkwardly in the parlor, his long legs making the furniture appear small and their presence there, together, making the room feel terribly close. She could see his eyes as he handed her the folded letter and feel the gaze of his eyes on her as she read it that afternoon.

I think not, she answered, and noticed her mother smile slightly again and shake her head as she drew water for cleaning.

Later they were together in the garden. Alexander was turning an unlit cigar between his lips as he sat reading a recent issue of *Harper's Weekly*. Beside him a small stack of his own newspapers sat pressed against the new grass. Sarah reached down and picked one up and began to leaf through its pages, careful not to get the smudged ink on her dress. Then in the corner of the third page she saw the banner headline.

WELCOME THE BOSTON LOWELLS IN A MATCH AGAINST OUR OWN NINERS BASE BALL CLUB. WEDNESDAY AT 4 PM. ADMISSION 15 CENTS.

She lingered there a moment with the paper open, then folded it and set it on the grass beside her. She looked across the yard at the patterned shadows and the avenues of lawn that dissected the patches of tulips and crocuses. She could see the bare woody roses clinging to the white lattice and just beginning to swell with spring growth.

Perhaps I will, Father.

What's that dear? her father asked, looking over the newspaper he held in front of him.

Perhaps I'll come with you. To one of your base ball games.

As she said this her mother, still in her Sunday dress but squatting down to pull thin weeds from between blocks of weathered brick—turned and smiled again. Her father looked back down to the newspaper he held in front of him and with the unlit cigar gripped in his teeth said, I thought you might.

Now, some weeks later, the playing field was almost perfect. It was a flat plane of grass that seemed to be laid out like a blanket for a summer picnic. There were thin lines of worn grass marking the base paths, connecting bright white canvas bases anchored to the ground with railroad spikes. A split-rail fence marked the boundaries. Sections of the top rail were missing and at least one post was broken and ready to fall. A horse was tied to a post down the first-base line directly across from the Terryville town library. Several people stood on the porch of the apothecary in animated discussion. A boy rode by on one of the new three-wheeled cycles and the horse shuffled uneasily where it stood.

The sun was directly overhead and the sky was the uninterrupted blue seen only in summer. The home plate was white—freshly painted—with the footprints of children already across it. Twelve-inch-wide wooden planks lay stretched across nail kegs on both the first-base and the third-base sides. These would serve as benches for the competing clubs. The noon whistle sounded at the Terryville textile mill. A group of wagons passed, obviously traveling together, and pulled up at the fence that surrounded the field.

A bit later another wagon pulled up and carriages pulled together on a section of the field where the grass had been worn down to dirt. Two more boys on horseback rode up and dismounted and tied the horses to the fence. People began to gather at the fence—a few at a time—from different directions. They were talking and laughing, drawn somehow to the empty field, and they stood along the length of fence and gathered on the grass and the slopes beyond the fence. Gathering for the contest were women with parasols to protect themselves from the summer sun, men in silk derbies and white shirts, children running—hopping the fence and sliding back through. Off the right field side, down the line that connected the home plate to the first base, the grass sloped upward pretty severely for thirty feet or so and families began to lay blankets along the slope and children rolled down from top to bottom, clenching their arms to their chests and then dashing back up to the top. In direct center field a small group of men leaned on the fence smoking; one of them was turning the pages of the *Morning Star* and the pages flapped like a wounded bird in the gentle breeze that occasionally picked up across the field and the man struggled to hold it still enough to read.

From behind the home plate two men in gray uniform shirts and long trousers entered through an open space in the fence. They carried canvas bags under their arms and one carried two wooden bats over his shoulder. Behind them a rotund gentleman carried two wooden chairs and a small boy followed behind him and shouted indecipherably into a megaphone— until the man turned and told him to stop. The two men in uniform walked and faced each other about thirty feet apart and began to throw a baseball back and forth, the sound of the ball slapping their palms break- ing the dull drone of the afternoon. Workers from the mill walked across the street to the grass and sat eating cold sausage sandwiches and watch- ing the men toss the ball.

Joseph dipped the last piece of his biscuit in the gravy and put it with two fingers into his mouth. He dabbed his mouth quickly with the white napkin, put a quarter on the table, and said, Thanks Jenny.

The bell clanged on the door and it opened and he heard, Okay Joe, as he was halfway down the wooden steps.

He was outside Jenny's Café and he had a bat over his shoulder and his uniform shirt tied around the end of it. He crossed the street to the field. Joseph's hair was cut short and combed neatly to one side. His shoulders were broad and the undershirt fit him tightly around the neck and the lines of muscles ran along his neck, shoulders, and back. He had long legs just like his father's now, and each strong step covered the ground in big strides. He could see Jeffrey Stokes and Ned Conway already throwing to each other on the field and he could see that the other team was arriving, quickly now, on wagons and horses, and was already gathering together and discussing the game. They were all parked together on the far side where Taylor Road ran along the grass close to the field. A couple of them were jogging in his direction while Mike Harris wrestled a bag full of equipment onto his shoulder and followed behind.

Joseph approached the split-rail fence—placed both hands on the top rail—and swung his legs over onto the playing field. A boy, maybe eight or nine years old, yelled out, Rebel Joe Tyler! Three hits today, and Joseph smiled and tipped the bill of his cap toward the boy. When he was in the middle of center field he stopped and knelt down to tie the loose lace of one of his base ball shoes and to watch the activity of the field around him.

The sound of the ball, the rumble of wooden wheels across the cobbled streets, the conversations and the laughter that drifted in on a breeze and then silenced just as quickly kept him there on his knee. He could see the smoke-stacks of the mill in the west and groups of people along the steps of the storefronts. He could see Jenny standing outside in the sunshine in front of her café, away from the hot stove, wiping her hands on a white apron and breathing in the clean summer air. He watched her greet a family that walked by and they slowed to talk and then continued down the road.

He thought of the pasture in Virginia where he and Terence had played the same game. Before the war. He tried to see it clearly but he could not. He could see only the tangled wood of the wilderness and the choking canopy of dense trees that seemed finally to inhale all the light and leave only a close and cramped darkness. A darkness from which there had seemed no escape. And yet here he was. How was it that he had been deliv-ered from the wilderness to this?

He saw Terence's face, but then suppressed the image. He could not think of it any longer. Could not think that Terence had not emerged from the woods into the light like he did, to sit on this field—that Joseph had walked from the woods and Terence had not. He had heard from Virginia that Terence had never returned to Fernwood. Now all this time had passed and Joseph still waited to hear his voice, expected him to walk from one of these crowds and greet him. He looked at the faces of the boys on every ball club and expected to see the face of Terence Hooker among them. But the image of the face lingered only in his own eyes and he could see it clearly on days like this when the sun shone full and the sounds of the game they loved filled the air.

He returned to the moment. To the level grass in front of him. To the warm wood clenched in his hands. To the perfect flight and sound of the ball as it was tossed from one to the other. And then he could see Terence's face again, his smile, he could hear his laugh rise over the laughter of the swelling crowd. Had he died that day in the wilderness or was he consumed by the fires? And he could see the gentle smile of his friend amid the choking woodland and he knew in his heart that Terence could not have survived the black battles of Virginia and that his soul had been unanchored in the flames and Joseph looked upward to the clear sky and thought, You can see the world now from where you are. You can see this field and you'll watch this game won't you Terence Hooker and you'll watch the ball spin from my hand and you'll laugh as the strikers miss and you'll hear them call my name as sure as this grass is green. Terence had said that—that it would be better if they could see us, the dead lookin down at us. Was he dead? Was there a grave somewhere? He didn't even know for sure. He was just gone—that was all.

Joseph looked back to the base ball field and lifted himself up to walk toward the infield. He was greeted with handshakes and quick claps from his teammates and he saw Alex Cooper arrive on a horse and dismount and walk toward the field. Cooper greeted his clubmates and then went to talk over the rules and such with the other club and Joseph started a toss with Mike Owens who had just joined them from Boston and had made some spectacular plays in the outfield. He was a short man with a slight trace of an Irish accent, but he was swift of foot and tireless in competition. His laugh came easily to him and it was a loud one and Joseph had liked him from the start. The two had had dinner together the past week at Jenny's and laughed quite a bit as they talked about the games and the different players they had seen. Owens had been on two clubs—the Tri-Mountains of Boston and then for a short while he was on the second nine of the Brooklyn Stars— before joining Terryville. He knew quite a bit about the development of the game. After an hour or so of baseball talk Owens had leaned over and said to Joseph with a broad smile, She was there again, Reb. At Thursday's game.

He pretended not to know, but of course he had seen her. She had come late in the game and stayed only for an inning or so. She had been at last

Tuesday's game against the New Jersey team as well, and he thought he saw her at the game against the Troy club. If she was there, she had seen him hit a triple and a home run and she had seen them carry him on their shoulders from the field. She stood with her father, or a reporter from her father's paper, and then sometimes a female friend. Joseph had not acknowledged her—had not had a chance to talk to her although he looked for her after every game. He surely did not know what he would say if he did have a chance. She was gone, though, by the end of every game.

She's there with her father, Joseph answered.

She's there to see you, Joe Tyler—I've seen her watch you play. You had better pay attention the next time, man. Let me know if you're not interested, friend, he had laughed as he took a sip of rum.

Joseph's attention shifted back to the field and he looked quickly to the crowd but did not see her. The other team began to walk onto the field. They had white uniforms with gold stripes and gold hats. Some of them were singing as they arrived on the grass and Joseph and the players on his club greeted them with handshakes and exaggerated stories. This club was from Albany and they had already met five times this season with Terryville having a three to two edge. Joseph pulled on his uniform shirt and buttoned it and the word Niners could be read across the chest. The Terryville Niners wore blue and gray uniforms and gray caps and together they looked like a new regiment, fresh recruits—but to the game—to the new bursting life of the game. Twenty minutes later the man with the megaphone yelled out for the contest to begin and Joseph's club took to the field.

Joseph was going to pitch this game and when he took the base ball in his hand he felt the familiar thing. He couldn't tell what it was. If you asked him, he couldn't explain it. Perhaps it was the angles—all leading to a central spot—linear paths of worn grass connecting to the white plate, divided by the slash of sun. All of this was collected by the grass and breathed out across the field. Depending on how the grass was bent or how the wind swept it, the colors were deep green—almost black—or silver-gray and all shades between. It was not the colors of the field but the colors of the sun and the breath of the wind that lay beneath them. It was the color of

Virginia. In the outfield the shadows of the fence offered warning to the fielders that they were close and as they ran the silent grass would turn into the scratch of gravel before the catch—before the fence.

The sounds—the low chatter from clubmates behind and around him—the calls, the whistles from the players along the wooden benches—were like music to him. The laughter from the growing crowd of spectators—word-less conversation that rose up and across a field of colored hats and derbies, undulating like an unsettled sea. In the drifts between the waves of varied sound boomed the deep gravelly voice selling peanuts and buckets of beer from the breweries in Utica. The sound of the ball—hand to hand—around the field. The fresh beginning—success or failure undetermined and pre-cise—ordered and clear. Joseph did not know if it were any of these things as he dusted the front of his uniform shirt with his palm. He knew that this was right. This was where he should be, for whatever reason. On the base ball field he felt almost complete—almost right.

He thought for a moment of his father, gazing down the length of a stone wall along the field ready for planting. He could see the back of his father's head and the long shadow cast along the grass of the meadow. This was his field. This was Joseph's wall. He wished his father could see the thing that he loved. He wished his father could help him with the building of it and see it as plainly as he himself could see it. He suddenly, overwhelmingly, wished that his father were here with him now—could see him on this field where his place was as certain as that of Caleb's on the working pasture. For a moment he understood the correctness, the cer-tainty of the stone walls. If only his father could stand here and see the correctness of this—this field and Joseph's presence on it.

There was the lack of thought that overcame him. The clarity of sense required to play the game well. The loss of memory—the absence of any-thing but the moment. He had experienced this in battle—but it was a suffocating absence of anything but the immediate, the terror of the next moment—no reality beyond the reach of the saber or the cannon, none but the thin blade through skin and bone and the black smoke of guns and the whistle of lead. None now but the suddenness of bat against ball and the still concentration that exploded with instinctual, reactive motion.

Joseph could see that the catcher was ready as he clapped his hands together and showed Joseph his white palms. He saw in that moment only the hands, as if there were a hole in the scene around him through which he would throw the ball. He stood bent toward the target, drew his arms back—felt the familiar painful tinge in his shoulder—and hesitated for seconds. His balance was back and his left leg lifted slightly and the direction of his body changed as he leaned in toward the hands of the catcher—stepping forward with the motion of his body moving him there—the ball rolling off his fingers and his feet landing firm at the very instant of the sound, of the white ball hitting the catcher's hands and the rotund umpire calling strike from somewhere behind them.

He looked at the striker. The man was smiling with white teeth that seemed too big for his mouth and he could see the red letters scribed across his chest and then the bat banging on the plate and the shaking head of the striker as he collected himself and raised the bat to be ready again for the thrown ball. Joseph was aware of voices that drifted into his awareness and then quickly away as he focused on the hands of the catcher and the short shadow of the striker across the white plate.

Joseph wound up and threw again and as he did the batter swung himself around and fell to the ground and when he rose up, dusting his white trousers off with a free hand, he was no longer smiling. Joseph could see only the white teeth, the gold letters and the hands. Once more he coiled his body and let the ball fly toward the hands and he watched as the bat swung wildly again and the ball slapped in the open hands of the catcher. The next batter was the same and was retired with three missed balls, another hand down, and the game went on like this. Pitch after pitch, inning after inning the process was repeated and Joseph was aware of the growing excitement of the crowd and the quiet as he threw the ball. Very little like this had been seen. Hitting had dominated the game. The people watching were uneasy—unsure how to react. Only after the last pitch—after the catcher caught the ball, tossed it on the ground at the feet of the helpless batter—was Joseph aware of it all. Not one striker had reached base. Only two pitches were called anything but perfect. Only three balls had been even hit to fair territory. He was aware then of the applause and the shouts of Rebel Joe—Rebel Joe. He was aware of the metallic voice over the megaphone shouting across the crowd, Down in order—perfect pitching, and some other indecipherable words that floated across the field and away. Alexander Cooper reached him first and lifted him off the ground and then the other clubmates joined him in the middle of the field. He could see over their heads as they swarmed him and he looked across the sea of colored hats toward the stores and the mill beyond. Farmers outside town hesitated in their work and looked up toward the unfamiliar noise and then returned to their plows and their labor. Joseph looked across the crowd but he could not see her. He was being lifted to the shoulders of the men but he strained to find her eyes in the crowd and he could not.

Reporters gathered around him with pads and pencils and asked him what he felt. He could see the boy from the *Morning Star* but she was not there with him. Tables were being set up for a feast after the game and later that night the clubs would meet and celebrate again at the tavern and the newspapers would carry the story of the perfect pitching on that perfect afternoon but Joseph thought only that she had missed it and because of that the moment would be ordinary.

The next morning he was sitting at Jenny's when a boy brought him the newspaper. You're in here mister. There's a picture of you on the second page.

Joseph opened the paper and in the corner he could see a dark photograph of himself as he pitched the ball and as he saw it he remembered. He remembered the open newspaper left on the wooden table so his father could see it. Nothing was ever said about it. Nothing.

Will you sign it sir?

Sign what?

I have two copies. Put your name on the picture. Write your name. I'll give you this other one.

What for?

So I can tell my friends that I know Rebel Joe Tyler.

You don' know me son. Why would you want my name written on the picture?

So I can show my friends. Even my daddy's a big base ball fan. I can tell him I talked to Joe Tyler.

You can talk to me anytime you want son.

Just the name would be fine sir.

Joseph looked down at the paper as the boy handed him a writing pen. It was him all right. First time he had ever seen a picture of himself. He signed JOE TYLER across the chest and handed it to the boy.

Thank you, the boy yelled as he ran down the street holding the signed paper in his hand. As Joseph walked down the street that morning he hesitated and then sat on a wooden bench that overlooked the river. He pulled the paper from his pocket again and unfolded it. He sat there looking at the picture for a while and he thought that someday he would leave it on the table again for his father. He looked at the image of himself in the black shadows of ink and thought of that first picture of a player he had seen. He could see every line of it like it was yesterday and he remembered it was that picture as much as anything that brought him here. He sat on the bench for an hour or so and watched the traffic of wagons and carriages go by and many of the people who passed shouted to him, especially the children. He felt a calm—a gladness in his heart—and being aware of it, he thought back to another time and he could see it clearly.

He could not recall how old he had been—as early in his childhood that he could remember. He could feel his father's hands as he was lifted and he opened his eyes to see his mother's face as well as his father's. She was smiling as they tucked a blanket around him and made sure he was covered well as they lifted him and carried him from his bed. The great room was lit by a single candle and a new fire had been started in the fireplace. The first light of morning was just seeping into the room. He could not remember how old he was—four, maybe five years old—he was not sure but he could see it as if it had been a month ago. He remembered the excitement of being awakened in the dark and brought from his bed in blankets.

Come Joseph, there's something for you.

Joseph saw his mother slip on a coat and he could see his parents' breath in the morning air. His father carried him to the door and his mother asked him to close his eyes and so he did. He felt himself pass through the doorway and out into the cold air as he kept his eyes closed tight.

Okay—open your eyes Joseph. Look . . . look at this, she said, and her hands were open to the fields and pasture of Blackstone.

Joseph's eyes looked away from his mother and to the fields, and instead of the brown and gray of winter—there lay a blanket of white over everything. Everything was equal—rock to field—hill to pasture—soil to water, all white. It was the first snow he could remember—perhaps the first he had seen. The three of them were under the cover of the porch as they watched the increasing snow cover everything.

Close your eyes again, Joseph. Listen.

He had closed his eyes and listened and he heard nothing but the rattle of a windowpane and then nothing at all. Then he remembered hearing the whisper of snow on snow—the thin whistle of the winter wind.

See it Joseph—how lovely it is. Close your eyes and see it with your heart Joseph and remember what you've seen. She was leaning on the porch post with a coat wrapped closely around her shoulders. He could see flakes of snow settle on her hair and then vanish. She walked toward him.

Think sometimes, Joseph, of mornings like this. Hold them in your heart.

He had looked out over the blue shadows and the moon that sat as if under water through the falling snow and he closed his eyes again and he could still remember the quiet sound and feel the strong hands of his father as he held him there. As he sat on the bench now he could recall it—the magnitude of the quiet—as a child might—and he was glad that he could feel that morning still lying written across his heart.

They played three more games that week, finishing up on Friday afternoon. The first two were against the Lowells from Boston and they split those games. Then on Friday they played the Mutuals and Joseph pitched again. He had struck out fourteen but he got wild with his throwing in the seventh and he pitched poorly after that. He gave up consecutive doubles before retiring the side in the eighth and he could feel the pain in his shoulder growing more severe. Alex Cooper walked in from the second base and asked him if he'd had enough, Guess I'd like to finish what I started, Joseph answered, and Cooper tipped his hat to him and trotted back to his bag.

Just let em hit it Tyler, the centerfielder yelled in. We'll take it from there. Joseph pitched to the final strikers and allowed only one hit and the runner was thrown out at second and the game was over with the Niners winning with a score of 18–17. Joseph had two hits and pitched well enough to win despite the growing pain in his shoulder. Cooper had the ball in his hands as he walked to the pitching box to congratulate him and a couple of the other players came in and shook his hand. As they did, Joseph looked over their shoulders toward the crowd of spectators and through the small sea of faces he could see Sarah. She was talking excitedly to her father who was smoking a long cigar and laughing through the clouds of smoke. They were beginning to sink into the crowd, away from the split-rail fence, and Joseph pushed through the players and across the grass toward her.

Sarah. He called her but she didn't hear him, or at least didn't turn toward him.

He called her name again and he saw her father and she hesitated and then turned in his direction. Her father took off his hat and they both approached the fence where Joseph now stood. She was wearing a broad hat made of white straw and a white sweater over a blue dress. As he was about to speak to them, her father was called in a different direction and Joseph and Sarah were left standing alone. Clouds had begun to form in the late innings and Joseph could feel the first trace of rain.

Miss Kingsley, he said, and she smiled. Joseph removed his cap and held it in both hands.

Excellent game Mr. Tyler, she answered. You look tired though. Are you tired Mr. Tyler?

Yes, he answered honestly and then added, Well no—it's just a game— not much to be tired about. He could feel the sweat cool on his forehead and wiped it away with the back of his hand. He leaned with one hand on the fence.

You do work hard at it, she said.

Yes maam. I try to do it well as I can.

She looked at his strong hand gripping the fence tightly, nervously, and placed her own on top of it. Joseph, she said quietly. I would like to talk to you. To find out more . . . about the war, if you don't mind. And I would like to know how you came to be so adept at this game.

He couldn't take his eyes off her as she spoke and he did not respond. He let the weight of her hand sink into his—tried to feel every spot where the hands touched—and then he felt her pull away.

Perhaps not then, she said.

Yes, of course, he said quickly. I would like to talk. I mean for us to talk.

She laughed softly. You're much more comfortable on the field aren't you Joseph Tyler? How's Sunday afternoon?

Yes, Sunday is fine. What time can I, shall I come? he asked and she walked to take her father's arm and as she did she said, Two o'clock would be fine.

Joseph could hear someone calling him and he turned to see Cooper and Owens loading gear onto a wagon while other men were setting up pots of chowder and barrels of beer and laughing and slapping each other's backs and recalling the game and other games. He watched and he could see them as if they were in slow motion. The first rain began to fall—the men were gray, muted, and almost formless, colorless—a washed out background against the vivid image of her lips, of the folds of her blouse—of the shadows cast across her face by the broad hat.

He remembered the first time he had felt the weight of a bat—that clear weight that connected him to a future, uniquely his—in his hands, elevating him from the stark reality of stone and soil. He remembered the first feel of the base ball—the texture of the stitches against his fingers—the clarity of his love for the game. This all fell away—diminished—insignificant. He could feel only the gentle weight of her hand on his. Warm—his own sweat absorbed in the pores of her skin, her palm—the coolness of the split-wood rail on his own palm, contrasting with the sweet warmth of hers. The weightlessness of it. He could see nothing else clearly—everything was changed.

That night he awoke—twisted in his blanket—drenched with sweat. He had felt the hands of Jacob lift him. Jacob was yelling,

Lets go, lets go, and as Joseph rose from the ground he could smell the carbon smoke and he was choked and slowed by it and as Jacob ran ahead Joseph could see him disappear over a ridge into a hollow and as he reached the edge of the deep swale and looked into it he could see Jacob standing there with his arms outstretched and falling backward into the darkness and Joseph reached for him but their hands would not touch and Jacob's eyes were fixed on Joseph's as he drifted into the black space and vanished. Joseph felt his own hands on the cold floor of his room and could see from the lightless window that it was still night and he had many hours to go before morning.

On the following Sunday they sat together on the couch in the parlor. Sarah's neice, Sophia, who had just turned ten, played the piano for them. It was Mozart and the simplest measures of Chopin. A pitcher of water sat on the table loaded with sliced lemons and sugar. Three glasses stood on a knitted napkin that was draped across the table. The sounds of the notes bounced off the wooden floor and plaster walls and Sophia's small fingers hesitated over certain notes—then played several notes and chords confidently and easily.

Joseph loved the sound of the piano—loved to watch the tiny fingers dance across the keys. He watched the little girl—her hair pulled in a single braid behind her head—Sarah sitting inches from him on the couch with her hands folded in her lap. He could sense the cushion depressed where she sat. They occupied the same space—listened to the same music. It was new to him, this music, and he felt overwhelmed with the sound of the notes—the texture of the soft hammer on the taut strings. He wondered, though, how it it sounded to her—how these notes sounded in her ears—what effect on her heart—and this was as important to him as the sound itself. Its effect on Sarah.

He looked at the young girl and could see that she was smiling broadly. The notes were building toward some climax—the melody dipping and changing and then repeating. The walls were washed with the window light and he saw the shapes of flowers along the papered wall and he watched as the light slipped over Sarah's face while she watched her young cousin play this music—and he knew that his world was within this room, and whatever went on outside that window at this moment mattered not at all. He could feel the thump of the singular notes.

How could this be? he thought. He could see the white lifeless face of Roger McCleod and he felt suddenly that he should be here with them in this room and hearing this music. He wondered if Roger had sat in this spot. The words, the letter—took on new life, new depth as he sensed the source in the pale shadows of the room. And he felt himself suddenly small—insignificant. As he had often felt in battle.

Joseph wondered, as he sat, how this music and this moment fit in his life. How could this little girl be of the same species as the killers in the field, of Joseph himself? Where was this music before Sarah? Where would he keep it now in a spirit so filled with sorrow and with anger? The music was like base ball. It was something that could not be explained to those who hadn't experienced it. It existed in the moment, but lingered after and was savored truly only in its own resonance in the human heart. But even as he sat there this day and did not speak to Sarah—it occurred to him that she was the moment and all the moments to come. That as the music had altered his view of the human spirit, she had altered the spirit itself and now there was no future without her. There was nothing ahead without her in his poor sight and that thought scared him more than any battle or any memory, because now there was truly something to lose. Something that, once lost, could never be replaced and as he acknowledged this in his heart he was overcome with a sadness. As the last notes thumped and rang across the room he was suddenly lonely.

The music ended and they both clapped and smiled and stood and Sarah hugged her giggling cousin. Sophia curtsied politely and more than once, pulling the pink folds of her dress from her sides, and then excused herself and ran from the room, leaving them alone. They sat again together on the couch. The shadows of afternoon filled the room and it was cool. The window beyond the piano was open slightly and a primitive screen kept a moth at bay although the gentle rattle caught the attention of both of them.

Persistent, she said, and he smiled and nodded.

I haven't heard music like that. She plays real good. I've read about Mozart—but never heard the music.

Sophia is considered quite accomplished for her age—perhaps a prodigy.

Guess I don' know what that means.

Sarah laughed and looked toward Joseph on the couch. It means she's quite good and she's quite young. She's been playing since she was four years old. Sarah hesitated and then said, And she loves it—which is what's so important, right? Like your base ball.

Maam?

You love your game don't you? I suppose you were something of a prodigy. She had settled into a corner of the couch, a white silk pillow on her lap and her hands folded on the pillow.

No, I just enjoyed it right away. Like I discovered it or somethin.

As he said this he thought for the first time that it was just a child's game and he was suddenly embarrassed by it, but he couldn't lie to her. I do love the game. I caint say exactly why but it seems to be just the right thing for me—and I guess I'm pretty good at it. It seems to—fill me up, I guess.

She watched him closely as he spoke and she was struck by the simple honesty of his words and the eyes that never wavered from hers as he spoke. When did you start to play?

As a boy, in Virginia. My friend—Terence Hooker was his name—traveled to New York, and he had a cousin who knew the game and showed it. One time Terence brought back a ball and we made our first bat out of an old ax handle. We had seen a picture of one and we carved it ourself and started to play.

As they sat together in the late afternoon, he told her of the games in the Virginia fields and in the shadow of Stone Hill and how the boys would come together for games and such, and she listened to every word—to each long southern syllable as it rolled from his mouth. She watched the curl of his lip and the movement of his eyes—upon her—and then on his own hands as he demonstrated how to grip the bat—and they sat like this for hours in the fading light of afternoon.

Sophia came back into the room and begged them to join her outside in the garden, and ran again from the room singing and almost spilling the lemon water, her pink dress flying around her as she filled the doorway of the room and vanished again—leaving Joseph and Sarah alone in the dim light. The low sun now washed azure across the surface of the piano as they talked.

He told her all about Virginia—the rugged hills, the spring meadows, the rivers. He spoke of Stone Hill and of Blackstone Farm and of his father. But they were words, nothing more. The words fell short. Descriptions of something cherished—protected. She pursued.

What of your father—where is he now?

Blackstone. I had a letter last year with a sentence or two and nothing more. When I write he doesn't write back. He never had many words to offer though. Guess he never will say much. Joseph hesitated. I'll need to go see him soon.

She reached out her hands and held his fingers in her palm. The pillow slid silently to the floor as she moved slightly closer. She noticed the length of his fingers and the coarse strength of his hands—the thick tendons of his wrists that vanished in the stiff white sleeves.

Why haven't you seen him—gone back to see him?

It's difficult for us. Always has been—least as far as I can remember. Since my mother died. He doesn't like the base ball at all. Doesn't understand what I'm doin up north. I'll go back—to see him—but I guess I caint stay.

Joseph looked down at their hands enfolded together.

It was before the war. Too much is changed.

Or perhaps nothing has changed, she said. She stood to enjoy the fading light from the window. I don't think folks change all that much. They just discover things they didn't know about themselves. Like this music, Joseph. You've heard it for the first time but I can tell by your reaction that the sound is familiar in your heart. Some folks listen a thousand times and never hear it like that.

She was still standing in the light of the window and she turned and pressed the folds of her dress down as she spoke.

I should like to hear more, she said. I should like to hear everything.

There isn't much more.

She looked at him and then turned again toward the window and sighed. It's getting late. I'm to help mother with supper.

I'm sorry—I didn't know it was late.

It's quite all right. Will I see you this week? I should like that.

Yes, if I could I mean. I have three games but I'll see you.

I'll come to at least one of them. I'm just starting to understand the rules I think.

He took her hand in his and said, Thank you, Sarah, and walked from the parlor to the hall and to the horse that was tied at the gate. She was watching from the porch as he rode away and he kept looking back until he could see that she was gone from the door. He tried to remember the tune that had been played on the piano but he couldn't so he whistled something else as he rode through the village of Rocker Falls toward Terryville and he urged the horse to move faster until he could feel the sweet air rush across his face and the rattle of the wooden wheels drowned out all other sound.

They began to see each other regularly. Slowly, she began to get glimpses of the things she knew were etched on his heart. She would wait for him after the games and they would sit on the grass and talk, and on Sunday afternoons they would sit in the parlor of her parents' house. They had come to expect each other's company and as their relationship grew from friendship to much more, their feelings about the things around them changed as well. Sometimes they would walk the narrow streets and alleys down to the river to watch the boats drift by and watch the play of the sun across the water and Sarah thought she had never seen things in quite this way. But he always could. He always seemed to notice the color of the water, the message written across the sky.

There'll be rain tomorrow. Maybe even tonight. Don't look like we'll get a game in.

How can you tell that?

And he would look up and put his hand toward the horizon. Look at the clouds all twisted up in the west, he said. Look at the sky beyond them and you can see the color run straight out like it's been painted on a ceiling. That's the light bein dragged along the bottom of the clouds. It means there's thick cover. Thick cover means rain, Sarah, and plenty of it.

There was a place where they could sit in the shade of an elm and they watched as boats of all sizes floated by, sail and steam, small and quite large. Flat barges loaded heavy with barrels and crates with men walking or standing along their surfaces as if they were standing on drifting islands recently freed from the shore.

Thomas Eagan and Mike Owens work the barges, he said. They load and unload the wooden crates. It's heavy work but they seem to think it's good work.

I know Owens from the club, but who is Thomas Eagan?

New player. Say he can throw a ball on a line from the outfield while still runnin. Haven't seen it yet, but workin the barges can't hurt. A man's got to be strong to do that. I'm sure there's a lot of things I haven't seen in this game.

You think there's more to it?

I believe so, he answered, and he took her hand and they walked again on a thin trail along the river. They were quiet as they walked, listening to the sounds of commerce along the river's edge.

Watching children throwing sticks into the flat water, imagining them great ships in an infinite sea. She spoke to him softly as she led him to a bench that had been built along the river's edge at a point where it began to bend and widen toward the city's harbor. Tell me more of Virginia. Tell me about Blackstone, she said and looked at his sun-colored face and watched as his eyes met hers and then looked out toward the unsettled horizon.

He took a deep breath, let his chest rise and settle, and put his hands flat on the bench at his sides. A breeze picked up across the water and pushed the hair from his forehead. There's not much to tell I guess. Or too much. It's all I knew. Blackstone and the Blue Ridge was all there was. The sun rose over the east pasture and set early over the hills. In between there was work, I guess. I guess that's all there is to it.

No, Joseph, there's so much more, Sarah said as she stood and looked across the river. Tell me how you felt. It's who you are, Joseph Tyler and I should like to know.

He pulled his arms up and rested them on the back of the bench. He would like to tell her everything, to have her understand everything. Black smoke came from a steamer and he watched it as it was pulled apart and made part of the clear sky.

I could always see the hills. Always. Even from my window I could see them and I felt sometimes they were there for me. Like they was somethin special put there for me. They never changed and they never stayed the same.

He paused as she sat again next to him on the bench. She could not take her eyes off his as they scanned the river and the horizon and saw things that were not there.

They lay—like the folds of your dress—shadows and colors that never seem to end. And the colors never stayed the same. In low light they were surely blue—a thousand shades of blue, and in the full sun, in the summer sun, you never seen so many colors green. There's yellow that turns green and black that's green. There's the blue-green of spruce that stand out like jewels in the forest—like somebody put them there on purpose to show off another color.

He hesitated and then continued.

I used to wear the mountains like a cloak, Sarah. I used to pull them across my shoulders as I worked the field, like they was wrapped around me and I swear they gave me strength. It was like God hisself put the weight of his hand on my shoulder as I worked. I remember my mother sayin that if you couldn't find God in this valley then you sure won't find him inside any church building.

Joseph stood now, leaving Sarah on the bench following him with her eyes as he paced slowly along the path at the river's edge.

I remember she loved Blackstone. I can remember her. She was nothin but kind to me.

I was only a small boy but I remember. Following her and listening to her soft clothes in the tall grass. She would hand me wildflowers that she cut from the ground and together we would place them in a basket. Long stems and leaves busted out of all sides of the basket and when I was sure it was full she would hand me more. She would hold them up to the sun and show me how the light passed through them and I remember once she said that in the cities they have churches and buildings with stained glass but, she said none so beautiful as this. Men work hard to fall far short of God's work, she said.

Joseph stood now—quite still. The traffic of the river had quieted and Sarah now rose to stand next to him. She stood close, so that he could feel her leaning toward his arm.

When she was gone, he continued, I never thought I'd see these things again. Not in this way. But I did. I think finding the game was part of it. Feeling the lightness I felt when I played the game . . . helped me see things again. There was a trail that led to the field where we played. The first part was rough and narrow, but as it got closer to the river it opened up and there were tall pines as far as you could see, and a thick blanket of needles that lay like feathers on the ground. I would walk through this part trying not to make a sound as I walked. Trying not to startle the deer or the bear or the fox. Sometimes I would take my time. Sometimes the sun was so strong it would flood down through the thick pine in great shafts like a waterfall and I would find a spot and lay back on the needles and let the filtered sun wash over me, only me. All this, I remember thinkin, all this goin on for me. And then we would play the game in an open field and it would all just come together. Where we played, if the wind was right, you could hear the Salmon River as it fell over the rocks.

The Blue Ridge was always there. Terence Hooker was there. We loved the game together, he and I. It lifted us both, it did.

Joseph was suddenly quiet. Sarah let her hand touch his and their fingers entwined gently. Your father? Joseph. You speak of him so little.

My father's a quiet man. He never could see no colors after my mother died. He worked is what he did. He worked the fields and built the walls. I know he saw the beauty of the stone, I know he did. But he never said. I don' know what the walls meant to him for sure. Sometimes it seemed like he saw the earth like . . . like a stubborn mule and these walls were like a yoke across it. Like if he could, he'd drape a wall across the whole earth and then be done with it. Like end to end was a life.

A family was walking down the path dressed in Sunday clothes and carrying a basket for a picnic. Joseph and Sarah greeted them and stepped out of their way as they continued down the path.

We best get back, Joseph said.

She thought she could see tears in his eyes but he quickly blinked them gone. And what do you see now, Joe Tyler?

He didn't answer right away. He looked down. I caint see clear now. I see the war. I can hear men cryin. Caint always hear the wind anymore, or make out the sound of the river.

He was looking at her now.

But I do see you, Sarah Kingsley. I see you somewhere beyond all this, like through some kind of tunnel. Like I can see you but I don't know if I can get there.

Sarah laughed quietly. I'm right here, Mr. Joseph Tyler. And I think I should like very much for you to find your way through this tunnel of yours. But for now we'll walk back to the house. Mother will have supper almost ready and I have my own work to do. Will you come next Sunday?

If you'll have me, he answered. I don't mean to take up all your time.

Somehow when I'm with you it doesn't seem like time's being taken up. Like it's a fine use of the moment.

I'm glad to hear that, Sarah. I believe I cherish every one of these moments more than you do.

They walked back to the house and Joseph bid her goodbye at the porch. Next Sunday, then, she said, and closed the door behind her.

Joseph stood for a while at the porch steps. For the first time he noticed the fragrance of the potted flowers and he breathed it in deeply before he turned and walked down the stone path toward his carriage. He closed the gate with both hands so the latch snapped easily into place, leaving the quiet of the afternoon undisturbed.

The weeks turned to months, and the winter brought another spring—a new season of the game. She loved to watch him play and sometimes she would even linger after the matches and join in the pleasant celebrations. On most Sundays he returned to her house to spend the afternoons with her. Joseph opened up a little more, but for the most part he remained quiet, and she patient. Sarah could feel him moving closer to her—yet still holding back. Protecting a part of himself as if it were a raw wound that could not bear be touched. No different, really, from the wounded flesh she had gently bandaged in the hospital—quickly pulled away in fear and pain. She would sit with the boys then—read to them, listen to them—until her touch was trusted, and even in its offering, somehow healing. Joseph loved to listen to her. She showed him new books and read to him from them and he would often leave the house in late afternoon with an armful. There was a small room off the foyer that was lined with thick shelves that held hundreds of books and Joseph loved to look at the books and read the titles embossed in gold and silver along the bindings. He would pull them from the shelves and wipe the dust from them, with his sleeve. Sometimes they were stuffed with notes written in the hand of Mr. Kingsley or his wife. Some were familiar, many of the classics—the histories—but most were not. Titles like *Hiawatha* and *Wuthering Heights*. A journal from a man named Thoreau about living in the woods. Joseph stood one day waiting for Sarah and opened a large volume that he thought was about fishing or the sea. It was heavy in his hands and he turned the thin pages carefully with his fingers. It had a curious title and so he turned to the opening text and read.

Call me Ishmael. Joseph read on and could not stop reading. He barely noticed Sarah as she entered the room and his eyes did not leave the page until she coughed quietly.

Have you read Melville?

No.

Take it with you. It's one of father's favorites, she said and put her hand gently on his shoulder.

Have you read it?

No, not yet. She hesitated and then continued. Joseph, I have something to tell you. I am going back to school, to teacher's college. I'll be leaving at the end of the month.

Joseph was surprised—stunned.

I didn't know, I mean, that's good, isn't it? You'll make a wonderful teacher.

I hope so. I won't see you, though. The college is miles away and there are—no men allowed, no visitors.

How long?

I have a semester to finish. A few months. It might take me longer. I don't know for sure. It's a new program—very exciting.

I am happy for you, Sarah. You know that.

I had hoped so.

Will I see you when you return? Will you let me know when you're back?

Of course. Besides, you'll have to return my father's book now won't you?

He smiled and she put her hands gently on his arm.

You'll need to get through this tunnel of yours, Joseph. When I return perhaps.

He didn't answer and they moved to the parlor and sat and talked quietly as the afternoon sun slid through the polished room. When it was time to leave he found he was unable to say goodbye. He squeezed her hand gently and then turned his back to her and didn't look back. It didn't do any good to be looking after someone. Terence had said it would be okay as long as he looked. But it wasn't. He squeezed the book in his hand as he walked. It wasn't.

Later that night he sat alone in his room. He lit a single candle and pulled a shawl over his legs and opened the book she had given him.

Once more. Say you are in a country; in some high land of lakes. Take almost any path you please, and ten to one it carries you down in a dale, and leaves you there by a pool in the stream. There is magic in it.

The flame of the candle fluttered and he brought it closer to the page and he read through the night—and into the morning—of the sea, and of the great whale—until Cooper came up for him and they left for a ball game and as he rode the carriage to the field he thought of the sea and of Sarah and of the thousands of things that he did not know. It was the summer of 1869 and he thought little about the game. Except for the moments he spent on the field, his thoughts were of Sarah. And of life's possibilities.

Rocker Falls, New York

The fabric of curtains wafted on a thin breeze that slid silently between the slice of white moon and the darkness of her bedroom. She turned and, wrapping her arms clear around her pillow, pulled it to her shoulders in full embrace. Her eyes opened. A shutter wrapped against the old wood of the window and she rose to clasp it and then returned to sit on the side of the bed. Despite the darkness, this room was so familiar to her she could see everything clearly as if the image of the room and the objects within it were etched in her memory, and would remain there always. Now completely awake, she watched as the weak light of the moon saturated the room as if the last oil of a lamp were being burned off and at the final second—the light was sustained, and the flame lingered long enough to turn the world to silver apparition.

This light was familiar to Sarah. She woke most nights before morning. Restless—twisted in her quilt—wide awake. And more often than not, and much more lately—her thoughts were of him—of Joseph. This night she could see him clearly. An image left from the previous afternoon. She had been there at the game, among the hundreds. She watched them in their grand uniforms. She watched and tried to understand the competition, but mostly she watched him. It was late in the game. The score was tied at twelve and it was the last chance for the Niners. The two strikers before Joseph had reached base with clean hits and one stood on the third and the other on the first base. The other team, a Boston club, brought in a special pitcher as Joseph walked up to the plate. The first throw was very fast and quite wild and she had watched as Joseph fell straight back onto the ground and then rose, dusting himself off. She looked to see his face. To see if he was all right—and she could see that he was smiling—laughing amid the cloud of dust and hollering something out to the pitcher and she could see the pitcher turn quickly to look at his outfielders and then turn to face Joseph directly. She watched his arm rise slowly and then whip down in a circle to his waist. She watched Joseph's smile melt, and then freeze in a determined grin as the bat flew from around his shoulder and the ball erupted in its path and she could see only the shadow as it crossed the pitcher's face and shot into the grass between the fielders with such ferocity that the fielders did not even move until the ball had vanished into the taller grass of the outfield and the extra players on the Boston team rose from the bench and hollered at them to give chase. They waved their hats and almost came onto the field and Rooster Nash was the first one to greet Joseph as he crossed the white canvas of the home plate. The rest of the Niners were all jumping up and down and hollering. And she watched Joseph. She watched his face. She could see the elation—the joy in his expression. Would he ever feel that again—off the field? They never found the ball, she thought.

She recalled, in her sleeplessness, one of his early visits. She had asked him to read Roger's letter to her—that she might hear it from a soldier's voice. She had told her that she would close her eyes and try to imagine that it was Roger McCleod reading these words to her—given one last chance to speak to her. Sarah could see him—sitting with her in the parlor. It was afternoon. Joseph opened the letter carefully in his lap and she saw it so small, worn, familiar in his hands. She watched as he slowly pressed it in his lap with his palm and began to read it out loud in the late light of afternoon. She closed her eyes and listened to the words—and they enfolded her like an embrace and as she listened she opened her eyes to look at Joseph and she could see in the gray light that his eyes were closed as well. She began to weep silently as she watched him recite the letter word for word—pretending to read—and she imagined him lying on the cold ground of prison, reading it. In the nights when all else was filled with sadness and rage, he had said, he would open the letter and read it to himself and he could feel the words rest on his heart and he would be able, finally, to sleep.

Now, as she sat again alone in her room, she could see him with the fire at his back and her Roger in his arms and she could see him with the letter in his hands, surrounded by war—death, and clenching it as if it were a lifeboat, he had said, and he would cling to it as he would the shore and tears formed in her eyes now as she thought of him reciting the letter with closed eyes in the dim parlor that day. And here, in her room—embraced by night—she wept. For Joseph—and for all he had seen. For young Roger who had not returned. For the boys in the hospital whose limbs and lives had been torn from them—whose sad letters she had read and written. And finally for herself. For the love she was beginning to feel for him and the long road to his tired heart. Would she ever be able to make him smile like she had seen him smile that afternoon? Was there any joy for him besides that?

She lay back on her bed and cried. She would try. She would finish her schooling and see if the time apart would help them. There was no road too long. She was determined to try. And as the first hint of morning swept into the room and spilled dim shadows along the walls—she quieted. And with a determined breeze filling the curtains of her window as it would the sails of a ship—she rested—and finally slept, in the hours before she was to leave.

III.

To the garden. The world anew ascending.
—Walt Whitman

It was September and Sarah had been gone for almost six weeks. In her absence, he concentrated as much as he could on the game. It seemed like the only thing he had any control over and he always enjoyed his time on the field. He had received one letter from her and written many. Her words were sweet and brief. She seemed to like school. She asked about the games.

The Niners were due to play a team from Maryland and Joseph had heard how some southern boys had joined the club—from Tennessee and Virginia—and he heard the club was doing well on its tour against the teams from New York and New Jersey. There were now about twenty-five base ball clubs in the area of New York and there seemed to be more sprouting up every time you turned. Joseph couldn't wait for the club from Maryland, to see how the southern boys were doing with the game. He heard there was a club in New Orleans now too.

He was on the field early with Mike Owens and they were tossing the ball back and forth and taking little hits that some called "pepper" from one bat to the other. The Maryland club began to show up in groups of two and three—in carriages and on horses. Some of the men had stayed together in an inn next to the train station, while others were just arriving this afternoon. Joseph watched them closely as they pulled base ball equipment from carriages and dragged bags of bats and balls from behind the seats of the carriages toward the field. He listened for familiar accents and he heard a couple of unmistakable drawls from the varied conversations across the field.

Two more men rode up on a small carriage and Joseph watched them unloading a couple of canvas bags. He could see that the face of one of the men was disfigured—badly burnt and distorted—and he looked away quickly. He had heard that there was a boy playing in Philadelphia who only had two fingers left and a one-armed man up in Buffalo playing for one of the small clubs up there, but other than that the game and the war had not intersected for Joseph. He did not know if this wound was from the war, but it was not old, and he figured as much.

More boys began to show up and the club managers called all the boys over to talk as they did before each game. They discussed the latest rule changes and the arrangement for food and drink after the match and they shook hands and took to the field. Joseph noticed the man again. The skin of the left side of his face was pink and thick and his one eye was almost closed. The boy was laughing, though, and talking out of the corner of his mouth from a twisted smile. Joseph looked away again and took to the field.

He was playing center field today. His speed was famous around the clubs and he caught everything he could get to but his success at pitching kept him from the outfield most games. They were playing with the new fly rule—that if the ball bounded before it reached the fielder the runner was safe—so the outfielders were becoming more and more important and the skill of catching a ball in the air was a key to a club's success. With bare-handed catching, this was another rule to favor the striker and would account for a lot of high scores. There was some talk of gloves. Word was there was a catcher in Cincinnati who was wearing some kind of glove fashioned from leather straps, but most of this talk was laughed off. Bare hands was the rule.

The first batter popped the ball lazily to the infield and there was one hand down when the boy with the burnt face approached the plate. Joseph could see that although the left eye was badly damaged it was still in use and the striker was set in full concentration. He watched as the boy set his feet and peered across the field like a hunter would look across the wood-land for a sense of prey. He seemed to look at each fielder as he set his feet, balanced, on the ground and steadied the bat in his hands. He watched as Alexander Cooper moved three steps to his right off the second base and he saw the quick movement of the bat as the ball was hit sharply to the exact spot that Coop had just been standing then rolled to Joseph over the rough ground. Joseph threw it in to second base and the runner clapped his hands together and yelled from first, Shouldn't have moved.

Joseph could hear a trace of the South in his voice as he yelled. Coop yelled back that the damn ball appeared to be aimed.

The boy on first yelled back, laughing, from the corner of his twisted mouth, Well I sure as hell weren't gowna hit it where you stood, and a shiver crept across Joseph's shoulders as he recognized the voice—and the unmistakable arrogance. It was Billy Spence.

Hold on, Joseph called out, and the men turned to watch him trot toward the first base. Joseph stopped a few feet from Billy and stood still. Joseph could see that along with the pink swollen scar and the features that seemed to be pulled and smeared across the side of his face, Billy had no hair. Joseph took his own cap off and fought back tears as he spoke.

Billy Spence.

The boy looked at Joseph for a long moment through thin and squinted eyes until the mouth twisted into a smile.

Joe Tyler.

There was hesitation and then the two embraced there on the field for seconds and then stepped away from each other.

Surprised you recognized me, Billy said.

I almost didn't—but I never seen a man could aim a ball like you, Billy. Never did and never will. Joseph paused and was shaking his head from side to side and trying to look through the distorted skin to see the boy in front of him. What happened?

Served with Pickett at Gettysburg. I was one of the lucky ones.

There was silence and then the other men started to call for them to get back to the game and Joseph returned slowly to the field and he could hear Billy Spence hollering to the next striker to move him on the bases and the game continued.

In the ninth inning the score was tied 32–32 and there was one hand down when Coop called for Joseph to come in and pitch. Show em your stuff reb, Cooper said to him quietly as he tossed him the ball.

The first batter was the Maryland pitcher, Clinton Bogues, and Joseph served up one of his slow pitches that seemed to float and die in the air before it reached the plate and Bogues grounded it weakly to the third base and was thrown down easily by Mike Owens. There were two hands down as Billy Spence picked up the bat and walked slowly to the white plate that had been driven in the ground with two spikes.

Seems familiar, don't it, Joe Tyler?

That it does, Billy. We been here.

Well show me what you've learned—what you got, Billy said, and put the bat under his arm and spit in the palms of his hands and rubbed them together before he gripped the bat.

You seen what I got Billy, I just got more of it. They both laughed and it was if none of the other boys existed on the field and the two of them were there together facing each other in an old contest. The months, the years— vanished.

Well, you're right there Joe—I seen it.

I aint movin.

Didn spect you were. Suit yerself Joe Tyler.

The first pitch was thrown low and bounced off the ground before it even reached the area of the home plate. Joseph shook his head as the catcher retrieved the ball and tossed it back to him. This time Joseph took a moment. Not a moment, really, but seconds. Enough in the pace of a contest to pause and to see more clearly the task. Like the moment his father would pause to see the stone and the light across it. He set his feet and breathed in deeply and let the air out of his chest slowly. The ball was held in both hands at the level of his chest as rocked gently backward. Joseph let his right arm drop quickly and then whipped it forward to his waist and let the ball fly from his hand just beneath the belt, toward the home plate and Billy Spence. Spence watched with his squinted eyes and let the bat move as if unavoidably drawn to the ball. Joseph's eyes followed the sagging flight of the white ball as it turned toward the plate and he could see it in the instant it cracked against the wooden bat and he could see that the direction of the ball appeared not to change but that the round object grew larger again and at the last second, through instinct only, his hands jolted up to his face and he felt the ball slam against his palms and fingers and his hands were forced backward with the force of the ball's movement, and his hands hit his chin and he was aware of the ball rolling from his fingers to the ground. He reached down, picked it up with his right hand and in the same motion threw it to the first base, but he could see Billy already touching the bag with his foot and clapping and smiling broadly with the half-grin that now seemed as full as any man's.

You should've moved Tyler.

If I had, it would've been a two-bagger, Joseph called over, shaking his head. That is the damndest thing.

He shook his hands because they ached slightly from the force of the struck ball. He rubbed the base ball between his hands when it was thrown back to him. Damndest thing, he said again to himself as he readied for the next striker.

After the game they sat together under the broad, thick canopy of sugar maples and cottonwoods and sipped beer from thick mugs. Terryville had gone on to win the game in the bottom of the ninth and now the clubs were eating and drinking together and sharing stories about the game. Some of them were true and some were not but they all were part of the fabric of base ball as it grew every day in contests like this one across the country. Joseph sat for a while silently next to Billy Spence. He tried to think of what to say but he was uncomfortable and hesitant. In the shade the wound looked even more horrible and if it hadn't been for the game Joseph knew that he would have never recognized Billy.

Billy drank down a full beer and put the mug in the grass between them as he belched loudly and chuckled. You fight? he asked Joseph.

Pegram's brigade. Mostly in the wilderness. I didn't last long though. I took a shoulder wound and ended up a prisoner.

How was that?

Wasn good.

How'd you end up in New York?

Prison. I guess the prisons down there were full so they shipped us up here. They put us in a train and let us out at Elmira. Not everyone survived the trip and those who did weren't too sure they were the lucky ones. Spent some months there—in that hell pit—till I got out, but that's another story. Anyway, I met up with Alexander Cooper there after the war was over and I hooked up with him to play ball.

How bout any of the other boys? You heard?

No. I aint been back but I aim to go soon. Your family? They all survive?

Lost a brother at Shiloh. Might as well of lost my folks. Breaks their hearts to see me so I think they're glad I stay away . . . You? How bout Terence Hooker? You guys were like brothers.

My father's still at Blackstone. Hooker was with me—but I lost him. We joined up together in '64 but we got separated and I lost him.

Killed?

I don' know. He went out on patrol and never came back. We were attacked that afternoon and had to scramble and I never saw him again. I give em my boots and never saw them again neither.

Maybe he'll show up. I hear stories of fellas just comin home now.

Don't guess so.

A black dog came and sat in the cool grass next to them panting. He licked at the empty beer mug and Billy chased him away.

Joseph looked at Billy's eyes. What happened to you?

I was in the first charge. Pickett was a damn crazy man but we loved him and we'd follow him into hell if he'da asked us and that's pretty much what we did. I saw the damn cannonball comin and I dropped down and I thought I was a dead man but the thing fell short and opened up the earth in front of me. Somehow the grass was burnin and my damn hair started on fire and I continued the fight—brought the fight right to the yanks with my head on fire. They tell me I was still runnin at the yanks and they stopped firing their rifles as they watched me and I guess I fell and passed out after that. Don't remember much else. When I got home my mama couldn't even look at me and I was walkin around like a freak and I couldn't much figure what to do until I heard about the new base ball club and I went and tried out. They put me on the second nine until I showed them how I could hit, just like I showed you Joe Tyler and I've been on the first nine since. With the bat in my hand, it don't seem to matter too much. On the field I'm just one of the boys.

I'm sorry.

I can still hit. I'm here, aint I? That what you're sorry about?

Joseph laughed quietly. You sure can do that.

Gilmore, third baseman, was there. He was behind the wall at the battle with the Pennsylvania artillery.

You talk about it?

Not much—don't think it does much good to talk about it.

I don't understand much of it, Joseph said as he looked up to the cover of leaves over their heads and watched a breeze shiver through them. The black dog returned and lay in the grass next to them and slept.

Don' spect we ever will, Joe Tyler. Guess it aint for us to understand. Damn, somehow I knew I'd see you again on a ball field Tyler. You see how the game's growin?

I've seen it. I love this game.

There was five thousand people at our game in New Jersey last week, maybe more. There was ladies there and rich folks and kids. That's what to think about. I'll spend the rest of my life with people turnin away from the sight of my face but I thank God for the chance—to walk, alive from the field of battle—to play this game again. To feel the sun on my neck and look for the gaps in the field between the fielders and run like hell once the ball's struck and watch em chase it. God I love that. I can still feel the sun, still taste the beer, still see clear as day that ball skate across the green grass. That's what to think about now. Everything else is behind us.

They talked like that for over an hour. The Maryland team was heading back to Brooklyn to play the Excelsiors and Terryville had two days off before their next game against Hoboken. The two shook hands and then embraced again as they said goodbye.

Wasn't so long ago was it? Joseph said, and Billy Spence said yes it was and walked toward the wagon with a bag of base ball equipment draped over his shoulder.

Joseph worked that night stocking the shelves and cleaning in the grocery. With Sarah gone he did everything he could to keep busy and he had taken on extra hours. The next day he traveled to Rocker Falls. It was less than an hour's carriage ride in good weather and the sky was clear and Joseph had taken this ride so often that he recognized every tree as he passed it along the road. As he approached the village he could see the new schoolhouse and the post office and he rode past the houses tucked together, each with small lawns and rows of flowers along stepping-stones and statues and flags and a few folks recognized him and waved as he passed.

He rode past the *Morning Star* office and across a small wooden bridge that crossed the diverted river leading to the textile mill and a new factory that was being built. Stones had been pushed and mortared along the steep banks of the ravine and the water ran in a thin line toward the mill and disappeared in a fierce waterfall. He could hear the sound of the water and he looked up and as he did he could see a broad open gravel space with thin patches of grass emerging here and there along it. He could see on the far edge of the clearing, in the shadow of the large mill, a group of boys playing ball and shouting to each other as they played. Joseph pulled up the carriage on the bridge and watched for a few moments before he continued to Sarah's house. Everything else is behind us, he thought and listened to the clatter of the wheels along the road.

When he arrived at Sarah's door he allowed himself to hope that she would be there—that the door would swing open and she would be standing there smiling and invite him in. But he could see through the thick glass lights along the door the blurred figure of Alexander Kingsley.

Joseph, he said immediately. Come in. We're delighted to see you—do come in. Delighted—it's been very quiet.

I haven't heard . . . from her, sir. In a few weeks. He was saying this even as he entered, still shaking her father's hand. I came to see how she is, how you all are.

Like you, Joe Tyler, we'll be better when she's back. They're very strict there. During exams they are only allowed to write to family. We received a letter on Tuesday, I believe. Most of it was asking about you, I'm afraid, he called this back as he left the room. Let me tell my wife you're here.

She'll be anxious to see you again I'm sure.

When Mr. Kingsley returned he was smiling.

Mrs. Kingsley will see you in the garden if you don't mind. And then he added, holding his hand to the side of his mouth in a joking manner, This is where she does all her profound thinking, I'm afraid.

He led Joseph down the narrow hallway covered in framed photos and other small pictures through a bright room that led to the kitchen—and out through the screen door. They were then in an outdoor corridor formed by the space between the house and the carriage house—cool and narrow as it emptied to the backyard through an arch painted white and covered with the woody tendrils of ivy.

As he passed under the arch following Sarah's father he noticed the detail and it reminded him of some of his own father's woodwork and he slowed slightly to admire it again before entering the full sun of the yard. As he entered the yard he could smell instantly the fragrance of blossoms and saw the sun washing across a multitude of flowers in masses and in rows: daylily, hibiscus, sweet william, and the deep purple and pink of bleeding heart filled the shadows along a white lattice fence that bordered the entire yard. He saw Mrs. Kingsley's back half shielded by a straw hat that not only covered herself but shaded a large part of the ground around her. On the hat's brim were tied sprays of dried lavender.

There was a path made of irregular clay bricks set in a herringbone pattern and the spaces between the bricks were swollen with thick moss. Along the path sat a tin bucket filled with dry green weeds from the garden and the woman continued to work with a pointed tool that chewed into the soft soil and loosened the roots of unwanted growth.

One moment please, he heard her say. If I leave this now I'll not get back to it.

Joseph turned to look across the yard. A structure of great white beams, a pergola, divided the sunlight into linear shafts along the thick grass, covered in climbing roses of red and pink and shading a small fountain where silver water trickled from an overturned pitcher held carelessly in a child's hand, all carved or molded from stone, chiseled like his father had done so carefully shaping wood.

The woman rose and turned to them, wiping her palms gently on a burgundy apron that hung around her waist and up around her shoulders. She wiped her hands together and used both of them to fix the position of her hat on her head before she reached them both to him, saying, Joseph. Good to see you again. We've been learning more about you . . . in the letters since she's been gone. Do you enjoy my garden, then?

It's beautiful, Joseph said.

The woman watched him collect the colors of the garden in his mind. Ah, Virginia though, she said. You have beautiful azaleas I have heard, and the woodland trees must be magnificent.

Joseph nodded, thinking of the dogwood and the wildflowers that he had taken so much for granted. He looked at Sarah's mother and was startled, as he had been the first time he had seen her, to see Sarah's eyes and the soft curves of her face, though rounded and textured with time. She had white hair, no trace of color, and it was in magnificent contrast to the sun-darkened skin. Seeing her made him miss Sarah even more.

Did you plant them all? He asked this as he knelt on the path to feel the soft silver of the woolly lamb's ears that touched the edges of the brick and seemed to shine from within.

With Sarah's help, every plant. I'm afraid Mr. Kingsley isn't much of a gardener although he does quite admire roses. She reached deep into the pockets of her apron and out of the left one pulled small pruning shears. The men watched as she walked to the rose trellis and cut the stems of three blossoms from the bush. She laid the green stems in the shallow pool of the fountain. I'll bring them inside later, she said. Come and sit. Alexander, would you get us a pitcher of iced tea? I made some this morning Mr. Tyler and I'm sure you'll enjoy it.

Thank you maam, was all he could think to say as they sat there in the garden.

They sat quietly for a moment as Mr. Kingsley left them and went into the kitchen.

She's harmless, Joseph, he heard him say, but watch yourself. It will be like facing a wild pitcher. He heard Mr. Kingsley laughing as the screen door slammed shut behind him and startled a bluebird that fluttered up from the rosebushes and disappeared in the clear sky beyond the white lattice.

Pay him no mind, she said, smiling. She continued, Many of the neighbors think my gardens are quite scandalous. I believe there should be a random element, not so ordered.

He nodded. I wouldn't know, he tried to say.

I have no problem letting the pink goat's beard spill into the rudbeckia and the red and yellow roses mix as they please, you see. I think it's wrong to work so hard at order, as if order had any real merit in the garden.

She used her palms to press the apron across her knees.

It's too much, she continued, to have everything so ordered, so neat, and when we turn our backs the flowers mix anyway and who are we to say they shouldn't? At least that's how I feel.

She hesitated and looked closely at Joseph's face. And what about you Mr. Tyler? Do you like things ordered? Or do you enjoy the random nature of things?

I wouldn know about these things maam, Joseph answered. All I know is your gardens look beautiful maam and if they're random, then random's fine with me.

She chuckled to herself and fixed her hat to keep the sun off her face. According to Sarah, you know a great deal young man.

How's that?

She's quite taken with you, you know—and she believes you see many things quite clearly, and understand more than you own up to.

Joseph thought on this. He was growing uncomfortable, but he saw no way out. I guess I believe there is some overall plan to things—that somehow God sorts out random and order when he wants to, and lets it be when it oughta be.

Interesting, she said. She was watching him, watching his eyes and obviously waiting for him to say more. With her fingers, she pulled some hair from her eyes.

I've surely seen the face of God, Joseph said quietly, across a Virginia pasture on April mornins, and in the last light a day. Like the breath a God rustlin through the trees at last light. Joseph hesitated, and then continued. And I've seen across the faces of men . . . no sign of the shadow of God . . . may's well been creatures as men—and not any creatures that no God would claim. I've seen both these things as clear as I see you right now, Mrs. Kingsley, and I tell you, I have a hard time with it. A hard time puttin things in order. Seems sometimes the livins random—and the dyin—the dyin seems ordered.

And you think these things should be reconciled? That they can be?

I always thought I would see the whole deal one day, and be able to feel it clear. . . . But the only time anything's clear is when I'm playin base ball, and when I'm doin anything at all with Sarah.

Mrs. Kingsley laughed quietly as she folded her hands together on her lap. Her expression became more serious. Do you think you know Sarah? she asked. Do you think you understand her?

No maam, Joseph answered, and he watched the mild surprise in her face. I really don't know much at all maam, know much less than when I was a boy on my father's farm. But I understand some things now—that it's not the knowin that's the thing, but tryin to know, tryin with all your heart to understand a thing, so that there's a measure of it in your heart, whether it's known or not. That we let it through the understandin of it . . . and let it rest in our heart. With your daughter, Mrs. Kingsley, with Sarah, well she wrapped herself so tight around my heart . . . and I aim to take full measure of her . . . as long as it takes, and hereafter, cause there's God shinin across her face if ever there was . . . and when I look upon her, maam, there's order and there's random and there's roses and everything else you could think of that you could call good, rolled up in one.

Mrs. Kingsley let out a great unexpected laugh and put her arm around him and said to her husband as he brought the tea with three glasses of ice that had been shaved from a block delivered the day before: Sarah was right dear. He knows a great deal, for a young man. Her mother rose from the bench where she had sat next to Joseph. Now I have an idea what they were talking about, all those afternoons in the parlor. Bring the roses in dear, when you come in, would you. I've had too much sun. The blue vase I think, is empty—and she walked from them toward the house.

Alexander Kingsley put his arm around Joseph's broad shoulders. You okay son? He was smiling and lighting a cigar.

Yessir.

Would you like a cigar?

No sir. Thank you.

You've been playin well son. I saw the end of Monday's game. Quite a catch.

Thank you.

We're printing the statistics in the paper now. Have you seen them?

No sir.

Stop by the office someday. I'll put some aside for you.

Thank you.

Do you know where it is?

Yessir.

Very well then. Can you sit for a while?

No—I have to work at the grocery tonight sir.

Well then another time son. I'll show you to the door.

As Joseph was leaving Mr. Kingsley spoke to him again, this time with his hand on Joseph's shoulder. I trust your intentions with Sarah are noble, son. She has been through much.

Yessir. We've all been through it sir. And he almost saluted as he turned away and the door was closed behind him.

It was October when she returned for a few weeks. The Niners were in the playoffs for the regional title and he had spotted her as he was taking the field in the second game against the Philadelphia club. She was with her father and they both waved as he stopped and looked their way. He walked toward the grandstands that were set out with red, white and blue bunting and stood at the field's edge. There were a few hundred fans sitting along narrow benches and all talking at once, it seemed.

Sarah, he called. And she made her way toward the front of the crowd.

She put her hand out and he held it firmly between his. Neither of them said anything more.

Lets go, reb, somebody called, and there were whistles and laughs from the crowd as he stayed for a moment holding her hand, and then cheers as he returned to the playing field. The game was won by the Niners that afternoon, but Joseph could barely concentrate and could not even remember the score when he was asked later. He recalled striking the ball—but he couldn't even remember running the bases. He could not find her in the crowd after the game.

When he arrived at her house her father answered the door with a broad smile and said, Joe Tyler. We were just talking about you. Come in.

He looked around the room but Sarah was not present. There was a man in a dark gray three-piece suit sitting on a chair by the ornate fire-place. He held a derby hat in his hand and a bow-tie was loose around his collar. He had a neatly trimmed mustache that ended in a thick beard and his hair was parted in the middle and neatly combed and oiled. As Joseph entered the room behind Mr. Kingsley, the man rose from the seat and extended his hand, Rebel Joe Tyler. Pleased to meet you son.

Alexander Kingsley put a hand on Joseph's shoulder. Joseph this is a fellow newspaperman—a friend of mine—Mr. Henry Chadwick.

Joseph recognized the name immediately. Pleased to meet you Mr. Chadwick, Joseph replied.

Henry Chadwick was a reporter who had been writing about base ball since the forties. He had helped write the rules with the old Knickerbockers and was already hard at work on a book of rules. Some of the boys already called him the father of base ball. He was very critical of many of the new developments in the game. He preferred, as he wrote in his columns, the short well-placed hit over the long ball. He did not believe the players should be paid shares and he fought desperately against the wave of professionalism that was taking over the games. In his articles he celebrated the purity and gentle nature of the game of base ball and Joseph had enjoyed reading his column.

I've enjoyed watching you play, Joe Tyler. They say you learned the game down south.

Yessir, Joseph answered. We knew the game—but we got the rules from up here. We were busy playin and I guess folks up here was figurin out what it was we were playin.

Chadwick and Sarah's father laughed. Chadwick said, I saw Alexander Cartwright play in '46. He made up most of the rules. Paced off the bases himself—thirty paces. Now there was a gentleman base ball player, son.

I've heard that sir.

The game was all skill—thinking—small hits to different fields. It was considered bad taste to try to get the batter, out you know. It was a striker's game.

I've heard that too sir, but I guess the hitters had their chance and now us pitchers are havin ours sir. Seems like there's more to it.

I guess so, Chadwick answered, and asked Joseph to sit down. Sarah's father opened up a box of cigars and offered one to each of them but Joseph said no thanks and sat at the edge of the couch. There was still no sign of Sarah.

I've watched you pitch, the snap. It reminds me of Creighton.

Thank you sir. I've heard he was the best.

I was at the game. Brooklyn, October '62. Don't think I ever saw a ball hit that hard in those days. We were watching the ball and Creighton was rounding third and as I looked up I could see him stumble and fall and then he lay there flat on his face while the fielders still chased the ball. By the time anyone reached him he was dead. Just like that.

I've heard that, Joseph said. Never was sure it was true.

I was there, son. They say it was a burst internal organ, appendix maybe. I say he reached too far—just over the edge of the game—and it killed him.

Guess you know better than most, Mr. Chadwick.

Chadwick looked at him with his dark eyes and Joseph felt like he was looking right though him. Have you heard about what's going on out in Cincinnati son?

Heard somethin. I don' know much about it.

There's an advertisement in our newspapers looking for professional players. Seems like Aaron Champion has hired old Harry Wright to put the best players available on a full payroll. What do you think of that son?

Don't think about it at all sir. I just love the game—and I let other folks figure what's best to do. I don' think my shoulder's gonna last much longer anyway sir.

Well son, I'll tell you what I think.

Joseph thought that Mr. Chadwick must tell an awful lot of folks what he thinks whether they're interested or not.

I think if Wright fields the Red Stocking team with professionals—the game as we know it will be over, that's what I think. He hesitated.

Mr. Kingsley lit his cigar and joined in, You're exaggerating again, Henry, he laughed. You think these boys can play this game like gentlemen if they're living like peasants. I don't think so Henry. The game is growing too fast to try to keep it an amusement for wealthy patrons.

It will lose much more than its innocence if we let all the players become professionals. That I'll guarantee you, Alexander.

Joseph rose from his seat. I understand and I don't disagree sir. This game has meant an awful lot to me and it never meant anything about money. But folks got to live.

Exactly. But keep the game separate. That's the game we both love.

At that moment Sarah entered the room. She was surprised to see Joseph with her father and Henry Chadwick. I didn't even know you were here, Joseph.

I'm afraid we were talking base ball Sarah, but I do believe Joseph would rather talk about anything with you. Her father smiled and flicked an ash off his cigar. We'll go outside in the garden. You two can sit here.

Pleased to meet you Joe Tyler. I enjoy watching you play the game.

Thank you sir. I enjoy reading what you write.

Remember what I said about the Cincinnati Red Stockings. Our game will be over after that. I guarantee you everything will change.

Yessir. I'm not sure you're wrong if it's true.

The two men left the room and Sarah came and sat next to him on the couch.

You didn't wait after the game, he said.

She looked down before she spoke.

I've not felt well this week. Well, no, it's not that.

Joseph could see her face was drawn and sad and he felt in his heart an unfamiliar sadness.

Tell me what it is Sarah.

She lifted her head and looked at him.

You know I care for you Joseph, but you seem so . . . so unhappy. Except when you're playing base ball you seem so sad. I feel I know only half of you, and the other half is still back in the war. Even your letters are like this. You hold so much back from me.

It's hard, Sarah, for me to forget it. I think a lot about the war, and I caint talk about it much, specially to you. It's like I need to keep it separate.

She rose from the chair and pressed the folds of her dress down as she stood. Well, I think you'll need to talk to me about these things or we'll never get past this, and then there's no reason for us to see each other anymore is there Joseph? Things can't be separated. These are the things that make us who we are. All the good and all the bad. That's who we are. And you and I will be no more than friends if you keep me from knowing that part of you.

She turned and walked from the room. She held her hand to her eyes as she left. Show yourself out Mr. Tyler. I'm sure you must have a base ball game to attend.

Joseph stood and watched her leave the room. He wanted to call out and follow her, but he couldn't. Chadwick was putting his coat on in the hall and Joseph tried to leave quickly—before he was seen again.

Remember what the game was, Joe Tyler. It won't be better, and we'll lose what it was.

Joseph didn't say anything as he closed the door behind him and hurried down the path and away from the house. He had games to attend, she was right. He would play, because that was what he did. The game he loved, clearly.

It was later that same month. The playing fields were already thick with frost, and slick, and the nights came early over Terryville and Rocker Falls, New York. She was leaving again—for more exams at school—and on the afternoon before she was to leave he called on her again. It was raining and cold as the fall slowly gave in to winter and she invited him in and took his drenched coat and draped it over an iron stand by the fire. He wore no hat and his hair was matted against his head and she had to laugh quietly at his appearance. Sarah and Joseph stood in the room together and this time he took both her hands in his and spoke quietly.

I'll find a way . . . to speak of all this.

Before he could say more she took one hand from where it rested in his and held a finger to her lips. Don't speak unless it is from the heart, Joseph. It is wrong of me to ask you to put into words that which is burned into your soul. Forgive me.

She did not take her eyes away from his while she raised her hand and placed it gently on his bearded cheek. It is just that it is something that lies between us, Joseph. And I fear it always shall.

She pulled her hand away and folded her arms in front of herself, shivering from the dampness of the day. She turned slightly away, to feel the warmth of the single log burning in the fireplace. She could hear outside that rain persisted. Without turning back to him she said, But I have no right to ask. I'm sorry.

Joseph moved away and sat down in a high-back chair near the fireplace. His elbows dropped to his knees and his hands were folded together under his chin. He rubbed his knuckles slowly on the trimmed hair of his beard and thought how far he was from the battlefield. Sitting here in this room with her must be a different world from that one. The sweet smell of her, the sweet smell of Sarah was enough for him at this moment. How could he possibly put into words what he thought and what he saw? Why should she hear this? How can this gentle soul understand the battle and the rage.

The war is over, he said. I'll leave it be.

No, Joseph. Not for those of you who fought it. It rages still—and I should like to help you. To help carry you from this fire that still burns inside you. I want so much to understand, so that I might be of comfort to you.

She let her weight settle into the chair near him. She held her hands folded on her lap, twisting the fabric of her dress in her fingers. But you need not tell me anything. It's only that I believe the unspoken words are often harder to bear than those that are spoken—and if I could, Joseph Tyler, I would share that burden gladly.

She rose and walked across the room toward the window. Her back was to him. She did not want him to see her tears. What help could tears be? The rain had lessened and the sky was white with streaks of returning light.

Joseph spoke, very slowly, without lifting his chin from his hands. She leaned on the edge of the piano as he spoke and she watched him. His eyes closed slightly as if straining against a light too bright and he looked straight ahead, not at her, as he spoke. These boys—who are now in the ground. These boys should be here with us. They should know again the lightness of the spirit like I do at times. I know there were causes and maybe some of them were worth a fight—but these boys who lay in the ground ought to have understood better. It ought to have been more clear how bad the dyin would be. I caint help but think their mothers and their wives and their daughters should have kept them home and they'd be dreamin dreams now like I sometimes do. Between the nightmares I do dream and I wish these boys could dream again.

He hesitated and looked directly at Sarah. Virginia was all I knew—and the fight came to us. I was a kid and I could see the dust of the cannon and the wagons risin over the ridge and I would sit with Terence and we would wonder how it would be—ridin horses—with brave men into battle. In the end it was nothin like that at all. There was just fear.

He paused and breathed, as if thankful he could.

I read now in the papers about the great battles. Well, there were no great battles that I saw, not to the soldier—just tryin to live—to cut another man before he cuts you, shoot before gettin shot. To watch the surprise on a man's face as his life flies from him. To see tears in the enemy's eyes—to be so close you could actually see the tears. I don't see that in the newspapers. That's what the war was.

He stood now and turned his back to her.

The whole story of the war was written across Terence's face the last time I seen him. He was going—volunteered I guess—and he wanted to be brave and to know some of the glory—but I could tell that what he really wanted was to stay with me in camp. Splittin wood and stackin it and buildin some kind of stockade. We used to split wood together some-times back home. One would help the other so we'd get finished earlier to play ball before the sun went down. I could tell as he was leavin that that's all he wanted really. To stay with me and split wood and leave the glory to someone else.

Joseph paused again and turned to face her. There was a pitcher of sar-saparilla and Sarah poured a glass for him and he drank half of it down before he he set the glass on the small table and continued.

Your Roger—he was scared. I could see it in his eyes. The fire was close and his hair was singed when I got to him. I bet he was lyin there thinkin of you, Sarah, as he waited to die in those flames. I couldn't do much. I saved him for a few hours before he died.

She turned to the piano and picked up the framed picture he had seen there on the first day he walked in this room. This is him. This is Roger.

Joseph held the picture in his hands. He did not tell her, but it looked nothing like the man who lay waiting to die on the battlefield. He had been very changed. He said, He was a good man, your Roger.

You didn't know him.

I read his words. I couldn't save him—but I swear his words saved me. I meant to save him and was him saved me.

What a noble thing to do, Joseph, she said as she took the picture from his hands. After all you had seen—to pull the enemy from the fire. He was a good man, Joseph, and so are you. You did the right thing when the world around you was all wrong. Filled with wrong.

After I read the letter—I wished even more that I could've saved him, could've let more than his words live. Maybe I coulda done more. I don' know. I think sometimes of what I coulda done.

They sat then, together in the parlor as the light of another day faded. Across the autumn sky the sun appeared low on the horizon, wringing the last rain from the thin clouds.

I caint talk about it, and I caint keep it no longer Sarah. It aint easy to talk about.

You can talk to me, Joseph. About the war . . . about everything. I would like that very much, Joseph Tyler. I should like to hear all of it— every thought, every word that's been pressed to your heart.

I'll find a way then. I'll find a way. He let his shoulders sag into the cushion.

She placed her hand gently on his. The rain had stopped and they sat there together as the orange sun gave way to a silver moon that lit the village streets, the square lawns, the fences—and ran like water through the canyons between one layer of brick and another—curling finally over the thick paint of the windows and lay spilled across the wooden floor of the room where they sat—fervent and alive.

I should like that very much, she repeated and rested her head on his shoulder in the silver light.

A Thing Sacred

In the tranquil landscape, and especially in the distant
line of the horizon, man beholds somewhat as beautiful
as his own nature.
                    —Ralph Waldo Emerson

I.

New York City, 1871

A light rain had fallen during the night and puddles of water lay like a thin membrane against the cobblestone curbs and in the ruts of the gravel street. Shop owners were opening their places of business and the jingle of entry bells could be heard as the doors were opened and left open to air. Some of the storefronts were being decorated with green and white bunting in anticipation of the St. Patrick's Day celebration. It had been a very good year for the city businesses and the coming year would be even better as New York recovered from the financial exhaustion of the war. Veterans hung red, white, and blue sheets from the windows of their apartments. Some were in their old uniforms for the city celebration and while many of them fit, others were pulled to bursting around thickening waists and shoulders.

Joseph walked down Thirteenth Street away from the train station with his hands buried in the pockets of his trousers and his collar turned up against the chill air. One hand was wrapped around the written notice he had received asking him to attend a meeting of baseball players at Collier's

Café in New York, and he had left Rocker Falls early this morning.

New York was a conglomeration of new construction carelessly mixed with old. A combination of brick and timber—of the soft brownstone from Portland, Connecticut, the polished glass of the northern mills, southern pine used for framing—the place was exploding with construction and Joseph looked around him in all directions to see the sometimes passionate, sometimes casual architecture of the burgeoning city. He looked into the great glass windows and saw women cleaning tables— men and women cleaning—setting up displays of dry goods—cooking in open kitchens, dragging tables to the brick sidewalk to display items from across oceans and across the quiet continent. He could see them sweeping floors, shining metallic things—the shop owners were talking, laughing with each other—and it reminded him of the few quiet days in camp—the mornings when battle was far away and the soldiers were allowed to be boys—and he tried to remember a still morning at Blackstone when the only sound was the slap of a beaver's tail on the deep river, but he could not hold the image in his mind.

He rounded a corner onto Broadway and then he could see the finely carved wooden sign, painted gold and blue, that said COLLIER'S CAFÉ—FINE FOOD AND SPIRITS and a black iron lamp unlit on the sidewalk in front. He could see that it was not yet open and that none of the other men had arrived. Disappointed—or relieved—he continued down the great wide street so appropriately named Broadway. By now the streets were full of carriage traffic and there were enough people on the sidewalks to crowd and small lines and groups formed at the tables set out by vendors. On the corner ahead he could see a man of perhaps his own age sitting legless on a short stool—leaning against a stone fence and setting up to play an accordion. He was wearing a jacket from the 2d Regiment, New York, and civilian trousers knotted under the stumps of legs. A Union cap with a cracked bill sat awkwardly on his head. Joseph stopped and watched him from a distance—waiting for the music. The man began to play "Sweet Evelena" and then "Annie Laurie," rocking from side to side on the stool, an empty tin cup on the sidewalk in front of him. Joseph wanted to approach him—to put money into the cup, a hand on his shoulder—a shared tear—what battle? what year?—and then he was struck with the terror that it might have been him—not legless but slashing with saber, or firing low and blind into the thicket at unseen soldiers—at shadows—sitting this boy on his stool forever, putting the sorrowful accordion in his hands and filling his life with the constant reminder of death. And for what? Because he had wanted to leave his father's farm—because Virginia had gone to war and had dragged him with it—and he thought of Blackstone again and he swore to himself right there that he would go back. He would go to see his father and to tell him that he understood— that everything was becoming more clear. He swore he would bring Sarah with him to see the farm, to meet his father. He walked to the legless soldier and dropped two coins in the cup and heard them rattle around to the bottom. Joseph hurried on by. The man looked up and followed him with his eyes, but Joseph could not look back and tucked his hands deep into his pockets and walked on down the street.

You too, he heard someone say. It was the man calling after him. There are pieces of us all left out there brother.

But Joseph kept walking until he was lost in the sounds and nervous activity of the city—absorbed into the swelling crowd in Long Acre Square.

He lost track of time. He walked for over an hour, down to the port to watch the ships being unloaded, the men working feverishly at hoists and chains, to the fish market where the carcasses of unfamiliar creatures lay bleeding and dripping from the sea on thick wooden tables, the choking smell both sickening and compelling. Negroes were unloading sacks of fresh fish and big-armed men were slashing fish with large and small knives—as if the knives were extensions of themselves. In their white, blood-stained shirts they were sweating, despite the cool March air.

He walked past the workingmen and along the shore away from the pier. He walked past the silver piles of quivering fish. He walked away from the noise that suddenly seemed unbearably loud and seamless—like the noise of battle when the sound of artillery and rifle and the screams of men blend into one suffocating din from which there is no escape. But here he could remove himself, and the noise subsided and gave way to the quiet clap of water along the shore.

There was a jetty formed of angular stone piled shapelessly and extending outward from the shore. He could not see its end from where he stood and where it blended with the near horizon it sat amorphous, suspended in the exchange between water and sky. He walked onto it carefully, finding safe footing on the slick stones and finally sitting on the cool surface of a large flat face. This stone seemed to have been dropped from above onto the smaller ones, and he wondered at the construction of the stone jetty—compared it to the smooth walls of Virginia—to the walls of his father. He sat listening to the water licking the polished stones in the crevices and miniature canyons formed by the careless placement of rocks in the water. He could see shining jellyfish, suspended in the lazy current, bounce off the unexpected stone and drift away into the deeper, uninterrupted darkness of the sea. The water teemed with life—small enough to hide on the green growth of the submerged stone—to drift on the current—to be lost in the shadows of the sun and the rocks and the sea—but life no less. He had never been to Virginia's shore but promised himself at this moment that he would see it. How far, he thought, he was from Blackstone. The game was the link—the thread from past to present. How much had changed? The war, baseball, and Sarah—this was who he was now. How could he reconnect with a past that seemed so much like another life? Yet he wanted desperately to connect. To bring it all together, his present and his past, and have it all come together—to sort itself out—to feel connected again. To see it clear like he could see the life in the water—riding the repeating tide, suspended by the stars and the moon, connected to the living jetty.

He knew now that it was Sarah. That she held the key. With her, he could make himself whole again. Without her he would be scattered. She cared for him, he knew. But did she love him? Did she feel any of these things he felt for her? Did she feel emptiness in his absence?—energy in his presence? Did she understand how he felt? Had he told her clearly?

Today he would. After the baseball meeting they were to meet and attend the symphony together at Lincoln Hall. He would tell her everything he felt—everything. If his feelings were not returned, he would prepare to leave for Virginia. Either way, nothing would ever be the same. He heard the loud horn of a ship as it slipped into view on the open sea beyond the jetty—watched as it melted into the liquid horizon—and turned back to walk toward the city along the rocky shore.

Sarah was fixing her hair by pushing a long silver pin through a French braid at the back of her neck. Both arms behind her, her body filled the powder-blue silk blouse as she looked at herself intently in the mirror. Her waist was thin and the dress lay in light folds over the corset and over her hips and she pushed it down with the palms of her hands. A white sweater with tiny pearl-like stones along the neckline lay on the bed beside her and she picked it up and pulled it over her shoulders without putting her arms in the sleeves. Her thin fingers buttoned a single white button at her throat and the rest of the sweater lay like a cape.

She was unhappy with the color of her hair and she thought of that this morning, as if it were more important on this day than on others. It was not quite blond, not quite dark, but somewhere in between. But she did not linger on these thoughts long as she looked at her image. It was reflected in the tall glass and framed with carved mahogany that was deeply cut in its carving; and the crevices of the wood were dark with oil and contrasted beautifully with the rolls of lighter wood protruding along its surface like the curls of a young girl's hair. The weak morning sun washed across it from the unshuttered window. The glass of the mirror was the new silvered kind from Germany and presented an unblemished image of Sarah as she stood in front of it.

She took a deep breath and stood still in front of the mirror. Perhaps I am pretty, she thought. Perhaps I am not so plain. Perhaps to him I am beautiful. She thought of Joseph now and let her weight and the folds of the dress settle onto the edge of the bed. She folded her hands on her lap and looked toward the slats of sun and the window. She could see clouds absorbing the white morning sun and listened as a mild breeze pushed the stiff branches of oak clattering against the brick walls and the wood shutters of the house. The polished stones sewn into the fabric of her sweater reflected the mixed light and seemed to be ablaze along her neck. The dog, Sherman, jumped up on the bed and lay next to her, thumping his thick tail on the mattress as she petted the long hair of his neck.

Joseph. He was different—she knew that. He was less polished than Roger had been, but at the same time he seemed so refined in many ways and when he spoke to her it was if royalty were speaking. His words were sometimes awkward—but every word seemed to be just right for what he was saying. He seemed to feel every word as if he were speaking at all times from the heart.

Roger—she had loved Roger as well. He was a good, kind man and she had thought that she would never feel any love again when she had heard of his death. But she remembered Joseph that first day when he had brought the letter and had stood awkward in the parlor. Even then, through the pain that she felt on hearing again of Roger's death, she felt something else for the humble boy who had gone through so much to bring her the letter—who had carried the letter for so long.

She remembered how she wept as she read it that first time and the many times since. But she remembered also, that afternoon in the parlor, when he had recited the letter word for word—eyes closed—each word as if falling from his tired soul. I can sometimes see us together in my dreams. She heard the words now as if they had been just spoken.

There was such honesty in his eyes—that light when he looked at her. And the words that spilled from him when he spoke of Virginia and of his father—those long southern sounds as he told her stories of his mother. She would rest upon those words and hoped secretly that the stories wouldn't end.

And then the other thing—the base ball. She went first out of curiosity and then to watch him play the match—to try to watch his eyes as he played and the graceful movement of his body and then after the match— to see the face filled with so much satisfaction, as if the playing of the game of base ball washed away all the pain of war and death and sorrow that was clearly written on his face at other times. Did he feel that with her? Did he love her as she loved him? She loved the part of him she knew. Now she must discover the rest of him. The part he left in the mud and brush of Virginia. The part that his friend Terence Hooker had taken with him on that day he vanished onto the wilderness trail. When he had promised not to look away.

All this past year they had grown closer. The courtship brought her to almost all of the games and she had sat with him during the late weeks of the '70 season when his shoulder had hurt too much for him to play. Watching with him, she came to love the game even more, as if seeing it through his eyes she was able to understand better its awkward perfection.

When this past season ended they had enjoyed even the coming winter, as if their affection for each other had grown in direct proportion to the shortened days and the early darkness of the winter nights. She could hear his laugh, as she had tried to show him how to skate that first time and they had fallen together like children, laughing, his long legs twisted beneath him. She smiled now as she thought of this.

The dog nudged his nose under her arm, for she had stopped petting him, and she rose and pressed her skirt down and straightened the blouse around her neck and thought that she would have all these answers by the end of this day. She was meeting him in the city this afternoon. Joseph was attending a base ball meeting and then she was meeting him and taking him to the symphony for the first time, and before the day was out she would tell him. She would make sure he knew how she felt about him. He liked things clear, she thought, and he shall have that. She walked out of the door of the room with the dog at her feet, down the narrow stairs, and out to the carriage that would be waiting for her beside the carriage house. Clouds stretched across the diluted sun and it was just beginning to rain. She and her father would take the carriage and then the train to Manhattan.

By the time Joseph returned to Collier's Café on Thirteenth and Broadway the rain had resumed and he hurried through the door, wedged open with a broom handle. His clothes were damp. As he entered he could see a group of about a dozen men gathered around three tables that had been pushed together. The smoke of cigars floated lazily to the tin ceiling and a short, very heavy man was bringing a tray of thick glass mugs filled with brown beer to the tables. He noticed that two of the men were wearing base ball caps and he also noticed that most of the men had mustaches and a few were already wiping the white foam of the beer from the drooping hair at the corners of their mouths. From out of a darkened corner Joseph immediately recognized Harry Wright from the Cincinnati team.

Wright emerged from the shadows and shook his hand vigorously. Welcome, Joe Tyler, he said, Or should we be callin you Rebel Joe? he laughed.

Joseph would be fine.

Joseph recognized most of the players around the room. They represented the big clubs. Two of them stood to shake his hand and another said, Come and sit, Tyler. Pour the man a beer, Mr. Kerns.

Joseph pulled up a wooden stool in a space between the other men. The blue smoke was thick and lay like liquid over the table. The surface of the table was strewn with black derby hats and hunks of yellow cheese. A crude glass jar held pickled cucumbers and was being passed from man to man and the men were taking them, dripping from the jar, and salting them and eating them that way and wiping their mouths on white towels and then washing the pickles down with the brown beer. Two more men entered the café behind Joseph and he recognized them from the Mutuals in Brooklyn and nodded silently to them as they took seats around the table.

Harry Wright took a deep breath of cigar smoke and began the meeting with a slap of his palm on the wooden table. Joseph noticed that he didn't have a beer, as he was a well-known teetotaler. Forty thousand people— maybe more. A couple of years ago they said fifty thousand for the championship in Philly. You hear that gentlemen? Fifty thousand people pushin each other out of the way to see us play ball.

There was murmuring and small conversations around the table and then someone asked Wright what he had in mind. Joseph rested his head by leaning it on his open palms, his fingers wrapped to his cheekbone.

We're talkin about money here, gentlemen. We're talkin about the future of the game. The Red Stockings made a lot of money . . . for our-selves . . . for all of you. This is just the beginning gentlemen.

A waitress with a young-looking figure but a face that seemed to carry a line for every day she lived brought a glass of beer and put it in front of Joseph and the other new arrivals. Some of the beer spilled on the table and it was sticky on his hands as he brought the glass to his mouth and sipped the bitter brown liquid.

We can't let the park owners and the gamblers take over the game. It's ours. It's us the people are comin to see. It was Gus Hawley from the Atlantics talking and he stood as he talked and walked around the table. Teams are sproutin up everywhere. New Orleans, Tennessee, Colorado — all playin ball in front a thousands. Ladies are comin out, kids are playin on the sidelines—it aint just a game. There's money to be made gentle-men. The only question is who's gonna make it and how much.

Harry Wright stepped forward and put a hand on Hawley's shoulder, *Gentlemen,* that's the key word here. Like Chadwick says, we have to keep it a gentlemen's game . . . but that doesn't mean we can't make a good living at it. We have to keep control of the game . . . not give it up to rowdies. We have to be in control of the rules . . . and the gates . . . and the future.

He hesitated and put his hands deep in his pockets.

I tell you, gentlemen, when we play in Cincinnati the trees around the field are full like human fruit, every branch carries kids, the grandstands are full with ladies, and the damn people selling food are making a killing —and it's our game boys, it sure is.

The room felt as if it was growing smaller to Joseph and the smoke made him feel nauseous. He stood up, pushed his chair from the table, and moved to an open window that looked out onto the street. Across the street a young girl was pushing the puddles of water away from the door of a storefront with some kind of broom toward the street and the water was collecting and draining into the city's clay pipes and into the rivers and bays that surrounded the island of Manhattan. He watched a carriage rattle by, pulled by a huge speckled horse. In the seat was a woman and a young boy and the horse followed slowly the tracks of the trolley and Joseph watched the thick hooves of the horse slosh through a deep puddle in front of the café. The boy, bouncing on the leather seat, turned to Joseph as they passed and Joseph looked at him. He was perhaps thirteen—maybe younger. He was Joseph's age before he left Blackstone and Joseph thought of this as he watched the boy. As the boy looked he reached into a pocket of his coat and pulled an object from it, and tossed it up and caught it and then sort of saluted with his thin hand to his cap as the wagon passed. It was a base ball. The boy looked once more at the figure of Joseph in the café window and then the wagon turned down the street at the next corner. Joseph watched until the carriage disappeared, then turned and sat again at the table.

He tried to listen to the discussion. Kerns was talking now about staying organized. There were arguments, laughter, but Joseph couldn't get the image of the boy out of his mind. He could see Terence—the green field at the base of Stone Hill. He could smell the river. He could see Terence swinging the bat at the dangling sock in the barn—could see the hay drifting through the air and settling in their hair and he could hear Terence's laughter instead of the laughter of the base ball men. And then he heard the sound of the pipes.

He looked to the window and then rose again and leaned on the wood of the sill. A couple of others followed until most of the men were standing at the window as the sound and the parade approached. He could see the green banners held high on wooden poles. He could see the street filled with men marching toward them—the pipers filling their bags with the air of their lungs and emptying them to the street in song that sounded like wind through a stone tunnel. Joseph could see the green flag with the gold harp of old Ireland waving off a long staff, held by a group of boys who almost ran past them. He could see some men in uniform marching, holding high the battle flag of Meagher's brigade, marching without smiling.

A glass or bottle shattered on the sidewalk in front of the café. The street was now filled with the parade. Women were walking arm in arm and singing. Men dressed in uniform were walking, some with crutches and some being pulled in carts—wounded in the fields of Virginia and the fields of Pennsylvania, marching now as sons of Ireland. A group of soldiers walked by the window and looked in to see the men at the window and per- haps mistaking the base ball caps for military caps—they saluted as one, in perfect military form, and Joseph without thinking raised his hand and saluted. Someone standing beside him said, Who you salutin reb?

Joseph dropped his hand quickly to his side. He turned from the window and returned to stand near his chair. He was not sure who had said it.

Lets get back to the business, a man was saying and most of the men returned to their seats and slapped each other's backs and ordered more beer. Someone said, The National Association of Professional Base Ball Players— that's what we'll call ourselves.

Joseph turned back to the window and could feel the smoke and the room shrinking still around him. I'm sorry gentlemen, he said, but I caint see it. He grabbed his coat and pulled it over his shoulders. You're right when you say it's more than . . . more than just a game.

He looked around at the men who were sitting and looking at him and listening to what he would say. Joseph took a breath and leaned a moment on the stool.

It's more than a game to me, gentlemen. But it sure is much more than a business, Joseph said, and that part I have to keep clear.

That's cause you're a country clubber, reb, one of the men offered, and this game's a city game. A couple of the men agreed quietly but most of them were silent. They watched Joseph, saw a little of themselves in him, of the game they loved—the purity of something they had discovered as young boys.

Damn, that aint true. The seed may have been planted in the cities, but this game is grown in the fields and the pastures all around this country and when a boy holds a bat in his hands for the first time and he feels the weight and the balance of it, when he feels how smooth the skin of the wood is, when he catches that ball and feels the cold hide against his skin—that sure aint about business. You men seem to have lost that, and to me it's never been clearer. He finished the inch of beer in his glass, pulled the coat on, and said, Good day gentlemen.

The door had been closed against the rain and he opened it with some effort and heard a bell clatter as he did. He pulled the collar of his coat over his neck and pulled his shoulders up and walked into the rain. Then he heard a voice behind him calling his name and he turned and saw it was Harry Wright who had caught up with him.

Wright put a hand on his shoulder and pulled him under a canvas awning. I know what you're sayin Tyler. Most of these men know. But it's the future. It's like a train goin by that you gotta jump on or get run over by.

A quick glance at his watch told Joseph that he would just make it to meet Sarah. He said, You're a good man, Wright, and I aint never heard different. But I think I'll just step out of the way and let this train pass me by. Just let it pass. I still got the game in my heart, and that's where it's always been anyway, and Joseph shook his hand and turned, hurrying down the street from where the Irish parade had come. He passed a couple of stragglers carrying green flags and bottles and singing as they walked. The closeness of the sky thick with rain and his steps along the gravel and then on the cobble made him think of the marching. Of the steps—the fear of falling and dampness and the illness that would surely follow in the camps. As he walked this day he thought of the letter—and then of the tangled thicket as it burned—and he could see the letter itself burst into a ball of flames and disintegrate into the air and he could see the words left written in the air, *For surely you are more than a man should ever have,* and he hurried his step toward the theater. He didn't think about base ball or the meeting as he walked. He thought only of Sarah.

He was late and she was waiting for him at the entrance of Lincoln Hall on Broadway. She took his hand and they went quickly through the gothic doors and were ushered quietly to their seats. Gas lanterns hung every twenty feet along the wall and as the musicians entered from backstage and took their seats on the wooden chairs arranged in a gentle arc along the stage, a limping man went from lamp to lamp turning the small flames down until they glowed orange like October moons along the foil covered walls. Dull bronze masks of faces sad and smiling alternated in the spaces between the lamps and cast elongated shadows that seemed to lunge upward to the vaulted ceiling—ultimately lost in the patterns and design of the ceiling itself. In the center of the theater the ceiling came to a vaulted circle, a cupola—and the rounded plaster within the circle was painted with a fresco of trumpet blowing angels with great, long instruments all pointing upward toward the room's pinnacle and there were white clouds of unpainted plaster as well.

The darkened room was now silent except for the shuffling of chairs and the occasional cough and Joseph felt it necessary to clear his own throat and as he did and returned his hand to the chair, he felt Sarah's hand rest on top of his and her fingers nestle their way between his own like water into dry earth. The dim stage light brightened and a short man entered from behind long red curtains and everyone in the theater, including Joseph and Sarah, applauded and then were silent again. The conductor rapped his baton three times on the wooden podium and raised both arms as if to declare something—then jerked them quickly upward—and as they went up the gut was dragged and pushed across the strings of cellos and the air above them and around them was filled with sound reverberating like the wind through leafless trees and across a frozen earth.

The men's chins were tucked over the great instruments that stood on thin wooden pedestals that seemed too small to support the massive cellos—and the instruments stood like ballerinas with pointed feet and moved gently as the notes changed and fingers climbed the taut trail of strings—then descended again. The light of the stage lamps flickered and splashed across the hard wood of the cellos as it would across a still pond at twilight—and Joseph's fingers curled and he was unaware that he held Sarah's hand in his. She glanced at him, but the glare of his eyes never left the stage and he might as well have been alone.

The music continued, almost predictably—and Joseph's hand pulled from Sarah's and his own hands were interlocked and he let the weight of his head rest on the knuckles of his knitted fingers as he watched the musicians and let the sound from the stage envelop him.

As he listened it was if he lay against the cool grass of Virginia's spring and the stars streaked across the black sky and reflected off the timid eyes of deer and shone in the yellow eyes of foxes and the fecund ground was flush with flower and the air saturated with fragrance. The music rolled along quietly—swelling—thick—and then quite suddenly exploding and Joseph shifted his weight in his seat as if he were physically lifted and he looked quickly at Sarah whose face seemed to shine with the gold gaslight and whose gentle hand moved again to his. Other instruments, then all instruments joined the swelling of resonant sound along the pale yellow walls—all the instruments separate but harmonious joined in symphonic union across the molecules of air that danced with sound across the theater as if it were a chamber and the air had turned to water and the human souls swam through the water and to the harmony of sound like fish to algae— and the yellow liquid light enveloped them, keeping silent their souls that they might ride the wave of sound across the chamber. And Joseph saw them—the bodies lifted, legless, armless—upward from the bloodied fields toward some shimmering surface—floating upward through the liquid chamber. As if he was removed and they whirled around him and he closed his eyes and shook his head from side to side to lose the image and hear only the music lifted from the stage. Sarah moved closer to him.

The music rose up as if from beneath. It was the warmth of the Virginia summer rising up from the ground. It was the union of spirits in terrible battle. The bow slid slowly across the strings of a solo violin, the player's chin tucked to the smooth wood whose surface glimmered with the yellow light. It was the sun washing across a piano and spilling onto the full form of Sarah. It was the voice of Terence through the woods. It was Sarah's eyes seeing him, seeing Joseph. All the violins joined in seamlessly—slowly— then in vigorous unchecked passion. It was the unbraided strands of her hair left for him to push into place with his fingers along the back of her neck. It was the silk dress between his trembling hand and her pale skin. The low note of a single cello now—growing louder. It was the moment—no, the second before the pitch when all men's muscles are tense and all eyesight riveted. It was the unchecked motion of the bat and the unseen instant of stillness—when the ball is met. It was the sudden flight of birds upward from the field.

There were strings joining to form notes of music he had not imagined. It was the trace of snow beneath spring grass—the moments between sunset and darkness when the light of the living earth is given up in silver— bequeathed to the stars. It was the weight of stone. It was the words of the letter—Roger's words unanswered. It was the lilt of his father's voice at supper when the day's work was done, and done well. It was kindness, human kindness. It was the faint laughter of his young mother—the wash of sun across an open field—beyond the woods, turned gold. Low mournful drums—it was the game—the clarity of the game to him. It was the lightness of her—it was the weight of stone.

The music built to a crescendo and then faded just as quickly, and then there was applause and Joseph joined in it and watched the men on the stage as they bowed and stood, and bowed again. The lights were turned up and the shadows shrank and vanished and the musicians left the stage while the crowd still stood and cheered. The conductor entered again and bowed and then the musicians followed suit and the applause rose up again and Joseph could hear people yelling bravo, until finally the applause subsided and the men filed from the stage and disappeared behind the long curtains.

He was trembling and almost unaware as Sarah took his hand and led him down the corridor. They walked through the wide doors of the theater and into the gray light. Joseph looked to the buildings across the street and to the early-evening sky and the fabric of clouds stained with pink and with red from the slanted light of the sun, the earth, dull silver sliding slowly toward darkness. He could feel her hand in his, her warm skin against his palm, but he did not look at her or speak until they were on the street and walking. The rain had stopped for now but the ground was lit yellow with the light from windows and the light of a few streetlamps across the saturated ground, mixed with the last light of the sun, and they walked, a meadow of color brushed across the ground. He began to lead her and they walked to a clearing of grass between two buildings that formed a small courtyard. He led her to a bench and asked her to sit with him there as he pulled a watch from his pocket. They had plenty of time before the train.

Since he was so quiet she didn't speak at all for a moment. Her hands were folded on her lap. Joseph pulled the sweater higher onto her shoulders and asked her if she were warm enough and she answered that she was fine. The grass at their feet was thin and he could see the relentless seedlings pushing their way into the cracks of cobble and stone and gravel. He could see it growing toward the street, reclaiming the dormant earth —only to be trampled by wagon and horse and trolley. In the dim light he put his hand gently on the back of her neck and let the tips of his fingers touch her warm skin. She relaxed toward him and let her head rest on his shoulder. They sat silently for a few more moments, watching the light along the street, until Sarah spoke quietly.

You liked it didn't you? I knew you would.

His hand dropped from her and he sat with his elbows on his legs and the weight of his head on his fists. I can't seem to reconcile it. Can't reconcile it at all. I can see the wicked deeds of the battlefield. I can hear the cries of the boys. I can almost see them tremble with fear—and I caint reconcile it. When I think on these things, when I see Terence's back disappear between the trees like it was a minute ago, I am damn sure that there is no God. No God could make man to be this way. In what image would we be then? In whose image?

He sat back and looked up at the darkening sky. It was thick now, but not quite dark enough for stars. It was like a dark blanket, a heavy sheet that you could still see through but you couldn't quite make out the images.

But then this. I see this and I hear it, Sarah, and I don't understand. I watched the fingers on the strings. I hear the sound that could not be made or could not even be heard or understood if there was no God. No God to separate us from the beasts—but that's what we were in the wilderness there, no more than wolves, no more than hogs, snakes that slid from dark to dark. There was no light in the woods. Just the darkness. There was no song to carry us up but the beat of drums, like the beaver's signal on the flat water, the coyote's howl. We were no better and most times far worse.

He hesitated. He could not look at her but had to keep talking.

I don't even know who I killed. I never thought too much of it. Don't even know why. But I can see some of the faces. I sure can still see the faces of the men I killed.

She could see he was fighting back tears and she pulled his head to her shoulder and enveloped him in her arms and as she did, Joseph began to weep and his body shook as he wept.

I am so ashamed, Sarah, she could hear him say. I got so much shame in what was done. I am so far from who I should be, so far from God I'm afraid I caint get back.

Ashamed of what, Joe Tyler? You were a boy. Ashamed of soldiering? It was the duty you were called to and there isn't a man alive who could blame you for what you've done.

No one called me. He sat up and wiped his eyes with his sleeve. We seeked it out, Terence and I. We couldn't wait to join the fight. Could feel it risin around us.

She looked down and shook her head slowly. You were boys, she said.

He had stopped crying and sat straight on the bench with his hands crossed in his lap. He looked down at his hands. They were trembling and he clasped them together as he spoke.

In the woods, I became good at killin. I could hear men in the thicket and it was like I could sense where they were. It was like I could sense their fear and I used it. Never thought much about it. I killed to survive, to save myself. I had no real cause. Virginia was nothin to me cept the length of my father's walls along the field. Virginia was the blue hills beyond the river and face of Stone Hill, and I became determined to see that again, and that was all. I never had no bicker with negroes. I never even knew any negroes cept the ones who played ball with us and they were freed before the war anyway. I killed for no other reason but to smell the fresh-cut grass of our pasture again. To be able to hit a base ball another time. I killed so I could get out of those woods and breathe air again without the bite of carbon smoke in it.

He stood and put his hands in his coat pockets. A man was lighting the gas lamp near them and the flame turned the ground beneath them to amber. The light illuminated her face and he could see that she had been crying as well, but he did not go to her though he longed for nothing else. He held his ground a few feet from the bench and continued speaking.

I don't know how to get around it. By the time the battle was done for me I felt nothing. And then I read the letter . . . from Roger McCleod to Miss Sarah Kingsley it said on it. I read it for the first time all the way through in Elmira. I lay there almost starvin, full of hate, full of rage.

And when I read that letter that first night I swear it was the only thing that kept me alive. Not Roger's words so much, and not you really—I didn't know who you might be—but the feelin in it. This man had just died in this war and all that was left of him was these words—kindness, words of love. I couldn't stop reading it and it got me through that night and a hundred more.

He turned from her and spoke again.

Since then I thought of you. Since then I've tried to get my arms around life again, to embrace the moments of life again. With all the suffocating brutality that I've seen, it's Roger's words that kept me, that led me to you, Sarah, for me to sit at your side and hear this music. To sit and listen to human beins make this music. To watch the hearts of these men laid out, like my father's walls . . . perfectly laid out, cause surely that music comes from the human heart and surely it was God put it there and it's God whispering in their ears and moving their fingers.

And you, dear Sarah. . .

She let him speak not another word as she burst from the bench, across the space between them and into his arms. He lifted her as she came to him. . . . And you, he said, My sweet Sarah. You are the song on my soul. How can I reconcile all this. How can I let myself be so happy, let myself think that we . . .

She stopped his words with a kiss and let her body push itself toward him, deeper into him until she was weightless in his embrace. They held each other long in the false light of the lamp and heard nothing except the breath of the other as they stood, slowly rocking, in their embrace. A wagon rolled by and the laughter of children startled them and Joseph took her hand, pulling away from her gently and said, We'll walk.

As they walked through the streets of Manhattan toward the train station, they delighted in the sounds. The clatter of wagons and horse trolleys, the laughter of children chasing one another—excited in the growing darkness, the smell of the fish on the breeze. Other couples like themselves passed and some of them greeted and some of them ignored the others passing, lost in each other. Joseph and Sarah held tight to one another's arms as they walked slowly through the canyons of brick and stone.

They walked completely silently for several blocks until Sarah spoke. Both of her hands were on Joseph's forearm and her face was turned slightly toward his. She looked at his eyes as she spoke. You try to understand too much, Joseph, she was saying. We have to be content with the mystery. It's, I believe, the mystery that is God. How can we ever understand his plan for us when we can't even understand ourselves?

They walked. Joseph was silent.

You think Joseph, that you can see God's face across the Virginia morning, but that's not God, Joseph. The way you feel it, the way you explain it to me in the words that come from your heart and nowhere else—that's the presence of God. The way the morning—the music—fills your heart.

She paused and then continued. I don't pretend to understand war—why men would kill each other—but I know that God is there somewhere, even if he resides in the broken heart and the broken spirit. Our failure to embrace him may lead us to the battlefield, Joseph, but even there he's present, I believe. Your tortured soul, Joe Tyler. Your bravery . . .

There was no bravery, Sarah, only fear, only desperation. He looked away and then continued. There were times out there, many times, when we weren't much men at all. When nothin outside the moment existed.

Nothin but the struggle to survive. The next breath. There was no time to mourn friends, no time to care for the wounded, to remove the dead from the field. Only to do what was instinctive, what you knew must be done to live. There's no God in war. I know . . .

I don't believe it, Joseph. I don't believe that's true.

But you don't know, Sarah . . . you haven't been in battle.

As soon as he said it he was sorry. He could not see her chin drop slightly and her eyes glance to the street.

Sarah, I'm sorry, he began to say.

No. She put her hand up. No. You are right, Joseph. I do not understand what it is like to be in battle. But the war touched all of us and I know . . . She folded her hands together in front of her. That men are not like other animals. Because there is God in the human spirit. Joseph, listen, she said as she turned to face him. Two starving wolves, wild boars, come across food . . . a fallen prey . . . whatever it might be . . . and they will almost certainly fight savagely for pieces. Almost certainly kill to survive. The strongest will survive and eat, and the lesser will fall and starve and surely perish.

She hesitated a moment, then continued in what had become almost a whisper, But two starving men, Joseph. Two starving men can choose to share . . . that they both might eat, however poorly. And that, Joseph, that is the soul of man. That lifts us.

She sighed. Or this, Joseph. She put her hands gently on his arm. One man . . . one man can choose to go hungry that the other might live. This I've seen. I know this occurs countless times. And this Joseph, this is the breath of God across the human spirit. This elevates us, protects us from ourselves.

Joseph looked down at the road in front of them, and then directly at Sarah. I have seen men step in the way of bullets for other men. I have seen men weep at the pain of other men, men who were strangers to them, men they barely knew. I have seen that. They walked quietly again and then Joseph's thought returned to his friend and he repeated, I should've gone with Terence. I should have stopped him.

You couldn't, Joseph. It wasn't yours to do. I know you, Joseph, and I know your bravery. I know your kindness to Roger, and the letter, that led you to me. What is that if it's not the hand of God? What is it that brought you to me?

He stopped walking and looked at her eyes glistening with tears and wiped them dry with the back of his hand. In the light he could see her skin white, a light trace of freckles across her cheekbone, and her dark eyes that seemed to shine from within her.

I truly believe, Sarah Kingsley, that I have done some good in my life. Leastways I have not been so bad as I would not have the right to stand here in your arms. I truly believe that there is heaven on this earth when you speak kindly to me and it is like I have seen the sun for the first time when it casts your shadow into mine.

Joseph, she said, and they kissed again before walking. Do you ever wish life were a moment?—this moment?

He said nothing as they walked but he thought that she was right. That there was nothing outside this moment and the moment was full with them. The shadows were deeper and longer and the natural light had melted into night as they walked. Now only the yellow light and the white light—full with the shadows from within the rooms—shone from the windows of the shops and offices and mixed with the silver stone that was set in the sidewalk. Music floated in and out on the breeze off the bay as the doors of cafés opened and closed. Joseph and Sarah stayed very close, arm in arm now as they walked. They heard the clatter of horse hooves on the cobblestone street and turned to see a cart being led by a gray horse pass them, a lamp swaying with the animal's tired gait and splashing the street with light and then receding to black and then light again, as the lamp swayed with the movement of the cart. It was darker when the light left, he noticed. Darker than even before the light. When the eyes became used to the light, the returning darkness was even more black and deep. He spoke to her, telling her he could not bear to allow himself to think that she might love him, want to be with him, and then to lose her again.

I'm not sure what to do, Sarah. The base ball—seemed so right—

seemed to be the thing for me to do, but it's beginning to feel empty. They
are turning it into a business—that's what the meeting was about. But I
find it's only the matches that you come to that I feel right about what I'm
doing. Base ball is losing something. And I've heard from my father and it
seems he's not well. He's asked me to come home—to come to Blackstone
to help him and I know how hard that was for him, to ask me for help. To
reach out to me at all.

Joseph was walking faster, and talking as fast.

But what about you, Sarah? How can I leave when with you is how I
am alive? And what is Virginia to you.

She stopped walking and pulled his arm to stop him. There is nothing
for either of us, she said, without the other. And then—then there is everything for both of us. We are a circle, you and I. She spoke with her eyes on
his. A peculiar one, but a circle nonetheless. They embraced again before
they walked.

As they approached the train station, Joseph looked at his watch. They
were still early and Joseph did not want the evening to end. Her father
was to meet them for the trip back and they would not be able to talk like
this. He felt as if a wellspring had been opened and the thoughts that
weighed on him poured out to her.

I want you to understand, Sarah, that my life caint be nothin without
you in it. But I don't know if I can . . . A dog ran by in full chase and they
stepped back toward a brownstone building and out of the way. Joseph
could feel suddenly the familiar dull pain in his shoulder and he brought
his other hand up to it and squeezed it firm and the pain subsided after a
moment. I don't know if I can get around it all, separate it all.

He was leaning against the cold stone and she stood before him. There's
been moments, when I'm playin ball—that it all sort of seems clear, sorted
out. But then it comes back to me. I can still see your Roger leaning
against the tree with the flames licking at his boots. I can see him look at
me . . . I can still see him and thousands like him.

And you saved him from the fire, Joseph . . . an awful death. And the
last thing Roger knew was your kindness to him. She was crying as she

spoke. Even in that horror, you found a way to do right. And God led you here, to me, Joseph Tyler, so that you could sit at my side and listen to the music of Haydn, so you could stand before me on this night. So I could hold you until all the pain of the past drops from your soul and our lives are forever joined. For your act of kindness to Roger, you were given the letter. So that we might stand here together. Oh Joseph, can't you see?

It was as if now he looked upon her for the first time. That seeing her at this moment—flesh, hair, eyes that shone with the moon's reflected light—that this was his first true glimpse of Sarah. He saw her as one would see the first smile of an infant, recognizing that the world has changed due to his part in it. Her flesh was not flesh—for flesh he had seen, torn and folded from muscle and from bone, and blistered with intolerable heat. This flesh—her flesh—seemed suspended between the real and the imagined. Her hair at this moment held no physical texture, no familiar color—but existed solely to frame the tender face and lie perfectly along elegant bone. The shadows caused by the yellow light of the street-lamps as it washed across the features of her face lay drawn across her neck and shoulders and now he could see the deep black eyelashes dance quickly up and then down as she lowered her gaze to the street.

His hands went unconsciously to her shoulders, to her back, and he pulled her to him and she seemed to come to him without moving, like a rising tide ascending the shore—imperceptible but complete, and they were suspended there—enfolded. He felt her soft warmth envelop him. He was stone on stone and she—the light across him, her beauty revealing his own. She was the celestial, the unknown, and he the familiar—the earth, the stone, the ice melting and running in rivers toward the unseen source.

She could feel him hard against her and she raised her mouth to his and he took her chin in his palm and opened his mouth to hers and breathed in the scent of her skin, the universe of her hair. He let his chest press against her breasts through the thin blouse and he could feel her rise up to him and he could feel her warm breath across his face and he could say only her name—over and over again. He felt a weight being lifted from him as he spoke her name between breathless kisses and felt her body push closer to his—felt the spaces between them melt and fill with each other, and he heard her say his name, and repeat his name as if those were the only words necessary and as if they represented long sentences and revealed ancient mysteries in their revelation.

Then there was quiet laughter and he turned quickly to see two people passing through the uneven light of the streetlamp and he allowed himself to straighten and pull gently from her although they still stood embracing. Her forehead lay weightless against Joseph's broad chest. She was breathing softly against him and he could feel the tender rhythm of her heart, the labor of her lungs with the palm of his embracing hand. She, in her gentle breathing, represented all life to him. He did not want to move. He could not believe the fullness of this moment—as if nothing else, nothing at all existed. He could think of nothing to say. Words would destroy this moment like rifle shot. He wanted to let it float there like a bubble of oxygen to a drowning man. And so they stayed like this, embracing, for some time until she said softly, We should walk, Joseph, and she placed her small hand in his.

They fell back into step along the granite curb, much as they had walked before, in and out of the pools of light, past the brownstone buildings. Now they held more closely to each other and wondered to themselves how different everything looked—how different it was. The yellow light that bled into the darker shadows, the tall thin poles of the gas lamps, the people that passed them with silent greeting and laughter seemed somehow exaggerated, as if they were watching a play—a performance just for them. In this moment everything had changed. Everything was new. All things existed only in their particular relationship with Sarah and Joseph as they walked together down the streets of New York. But for this, nothing at all mattered.

II.

Joseph entered the King's Tavern and walked to the table where they sat. Owens and Nash were playing cards and Alexander Cooper stood and greeted Joseph with a firm handshake and a hand on his shoulder. Two of the other boys were sitting at an adjacent table drinking beer from thick jars. They raised their glasses to him and continued a quiet conversation. He could smell stew cooking from Beezer's kitchen and it mixed with the smell of the burning wood in the fireplace.

Sit down, Joseph, Cooper said. Mr. Owens is giving Rooster a lesson in charity I'm afraid.

Hand aint over yet, Rooster said without looking up from his cards.

Joseph was still standing and he leaned on the back of one of the chairs. I got somethin to say boys.

Cooper thrust the fingers of his hands into the vest of his burgundy vest and pronounced, Well I guess you should go ahead and say it then Joe Tyler. Don't appear to be any stoppin you anyway is there? Hands down a minute boys, he said as he turned to the table.

Nash and Owens lowered their cards and looked up through a pillow of cigar smoke. Owens waved his hand in the air to disperse the smoke and said, What is it Joe?

Joseph cleared his throat and spoke. You boys have meant an awful lot to me. I appreciate the chance you gave me to play. I appreciate wearin the uniform of the Niners with you all. Your friendship. Joseph looked down the length of his legs to the dusty floor and continued. But it's time I move on. Time I headed back to Virginia. To Blackstone farm.

Mike Owens dropped the cards flat onto the table. You've just started in the game Joe. The game's just started.

I know Mike, but it's changin—and it's not for me. The game'll go on fine without Joe Tyler. It just aint right anymore.

Cooper pulled up a wooden high-backed chair and settled into it. Guess I could see it comin Joe. You've got a new wife. Things change. Seems like a long time since Elmira Joe. Since I ran into you at Mrs. Albright's inn.

Has been a while Coop—and I sure owe you for what you've done for me. You think she'll like Virginia Joe?

No tellin. Says she wants to go, though. Wants to help me go home, she says.

That's a good woman there Joe Tyler, Mike Owens offered.

Joe—tell them. Tell em what you told me about runnin from Elmira Prison. Tell the boys your story one more time.

He told us Coop, Owens and Nash responded. And so did you. We know about the game—bout how he ran with the bullets flyin over his head. But I guess we'd like to hear it again from you Joe. We'll be tellin your story so it's best we get it right. They laughed as they said this.

Tell them again Joe, Cooper said, smiling. And leaning back in the chair and stretching his legs out along the plank floor he added, I believe I'd like to hear your story one more time myself Joseph.

So Joseph told them. About the fake limp and the prison games and the day they moved outside the fence to play. He told them about the late innings and how the ball flew off the bat of the young prison guard and how he chased it and saw the birch grove and the high ridge, and then he told them what he did. He told it slowly, in the same words he had before.

I could see clearly, he said. The way to run—the path to my freedom. Could see that with the jump I had—those yankee guards didn't have a chance of catchin me. And then I could see the path of the ball and as I watched it I ran—not for the woods but for the damn ball. I couldn't help myself and instead of runnin for my freedom I ran for the ball. And I caught it and fell and when I got up I saw the runner on base headin around the bases and, instead of droppin the ball and headin for the ridge, I threw him down at the plate. Dead out. Was into the trees before I heard him called down—but I knew it when the ball left my hand. He was down at the plate.

The men sat looking at him and Joseph stood completely quiet himself. Cooper had his hands knitted behind his neck and was looking at the ceiling as if he were listening to some music. Then Rooster Nash slapped the palm of his open hand on the wood of the table and burst out laughing and Owens, the cigar clenched in his teeth, joined him. Cooper slapped both his hands on his knees and laughed, Dead out. Isn't that the damndest story, he said. I believe I'll be tellin my grandchildren that one someday.

Joseph smiled and shook his head slowly from side to side. Guess I could've been killed makin that play. Don't seem so smart now.

And then he let himself laugh as he hadn't in many years. And the boys ordered up some stew and beers and Rooster Nash told the story to old man Beezer as he dished out the stew from a big silver pot with the bottom charred black, and the boys sat there and shared the wildest stories they knew. Stories from the game, and from the war and before that. They spent one last afternoon in the King's Tavern Inn in Terryville, New York, and every word they spoke would be remembered and repeated by each man over the next years of their lives. Complete with the hiss and crack of the resinous oak in the stone fireplace that was big enough for a grown man to stand in. And those last hours they spent together became a moment cherished in the long story of their lives.

The next morning he lay next to her. It was very early—the morning of the day he was to leave Rocker Falls. The white light seemed to emanate from the solid objects in the room. From a small chest of drawers, from an upright wooden coatstand that had been oiled, the black oil lying deep in the grain. All else pale, watery images of itself. A white porcelain pitcher sat on a table near the bed half-filled with tepid water. Two glasses stood beside it on a white cloth, the glasses unused. He was waking and conscious of the shapes and the light in the room. He rolled over to his side and felt her next to him—turned away in sleep. He gently pulled her to him.

These years seemed to have spun by like a northern summer. Since his winter with Mrs. Albright and his time in the game with Cooper and The Niners it had been over six years. As he lay waking here in the early morning he tried to pull apart the memories so that he could see them separate—like the lines so clearly marked in shattered stone. But he could not see them separate. Instead his love for Sarah—this thing that was so much like a wind that had lifted and carried him—seemed to fuse all the events and memories and light them the same. As if they were laid out and the light fell across them as it had against the stones of his father's walls—equal and correct.

They had been married in April, on one of those days when winter had been unwilling to relinquish its grip and the world was quieted by a cover of new snow—spring flowers closed and drawn from it. The horse-drawn plows had cleared narrow paths through the streets and the women were forced to lift their dresses over thinly frozen puddles and mud as they entered the church. Joseph had written to his father but there had been no response this time, and Sarah's family and his friends from base ball had filled the small church as he stood and waited for her, watching the snow spin outside the thin glass of the windows.

He could see, even now, Sarah approaching him through the uneven light—her hand on the arm of her father as they walked up the narrow aisle of the church. She wore her mother's sequined dress that caught the lamplight and caused it to dance around her. And in that moment, he had felt the past fall away from him—and then rise up and embrace him again like a morning.

He had stood with Sarah at the altar, and had felt himself standing beside her as if his life could not have brought him anywhere else. As if that first time he had ducked into the woods along the fields of Blackstone he had been headed here. As if the water of the Salmon River had emptied here. And as thin and hard as the path behind him had been, the one before him was clearly marked and the long shadows across it were being lifted by an altered light. And this light was always there now—always new—just as it appeared this morning.

As always in the morning he could feel the dull pain in his shoulder from the old wound. The cartilage had never properly healed, muscle pulling unnaturally against muscle. He put his hand to his shoulder and as he did he heard the sound of horses' hooves and the wheels of wagons against the cobble, growing louder and then muted and silent. And then the laughter of children and the sound of another horse and perhaps the slam of a thin wooden gate closing, and then silence again.

He rose from the bed, careful not to disturb her. He pulled his trousers and shirt from the headboard and put them on quietly over his night-clothes. It would be a cool morning. He left his shirt unbuttoned as he sat on the edge of the bed and put his hand on her head and rubbed the hair from her forehead with his fingers.

She moved slightly at his touch, breathed deeply—gently—and opened her eyes. When she saw him next to her she reached her hands up to his shoulders and pulled him to her and held him there.

I'll write as soon as I get there, and then every day I'm there.

I should come with you, she answered.

Not yet. Let me see what it's like before I bring you there. Let me see what's come of Blackstone. Let me see what's there—for my father . . . for us.

But I'm your wife, Joseph.

And at the sound of that Joseph pulled her full into his arms. And I shall call for you to join me in a month. It's as long as I could bear, but I think it's best.

The room was now swelling with the morning sun as it shone in long slats of white across the bedspread, and the white walls and Sarah's face and the room seemed to be bursting with new light. I can't wait to be with you, Joseph. In Virginia, and then, Mr. Tyler, we shall never be apart again.

That I promise, Sarah Tyler. As sure as I've ever been about anything I am sure of that.

They held each other for moments and then he pulled away and sat on the edge of the bed and pulled his boots on. Sarah was crying as he tied the laces and when he was done Joseph put his hand on her shoulder. He could feel it trembling.

One month, he said. One month and you'll join me.

He held her face in his hand and then he stood and walked out of the room. He closed the door gently behind him. The dog was lying in the corner of the hallway and crawled nearer to the closed door as Joseph passed. Sarah's father was already waiting for him in the kitchen with coffee and sweet bread and they ate before they boarded the carriage to the train station. The morning was cool and he was glad he had left his nightclothes underneath. He thought for a moment—no bat, no ball—that was over for him. That part was behind him now. And would always be a part of him. And he would hold it in his heart where things are real.

III.

The average earth, the witness of war and peace, acknowledges mutely,
The prairie draws me close as the father to bosom broad the son,
The Northern ice and rain that began me nourish me to the end,
But the hot sun of the South is to fully ripen my songs.
          —Walt Whitman

The road was much wider—improved for the traffic of carts, new machinery carried on wagons from the harbors at City Point and from the trains as the South slowly rebuilt. Hundreds of jagged stumps lined the road like soldiers, where trees had been cut for the widening. Joseph sat high on the seat of the carriage next to the driver, an older man who had lost a hand at Second Manassas and could not farm or work machinery so he earned a fair living transporting people from the train station to the outer farms and the remote towns of Virginia. Along the road there were still reminders of the war—barns burnt and leaning and houses vacant. Other places where houses had been were now marked only by stone hearths and chimneys that stood like poor monuments to the families interrupted and dispersed by war. Thin fence posts sticking from the ground, stripped of their rails, and then black piles and piles of unburnt rails that the armies left behind. There must not be a fence left in Virginia, he thought, as he sat looking across the landscape.

They rode past a large plantation with the house boarded up and the land brown and unturned. Negro children sat on the porch and he could see a smaller house was full with a negro family and the land near the house was green with corn and a woman was hanging washed clothes from a line that ran from the house to the long branch of a cypress, and she turned and watched them as they rode by and Joseph raised a hand to wave but she did not respond and just watched them as they rode until she could no longer see the carriage. At a bend in the road the river appeared briefly; a broken pontoon bridge, left by yanks, lay across the shore half-submerged and silver with the years laying in the southern sun. There was a small clearing with pillows of grassy mounds along it and crude crosses made from thin wood lashed together. He could see a dozen men work-ing—excavating the graves and moving the bodies onto a flat wagon.

They're buildin a cemet'ry, the driver muttered, bout three miles from here. Got near five acres cleared and they're still clearin.

Joseph said nothing. The river disappeared and the road was crowded by oak trees and it narrowed so that the carriage barely passed through and the landscape began to look familiar to Joseph and he sat even higher in the seat of the carriage as he watched the river reappear and then vanish again as the road casually followed the river's path.

How long since you been back, he heard the man ask.

Joseph answered, Since '64—seven years. Joseph was amazed to think that he had been gone so long and as he saw the rolling hills appear and the thick pine he closed his eyes and then opened them and saw familiar markings of trees and boulders along the gravel road.

Stop here. Could you stop here, please?

The driver pulled up on the ropes grudgingly and the wagon clattered to a stop and the old man said, Time is money, and you better hurry if you have to relieve yerself—make it quick, or you'll spend the night in these woods. I got three or four more fares to do before the sun goes down and I aim to do em.

Joseph could hear him as he followed the path over the thick cushion of pine needles and through the laurel that had grown up thick and he searched for a clear path—and he could hear it, and then he could smell it as he pushed his way through waxy leaves and new growth and then to open air until he saw the silver surface of the Salmon River as it danced along shining rocks and pushed its way toward the James. Joseph knelt on a slick boulder that connected the dry shore to the water's edge and filled his cupped hands with water and brought it to his mouth and sipped the cold water and then again filled his hands and brought it to his face and ran the dripping hands through his hair. Then he noticed the tree lying awkwardly across the river with its roots thrown up from the ground, gripping nothing, and the bottom black and rotted. Good for diving, he remembered. Tears welled to his eyes.

It was the same. It was the same—as when he and Terence had stopped after playing ball—the same cool water ran like nothing had happened—like these last years had not happened. He looked around him, hoping to see Terence walk from a clearing in the woods—a wooden bat on his shoulder—to see Jacob leaning on a stone eating—complaining about the hardtack he ate—drinking water from a canteen and telling a story about the city in between gulps and laughter as if the war that was around them could not touch them—as long as they were laughing and remembering who they were and where they were from. The war had been there like an angry storm around them and their friendship had been a vessel in the storm. Maybe that was God then, he thought . . .

You comin or am I leavin without ya', he heard the driver yell.

Sarah would say there was God in the friendship. That friendship itself was a sign of God in all that horror—and Joseph stood straight up and thought of her and of his father and walked quickly back through the path to the wagon and the road back to Blackstone.

Almost left you in the goddam woods, the driver said, and then he cracked his whip gently on the horse's side and the buggy rattled onward down the road and he repeated as he drove, almost singing it, Almost left you in the woods.

When they rounded the last stand of black birch he could see the east field and the pond and then the house. He could see the sagging porch and one windowpane broken and a familiar brown shirt lying across the opening. Across the field the fences were gone and the barn door was open.

Stop, I'll walk from here.

He paid the driver fifty cents and took his bags and began to walk down the sloping grass toward the house. He walked past a huge pile of firewood that was gray and rotting, the logs fused together in decay, and he noticed there was no new wood cut—nothing for winter. He stopped midway across the field. A small area was thick with corn and the rest was a drift of knee-high grass. He stood and could feel the grass lick at the legs of his trousers and the wind roll over the hill behind him and pass across him and the grass leaned and followed it and then the wind subsided and the grass lay still. On the field's edge, the stone wall could be seen like a sunken pier amid the gold grass and the sun seemed to tumble across it and be thrown toward the porch and the house and he walked toward it.

The boards of the porch creaked as he stepped on them and he noticed the broken glass of the window still lay across the sagging boards in tiny pieces. The handle of the door was rusted and was black and orange in his hand as he pushed the door open.

It's Joseph. There was no answer.

He stood in the doorway a moment without entering. The familiar room lay in front of him like a picture. He was struck by the closeness. The plain wood and muted colors, as if color didn't matter. The table, the chairs, the lamps—only what they needed and nothing more. It was if everything else was false except the surfaces of the wood in the cabin and the pale light that dragged across it. He took a step and entered.

So it's you. So you've come home.

He heard his father's voice from the corner and he turned toward it. The tall, wooden chair was in the corner by the fireplace and there were the embers of a small fire and a pot of water was boiling over it and some of the water splashed and sizzled on the hot coals. The light in the cabin was poor with the brown shirt covering the closest window and it took Joseph a moment to focus on the figure of his father and when he finally did his heart sank at the sight.

He looked thin and pale and the clothes that he wore were faded the same color as everything else in the room. His father's legs were stretched toward the fireplace and his body seemed to sag in the structure of the chair. Joseph was still struck by his height, and the shoulders that still seemed large and powerful, but it was if muscle was settling into bone. His hair had receded and was awash in gray. Caleb leaned back in the chair and looked straight at Joseph's eyes. So you've come home, he said again.

Joseph let the bags settle to the floor and walked to him and put his arms around the broad shoulders of his father and his embrace was returned awkwardly but firmly, and when Joseph went to pull away he could feel the muscles of his father resist and embrace him harder and he let himself be held there until he could feel the muscles relax.

You'll be wantin some dinner by now I expect, he heard his father say and in the light he could see tears had come to his father's eyes.

Joseph felt his own eyes welling up and answered, Yes, we'll have some supper together, Father. And Joseph went to the corner where there was a small table and put his bags under it and turned again to face his father.

Din know if you'd come.

Lets have supper together, Joseph repeated.

Caleb got up from the chair and walked slowly to the dry sink and together they set the table with plates and spoons without speaking further, as if the years had fallen away like a passing moment and the light and the shadows that filled the room were the same light and the same shadows that had always lingered there. And then his father said, There's wood to split after supper. Plenty of light left. I caint keep up myself. We'll see if you remember how to split wood, Joseph. I put down three white oak near the pond.

I remember, Joseph answered, and they sat and ate fried ham and red-eye gravy and it tasted so good he remembered the meat in Mrs. Albright's smokehouse but they didn't talk anymore as they ate and they worked that night on the wood until it was quite dark.

Later that evening he wrote a short note to Sarah but, tired from the trip and splitting wood, he fell asleep with the note unfinished, his face lying on the broad wooden table that smelled slightly of the thousand meals served on it. When he woke it was early morning and he rose and splashed cool water on his face and walked out onto the porch. He stood for a moment there, and then set to work without eating. There was so much to be done.

Caleb had managed to sow the rows of corn, though they were not straight or finished. Some of the lower field was set with wheat, but not much. The farm was in great disorder. What was left of the fence leaned and was ready to fall. The horse barn was strewn with waste, the chickens underfed. The horse, Samuel, had been taken by the yanks—the hogs were thin with illness and Joseph set them on a diet of meal and pulled them out into the sun.

His first work was in the fields. The turned soil lay in uneven drifts and Joseph could tell that in many places the seed had not been set properly or at all. Between the rows the ground was already full with weedgrass, and a broken harrow lay where it had been dropped and forgotten weeks earlier. A small portion of the lower field had been set with wheat and Joseph spent the first week taking the hoe to the ground and purging the soil of the choking roots of weeds. When both fields were workable he set new seeds in the raised rows of corn and lugged barrels of water from Skull Pond on the small skid-sled and soaked and tamped the ground around the young plants and the new seeds. By the end of those first days he would return to the house soaked in sweat and sleep without eating. Caleb helped when he could, and he watched his son slowly recover the farm that was still their own.

On the seventh day Joseph walked the gravel road to town with some of the money he had earned in New York and although there were no horses available, he was able to purchase a work mule and on it he strapped a new-style tool called a "spring harrow," and sacks of seed for squash and pumpkins and a bag of peanuts and preserves. He was able to buy a half-pound of coffee. He also put out the word that Blackstone Farm was in the market for some beef cattle if any became available, and that they would be able to pay for them, and then before he started home he posted two letters to Rocker Falls and bought a small sack of dried apples, some of which he ate on the trip home and two or three he fed to the burdened mule as they walked.

The next day he set out the pumpkin and squash seeds between the rows of wheat and the clearing between the crops to keep the weeds down, and once again he carried the barrels of water up from the pond and soaked the dry southern soil. Only this time Caleb joined him, and together they hitched the mule and loaded the barrels onto the skid and Caleb sat and watched as Joseph pressed the soil with his boots and then kicked the caked mud off against the wood of the wagon.

That afternoon they spent at the edge of the woodland with ax and scraper, cutting new logs and skinning the bark from them so they could be run and stacked for rail fence around the pasture to the stone walls. Caleb helped him pull the bow saw through the wood to cut the logs to length and then the mule dragged them to the pasture's edge where some of the old posts and rails still leaned from the ground. Then the wood was stacked and leaned in crisscross fashion as if a bulging seam was being knitted along the ground and Joseph watched and admired as the new fence cast its tapestry of shadows along the spring grass.

They spent the weeks together working, Caleb with renewed interest and energy and Joseph with a passion he had rarely felt at Blackstone. And slowly the farm was healed, like a wound—and life returned to it as the sun swept across the old and the new alike.

Most evenings were spent in front of a low fire left from cooking, Joseph reading and writing letters to Sarah while his father slept in the tall chair with a blanket folded over the back to soften the place for his head. Caleb asked little about his time in the war and Joseph offered little. It was as if his father understood how bad it had been. As if he could see in his son's eyes the full measure of that time he had spent in war. But the base ball was different. Joseph had sent newspaper clippings about his feats on the fields of the game. And Caleb did seem to listen as Joseph would tell him stories of the games and his friends in the game. And he had even laughed the first time he heard about Joseph's escape.

Lucky you didn' get yerself killed, he had said. But he shook his head and laughed and he pretended not to remember it when he asked Joseph to repeat it on another night when the fire was low and they both had their legs stretched toward it.

What was that bout gettin out of that yank prison? he said.

And Joseph repeated it without changing anything and he could see his father's smile in the dim light and whenever he told the story his father would respond the same way.

Lucky you didn' get yerself killed, Joe.

The silence, though, the silence they had grown accustomed to, returned as if little had changed. And Joseph began to realize that his father's silence was as much a part of him as his work on the fields and on the walls. That words were only a small part of the way a man could speak to a son and a son to his father. But so much had changed. And Joseph was determined to find a way to bring the new and the old together.

He rose most mornings—at dawn—and walked out on the porch, coffee in his hand, the blanket from his father's chair wrapped around his shoulders, and watched the steel mist lift from the blue hills beyond the pasture. In these moments he lacked only her presence. A circle, she had said, was formed and now the ends dangled askew and distant—and waited their union. Here in Virginia—with Sarah at his side watching the light ride up the tall pine—to have her breath mix with his in the cool morning, watching the mist rise up—he would be complete.

Her last letter came Tuesday and confirmed she would be coming in May—an eternity now to him. He had told her of the new school and the need for teachers—and the possibilities there were for them. But mostly he told her in his letters of the farm and the hundred colors of green that washed the hills and the particular sound of rain on the porch roof. He tried to tell her of the lightness of his soul—as if on the wings of the geese that flew overhead and cast their perfect shadows on the fields—that her love, herself were wings. His awkward phrases fell far short of the feelings of his heart so he told her of his walks along the river and how he imagined them walking to a place where it pooled up black and deep, and they could sit and watch the silver fish ride the current past them in a silent morning. He told her how he could hear the rattle of piano keys as the water trickled through the smooth rocks and he wondered how Sophia was doing with her playing and if Sarah had been to New York with her father. And he asked her about base ball—what was happening in the game.

He was finished with it, he knew. It was becoming something other than what he loved—was becoming complicated. But he wanted to see where it would go. He loved to see the boys playing in the streets of Rocker Falls and in the streets of New York—and he was sure that somewhere in the fields of Virginia base ball was being played—just as he and Terence had first played it. Joseph didn't really begrudge the professionals, he just didn't choose to be one. He hoped the game wouldn't change too much from the game of the New York parks and the fields of Virginia and a hundred fields unseen. Joseph leaned against the porch post, brought his coffee to his mouth, and sipped. He tried to picture the flight of the ball cutting across the open field.

Suddenly he could see Terence emerge from the woods in full run—could see his slender form running in full breath—chest heaving—arms extended—to a spot ahead where he guessed the ball was heading—to intersect with his hard hands—and he saw him tumble full circle and stand holding the white ball, laughing, jumping in some sort of celebratory dance, and then Joseph focused on the white tail of a deer and then the deer as it darted across the field, leapt over the wall with all its graceful power, and disappeared back into the woods. He took another sip of his coffee, which was by now cool and tasted quite bitter, poured the rest of it onto the ground, tried to keep the image of Terence clear in his mind—but could not. Through that day as he worked he tried to call upon that image but he could not see Terence's face. An emptiness, the dull ache of a scarred wound stayed with him even as he closed his eyes to sleep that night.

The next morning he was awakened suddenly by thunder and a storm rolled through the valley quickly and then was replaced by a weak sun as he lay there. There were so many things he wanted to understand, but he knew for sure that he would not. That not all things were clear. He dressed quickly and before his father rose set out from the house. The morning was still damp and the ground was wet and slick under his feet as he crossed the pasture and entered the woods.

The trees were grown over the path so much that it looked more like a tunnel than a clearing in the woodland. The vegetation across the ground was thick and Joseph thought that no one else could've followed it. Except for himself and one other. The path finally opened up to the river and he followed its edge for a half-mile and then back up the slope until he saw the familiar stand of spruce that marked the edge of Fernwood Farm. Terence's farm. He passed under and around the gray-green foliage and then emerged at the edge of the field and stood and looked across it.

Black piles of wood emerged from the uncut pasture, where fence rails and posts had been piled and burnt for the warmth of an army of men. Across the field he could see what was left of the house, the walls charred black and the roof sagging into itself. As he walked closer he could see a few years' growth of grass on the roof itself, as if in a few more years there would be little sign that this home had stood here. Little sign that these fields had raised food for a family—for children—that boys had played games here. As if a tide had receded leaving a shattered and empty shell.

Joseph caught his breath and continued to walk toward the structure and then he entered onto the slanted floor through the opened wall at the end where saplings were forcing their way through the open spaces. There was still a small table sitting on the floor—a lamp hanging from a rusted hook on the wall. Joseph had heard only that they had used this house as a head-quarters. He wasn't even sure who it was who used it. And no one seemed to know what happened to the Hooker family. Moved on, some said. Killed, others said. Had Terence returned here? Joseph had asked. Did anyone know what happened to Terence Hooker? But no one knew. No one said.

Joseph looked around the shattered house. He could see what looked like a remnant of a map laying on the floorboards but as he reached to pick it up it disintegrated in his hand. In the corner of the space that had been a room he spotted a piece of painted wood and picked it up. It appeared to be a part of some kind of child's toy. Joseph looked out through a broken window toward the rolling hills and field that led to the wood-land. Perhaps Terence had come home. Perhaps he had seen enough in the wilderness and come home and taken his family away from the war. Maybe they went west. Maybe. But Joseph knew in his heart that this was not true. That somehow the war had torn the Hooker family from the ground and Joseph would never know how, never know why. He could see Terence walking away from him into the choking woods and then no more but this. The black, charred wood. The sagging roof. He put the piece of the toy in his pocket and walked out of the structure and started back toward home. There was nothing for him to do here. Nothing. He walked home to Blackstone. The morning rain had left the air cool and he felt a severe chill as he walked the remnants of the path that had joined the two farms and he could not get himself to feel warm. Soon the path would vanish as well and it was this that he thought of as he walked.

After lunch that day he walked to the low pasture as his father napped after morning chores. His father could complete few of the tasks of the farm and Joseph could feel him giving way—giving up more and more to his son. Caleb was now sixty-two years old and a lifetime of work and the recent hardships of the war had worn him down—like the old fence that leaned to the earth—as if being pulled. Caleb leaned as he walked— toward the ground—ready for rest—like the marching soldier weighed down with haversack and gun—wanting only rest. But there had been one night as they sat in front of the fire and Joseph thought his father asleep in the chair. Caleb straightened himself up and looked at Joseph and asked him in a quiet voice, Son . . . you and Sarah . . . do you dance?

Joseph didn't understand the question and asked his father to repeat it.

You and your new wife. Do you dance?

Well . . . yes. Not well . . . I mean, she is teaching me to dance.

And his father closed his eyes and smiled, and relaxed once again in the chair.

Joseph walked past the planted field into the higher grass where yellow and white daisies and purple loosestrife bloomed. He could see the mir- rored surface of Skull Pond and the huge rock that no longer looked any- thing like a skull at all to him. He had seen too many, knew their cold peculiarity. He walked along the edge of the woods to the spot where he thought the first stone had been set and pushed the grass away with his boots until it was revealed. Overgrown with brush and vine, it still stretched like a spine through the field, holding the ledge and the knolls of the pasture together like ligament and bone—separating woodland from pasture—following the dips and rolls of the field but holding onto itself stone to stone in a sleek silver stroke. It was the power of the human spirit laid upon the open field stone by stone. Each stone pulled from the earth to be lifted by men—by his father and by himself—into some order, into a form that brought new meaning, and redefined everything around it. He followed the unsteady line of the wall until it disappeared into the tall grass of the meadow.

In the shed he found the long scythe, the unnatural arc of wood and metal still hanging from a rusted hook. It was the same one he had used a hundred times to cut the grass for base ball and he knew its feel and its weight. Joseph returned to the wall and worked rhythmically, raising the scythe to his shoulders, sweeping the cutting blade through the coarse weed and grass—clearing the base of the wall until it was uncovered, revealed to the spring sun as if a blanket had been pulled from it. With his hands he pulled vines from the black crevices between stones and with shears he cut vines from its base until it lay clean in the pasture, dividing the land. There was a perfect texture to the rounded face of stone and he saw the last stone he had begun to set. It was laid on its side half-buried, sinking into the earth of the meadow from which it had come. It lay as if planted where he dropped it that afternoon. It lay untouched by any human hand.

A reg'ment's comin. He could hear the words like it was yesterday.

He realized that his father had given up on the wall on the day he had left—and in some way given up on himself. These years since, the wall lay beneath the meadow untouched. Thirty feet of wall still unbuilt— thirty feet of space waiting to be filled, defined. He lifted, using all his strength, the rock from its place in the earth and spun it around on a pointed corner, seeing a flat face that would sit firmly on the ground as an anchor. He pushed it into the space near the last stone of the wall and let it drop heavily into place.

This would be an anchor—he remembered his father's words. The wall is built on these foundation stones, and if they're weak, so then will be the wall—a man's efforts wasted.

Joseph stood back and wiped beads of sweat from his forehead with the back of his hand. He began to see more clearly the unfinished wall, sense the precise placement of the stone against the earth and he understood that he would complete his father's wall and that each stone would be some measure of himself and each stone would connect him to his father and to his father's father—fix him to this place where he had been born, where he had watched the earth reclaim his young mother—where it pulled even now at his father—and fixed him, fixed Joseph to the field, to the still pond, the rolling granite hills—to the meadows framed in ancient stone.

He worked on the wall the rest of the day—feverishly at times, as if he had discovered some timeless secret—pulling the stone to the wall—watching the shadow fall consistent on its surface until the sun was so long set that he could not see—and he noticed the yellow lamplight of the cabin. He made no mention to his father as they sat that night, but rose early and set to work before the day's light. He found the crude skid-sled leaning against the shed, shook insect nests and cocoons that fell black and dry from it, and dragged it to the field. There was a place by the pond where the earth seemed to spew stone—as if it were growing there—and he set to work loading cart after cart—dragging the boulders to a pile by the wall's end, where his hands would push and pull their way through them, seeking the stone for its certain place in the wall.

Joseph looked across the field to catch his breath. He crouched down and with both of his arms picked up a large stone from beside the base of a tall oak. Under it was an even nicer one and Joseph could see the perfect surface that would sit just right on the wall. The shovel didn't move it from where it lay, just barely exposed to the field, and he walked across the pasture to the shed and unbolted the plank door. The bolt was rusty and it screeched as it opened. Light from the door filled the small space and he could see, in the corner, tools stacked and leaning—hoes, rakes and the scythes. There were pitchforks and then finally, a thick iron bar hammered flat and still bearing the marks of the blacksmith's blows, just right for prying stone from the ground as he had seen his father do a thousand times. Pulling the stone like splinters from the flesh of the earth.

Joseph leaned forward and grabbed the iron bar with both hands and pulled it from the corner where it had leaned for years, and as he did, something—mice, squirrels—scurried noisily away in the unseen spaces below. He was surprised at the weight of the thing and remembered his father walking toward the house after working the fields, the huge metal bar across his shoulders and his thick arms leaning lazily over it to balance it on himself as the sun rested low on the Blue Ridge at his back. Joseph had never thought then how powerful were his father's arms from the work he set himself to every day.

As Joseph lifted the bar to his own shoulder and his eyes grew accustomed to the light he saw another thing lying in the corner against the frail wooden planks of the wall. It was rolled in an old horse blanket that was frayed from use and then from neglect, and it left the thing partially exposed. The weight of the iron bar dropped from him to the dirt floor of the shed and he pushed it aside with his boot as he leaned toward the thing.

He reached for it with both hands and wrapped his fingers around the coarse blanket and pulled it into the white light of the open door. He let the corner of the blanket fall loose and then unravel and the blanket dropped to the floor on top of the iron bar. The room darkened for seconds as the sun passed behind a thin cloud, returned in a breath and lit the space completely, and he held the thing in both hands toward the open door that exposed the green pasture. He held it up at his shoulder height in the light—the weight of it resting on his palms as if offering it up—receiving it—as if it were a thing sacred—cloaked in mystery.

The wood had been sanded so clean that it appeared to drink the sunshine in and the color of every grain, marking every year of an old tree's life. It shone golden and sparkled like the layers of granite and limestone in the hills and the canyons that surrounded him. He pulled his callused palm across the surface and let it slide over the barrel of the bat toward the thinner handle—the gentle slopes of Virginia's pastures and plateaus—and the sun slid across it in rivers of light.

Joseph's eyes followed every grain as he turned it, seeing his father's hands across the skin of the wood—imagining the cutting blade of the chisel, the patient pull of the file across the lines of grain. He imagined it taking shape in the muted lantern light, with the exhausting chores of the day completed. His father must have sat alone and worked at this thing in the quiet evenings, the war rumbling on around him, given to the task. Joseph turned it again in his hands, gently—with his thumb—and then let it freeze in a shaft of light from the door and he could feel the tears come to his eyes and his shoulders tremble as he looked at it. On the barrel as it thinned—before it came to the width that hands could hold—there were figures engraved with a burning iron and he could see it as it crossed the grain of the wood. In capital letters, J. T., followed by the date, 1864. It was the year he had left Blackstone. It was a father's gift to a son who had not returned all these years. It was a gift from a father's heart that superceded words—decades of things unspoken—from the father's heart to the hands of a son returned now to grasp it. The language of heart and blood—a song played across the fields and across the harsh winters—sent spirit to soul as it might have been before words.

Joseph leaned against the crude frame of the open door, the weight of the bat in his hands and on his shoulder. He could feel the southern sun full on him—and he slowly sank to the dirt floor weeping—great convulsive sobs. But not now of sorrow, not now of blood or of death—but of life. In joy he wept—for the life gift—in his incredible ability to feel—to love— to weep. For the field before him and the gift in his hands—for the breath of Sarah and the embrace of his father and the unimaginable gift of living upon the earth and the unfathomable gift of loving—even as the trees burn and the rivers quiver to a stop—even as the truth is draped in lies and the light of the sun is choked by the smoke of cannon—even then, the desire to live survives and the chance to love swells up and washes clean the battered landscape of the soul. And kindness—human kindness resounds.

Joseph gathered himself and walked to the back of the shed holding the bat, to another cluster of items—grain bins, burlap, and cloth—and he reached into the basket made of branch and vine by his mother years ago. It was now broken and leaning severely to one side, but he could see it on the table filled with flowers from the field and he could smell the flowers even now. He reached in and felt around until his hand grasped the old ball that he knew would still be there. Holding the bat in one hand, the ball in the other, he walked through the open door of the shed to the grass in front that overlooked the lower field and the unfinished wall. He held the weight of the ball in his palm—the bat poised over his shoulder and gripped with one hand. He felt the bat's cool grip and opened and closed his grasp of it.

It fit his hand perfectly as if molded to his grip. The ball floated inches up from his hand and his hand retreated quickly to the bat. It was gripped for a second by both hands and then exploded in forward motion, ripping through the air toward the ball until there was a sudden, almost silent collision and the ball leapt from the surface of the wood and flew up into the air above him—slicing across the blue sky toward the field.

He watched its flight—thought for a moment it might not end—and then watched its path decline toward the green pasture. He watched as the white ball hammered against the stone wall where he had been working, watched as it bounced toward the cultivated field, then to the meadow beyond where it vanished in the brown and yellow carpet of grass. Bluebirds fled from its path into the trees.

He held the bat over his head, brought it down to swing again through the air—and then again. The weight—the balance—was perfect. It was an extension of himself and as he held it his arms appeared as his father's, thick and strong.

It was perfect.

The sun passed again behind a thickening cloud and the shadows painted a tapestry of greens and yellows across the field and he saw every color distinctly—wedded to the grass and the stone and the sky. He heard every sound as an infant might hear it, and he walked—back across the field toward the wall. He leaned the bat gently against the silver stone and returned to the shed for the iron bar. Finding the large buried stone he put the bar under an exposed corner and with one push the stone heaved up from the earth and tumbled to the side of the pocket in the soil it had left. He crouched and lifted it and carried it to the place he had been working. He rolled the stone closer to the space and as he did he noticed it was the right size. It was large enough to anchor, yet it had good sloping sides that would fit into the last and accept the next easily. He lifted it and dropped it in place along the wall. It fell into the pocket of space as if it had been made for just that purpose. He went to move it slightly and it didn't move at all and he stood back from it. He could barely tell where he had just laid the new stone—it was already part of the wall.

Joseph stepped back and looked down the long length of the wall and at the work he had done and then ahead to the work still to be completed. As he did, he tried to measure how much he had accomplished in these last days. A great breath of relief and satisfaction came over him and he smiled as he stood and looked at his work. He couldn't tell where he had begun or where his father had left off. The wall would be finished, the work uninterrupted and the task complete. And it would mark their presence there and stand as a monument to their home, and to their work and to themselves. As he worked that afternoon the rhythm of the work became regular and his presence in the field natural and quiet, and the birds returned to roost in the tall grass of the field and the base ball he had hit lay there—and would then sink slowly into the earth and after many winters and many springs would become part of the soil of the field and would lie unseen among the sunken stone.

Blackstone Farm, Virginia, May 7, 1874

Joseph watched the dripping from last evening's rain—slowly rolling gems from the new roof to the dry ground below. He could smell from where he stood the fresh-turned earth—the wet clay exposed for the first time in centuries to the Virginia sun. He could smell the coffee in his cup as he brought one foot up to the lower frame of the porch rail.

Caleb, though slowed with stiffness, led the new horse across the field and down into the woods and toward the river. His house still stood at the top of the pasture overlooking the western field and Joseph could see it clearly from where he stood and from the window of his bedroom when he woke every morning. The new house was built with a stone foundation. Pulled from the field and mortared thick and deep, the stone foundation reflected the weather—shone in the sun and glistened with the dampness of spring and winter; turned black and silver as the sun set over the blue hills in the distance.

This morning the sky was almost cloudless; only a great white mass over the river valley interrupted the constant blue like smoke and seemed to drift and dance as in a breeze. He watched his father and the horse disappear into the dogwoods and looked toward the road for the wagon. There was no sign yet and he sipped his coffee, following the flight of a hawk over the foothills to the east. He could see the dust of the wagon first and then the wagon and then he could see Sarah holding the reins, stiff-backed and dressed in white cotton. She saw him and waved as she pulled the wagon to a stop. From where he was he could barely see the books she had bought for the school stacked in neat piles in the back of the wagon. When she dismounted she did not come up to him right away. She tied off the horse at the bottom of the hill and walked to the edge of the plowed field. Her hands were on her hips and she circled slowly, drinking in the morning and the field and the woods beyond. She looked up at the house they had built together—the strong stones and the detailed porch that Caleb had helped them create. Joseph looked back at her, pressing his hands to the railing—leaning toward her. She stretched her arms to the sky and laughed—turned back to the wagon for some of the books. Joseph smiled and set his coffee on the rail and approached the steps to head down to help her. He hesitated—looked once more below him. The leaves of the oaks were lit as if from below, while the pines were dark and thick. He could see the mountains rolling into the distance with the deep green fading to silver and to blue, and just traces of the cloud as if painted across the sky. He listened—the cry of the hawk. From where he stood—on his right—he could see the easternmost elbow of the Salmon River and the morning light dance upon its surface like diamonds.

There is a moment—maybe seconds—between the hawk's cry and the hearing of it. The sound travels along the canyon wall, through the thick needles of ancient pine, and then finally resounds within the living tissue of the human ear. The black shadow dances across the earth's rugged surface—the hawk's cry—and then the hearing of it. And in the seconds between—perfect silence. Joseph did not understand the movement of the sound through the atoms of air, nor the complex signals of sound to his brain. But he understood the moment between. He embraced it—and that was enough.

*To know baseball is to continue to aspire to the condition of freedom,
individually and as a people, for baseball is grounded in America in a
way unique to our games. Baseball is part of America's plot, part of America's
mysterious, underlying design—the plot in which we all conspire and collude,
the plot of the story of our national life.*
    —A. Bartlett Giamatti

May 2000

The blue sedan pulls off Interstate 64 and into the parking lot of the
Richmond Rivermen Stadium. The parking lot is already half-full with
sports cars and family sedans. Cars are pulling in behind them and someone
leans on his horn and there's a chorus of other horns and they finally find an
empty spot between a van and a station wagon. He parks the car and all
three boys jump out of the back doors and they're laughing and wrestling
and he asks them to settle down as he feels for the tickets in his pocket.

They are in a short line for a few minutes before a man takes their tickets, tears them in half, and hands them back. They walk up steel steps that
have been painted blue and to the doors that are numbered the same as
their tickets. The air surrounding the concrete and steel is cool, and the
sounds ricochet in the passageway and the father can feel the pressure
pounding behind his eyes from the long drive, and from the boys and the
noise along the steel steps that echoes off the concrete walls.

Thinking the whole thing might not have been a great idea, he pushes
open the steel doors. As the view widens the blue sky emerges cloudless in
front of them. The boys' laughter ceases. In front of them a perfect green
field drinks the sun and long black shadows wash across it and into perfect

rows of blue seats. The edge of the grass is framed in red soil like a picture and the deep green grass is dissected with perfect white lines that never quite intersect. The father and the boys hesitate, and then walk in and closer to the field to follow the sound they hear. In the outfield two men in white uniforms are tossing a ball back and forth and the path of the ball can be followed by watching the shadow across the field. As the ball reaches the glove there is a snap and the catching glove is pulled and the ball retrieved and thrown again. One man waves with his glove hand and the catch is stopped.

The two men stretch their shoulders and walk across the field toward them, toward the locker room, and before they descend the concrete steps of the dugout, one hesitates, looks at the boys and takes a few steps toward them. You guys play ball? he says.

The oldest boy says, No, not much, not really.

The player shakes his head slightly and tosses the ball softly to the boy's hands. Don't know what you're missin, he says, and disappears into the dugout.